Also by S... W9-AQF-575

The Montg...
Wait for Me / Trust in Me
Stay with Me / More of Me
Return to You
Meant for You
I'll Be There
Until There Was Us

The Shaughnessy Brothers
Made for Us
Love Walks In
Always My Girl
This Is Our Song
A Sky Full of Stars
Holiday Spice

Shaughnessy Brothers: Band on the Run
One More Kiss
One More Promise
One More Moment

Holiday Romance
The Christmas Cottage / Ever After
Mistletoe Between Friends / The Snowflake Inn
Holiday Spice

Life, Love and Babies
The Baby Arrangement
Baby, I'm Yours
Baby, Be Mine

Until *there* *was* Us

SAMANTHA CHASE

sourcebooks
casablanca

Published by Sourcebooks Casablanca, an imprint of Sourcebooks, Inc.
P.O. Box 4410, Naperville, Illinois 60567-4410
(630) 961-3900
Fax: (630) 961-2168
sourcebooks.com

Printed and bound in Canada.
MBP 10 9 8 7 6 5 4 3 2 1

For Sue and your love of all things Montgomery.

Thank you for your encouragement and your excitement about this book.

This one's for your Celeste.

Prologue

MONICA MONTGOMERY SIPPED HER CHAMPAGNE AS SHE watched over the roomful of celebrating people. Her nephew Zach had finally married his assistant, Gabriella, and she couldn't take her gaze from them. The way they looked at one another told everyone how in love they were. It made her heart happy. They were yet another couple her beloved husband, William, had helped along on their road to true love.

How had she gotten so lucky? William had approached her so many years ago because—he swore—after one look, he knew she was the one for him. Their life together had truly been perfect—even after almost forty years of marriage. He had followed up with matchmaking for their own sons and then branched off to some of their nieces and nephews.

Zach and Gabriella were his latest success story.

"I have to say, Monica, you're looking almost as pleased as your husband right now."

Monica turned as her sister-in-law Eliza sat beside her with her own glass of champagne. With a smile, they touched glasses.

"I am pleased," Monica said. "I can't remember ever seeing Zach look so happy. He was always such a serious young man."

Eliza agreed. "Being in love suits him. That's what I

wanted to talk to you about," Eliza said as she turned in her seat to look at Monica head-on.

"Really?"

"I want grandkids!" she blurted out.

The thought of her own grandchildren made Monica smile. "They are wonderful. We've got six of them now, and I'm telling you, it feels so good to hear those little voices and laughter throughout the house again."

"I want that," Eliza stated. "But...I think we must have done something wrong."

"What makes you say that?"

"Look at them, Monica." She motioned toward the crowded room.

"I can't find them."

"Exactly. It was like pulling teeth to convince Megan to wear a dress today, then it was a month's worth of arguing to convince Christian to take time off for the wedding, and Carter's been on the phone almost since he got off the plane yesterday," she said with exasperation. "I appreciate a good work ethic, but this is ridiculous. Even his father takes a break every now and then." She paused and looked at the dance floor again.

"Oh! Monica, look!" Eliza hissed. "Megan's dancing! Who's she dancing with?"

Monica looked a little closer and smiled. "That's Alex," she said. "He's a friend of Zach's. Actually, he was Zach's physical therapist after his accident, and they became good friends. William and I have met him on several occasions, and he is the nicest young man."

"You don't say..."

For a few minutes, they sat in silence and watched as Megan and Alex danced to a more upbeat number and then two slower ones. By the fourth dance, Monica's mind was starting to go to places normally only her husband's went.

Leaning in close to Eliza, she said, "You know, that's four dances."

Eliza nodded.

"Normally, if you're only being polite, you accept one dance. Two dances, tops. But four?"

"I have to admit, I don't think I've ever seen my daughter look quite so...smitten."

Monica smiled and then looked across the room to where her husband was standing and talking with his brothers. It gave her a little bit of a thrill to know he seemed oblivious to what was happening on the dance floor.

"They're holding hands!" Eliza cried. "That's definitely not something you do to be polite, right?"

"I wouldn't think so, but then again, it's been a long time since I've been on a dance floor with someone other than my husband."

They both laughed and watched as Megan and Alex blended into the crowd on the other side of the room.

Too bad, Monica thought. She wanted to watch them for a little longer because she was already thinking of doing a little matchmaking of her own.

Alex Rebat was exactly the type of man she would want for her own daughter—if she had one. So it only seemed right that he would also be the kind of man she'd want for her niece.

"Where is Megan working these days?"

Eliza sighed. "She's been at this company in Albany for about a year now. She has a contract with them, and she'll be there for another eighteen months. Maybe more. I hate it. It's so far away!"

"You're only a couple of hours away, Eliza. Last I checked, Manhattan wasn't that long of a drive from Albany."

"Fine, it's not. But...the way she works it might as well be on the other side of the country. All she does is work! She doesn't date, she doesn't socialize... I'm telling you, if I want any grandchildren from her, I'm going to have to pry her from the office with a crowbar."

"It won't matter," Monica said. "She can have all kinds of tech devices hidden in her purse to work on anytime and anyplace."

"That's not encouraging, Monica."

"No. But it's a fact. And believe me, as the mother of three former workaholics, I know what I'm talking about."

"So...what do I do? How do I get her out of this... this pattern?"

Before Monica could reply, her husband walked over with a big smile on his face. "Are you two lovely ladies enjoying yourselves?" William asked.

"We're having a wonderful time," Eliza said with a hint of whimsy.

William handed his wife a fresh glass of champagne. "Do you see how happy Zach looks?" He raised his own glass in a mock salute. "I do believe this match was one of my more satisfying ones."

"You're certainly a genius, dear," Monica said as she sipped her drink in an effort to hide her grin.

He leaned down and placed a gentle kiss on her temple. When he straightened, he said, "Your kids are too spread out, Eliza. They may be more challenging for me. But given a little time, I think I can figure something out."

Eliza was about to respond when Monica gently kicked her under the table.

"I'm sure you'll come up with something clever," Monica said with a sincere smile at her husband. "Now why don't you go see when they're going to be serving dessert. I believe my sweet tooth is calling."

With a loving smile, he bowed and said, "As you wish."

Monica watched him walk away, and out of the corner of her eye, she spotted Megan and Alex walking out of the ballroom smiling.

She sighed happily. "What are you doing tomorrow after breakfast, Eliza?"

Shrugging, Eliza looked at her curiously. "We're here for the weekend so Joseph can play golf with William and Robert once his father-of-the-groom responsibilities are done. Why? What do you have in mind?"

Monica gave her a sly grin. "I've learned a thing or two, and I think it's time for this matchmaking thing to have a female touch. Are you in?"

Eliza's eyes went wide, and then her smile matched them. "I do believe I am."

Chapter 1

Two years later…

"Dammit," Megan Montgomery cursed as she tried to pull her phone from her bag and ended up nearly tripping over her own two feet. She might be in a new city, but she was the same old klutz she'd always been. The airport was crowded, and she wasn't paying attention to where she was going, and all in all, she felt like a disaster. She murmured an apology to the people around her before stepping aside to read her texts.

Her cousin Summer Reed was meeting her outside baggage claim, and according to the text, she was circling the airport, trying to put her baby daughter to sleep.

Great.

The flight to Portland had been full, there had been a crying baby behind Megan, and the last thing she wanted was to be sitting near another crying baby—even if she was incredibly adorable and related to her. *Ugh*…her nerves were frayed. As if moving across the country wasn't stressful enough, it had to get off to a rocky start? She let out a breath and joined the throngs of people again—careful to pay attention this time—and merged into the stream heading to the exit.

Fifteen minutes later she had her bags and was searching for Summer's red SUV. Spring in Portland was nicer than in Albany, Megan thought as she waited. She was practically bouncing on her toes as she watched the flow of cars. Her emotions were doing their own version of a tennis match, bouncing between being nervous and excited about this new adventure.

Leaving the job she'd had for the past three years hadn't been hard—especially since she knew from the beginning it had an end date—but opting to work for her cousin Zach on the other side of the country was definitely out of her comfort zone. Megan liked to keep things simple. Orderly. She had been settled in Albany and figured that even when her job ended, she'd find another in the same city.

That hadn't happened.

Instead, she had been handed an opportunity she'd always wanted but never thought she'd get—working within the family business.

It was crazy. After all, she *was* a Montgomery, and it shouldn't have been a big deal. The only problem was… she didn't understand finance, she wasn't particularly suave, and she didn't have the business savvy of the rest of her family. She was a computer girl—a techie—but she was really good at what she did.

Still, the planets seemed to have aligned perfectly for this job with Zach to open up just as she was in need of one. Who was she to question it? It was the perfect solution to her employment dilemma, and it was going to be a good thing for her to do something new.

No matter how terrifying it currently felt.

The sound of a horn broke Megan from her reverie, and she saw her cousin pulling up in front of her. With a big smile on her face, Megan waved to Summer and immediately loaded her bags into the hatch. With a shriek of excitement, Summer gave her a fierce hug.

"I am so glad you're here!" she cried. "I have been counting the days until I could see you and squeeze you and look at your face!"

Summer had always been the excitable one in the family. She had a heart of gold and a zest for life that Megan never quite understood, but she was hoping to have some of Summer's excitement rub off on her.

"Come on, come on, let's get you in the car! I want to hear all about your flight and how you're doing and if you're excited about starting work on Monday and—"

"Summer?"

"Hmm?"

"Breathe," Megan said with a smile.

With a nod, Summer walked around to the driver's side and climbed into the car. Megan did the same on the passenger side, but not before peeking into the rear seat at her niece—that sounded much better than "first cousin once removed."

"I have some super cute stuff for Amber in my suitcase," Megan said as she climbed in.

"You didn't have to do that. You already sent that precious crocheted baby blanket when she was born." Summer smiled and added, "It reminded me of the ones Nana used to make. Do you remember?"

Megan nodded. Nobody knew that her great-grandmother had taught her how to crochet when she was just a little girl, and she found it to be fascinating and relaxing. She had come home from Nana's one day with the most adorable, soft, cuddly baby blanket, and her father had scoffed at it, told her it was ugly, and mocked her desire to spend her time making things he considered frivolous. At first she had been heartbroken, and she stopped crocheting for a while, but the next time she was at her grandmother's, she got pulled in again to the comfort of the soft wool in her fingers, the pretty colors, the rhythm of stitching, and the gratification of seeing a ball of yarn turn into something beautiful. So she had continued her creations in private, making absolutely sure nobody knew about it. Crocheting was her secret hobby, and she donated all the baby blankets and clothing she made to local hospitals and women's shelters.

In the past several years, she hadn't had as much free time to indulge as she would have liked. Sometimes her fingers just itched. For an instant she considered confiding in Summer, but then she thought of her father's scorn and everyone laughing at her, and the moment passed. "So…how far are we from your house?"

"It's about an hour's drive," Summer said as they pulled away from the curb. "Amber's a good sleeper, so we can talk all we want without worrying about waking her up."

Was it wrong that Megan wanted to let out a sigh of relief and a hearty "hallelujah"?

She did sigh, but it was a happy one. They were on the road heading to Summer and Ethan's house, where she was going to be living for the foreseeable future in their guesthouse. Which reminded her…

"I feel bad about this," she began.

"About what?"

"You finally got your mom and everyone to go home, and now I'm moving in."

With a light laugh, Summer glanced at her briefly.

"Are you kidding? This is going to be *way* more fun than having my mom here. You're the sister I never had! We're going to hang out together and work together and—"

Megan was about to respond when her phone rang. She smiled when she saw Gabriella's name on the screen. "I am in the car and on my way!" she said when she answered.

"Megan! We are so excited you're finally here! I wanted to ride with Summer, but things got hectic here, and then Zach was worried about me being in the car for so long, and…" She sighed. "I swear, you'd think I was an invalid the way he's carrying on."

"You're pregnant, and he's worried," Megan replied with a smile. "I think it's kind of sweet how he's so protective."

"It was sweet for the first two months when I was dealing with morning sickness. But we're nearly seven months in now, and I feel great, and he's making me crazy. Promise you'll distract him while you're here so I can at least go shopping by myself one day!" Gabriella said with a laugh.

"I promise. You say the word, and I'll keep him busy with codes and computer issues that will have his head spinning for days!"

"You have officially become my favorite person."

"I aim to please."

"Okay, so…it's going to take you about an hour to get to Summer's house," Gabriella explained, "and I'll meet you there."

"That sounds great! I'll see you then!" When Megan hung up, she felt a little more relaxed. This wasn't a move across the country where she didn't know anyone;

she was going to be with family, and that made her smile.

With the phone still in her hand, she knew she needed to let her own family know she'd landed safely and was on her way to Summer's. Her mother had been overly anxious about this trip—and not in an I'm-going-to-miss-you way but in an I'm-very-excited-for-you one. Which was weird. For all the years she had been hounding Megan about moving closer to home, she was suddenly her number one cheerleader for moving to the other side of the country.

Definitely weird.

With a sigh because all she wanted was to close her eyes for a few minutes and unwind, she turned toward Summer. "Would you mind if I give my mom a quick call? I should have done it while I was waiting for my luggage, but…"

Summer laughed. "Go for it. I know my mother went a little crazy when I moved here and was on the phone with me constantly at first. So I understand."

With a quick nod, Megan hit Send on her mother's number and waited for her to answer.

"Are you there? Was your flight okay? Are you with Summer?" her mother said as a greeting.

Her anxious tone had Megan laughing softly. "Hi, Mom. Yes, I'm here, my flight was a little less than ideal, and I'm in the car with Summer and Amber right now."

"Oh, she brought Amber with her? How sweet! You'll have to send me some pictures!"

"We're in the car, Mom."

"I didn't mean right now," her mother said with a bit of a huff. "So you're there and you're on your way to

Summer's, and…when are you going to start looking for an apartment?"

"Mom, we've talked about this. I'm only going to stay with them for a couple of weeks, and I thought it was okay for me to get here and relax for a few days before I had to spring into action."

"I'm just saying…you shouldn't rely on them for everything because they're already so busy with Amber and Summer going back to work, and…maybe you should ask them if they know of any vacant apartments near people they know. Plus, you'll need to make some friends of your own and maybe start socializing so—"

"You know what…our connection…bad…call you… weekend…"

It was childish, and she wasn't proud of it, but now was so not the time to deal with the whole lecture on her social life.

Beside her, Summer started to laugh, and Megan smacked her playfully on the arm.

"Megan? Megan, are you there?"

"Can't hear…go…soon!" And then she hung up and immediately turned her phone off.

Yeah, not her finest reaction to her mother, but her mind was spinning with too many other thoughts right now to add that to it.

Yes, she was living someplace new, was starting a new job, and was going to be meeting new people. And yes, it was a chance for a fresh start. None of this was news to Megan. Actually, she was looking forward to the opportunity. Her life in Albany had been…well, she was in a serious rut. She'd been working ten hours a day, six days a week, and the only people she'd socialized with were her coworkers.

Maybe socialized wasn't *quite* the right word. More like…saw them frequently—like whenever she came out of her office.

Which wasn't often.

Her muscles were starting to tense up again, and she forced herself to relax. This move was supposed to help her break out of her rut—force her to meet new people and be someone who didn't spend her entire life holed up in her office staring at a computer screen. All around her, people were meeting and having lives and falling in love and starting families. And as much as she argued how missing out didn't bother her, the truth was that it did.

Megan had always wanted to be the girl who had a ton of friends who went out for girls' nights and went away for weekends together. And then she wanted to meet a man and fall in love and have the kind of family she had grown up with.

Maybe it wasn't for everyone, but Megan wanted the American dream—it was a little outdated, and she'd learned to keep that ideal to herself because so many people felt like it wasn't something a modern woman should want. But she did. She really, really did. And the only way she was going to achieve it was to force herself to break out of her comfort zone and put herself out there—meet people. Go out. Date.

Sigh.

The last time she'd gone out on a date was…

Nothing was coming to mind.

"That can't be a good sign," she murmured.

"What's not a good sign is you talking to yourself when I'm sitting right here," Summer said. "Seriously, you can't let your mother stress you out like that."

"Easier said than done."

"Which part of the conversation did you in? The move? Finding a place of your own? Or the socializing?" When Megan gave her a quizzical look, Summer smiled. "Sorry, but your mom's voice carries."

"Oh." Okay, so this was exactly the kind of thing she wanted—a friend she could talk to when she was stressed out. "It was the socializing."

"I knew it!"

"Yeah, well, it was more the implication of what it entailed. It isn't just making friends, it's dating too."

"And that's a problem…why?"

"I've always been busy, and after my breakup with Colin, I didn't want to get involved with anyone."

"He was a major jerk, Megan. You should be relieved to be rid of him!"

"I am. I am. But…it wasn't easy to get over. Things were a little—"

"They were ugly and intense," Summer said. "I get it. But that was more than two years ago. You can't tell me you haven't dated since then."

"I've been busy." Unfortunately, she couldn't blame the lack of dating on her work schedule. It certainly didn't help, but it wasn't the real reason for her lack of interest.

It was Alex.

Yeah, there it was. And moving to Portland was asking for trouble, but Megan couldn't help it. Her family was surprised at how she had readily agreed to this move, but the truth was…she was curious. Curious to see if her memories of one incredibly hot and wildly sexy physical therapist and their time together were accurate.

Not that she was looking for a repeat performance. Not really. Okay, she totally was. But it was more than just the sex. Kind of. Megan had a feeling if things had been different and geography hadn't been against them, their relationship could have gone somewhere. At least that was what she'd been telling herself for the past two years. The logical part of her brain, however, told her that she needed to see Alex in person in order to know whether she was remembering things correctly or if she was still looking at him through sex goggles.

She groaned. Maybe seeing Alex was something she should ease into. No need to rush out and ask about him or look him up—but considering he and Zach were friends, they were bound to run into one another eventually. And for all she knew, he could be involved with someone or married. And just because she hadn't moved on didn't mean he hadn't.

Maybe there was a way she could casually bring him up without being too obvious.

The memory of how they'd danced together and then walked around the estate where the wedding had been held and talked and laughed played through her mind as her head rested on the leather cushion. They'd flirted from almost the moment he had walked over and asked her to dance. Then they'd gone walking through the garden that was lit with twinkly lights, and Alex had surprised her with a kiss. And that was the moment she knew she wasn't going to her hotel alone.

The man kissed like a damn fantasy.

To this day, Megan couldn't remember ever getting so completely *swoony* over a kiss.

Either way, Alex Rebat had turned her world upside down with one kiss and then proceeded to keep her there for two incredible days.

And nights.

They'd kept in touch for about three months after the wedding, but…she'd screwed up in typical Megan form. Just when she thought she was capable of being in a relationship, she'd gone and ruined it. Unable to help herself, she sighed.

"You okay?" Summer asked.

And the thing was, she probably could tell Summer about her fling with Alex. After all, what harm would it do after all this time? But now wasn't the time. She needed to focus on something—anything!—else.

But the image of Alex and her tangled up together refused to budge from her mind, and she wanted to growl with frustration. Why was she still thinking about it?

Because it was the most exciting weekend of your life!

Oh, right. That.

Maybe it was the dress her mother had insisted she wear when she normally didn't wear dresses, or the champagne she'd had when she wasn't normally a drinker, but everything about that weekend had almost felt like it was happening to someone else. Megan could still remember her shock when Alex had approached her and asked her to dance. Men didn't normally ask her to dance. She was the friend, the buddy, someone to hang out with or ask advice for dating *other* women. It was something she'd gotten used to, and even when she dated, she wasn't the overly romantic type. She didn't do the girly-girl thing.

And yet…the second Alex had wrapped his arms around her, it was what she wanted more than anything else.

Heck, if she ever ran into Alex again—and she was pretty sure she was going to—he probably wouldn't recognize her. Now he'd see who she really was: a no-nonsense computer girl who dressed for comfort and wasn't the least bit…girly.

Another sigh.

For the most part, Megan was okay with who she was. She didn't feel the need to read *Cosmo* and let it dictate the kind of woman she should be. But lately a little bit of discontent had been sneaking in.

It was probably because she was in need of a change.

It was the rut.

So here she was, out of her rut and starting a new life. Sort of. You can't take the geek out of the girl, but you can take the girl out of her rut.

"Okay, I didn't mean to make you get all quiet," Summer said. "Let's talk about something fun! We're going to get some takeout tonight, and Zach and Gabriella are coming over and we'll hang out and relax. Doesn't that sound great?"

Megan laughed softly. "It does. Sorry about zoning out there. I guess I'm trying to get a grip on too many things, and you know me, I can't ever seem to make my brain shut off."

"We are seriously going to work on that. Stick with me, little cousin, and I will show you all the wonders and benefits of taking time for yourself."

If only it were that simple, Megan thought.

"I have plenty of distractions to offer you. My

precious baby girl, for starters. She is a surefire distraction. And then there's Maylene."

"Maylene?"

Summer nodded. "Our dog. She's a pug, and she's incredibly playful and sassy, and when she's around, there is no way you can zone out the way you just did. She won't allow it."

"She sounds like the perfect dog for you," Megan teased.

"Oh, she is. And trust me, you'll feel like a brand-new person in no time." She smiled brightly before she let out another happy little squeal. "This is going to be so great!"

Megan wished she could be that optimistic.

"I now pronounce you husband and wife. You may kiss the bride."

Alex did his best to smile and clap with the rest of the people in the large Catholic church, but honestly, this was getting old. Not weddings per se, but...okay, yeah. Weddings. Six of them in the past two years, and he'd been a groomsman in all of them. And while it was great to see all his friends so happy and in love and starting their lives with someone, he was seriously getting tired of putting on the tux and standing to the side and posing for pictures and just...*ugh*.

Technically, he was the last single guy out of his circle of friends.

Was it hot in here all of a sudden?

He adjusted his collar—which was suddenly choking him—and watched as Violet and George made their way out of the sanctuary. With his smile firmly in place, Alex stepped forward to hook arms with the bridesmaid he was paired with—Kaitlyn. She gave him a smile that conveyed what she'd been hinting at all weekend—she was available.

Great.

That was another perk that had stopped being enjoyable about five weddings ago—the interest in a no-strings-attached hookup. It was like there was some sort of target on him, or maybe he was throwing off some kind of vibe, or maybe someone in the bridal party had a big mouth, but whatever it was, Alex had no interest in hooking up with anyone.

Been there, done that, and…

He was over it.

As annoying as these weddings had become, the bottom line was he was tired of watching from the sidelines. It was something he wanted for himself. He wasn't getting any younger, and at thirty-two, he was ready to settle down—a wife, kids, a dog…yeah, he wanted all of that. Last year he had bought a house with the mind-set that it was something he would share with the woman of his dreams and together they'd build their lives there.

But so far, he hadn't found anyone he would consider sharing a life with.

Okay, technically that wasn't completely true, but…

"Bridal party! We need you to quickly form the receiving line so we can start greeting guests and keep to our timeline for pictures!" Linda, the super-perky wedding planner, called out.

Alex watched as she moved everyone into position

before giving the all clear to her assistant to start letting wedding guests come out to greet them.

Great. More smiling. He was already over this day and wanted nothing more than to loosen his tie and go to his hotel room—*alone*—and watch a little TV, order some room service, and maybe work on his schedule for the upcoming week.

Not that it changed much. As a physical therapist, Alex worked with some of his clients on a long-term basis. Right now, he had four he had been meeting with every week at their homes for almost three months. Then there were his clients at multiple rehab facilities in and around downtown Portland. Those clients were more traditional—knee or hip replacements, recovery from surgery or car accidents—nothing that required long-term rehab. His private clients were of the more challenging variety. They had injuries that couldn't be dealt with in a four-to-six-week time frame. Which was why he met them in their homes.

These were clients who had started out in the traditional setting and then were able to go home but still had a lot of recovery time ahead of them. All of his current clients were great—eager to get their mobility back and resume their lives as close to normal as they could get. Their attitudes made Alex's work easier, and he enjoyed being able to help them achieve their recovery goals.

To be honest, most of his clients—although challenging at times—were a pleasure to work with. Only once had he been so challenged that he seriously almost reconsidered his profession.

Zach Montgomery.

Alex remembered the anger and hostility Zach had

thrown at him from the moment they met. It had been shocking and more than a little intimidating to take him on as a client. Zach's reputation in the PT world had preceded him. So Alex had gone in as prepared as he could—or so he'd thought. It didn't take long for him to realize that Zach's injuries were the least of his problems.

The psychological trauma from his injuries had been far worse.

Luckily, Alex had forced himself to hold his ground and push back, and now the two of them were friends. Good friends. As a matter of fact, it was Zach's wedding two years ago that had started this whole string of weddings Alex found himself in.

Not that one had anything to do with the other, but he could look back and say it was the first of many weddings for him to act as a groomsman.

Beside him, Kaitlyn elbowed him playfully. He looked down at her in confusion.

"You're frowning," she whispered. "We're supposed to be smiling. Linda's been watching you, and no doubt you're going to get a lecture when we leave here on remembering to keep your smile in place all day."

He nodded.

"If you'd like, I can make sure you keep a smile on your face all day…and all night," she said seductively.

Alex studied her for a moment—long black hair, big green eyes, and…he wasn't feeling it. She was tall and willowy, and yet…there was no pull of attraction there. So rather than answer her, he immediately turned back to the couple waiting to greet him as they made their way toward the bride and groom.

At that first wedding, he met the woman he'd never

been able to forget. Now, when Alex thought about spending a weekend with someone who kept a smile on his face, he envisioned a curvy and petite woman with honey-blond hair and big brown eyes.

Megan.

It was crazy to keep thinking about her. You'd think after two years, he would have stopped. And it wasn't as if he hadn't dated since then. He had. Just…not a lot. There was no crime in that, but Alex knew he needed to face some serious facts.

Megan lived on the other side of the country.

She was a workaholic who didn't believe in taking time off for herself.

And clearly, their weekend together must have meant more to him because he'd been the one to try to maintain their connection. They'd planned a couple of weekend getaways that had fallen through, but the one time he'd actually flown to NYC for a weekend, she'd never even shown up. It had become abundantly clear that he was more invested in the relationship than she was.

She'd been the one to say that they weren't meant to be.

At the time, he'd believed her. Hell, he'd had no choice but to believe her. But the more time that had passed, the more he thought about the things they'd talked about. The way she laughed and how she looked when she smiled and…

Yeah. He still had it bad.

Another elbow to the ribs had him feeling a little annoyed. "I was smiling," he hissed softly.

Kaitlyn frowned at his tone. "I know, but Linda told us to make our way outside, and you were just standing there."

"Oh," he murmured. "Sorry."

The rest of the day was like being on a damn conveyer belt—the bridal party was constantly being told where to move and what to do, and there seemed to be no time to sit and breathe. *Move here, move there, stop and pose, smile, stand here, look there…* By the time the first dance was over at the reception, Alex's head was pounding. Kaitlyn stayed close, and he was running out of ways to be polite.

"Excuse me," he finally said to Kaitlyn when they were allowed to leave the dance floor. "I see some friends over there." Alex didn't wait to hear her response. He moved swiftly through the crowd of wedding guests, walked straight out of the hotel ballroom, and kept going until he found the bar.

Waving the bartender over, he ordered a beer. He knew he couldn't stay out here long, but maybe by the time he finished his drink, he'd have a better attitude toward the whole thing. Paying the tab, he grabbed the bottle in front of him, took a long pull, and almost groaned with pleasure. Tension started to ebb, and for the first time all day, he felt some sort of peace.

His phone vibrated in his pocket, and Alex pulled it out and read the incoming text. His Monday client had the flu and needed to reschedule. No big deal. It meant he could sleep in on Monday.

Or maybe he'd take the time to go to the gym or play some racquetball with a friend.

Zach.

He and Zach had gotten into the habit of playing racquetball once a week, and until a few months ago, it had been a highlight for Alex. But since Gabriella had gotten pregnant, Zach had gone into hyper-protective mode and spent most of his time doting on his wife. The thought made Alex chuckle. He doubted Gabriella would mind if her husband spent a little time on his own. She wasn't the kind of woman who enjoyed having her husband hover.

Alex quickly typed a memo for himself to reach out to Zach when he got home tomorrow to invite him to the gym Monday morning. Hopefully, they'd get a chance to catch up and start playing together again.

Sounds like a plan, he thought.

True, he could text Zach now and put it out there, but…he had a feeling that if he gave his friend too much time to think about it, he'd make excuses and bow out. A late-afternoon call was the way to go. Maybe he'd even text Gabriella first and give her a heads-up. Alex had a feeling she'd do her best to get Zach to agree.

So he typed a second memo to himself to text Gabriella tomorrow before calling Zach.

He was about to put his phone away but stopped. Unable to help himself, Alex scrolled through his phone and pulled up the one picture that, if it was an actual photograph he held in his hand, would be worn around the edges by now.

Big brown eyes smiled at him as her sexy smile beckoned. He'd taken the picture of her while they'd been walking in the garden during Zach and Gabriella's wedding reception. They'd been flirting, and he'd kissed her, and everything about her had called to him on every level.

She was beautiful.

Probably not the smartest thing to be doing right now—staring at a picture of a woman he hadn't seen or heard from in almost two years, but weddings tended to put him in that mind-set.

Going back to the current reception wasn't appealing in the least, but leaving wasn't an option. Finishing his beer, he waved to the bartender as he stood and straightened his tux. He'd return to the ballroom; he'd socialize and eat some amazing food. Then as soon as he could, he'd head out, go up to his room, and thank God that it was finally over. No more weddings after this.

There would probably be an awkward moment or two with Kaitlyn—she seemed like the type who didn't take no for an answer—but in the end, he'd walk away and spend the night blissfully on his own.

And think about the one who got away.

―――∾∾∾―――

Alex put his luggage down, shut the door, and breathed a sigh of relief.

Home.

Looking at the clock and seeing it was after eight, Alex knew it wasn't too late to call Zach. Hell, he should have done it from the car, but he had left later than he'd intended, and then there was traffic, and basically, he hadn't felt like talking to anyone.

Until now.

Starving, he made his way into the kitchen and quickly put together something to eat. Sandwich made, he grabbed a bottle of water and pulled out his phone. Once he was sitting down, he first took a bite of his dinner and then tapped out a text to Gabriella.

His head might be spinning from his long day, but he at least remembered to try to get her on his side first.

He was hungrier than he'd thought because he wolfed down the rest of his turkey sandwich and jumped up to make a second one before even looking at his phone. Gabriella sent him a thumbs-up, so after taking his first bite of sandwich number two, he pulled up Zach's number and hit Send.

"Hey, buddy! What's up?" Zach said when he answered.

"I am in desperate need of someone to beat at racquetball tomorrow morning, so naturally, you were the first one I thought of."

Zach's laughter was loud and infectious. "Is that right?"

"Hell yeah!" Alex agreed. "My Monday morning client is down with the flu, so I have some free time. And other than the perk of kicking your ass on the court, I figured it had been a while since we'd hung out, and I thought it would give us a chance to catch up before you run to the office to play Corporate CEO."

Zach was still chuckling. "It has been a while."

"Since I've kicked your ass?" Alex teased. "Yes. Yes, it has."

"Not that, dumbass. Since we've hung out. Geez, when was the last time I saw you?"

"We played about two months ago—and that was only because we happened to run into each other at the gym. You'd been blowing me off for a while since you told me you and Gabs were having a baby."

"Wow. Has it really been that long? She's in her third trimester already."

Now it was Alex's turn to chuckle. "Um, yeah. I know. You've been in Mother Hen mode—refusing to leave her alone."

"She had morning sickness—"

"Which went away four months ago!" Alex heard Gabriella call out.

"Dude, seriously—"

"Okay, okay, okay," Zach said. "Maybe I was being a little…cautious."

"Zach, do you really think there is anything your wife can't handle? I bet if you asked her, she'd be willing to not only drive you to the gym but leave you there for several hours so she could catch a break."

"For your information, Gabriella and I enjoy spending time together," Zach argued lightly. "Don't we, sweetheart?"

"It wouldn't kill you to go out once in a while without me," Gabriella said loudly enough for Alex to hear.

"Aha! I knew it!"

"What is…? Okay, fine. You heard it," Zach grumbled and then sighed loudly. "What time tomorrow?"

"That depends."

"On?"

"What time you need to be at the office and how many games we are going to try to get in."

"I don't have any meetings until…" Gabriella was giving him his schedule. "Ten. So how about we meet up at seven?"

Alex grinned. "Sounds about right."

"Great. Then I'll see you in the a.m."

"Awesome. Oh, and Zach?"

"Yeah?"

"Be prepared to lose," he said with a laugh as they hung up.

Putting the phone down, Alex finished the rest of his

dinner. Just knowing he was going to have time to catch up with his friend left him feeling lighter—especially because it was going to be while doing something they both loved.

Competing.

Alex fell to the floor and let out a hearty laugh. Zach threw his racquet and cursed.

Again.

"Tell me again how you're not out of shape," Alex said as he caught his breath. "Because that, my friend, was almost embarrassing. I'll tell you what. I won't even count that one as a game. We'll call it practice."

"It was our third game," Zach said angrily. "You can't have a practice game after you've already played two."

"I'm trying to be gracious here."

"Yeah, well...screw you," Zach grumbled. "And your graciousness." He sat down next to Alex and let out a weary sigh. "Okay, so maybe—just *maybe*—I'm a little off my game. It has been a while."

Alex rolled to sit up and grinned. "You know that's all on you, right?"

Zach glared at him. "Excuse me for being concerned about my wife's health."

"And there is nothing wrong with that. Seriously, I'm not harping on you for that. I just think you got a little... obsessive about it. Gabriella is in great shape. She had some morning sickness—most women do—but she hasn't had any other complications. You need to relax a bit. That's all I'm saying."

"You sound like her."

"Then maybe you should listen."

"Screw you."

Laughing, Alex climbed to his feet and held out a hand to Zach. "Need some help, old man?"

Ignoring his hand, Zach immediately jumped to his feet and stormed over to pick up his racquet. "One more game, and then let's hit the treadmills."

"I've already beat you three out of three," Alex said with a smart-ass grin. "That's our typical game plan. Best of three."

"I thought you said the last one was just practice?"

He shrugged. "And you said it wasn't."

"Shit."

"I'll tell you what. I'll agree to one more and give you a chance to at least *try* to win. Either way, I'm still the ultimate winner here."

"Nice of you to be such a good sport."

"I have my moments. But…"

Zach cursed as he got into position. "Now what?"

"Just admit that even if you win this one, I am still the reigning racquetball champion."

Groaning, Zach bounced the ball in front of him. "What if I just said you are the reigning pain in my ass and I know I can run longer and faster than you on the treadmill?"

Alex laughed. "You're on."

Twenty minutes later they were jogging side by side and Alex was telling Zach about his weekend.

"So did you hook up with her?" Zach asked.

"Hell no. I just wanted to get out of there."

Zach looked at him like he was crazy. "You said she was beautiful and interested. Why not take her up on her offer?"

Damn. Alex had stepped into that one.

Two years ago when he had hooked up with Megan, he had promised her he wouldn't tell her cousin. Little warning bells had gone off in his head because, really, what difference should it make? Especially when they started seeing one another beyond that weekend. But he had honored her request, and then…it never came up. So how was he supposed to explain to his friend—whom he shared pretty much everything with—why he was suddenly so dissatisfied with hookups?

"Alex?"

Oh, right. An answer.

He started off with a sigh. "I don't know. I think I'm at the point now where everyone I know is married, and…" Another sigh. "I never thought I'd be the last one standing, you know?"

"I hear ya. Although for me, I never thought I'd be the kind to get married. I thought I'd enjoy being single, traveling the world, doing whatever the hell I wanted until I was too old to do it anymore." He paused. "And then came Gabriella."

"She's amazing."

"Don't I know it." They jogged in silence for a couple of minutes before Zach turned to him again. "So is that why you're done with the hookups? You've met someone?"

Now what? Another long breath escaped, and Alex kept his gaze straight ahead. "I met someone a while ago. I thought we clicked, but…" He shrugged. "It didn't work out. Met her at one of the weddings, and we had a great weekend together. We kept in touch for about three months, and then…"

"Damn. That sucks."

"Yes, it does," Alex agreed. "But here's the thing…I can't stop thinking about her. Why can't I move on? Clearly she has, because she hasn't contacted me, but—"

"Does she live around here?"

Alex shook his head. "That was the main reason I never saw her again. Our work schedules kind of prevented it, and, really, I could deal with a little bit of a distance, but not other-side-of-the-country long."

"Maybe call her again. Send her a text and feel her out. A lot can change. For all you know, she's no longer at that job or living in the same place. What have you got to lose?"

Alex shrugged. "I'll think about it."

Zach began to push the buttons on the treadmill to pick up his speed and incline.

"Great. Now let's see if you can beat me in this last sprint. Loser buys breakfast."

Alex immediately began to push his settings and grinned. "You're on!"

Chapter 2

IT WAS HARD TO FEEL GOOD ABOUT BEING COMFORTABLE when you worked with a supermodel.

Okay, Gabriella wasn't a *real* supermodel, but she certainly looked like one.

All the time.

Megan looked at her reflection in the mirror and sighed. Back home, she wouldn't think twice about wearing a pair of black yoga pants and an oversized sweater to work. Occasionally, she'd even pair the ensemble with a pair of boots rather than sneakers.

Another sigh.

Her hair was pulled up in a messy bun, and while some women could totally rock that look, Megan felt like she looked more like someone who was too lazy to do her hair.

Which…she was.

This was her third day at her new job, and the first two days she had put a bit of an effort into her appearance, but today it seemed like too much of a pain. And now she was regretting it because since she'd opened the restroom door and met up with Gabriella, she'd felt like a homeless person in comparison to her cousin's wife.

Not that she was begrudging Gabriella anything. After all, if you had it, you should flaunt it, right? It was just that Megan wasn't used to seeing a woman in her seventh month of pregnancy walking around looking quite like that. She looked at the tennis shoes on her feet and frowned. No doubt Gabriella would have on mile-high stilettos. How she managed to walk around in those things was still a mystery. And her wardrobe looked like something off a New York fashion week runway—and she was pregnant!

After another look in the mirror, Megan realized that her sweater made her look like *she* was pregnant.

And not in a fashionable way like Gabriella.

"Damn," Megan murmured. It was blazingly obvious she was going to have to do something drastic like—*gulp*—go shopping. The thought was almost more than she could bear. With a little luck, maybe Gabriella and Summer would go with her. She'd bring it up later that day when she met her cousin for lunch.

Knowing there was nothing she could do about her choice of clothing at the moment, she made quick work of fixing her hair a bit and putting on some lip gloss. Feeling mildly appeased, she zipped up her purse and decided she couldn't stay in the bathroom forever. She looked okay, but it was a far cry from what she knew was waiting for her on the other side of the door.

And it was only slightly better than how she had looked five minutes ago.

Pulling open the door, she stepped out into the massive reception area and made her way toward her office.

"Good morning," Gabriella called out when Megan walked by her desk. "Coffee's made, and there are blueberry muffins if you're interested."

"Blueberry, huh? What's the occasion?" she asked as she looked around for them.

Gabriella laughed softly. "I was never a cake person, but this baby craves it. So I try to compromise and at least make ones with real fruit to ease my guilt."

Following Megan's gaze, Gabriella pointed toward the platter of muffins.

Megan took one and bit into it, nearly groaning with pleasure. "You made these?"

With a nod, Gabriella replied, "This morning. Zach had an early meeting in Vancouver, and once I was awake, I realized what I wanted to eat. I swear, I never thought pregnancy cravings were real, but this baby of mine is proving me wrong."

Pouring herself a cup of coffee, Megan smiled. "A friend of mine had her first baby last year. I remember going out with her and watching her order some strange things. We'd been friends for years, and I couldn't remember her ever eating most of the stuff she ate during her pregnancy. And you know what? She hasn't eaten any of it since."

For a few minutes, they ate in companionable silence, and then Megan decided to broach the subject of her wardrobe instead of waiting for lunch—and Summer.

"So I have a favor to ask," she began hesitantly.

"Okay."

"And I feel weird because you've all done so much for me already. I mean, the job, Summer letting me live in her guesthouse, and now you making me yummy food… I should probably just say thank you and work my own crap out for myself, but…"

"Megan?"

"Hmm?"

"You're rambling. What's going on?"

She sighed. "I think I need a new wardrobe."

Gabriella's face lit up. "Really?"

Megan nodded.

"And when you say a new wardrobe, you mean everything, right?"

She nodded again. "And I figured I'd ask Summer to help out too. Maybe we could make a day of it on Saturday or something."

Gracefully, Gabriella turned and put her coffee mug down before looking at Megan again. "I think that is the perfect plan. We'll talk to Summer about it over lunch, and since it's for you, Zach can't possibly have a problem with it."

"He's been a bit of a—"

"Nervous Nelly?" Gabriella said with a grin. "Yes. If it wasn't so incredibly sweet, it would be annoying. Don't get me wrong, I love the attention, and I love how concerned he is, but there are times when I need to go off by myself and shop or get a pedicure, and he's always right there with me."

Megan laughed so hard she almost choked on her muffin. "Please tell me he just sits with you when you get a pedicure!"

Gabriella smiled as she shook her head. "In the beginning, I think he figured he'd sit and watch. Then he tried it. Now he comes with me because he enjoys it!" She laughed. "Please don't tell him I said that! He'd die of embarrassment!"

With a zipping motion across her lips, Megan winked. "Well, whenever you need to escape without him, feel free to use me as an excuse. I have no problem covering for you."

"You have no idea how much I appreciate that or how much I am going to take you up on your offer."

They laughed as Megan finished her muffin and refreshed her coffee. With another word of thanks, she waved and made her way to her office, and before she knew it, she was up to her eyebrows in emails and phone messages from employees who were having issues with some of the new programs they were installing.

"If only they realized this is just the beginning," she murmured as she went to work. No one liked change, and learning a new operating system was even more of a challenge than some people could handle. Megan thrived on learning new things; she had worked with Zach remotely over the past month to get him ready for the transition, and she knew she'd have to work equally as hard to put the employees' minds at ease as she would to get the new system in place.

That was why she'd ended up working so many hours over the past few days.

"Hey! You ready for lunch?"

Megan turned to see Summer standing in the doorway. For a minute, she was confused. Ready for lunch? Glancing at the clock, she saw it was almost one.

She stood and stretched and then laughed when Summer hugged her. "Have I mentioned how happy I am that you're here?"

Megan hugged her back. "About a hundred times, but I love hearing it."

"I have to admit, there was a very real possibility of me not being here, but I'm glad Ethan and I compromised."

Looking at her curiously, Megan asked, "You mean the whole moving to North Carolina thing?"

Summer nodded. "Originally, we were moving there full time. But after we got married and talked about it, it was obvious how much he loved it here—not just Portland but working with Zach. So the house in North Carolina is our vacation home now. Plus, I found I kind of like being with this branch of the family for a while."

"It's really just Zach—"

With a smile, Summer grabbed Megan into another hug. "And now you."

That's probably one of the nicest things anyone has ever said to me, Megan thought.

"Come on—Gabs is waiting, and she's cranky."

"Uh-oh," Megan said as she grabbed her purse. "How come?"

"She's hungry and we're keeping her waiting," Summer said with a grin.

Together they walked to meet up with Gabriella, and as they rode down in the elevator, they talked about lunch options and eventually agreed on a small café around the corner from the office. Megan waited until they were seated and looking at menus to ask Summer about going shopping.

"Oh my God, yes!" Summer said with a huge smile. "I need a good shopping day!"

"Oh no," Gabriella murmured.

"What? What did I say?" Summer asked.

Putting her menu down, Gabriella looked at her patiently. "You are probably the *last* person who needs a shopping day. The last time you went to the mall, what happened?"

Summer played with her silverware and adjusted the napkin on her lap. "I…shopped."

"Really?"

Rather than respond to Gabriella, Summer looked at Megan. "I bought some dresses for Amber."

Megan was confused. "And that's wrong? Why?"

"She's barely three months old, and she doesn't need fourteen dresses," Gabriella said with exasperation. "Summer, your daughter is beautiful. Stunning. She looks completely adorable in everything you dress her in."

"But?" Summer prompted.

"But whenever you get within ten feet of a baby department, you tend to go a little crazy."

"That won't be a problem," Megan said, trying to defuse the situation. "I promise we'll pick places that don't even *have* a baby department. If anything, *I'm* the baby," she added quickly. "If you need to dress someone up, dress me! Seriously, I'm desperate. I normally wear yoga pants to work. It's been two years since I bought a new bra. I've never once been to a Victoria's Secret, and I wear old T-shirts to bed."

As she let out a sigh of relief at her fashion confession, she missed the nervous glances exchanged between Gabriella and Summer.

"Two years?" Summer asked. "Really? How is that possible?"

Megan shrugged. "I don't know…the one I have fits fine. I didn't need another."

"Everyone needs new lingerie," Summer countered. "We're girls. It's what we do."

"No one was seeing it except me, so…"

"Oh," Summer said, and then it hit her. "Ooohhh…"

What was the point in denying the truth? "Yup. So now you know why I need help."

"We're here for you," Gabriella said, reaching across the table and patting Megan's hand.

"This is going to be an all-day event," Summer said. "I can't guarantee I'll be able to stay away from home for that long—Amber will need to be nursed—"

"You can pump beforehand and bring the pump with you, right?" Gabriella asked. "Ethan won't have any problem feeding her while you're gone."

"She's fussy about taking the bottle," Summer explained.

"It's all right," Gabriella said. "If we schedule and plan it right, we'll stop for lunch, and you can run home while Megan and I eat, and then we'll meet up again when you're done."

"That will work. And I'll let Ethan know where we are, and if he needs to, he can bring Amber to me while we're shopping."

"Wait," Megan said as unease crept its way up her spine. "How long do you think this is going to take? I figured we'd hit Macy's or something and get everything there. We can be done by lunch."

Gabriella and Summer looked at each other and started laughing.

Megan wasn't sure whether she should be offended.

"Megs," Summer began, "trust me. There is no such thing as getting everything in one place. If you're going to do this, you're going to want to do it right."

"I don't need *that* big of a wardrobe. I do have some outfits I can still use."

The look both of them gave her said otherwise.

"Don't worry," Summer said soothingly. "We won't go too crazy, but we will need to cover the basics—a couple pairs of nice pants, some skirts, maybe some dresses, shoes, underwear, and then a couple of casual outfits and sleepwear."

"I don't mind the T-shirts," Megan grumbled.

"And you're going to want some fun outfits for when you start dating," Gabriella said with a smile.

"Um…that won't be necessary right away. I mean, I work a lot of hours and—"

"Maybe your last job was like that, but I can tell you right now Zach won't allow you to live at the office," Gabriella said.

"Neither will Ethan. They don't believe in working their employees like that. And trust me—don't argue with them about it. You won't win," Summer said.

So far, none of this was going like she'd planned— first the topic of shopping and now her work schedule. Megan picked up her menu and forced a smile. "Okay! What are we ordering?"

—◦◦◦—

"I think you seriously need to just give up. You've gotten soft. Maybe think about taking up something like…badminton. Or knitting."

Zach growled as he paced away and then back again, and all Alex could do was grin.

"It's okay. It happens to everyone. You know… you're old and out of shape. Maybe we should think about going for a stroll in the park where you won't exert yourself so much."

The words his friend was muttering were quite color- ful as they bounced off the racquetball court walls. Even though Zach had done better, Alex was still kicking ass, and as much as he was enjoying it, he could tell Zach no longer was.

"Fine. No strolling in the park. How about you pick the next challenge?" he suggested.

That perked Zach up. "And you can't complain?"

Alex laughed. There wasn't an activity the two of them had ever done together that he hadn't enjoyed. "Bring it."

"Painting."

"Not a…wait. What?"

Zach grinned. "We're painting the nursery this weekend," he explained. "And the guest room, bathroom, and hallway."

"Isn't it a little soon to be painting the nursery?"

"We're going with a neutral color since Gabriella and I decided that we want to be surprised by the sex of the baby," Zach explained. "Once we decided on that, we realized we were going to be seeing an influx of guests once the baby came, so we thought we'd spruce up the entire guest side of the house. I already recruited Ethan to come help me while Gabriella and Summer go shopping with Megan and…"

Everything in Alex stilled. "Um…Megan?"

"Oh, right. I didn't tell you about that," he said with a small laugh. "My cousin Megan just moved here from Albany. She's staying with Summer and Ethan and is working for me now because we're changing computer systems and she's kind of an IT genius. We're only a week in and…"

Zach's words faded away as Alex tried to come to grips with the fact that Megan Montgomery was here in Portland. Minutes away. It had to be a sign, right?

It had to be the reason why she was suddenly on his mind. The thought of seeing her, talking to her…touching her again, it had Alex's blood pumping in a way that racquetball hadn't.

"I'll do it!" he suddenly blurted out, and Zach looked at him like he was crazy. Which he was. After all, Zach had been talking about computer systems, and here he was shouting out about painting. And there was no guarantee he would see her. Yet. But there was at least a chance.

"Um…okay. Great. Do you want to come over tomorrow morning?"

No. Tomorrow was too long. Hell, Alex wasn't even sure how he was going to get through today!

"You know, it would save a lot of time and make the weekend more efficient if we prepped tonight. That is, if you're ready. Maybe call Ethan and we can get a jump start on it."

Not questioning Alex's sudden enthusiasm, Zach agreed. "I had planned on doing some of that tonight—taking off switch-plate covers, taping the trim, that sort of thing."

"How about I bring over a couple of pizzas and help?" Alex quickly suggested.

This time Zach laughed. "Dude, you're awfully excited about this. Is painting a secret passion of yours?"

No. But your cousin is…

He laughed nervously. "No…no, it's not that. I've been bored lately, and I had nothing planned for the weekend, and really, I am happy to lend a hand."

Zach didn't look like he believed him, but he didn't push him about it. "Great. Well…um…actually, Ethan,

Summer, and Megan were already going to come over tonight, but the more the merrier, right? I was planning on burgers. Why don't you bring the beer. And maybe ice cream for the girls. Gabriella's been craving all things chocolate."

"I don't think that's a pregnancy craving. That's an all-day, everyday female thing."

"Either way, grab the most chocolaty ice cream you can find—and maybe some butter pecan for the guys—and the beer, and I'll grill. Deal?"

Alex shook Zach's hand and did everything in his power to hide the goofy grin he felt tugging at his lips. "Deal."

They left the court and went to the locker room to shower and change before they went their separate ways—Zach to work, Alex to his morning client. He was going to have all day to think—obsess, really—about what he was going to do and say later on when he and Megan were face-to-face.

He'd have to play it cool and then...wait. What if she didn't remember him? What if—like he'd been fearing—their weekend together had meant more to him than it had to her?

"Don't go there," he murmured and then cursed. He was mildly disgusted with himself.

Why? Why after two years was he still thinking about this? About her? It was a weekend! Granted, it was a damn spectacular weekend, but still. He was a grown man who'd had more than his share of...well...great weekends. He'd been in relationships, and he'd been in love. Although right now he couldn't conjure up the face of even one other woman.

Only Megan's.

Knowing he had to get back on track, he walked in through the front doors and waved to Cindy at the reception desk. Then he made his way to the PT room to set up. His client today—Nathan Adams—was suffering from degenerative disc disease. He and Alex had been working together for months out of Nathan's home. Three weeks ago, Nathan had been in a car accident and was now dealing with not only his preexisting issues but also the injury from the accident. Alex had scheduled them for a two-hour session rather than their usual one hour because he knew they were going to need to take things slowly. This was their first session since the accident, so Alex wanted to have time to talk with Nathan about how he was feeling before they got started with movement and exercises.

As he set up his station, Alex chatted with other therapists and found that being around like-minded people was enough to get him focused on the job rather than his personal life. He loved what he did—loved helping people—and the dream was to someday have a facility or practice of his own. While he was building his client list, it wasn't enough to support him yet. After all, the goal was to get the patients well enough that they didn't need him anymore. Working for others wasn't an issue—not really. But there were times when Alex wished he could be his own boss, buy his own equipment, and try some new therapies the more traditional facilities tended to shy away from.

Someday, he thought.

The house he'd bought had a space over the detached garage that was currently set up as an apartment, but he'd considered transforming it into therapy space. It was basically a large studio apartment with a small kitchen area, but it had a massive full bathroom with a spa tub and separate shower. Alex knew with a few modifications he could turn it into the perfect space for clients. The only drawback? It was on the second floor. There was no way most patients would be able to get up there.

In the past several months, he'd tried to come up with ways to make it work—adding an elevator seemed the most logical option—but the cost to do so was a little more than he wanted to invest, and the change would mean losing space in both the garage and the apartment. And right now the garage was fully utilized for his second car and storage. The space had been a perk when he purchased the house, but now it sat vacant. Eventually he'd figure out what he wanted to do with it.

"Depressing thoughts for another time," he murmured and decided to get his head focused on what he was here for. Therapy.

Placing a stack of towels on the table beside him, Alex looked up as Nathan was wheeled into the therapy room by one of the nurses. Damn. He looked rough. There was still a lot of bruising on the man's face, and as he got closer, Alex could see him grimacing in pain. Today's session, unfortunately, wasn't going to ease anything.

There was going to be cursing and crying and probably a whole lot of begging for them to stop. Alex was sympathetic to it, he was, but he knew if they could get over these first few sessions, they'd start to see results, and the healing would begin.

He smiled broadly as he walked over and held out his hand.

"Nathan! It's good to see you, buddy!" he said. "Are you ready to get started?"

———~~~———

"So then I was thinking how I could get from the pool to the house without anyone seeing me," Summer was saying while laughing. "And Megan grabbed two cushions from the patio set, and we ran into the house!"

Megan wiped away tears as she laughed at the memory. "It was the last time either of us dared one another to go skinny-dipping!"

Zach was standing in the kitchen putting the meat on a platter while Gabriella stood beside him slicing tomatoes, and they were laughing too. "I'm glad I didn't witness that," he said. "Although I'm sure Ryder wishes he didn't remember it!"

"No one was supposed to be up," Summer argued lightly. "We thought we were so smart going out to the pool when everyone was asleep. We had no idea Ryder had snuck out and was trying to sneak back in!"

Beside her, Ethan leaned in and kissed her on the cheek and then bent to kiss baby Amber on the head. "Tell all these stories now while our daughter is too young to understand them. I don't want you giving her any ideas."

"Oh, stop," Summer said, playfully swatting him away.

"Although," Megan said with a grin, "Amber is going to have a new cousin soon. There's no telling what kind of mayhem they'll get into together. Especially if this new cousin is a girl."

This is good, Megan thought. It was a Friday night, and here she was laughing and hanging out with her cousins and their wives and feeling very relaxed. Happy. She'd survived her first week, and she hadn't worked beyond five o'clock any of those days. Gabriella had made sure of it. Although now would be as good a time as any to talk about the things she needed to do starting next week.

"I think I need to look at cars," she said.

"What's the rush?" Summer asked. "You know you can borrow mine anytime."

She smiled at her cousin. "And I appreciate that. But this is something I'm going to have to do eventually."

"Well, of course it is," Gabriella commented. "But you've only been here a week, and I guess we're just making sure you're not overwhelmed by all of us and looking for an excuse to not be with us."

Megan laughed. "Guys, don't be silly! That's not it at all! I know I'm going to be living in Portland for a while, and I want to start making my own way. I appreciate the hospitality, and I love being here with you. But I'm a practical person, and I don't like to feel like I'm not pulling my own weight. I don't want to be a drain on anyone, and honestly, I feel bad enough about the timing of my move."

"Why?" Zach asked.

With a sigh, Megan looked over at Summer and Ethan. "You guys just had a baby and have had people in your house ever since. I would think you'd be looking forward to having the place to yourself by now."

Summer waved her off. "This is different. You're living in the guesthouse, and you're working. My mom wanted to stay in our guest room so she could help out when Amber woke up at night."

"But she was here for a while, right?"

"Yes, she was," Summer said with a small laugh before she turned and looked at Zach. "Do you remember how long Mom stayed when Amber was born?"

"Didn't she leave like two weeks ago?" he asked.

"No, more like a month, but she was here for almost two! And don't get me wrong, I appreciated the help, and I loved how she had time to bond with Amber, and it gave me time to sleep, but…oh my God! It was glorious when we had our first night of it being just the three of us. Right?" she asked Ethan.

He nodded vigorously. "Your mother is a perfectly delightful woman, but there is something to be said for being able to walk around in my boxers in my own home." Then he chuckled. "I learned *that* lesson fast. You do *not* want your mother-in-law seeing you with morning wood."

"Dude," Zach murmured but then started to laugh. "I can sympathize, and yet…I almost wish I could have seen the look on your face!"

"It wasn't so much the look as the scream he let out," Summer said playfully. "Mom was mortified, of course, but later on she gave a nod of approval."

"*What?*" Ethan cried.

"Baby, you have an amazing body," Summer cooed as she leaned over and kissed him. "There's no shame in it."

"There is when your mother-in-law thinks that," Ethan grumbled. "It's just…wrong. And gross. And now I'll never walk out of the bedroom in my boxers again."

The look on Summer's face showed how much she didn't believe that statement for one minute.

"Anyway," Summer went on, "it was great having Mom here—and Aunt Monica and Aunt Eliza—but they were a little exhausting at times."

Zach laughed. "I have to admit, I was a little surprised that the aunts came and stayed for as long as they did. Nothing against you, Summer," he quickly corrected, "but I would have thought they would have waited to come when you had the christening and then stayed for a long weekend with everyone."

"I think it was an excuse for them to get away for a bit. There were several days when I didn't see them at all," Summer said.

"They did come over and spend a lot of time with us," Gabriella said. "They both were so curious to talk to Zach about how he was feeling and about the physical therapy he did after the accident that we finally referred them to Alex."

Megan choked on her drink and began to cough. Zach was immediately at her side, patting her gently on the back. "You okay?" he asked.

Slowly, she nodded and did her best to catch her breath. "Yeah…um…sorry. It went down the wrong way."

"You sure?" he asked, and Megan nodded again. He rubbed her back for a moment before returning to his prep work.

"Anyway," Gabriella went on, "we never found out why they had so many questions or were so curious about the whole thing, but they spent a lot of time talking to Alex." She paused. "Come to think of it, we never asked him what it was all about."

"You can ask him tonight," Zach said. "He should be here any minute."

And just like that, Megan started choking again. This time Ethan came over and patted her on the back until she caught her breath.

He carefully moved her glass away. "Maybe wait a while before you try that again," he teased. Everyone laughed, and Megan did her best to join in, but inside she felt like she was going to be sick.

"I'm good," she said after a moment.

"You didn't mention Alex was coming," Gabriella said as she began putting a salad together.

"I asked him if he could come help us paint this weekend, and he said yes and even volunteered to help out tonight."

"Well, that was nice of him," Summer said, placing Amber on her shoulder and rubbing her back.

"He's bringing beer and dessert," Zach said with a grin. Then he looked at Ethan. "And I thought we could shoot some hoops before dinner since the rest of the night will be a snooze fest of unscrewing switch plates and taping trim."

"Yes!" Ethan said with relief. "I was hoping there was going to be something else to do!"

"Hey, you volunteered," Zach reminded him.

"I know, but that's because I'm a nice guy and a good friend. Doesn't mean I wasn't going to be bored out of my mind," he clarified.

"Megan, did you meet Alex at our wedding?" Gabriella asked.

Immediately, she felt her cheeks warm and knew she was minutes away from a panic attack. "Um…I don't think so," she said and then quickly excused herself. It wasn't until she was in the bathroom that she finally allowed herself to breathe. She'd known she was going to see Alex eventually; she just wasn't expecting it to be quite so soon. Looking down at herself, she groaned. Sure, he couldn't come over *after* she'd gone shopping?

It was impossible to do anything about what she was wearing, and as she glanced at her reflection in the mirror, she cursed the fact that she hadn't even had the good sense to bring a little lip gloss or anything with her. Closing her eyes, she silently counted to ten and forced herself to leave the bathroom.

The doorbell rang as she was walking by the front door, so when Zach asked her to get it, how could she say no? Letting out a slow breath, Megan reached a shaky hand toward the door and pulled it open.

And basically forgot how to breathe.

Yeah, he was everything she remembered and so much more—sandy-brown hair, tall, lean build, and muscles that made her want to reach out and touch them.

Or lick them. Whatever.

He was wearing dark sunglasses, so she had no idea if he was as surprised to see her as she was to see him, but he smiled as he softly said, "Hey, Megan."

And just like that she was practically a puddle on the floor.

"Hey," she said and wanted to curse how breathless she sounded. Stepping aside, she motioned for him to come in.

"Thanks."

Her cheeks heated, and she couldn't make herself look directly at him. "Everyone's in the kitchen." And when she walked past him, she could almost *feel* him. Swallowing hard, she led the way to where everyone was and quickly took her seat. Then she took a moment to congratulate herself on not acting like an idiot in front of him.

"Alex!" Gabriella said with a smile as she walked over and hugged him. "Thanks for coming over."

He held up a grocery bag. "And I come bearing gifts!

I heard I couldn't go wrong with anything chocolate, so I found chocolate chocolate-chip ice cream with brownies in it. I hope that will work."

Gabriella looked at him before glancing over at Megan and Summer. "Will that work?" she asked with a laugh. "I may have to leave my husband for you! Thank you!" She kissed him on the cheek and immediately put the bag in the freezer. "What else was in there?"

"I bought some butter pecan and some cookie-dough ice cream in case the guys wanted some," he teased. Turning, Alex shook hands with Zach and Ethan and then came over to kiss Summer on the cheek. "Good to see you, Summer."

"Hey, Alex," Summer said with a smile.

He crouched beside her and smiled at Amber. "Look how she's grown," he said softly, reaching out to touch the baby's hand. "Hey, Princess. How are you?"

And right then and there, Megan's ovaries nearly exploded.

Taking off his sunglasses, Alex smiled at the baby and made a couple of funny faces before he straightened and took the beer Zach was offering him. "Thanks."

"Zach and I were trying to remember, Alex, if you and Megan had met at our wedding," Gabriella said. "Megan said she didn't remember, but I feel like I remember seeing you guys dance."

Megan averted her eyes, but she could feel Alex staring at her, and she didn't want to give anything away. So she busied herself with smoothing her sweater and pulling imaginary lint from her pants.

"We might have," Alex said casually, "but it was a long time ago, so…who's to say."

"Well, then let me reintroduce you," Gabriella said, oblivious to how awkward the moment was. "Alex, this is Zach's cousin Megan. Megan, this is our friend Alex."

With no other choice, Megan looked up, smiled at him, and offered a shy hello, and when he returned her smile, she was grateful to be sitting. Without the sunglasses, he was lethal.

Stepping forward, Alex held out his hand to her. He was close enough that only she could see the amusement in his eyes. "It's a pleasure to meet you, Megan," he said, and to the casual observer, it was a simple and pleasant greeting. To Megan, it was like a caress.

Swallowing hard, she put her hand in his. "Thanks," she said quietly. "It's nice to meet you too."

If his hand lingered a little long, no one seemed to notice.

But Megan did.

And just when she was about to sigh dreamily, Zach spoke up.

"C'mon, we've got about thirty minutes until the grill is ready, so let's go shoot some hoops!"

Alex let go of Megan's hand, but his gaze stayed on hers for a heartbeat longer. Then as if they hadn't just shared a moment, he turned and clapped his hands together. "Let's go! I'm looking forward to beating you at something else today!"

Zach kissed Gabriella.

Ethan kissed Summer and Amber.

Alex gave Megan a sly wink as he walked out the door.

He played basketball and won.

He joked with Ethan and Zach as they grilled dinner.

And he made pleasant conversation with Gabriella and Summer.

As expected, Alex ended up sitting next to Megan, and when his knee brushed hers under the table, he heard her soft intake of breath.

He'd missed that sound.

All through dinner, conversation flowed, and while Megan was polite to him, she also wouldn't look directly at him. At first, he was amused, but now her avoidance was starting to piss him off.

"So, Megan," he began, "Zach mentioned how you moved here from Albany. That's a pretty drastic move for a job."

This time she did glance at him and offered a small— but forced—smile. "My contract with my previous employer ended, and I was trying to find something new. So when my father and uncle mentioned that Zach's office was looking to change over its computer system, it seemed like the perfect opportunity."

Alex nodded. "So it was the job that brought you here then. Nothing else?"

She looked at him with mild irritation. "Well, the thought of working with family was certainly a perk."

"All the Montgomery offices are going to change over to this system, but we're doing it first because I was smart enough to snag my favorite cousin," Zach said.

Everyone laughed, and Alex saw the blush on Megan's face.

"I have to admit, the obvious choice was to go to San

Diego and be with Christian, but so far I'm pleased with my decision," she said.

"Who's Christian?" Alex asked with a little more aggression than he had intended.

"Megan's brother," Zach said around a mouthful of hamburger. "He's running the San Diego office my brother Ryder used to run."

"And what happened to Ryder? Where is he?" Alex asked, confused by the sheer number of Montgomery family members and where they were all located.

"Ryder is in North Carolina," Ethan answered. "He went there for a bit of a sabbatical and ran into an ex-girlfriend, and they reconnected and got married. She has a business there, so Ryder decided to relocate."

Nodding, Alex turned toward Megan. "Any other siblings?"

"I have another brother—Carter. He's a chef," she replied.

"Wow! A Montgomery who isn't in the finance empire?" Alex asked with amusement. "How did that go over?"

Zach was the one to respond. "I think everyone would have been a lot more upset if Carter wasn't a genius in the kitchen. He's got restaurants in LA, Vegas, and New Orleans, and he's looking to expand in the next couple of years. After the success of the first place, no one brought up his straying from the family business again."

Megan laughed. "Carter's lucky the whole chef–restaurateur thing worked out because my parents thought he was crazy. Even after the first place succeeded, they still thought it was a phase," she said. "When he started appearing on the morning talk shows and showing up in the tabloids as a 'celebrity chef,' they finally accepted his choice of career."

"Oh my gosh," Summer interjected. "Ethan and I went to Carter's place in New Orleans last year while we were on vacation, and I don't think I've ever had a meal like that."

"He knew we were coming in," Ethan explained, "and when we arrived, the servers were instructed not to give us a menu. Carter prepared a special meal for us, and it was…it was…I'm telling you, it was spectacular."

"I still don't know where he got his talent," Megan said. "My mother was never creative in the kitchen. I mean, she always cooked perfectly fine meals for us, but nothing on the scale of what Carter does."

"What about you?" Alex asked. "Do you cook like your brother?"

Megan's eyes went wide, and then she laughed out loud. "Oh God no," she said. "I am *not* someone who cooks. I know the basics, but I end up getting takeout or microwave meals way more than I should."

"You can't be that bad at cooking," Summer said. "I remember staying with you one summer during college, and we didn't eat out all that much."

"Sandwiches and salads," Megan said. "I make a mean sandwich, and I am practically a gourmet with salads, but if it has to be cooked? I can't do it."

"Oh, come on," Gabriella said. "You have to be exaggerating."

Megan gave her a look. "Are you willing to test that theory and let me make dinner one night?"

"Um…maybe we could…I mean…I'm sure we could try…" Gabriella stammered.

"What my wife is trying to say," Zach interrupted, "is she takes her meals very seriously these days, and maybe sometime *after* the baby comes and if she wants to lose weight, she'll consider it."

Megan laughed at her cousin's attempt at patting her on the head. "Oh, I can guarantee you'll lose weight, Gabs, if it's up to me to prepare meals. No worries. I'm your girl."

Conversation veered away from her brother and cooking skills and moved on to the plans for what they wanted to accomplish tonight and what they were going to try to finish the next day.

"We can move some of the furniture tonight too," Zach said. "I think between the three of us we can get it all done."

"We can help," Summer volunteered. "Well, I mean, Megan and I can. Amber's asleep, and if we all lend a hand, you'll get done faster and then we can have dessert!"

"Oh, sweetie," Gabriella said, "we are having dessert even if the guys aren't done. I'm already thinking of the ice cream Alex brought. *All* of the ice cream."

"But Megan and I can do stuff like take pictures down or strip the bedding in the guest room…you know, nothing major."

"I don't mind helping," Megan said.

"If you're sure," Zach said.

Everyone was in agreement, and once dinner was completed, Summer and Gabriella started cleaning up the kitchen while Megan went to help with the little stuff so the guys could start moving furniture. Alex waited a minute to see how everyone was going to disperse, and when he watched Megan walk in one direction and Zach and Ethan in another, he saw his opportunity and grabbed it.

"Why don't I start moving stuff out of the guest room while you get the tools and whatnot?" he suggested.

"Good plan," Zach said. "Megan can take down the pictures and put any of the knickknacks into drawers. And if you can get some of the stuff moved—we're going to try to put as much as we can in the office—I'll get Ethan started on taking stuff down in the bathroom, and I'll do the nursery."

With a nod of agreement, everyone sprang into action, and as Alex headed toward the guest room, he had to remember to breathe. He didn't miss the fact that she had practically dashed from the dinner table—no doubt to get away from him—but she couldn't avoid him forever.

Hell, he wasn't even going to let her avoid him for another five minutes.

"Hey," he said softly as he ducked his head into the room. Her big brown eyes went wide at the sight of him, and those soft pink lips parted as she gasped.

"Oh! I...I didn't think anyone was ready to start in here yet. I thought I'd...um..." But her words died away.

Smiling, Alex stepped into the room and explained the plan he and Zach had come up with.

"So...we're supposed to start moving stuff into the office?" she asked.

Nodding, he looked around. The room was large with a queen-size bed, two nightstands, and a dresser. There was a flat-screen television mounted on the wall along with several pictures. Megan was moving some things into the dresser drawers and was doing her best to keep her back to him. Alex chuckled.

"What? What's so funny?" she asked, still not turning around.

"You're going to have to look at me eventually, you know," he said casually and was pleasantly surprised when she did. She looked a little flushed and embarrassed, but at least she was looking at him.

"So you've been here a week already. How are you enjoying Portland?"

She returned her attention to her task. "I haven't gone out sightseeing or anything yet. This whole week has been spent getting settled in at work. Summer's been great with pointing out things on our way to work and all, but—"

"And you're staying in the guesthouse?"

"For now. I was relieved to have a place to stay right away. It takes some of the pressure off so I can focus on work."

Work. Yeah. That was a sore spot with him where she was concerned, and right now, he was kind of glad she wasn't looking at him because he was certain his displeasure was written all over his face.

"I'll start looking for a place of my own in the next couple of weeks, but it's nice to not have to think about it yet. As it is, I have to buy a car."

He looked at her oddly when she turned around to start moving other items into drawers. "Didn't you bring anything with you from New York? I know it wouldn't have been easy to drive cross-country, but it seems like you must have sold everything in order to move here."

"I did," she said as she closed a drawer. "The cost of moving all my furniture and keeping it in storage until I found a place wasn't cost-effective. I figured I would start fresh when I got here."

Nodding, he slid his hands into his pockets and waited to see if she would offer up any other information about herself without him prompting her.

But patience wasn't his strong suit right now.

"So, how have you been?" he asked, stepping closer to her.

"Good."

He chuckled softly. "Good," he said. "Me too."

She nodded and then moved to unplug the lamps. When she went to turn away from him, he placed a hand on her arm to stop her. She turned to him, and he saw every emotion she was feeling right there in her eyes. His heart melted a little, and he couldn't help but smile.

"Hey," he said softly.

That one word seemed to do the trick because she visibly relaxed.

"I was surprised when Zach told me you'd moved here," he said quietly, his hand still on her. He wanted to skim it down her arm and take her hand in his, but he knew it was too soon for that. "I wish you had called and let me know."

Megan took a step away, and he instantly missed the feel of her.

"Alex," she began, "it's been two years. I...it would have been weird to reach out to you after all that time."

"Why?"

"Seriously? What if you were involved with

someone? And why would I even assume you'd want to see me? After the way things ended—"

"Do you?" he interrupted, fairly blurting out the question.

She looked at him curiously. "Do I what?"

"Do you want to see me?"

Her brows furrowed. "I'm seeing you right now, Alex."

He laughed. "I know, but…did you *want* to see me? Did you think about looking me up when you got settled?"

Her hesitation wasn't encouraging.

"Alex…"

Then he stepped forward and reached for her hand. "Okay, it wasn't fair of me to put you on the spot like that. But I want you to know I'm happy you're here. I…I think about you a lot." His eyes met hers, and he saw confusion in those dark-brown depths. "I mean it. I hated the way things ended between us."

"I did too. But geography wasn't on our side, and then my job, and…I don't know… I don't expect you to feel obligated to make something more of it than it was."

Okay, *that* wasn't what he was expecting, and this time it was he who stepped away. "What's that supposed to mean?"

Megan sighed. "Look, I'm sure this is awkward for you because Zach's a good friend and I'm his cousin. No one knows about us, so there's nothing that says we have to do anything now—you're off the hook. Zach will never know, so we're free to be…acquaintances or something."

Was she for real? Did she really have no idea that was the *last* thing he was looking for? Hell, he'd practically lived his life in limbo for the past two years because he couldn't get her out of his mind! And now she was saying it didn't mean anything? "Megan, I—"

"Hey, man," Zach said as he walked into the room. "I grabbed a screwdriver and a drill for you. I think you'll need them to take the television bracket from the wall." Without any indication that he felt the tension in the room, he grinned. "Let me know when you're ready to start moving furniture, and we'll come in." Then he looked at Megan. "Don't worry about helping with all of this. Seriously. The girls are in the kitchen, and I saw my wife pulling ice cream from the freezer."

Megan smiled—a real smile. Not the forced ones she'd been throwing his way all night. "It's fine, Zach. I may not be strong enough to move the furniture, but I can at least help with some of the smaller stuff."

Walking over, he hugged her and gave her a loud, smacking kiss on her head before he left the room.

When they were alone again, Alex knew it wouldn't last too long. Things needed to be done, and he wasn't going to get the answers he wanted from her tonight. With a sigh of resignation, he said, "I'm going to work on the TV. If you could take those pictures and put them in the office, that would be great."

Nodding, Megan turned and immediately took one painting from the wall and then the other. They worked in silence for a few minutes, and then he needed her help. The television wasn't large, and he had carefully started to take it from the wall, but a second set of hands was required to disconnect the wires. "Can you give me a hand with the cords?"

She was right there and did what was needed. She was so close he could smell her perfume, and he had to fight the urge to inhale deeply. "Thanks," he murmured and quickly stepped away and took the television to Zach's office. And that's where he stayed for a moment to catch his breath and try to regain some focus.

"This is crazy," he mumbled. Leaning against the desk, Alex took a couple of deep breaths, let them out, and forced himself to clear his mind. He was pinching the bridge of his nose and trying to push away visions of Megan when Ethan stepped into the room.

"Don't tell me you're taking a break already!" he teased. "Dude, even Megan's moved more stuff than you."

It was the perfect way to break the tension, and Alex laughed. "Yeah, well…if I hadn't won the game against the two of you earlier, I'd have a lot more energy."

Ethan clapped him on the shoulder. "Nice try. But I'm on to you now, and I'll be making sure you pull your weight so we can get this done in one weekend."

"Don't worry about me, old man," Alex teased. "If anything, I'll be checking up on the two of you to make sure you don't hurt yourselves."

They both laughed hard at that.

Alex spotted Megan walking toward the kitchen, and he knew that for now, the only thing he had to focus on was moving furniture.

Chapter 3

"I THINK YOU FORGOT SOMETHING," MEGAN SAID AS SHE looked at her reflection in the dressing-room mirror.

From the other side of the door, Summer asked, "What?"

"The rest of this dress. It's a little—"

Summer laughed. "It's a little black dress, and every woman needs one."

Megan tugged at the hem and then shimmied around to try to cover things she felt should be covered.

Like more of her.

"Maybe the next size up?" she suggested. "It's a little snug."

"Open the door, and let me see."

Megan complied, and Summer gasped as soon as she stepped in. "Gabs! Come here! Quick!"

"It's too small, right?" Megan asked nervously, turning to look at her reflection again. "I'm normally a size—"

Behind them, Gabriella gasped. "Oh wow! Megan, look at you!"

Confused, she looked over her shoulder. "What?"

"That dress is perfect on you," Gabriella said with a smile. "I mean, absolutely perfect! Why are you hiding such a great figure under oversized sweaters?"

A great figure? Seriously? "Umm—"

"She's always had a cute figure," Summer said. "And now that you're not living at your job, you can start wearing clothes that accentuate your assets and go out a little more!"

"Um—"

"We could fix you up with someone," Gabriella said. "You seemed to hit it off with Alex last night, and he is one of the sweetest guys I know. I think the two of you would be a good fit!"

Summer's eyes lit up. "Yes! I could see you and Alex dating!"

Okay, things were starting to get out of hand, and if Megan didn't do something now, it was only going to get worse. Holding up her hands, she cut them both off. "I appreciate your…enthusiasm…for my social life. I really do. But I have so many other things to think about first that are way more important. I know you both mean well, but can we let this topic go for a little while?"

They both agreed—almost too easily—and then they were back to shopping. Megan decided to think about the black dress and was immediately dragged through the lingerie department, where she ended up purchasing more underwear than any one woman should own.

"Why am I buying all of this?"

"Because I have a feeling you don't own nearly enough of this kind of thing," Summer said. "If we're going to try to get you to lose the always-casual-Friday look, we have to start with underwear."

"Um…why?" Megan asked.

Summer sighed. "We have so much to teach you."

"If you feel pretty under your clothes, you're going to want to wear something pretty for everyone to see," Gabriella explained as they walked out to put this round of purchases in the car.

It was lunchtime, and this particular store was already their third stop.

"Any chance we can get some food?" Megan asked. "I swear I'm starting to feel light-headed."

Summer decided to go home and feed Amber, and as much as Megan was ready to be done, she knew the girls would fight her on it. So she and Gabriella picked a small Greek restaurant that was close to some of the boutiques they planned to hit next. They agreed that Summer would meet up with them two hours later, and once she was gone, Megan collapsed on the front seat of Gabriella's car.

"You're not having fun, are you?" Gabriella asked.

Shaking her head, Megan said, "Not really. I know this is something I need to do, but I didn't realize how exhausting it would be."

"We can call it a day if you want. Of course, then I'll have to go home and deal with the guys painting, and really, I'd like to avoid that. Just the idea of the smell of paint makes me queasy."

At the mention of the guys, Megan instantly pictured Alex in her mind.

Shirtless and sexy.

"Do you know how long they're planning on working today?" she asked quickly.

They were on the move, and Megan was enjoying getting to know her way around town as Gabriella talked about what was going on at home. "If I know the guys, they're going to want to get all the painting done today. And believe me, I don't doubt for a minute that they will—especially if they divide and conquer. The plan was to let them do their thing, and I was going to pick up some takeout—Chinese food or pizza—for everyone.

I just figured the longer we stayed out, the better. Less chance of slowing them down."

"So then no one should have to come over tomorrow," Megan said conversationally.

"They'll have to move the furniture back and rehang pictures and fixtures and whatnot," Gabriella went on. "But it shouldn't take too long. I'm sure if Alex came back to help Zach it would be fine."

"Why not Ethan?"

Gabriella slid her a sly look. "What's wrong with Alex?"

Great. Way to draw attention to the whole darn thing, Megan chided herself. "There's nothing wrong with Alex," she forced herself to say. "I just thought it would be Ethan coming over to help since they're so close."

"Normally I'd agree. But Ethan and Summer haven't had a whole lot of time to themselves since Amber was born. Like we were saying last night, they had Summer's mom there for almost eight weeks and then Aunt Monica and your mom there for two. I'm sure they would love a day with just the three of them." Then she paused. "I don't mean that the way it sounded."

But Megan waved her off. "It's fine. I'm trying to stay out of their hair as much as possible—and not just for their benefit. I'm used to being on my own, and I like my privacy and quiet time, so it's no big deal. Really."

"Honestly, I hadn't thought about this turning into an all-weekend event either," Gabriella commented. "Dinner last night was sort of spur of the moment, and I had already planned on today, but tomorrow means another round of takeout or something easy to make, and I'm kind of in the mood for something a little more…or should I say a little less…fast."

Megan chuckled. "Fast food is my middle name, but I get what you're saying. It's nice to sit down to a dinner you're not eating with your hands."

"Exactly!"

"Well, we have two hours to kill before we have to meet Summer. This Greek place we're going to is more of a sit-down place, right?"

Gabriella nodded.

"Then we'll make it a leisurely lunch and eat real food that requires utensils, and then we'll brace ourselves for another round of shopping."

"You're sure? Because the last thing I want is to torture you."

"I've never been a girly-girl," Megan admitted. "Much to my mother's chagrin. But maybe with a little help I'll learn to like it."

Gabriella's smile grew as she pulled into a parking spot next to the restaurant. "Stick with me and Summer. We'll have you loving it in no time."

Somehow, Megan doubted it, but she was willing to go along for the ride.

"But I do have an idea that might make the rest of today a little more…palatable for you."

Megan grinned. "I'm listening…"

"First, let me get some food in me, and then I promise that by the time I lay it all out for you, you'll never doubt my ideas ever again."

And even if she did, Megan thought, she'd never admit it out loud.

The pizza the guys had ordered for lunch finally arrived. The three of them gathered around the kitchen island and ate their first slices in silence. Then there seemed to be a collective sense of relief.

"Bathroom's done," Ethan said. "It took two coats, but I think in an hour or two, we can start hanging fixtures again."

Zach grabbed a second slice. "What about the guest room? Does it need a second coat?"

Alex shook his head. "Nah. The colors were close enough, and the paint covered the old color well. I have one more wall to do, and then we should be able to start moving the furniture back in. How's the nursery coming?"

"Slow," Zach said around a mouthful of pizza. "I'm trying so hard not to mess up the trim that I'm being overly cautious."

They talked about their schedule for the rest of the day, and once all the pizza was gone, Zach walked into the living room and sat.

"You know it's going to be that much harder to get up again, right?" Alex asked.

"Right now, I don't even care. I feel like I've been standing for days."

Ethan pulled his phone out and smiled.

"What's up?" Zach asked.

"Since the girls went shopping today, we left Amber with the nanny."

"Seriously? You got a nanny?"

Ethan nodded. "And she's a godsend. Anyway,

Summer went home for lunch so she could feed Amber, and she sent me a selfie of the two of them." He held his phone out and beamed with pride.

"That's a good-looking family, Ethan," Alex said. "You're a lucky man."

"Don't I know it." He paused and studied Alex for a moment. "What about you?"

Alex's eyes went wide. "What about me?"

Both Ethan and Zach started to laugh. "Did you see the panic in his eyes?" Zach teased. "Geez, relax."

"All I was asking was when you were going to stop doing the single guy thing," Ethan said with a smirk. "No need to get all tense."

Before Alex could say anything, Zach spoke up. "Did you call the girl you were telling me about?"

Alex looked at Ethan briefly and then at Zach. "Um… no. Not exactly." Great. Why did he have to add the *not exactly*?

"What the hell does that mean?" Zach asked. "It's a yes or a no."

"Wait, who are we talking about?" Ethan asked.

Rolling his eyes, Alex gave a condensed version of the conversation he'd had with Zach earlier in the week.

"Okay, then I'm confused too," Ethan commented. "Did you call her?"

With a sigh, Alex walked into the kitchen and grabbed a bottle of water before returning to them. "I sort of…" He paused. If he said he ran into her, it would seem suspicious that he had said this girl lived on the other side of the country and suddenly she was here. The comparison to Megan would be beyond obvious, and there was no way he was going to out their weekend to Zach without talking to her about it first.

"I started to, but then I decided against it," he said instead.

Zach snorted with disgust as he stood. "C'mon. Let's get back to it. I'd like to have all the painting done before Gabriella gets home."

That was it? Neither of them was going to say anything else?

Alex supposed he should be thankful, and yet...he almost felt a little let down. If only they knew how much he envied them—their lives, their commitment to their wives, their growing families—it was everything he wanted! And he had a feeling if she let him in even a little, Megan would see that he could be the man for her.

Walking into the guest room, he sighed. Focusing on the task at hand, he finished painting the last wall. When it was done, he washed out his roller and brush and then helped Ethan finish putting the bathroom back together. By that time, Zach was almost done in the nursery, and they talked about moving the guest room furniture back into place first.

"What about the hallway?" Alex asked. "I thought we were painting that too."

Zach raked a hand through his hair. It was late in the afternoon already, and no doubt Gabriella would be coming home soon. For the life of him, Alex couldn't imagine what kind of shopping took all day, but maybe they were making it last that long so they were out of the way.

"No, we need to move all the furniture back before

we do the hallway," Ethan said, interrupting Alex's thoughts. "This way if we bang into the walls or anything, we're not messing up the new paint job."

"Good plan," Zach said. "If the three of us get the furniture moved and all work on the hallway, we should be able to knock it out pretty fast."

They immediately started, and the only conversation was about furniture placement and putting switch plate covers back into place or moving drop cloths. It wasn't until they were each rolling paint on the hallway walls that Zach changed the subject.

"So what do you think of Megan?" he asked, and Alex nearly fell off the ladder he was on.

"Um…what? Why?"

Zach chuckled. "Nothing. Relax. Geez, you're jumpy today," he said and then focused on rolling for a minute. "It just occurred to me that with Megan being here now, you'll be hanging out with her too. It would be great if the two of you got along and all."

"Dude, are you trying to fix me up with your cousin?" Alex asked and secretly prayed it was the case because it would make things so much easier to have Zach on his side as he tried to convince Megan to go out with him.

"Hell no!" Zach cried, but with a smile. "I don't believe it's ever a good thing for a friend to date a family member, you know?"

Ethan looked at Alex. "True story. Zach was the biggest pain in the ass when Summer and I first got together."

"That's because you kept it a secret," Zach snapped. "You went behind my back and hooked up with her. It was kind of a betrayal. You don't do that to a friend."

Suddenly Alex felt a little uneasy with the whole situation. Granted, he and Zach weren't as close as Zach was with Ethan, and Megan was Zach's cousin rather than his sister, but…still. Judging from the arguing that was going on—and this being more than three years since it happened—Alex knew there was no way he was going to risk being on the receiving end of Zach's ire.

At least not until he knew where he stood with Megan.

Alex let out a loud whistle to be heard over the yelling, and both Zach and Ethan stilled at the sound. They looked up at him with annoyance.

"I think it's safe to say that things worked out," he said diplomatically. "Your sister and Ethan are happily married and have a beautiful daughter, and it shouldn't matter how or when they started dating…"

"I still say it was a crappy thing to do," Zach murmured.

"But," Alex went on, ignoring Zach's comment, "the important thing to remember is that Summer is a very happy woman. And really, isn't that what you want for your sister more than anything, Zach? For her to be happy and have a man who loves her and takes care of her?"

Zach mumbled something incoherent, and when Ethan was about to argue with him, Alex cut him off.

"Personally, I could only wish my sister would find someone who treated her as well as Ethan treats Summer."

"How would you feel if it was your best friend?" Zach grumbled.

"Considering my best friend is happily married with two kids and another on the way, I'd probably be a little upset. But before he was married, I don't think I would have had an issue with it."

"Trust me," Zach said, "you would have."

"Maybe. But I guess we'll never know," Alex said as he began to roll out more paint.

They finished painting in relative silence, and what he took away from the whole conversation was the fact that Zach Montgomery obviously held grudges.

"I don't think I can move."

"It's okay. You don't have to."

Summer shook her head lazily. "No, no, no…I really do. I have to pick up Amber before we head over to… to…wait, where do I have to go?"

"Gabriella's," Megan said sleepily. "But don't do it. Have the nanny bring Amber here. We'll start her young."

"I knew we'd win you over," Gabriella said.

"Had I known something like this was an option, I would have asked for this instead of the shopping."

They were each sitting in a massage chair of a nail salon after having manicures and pedicures. Megan had never understood the appeal of it.

Until now.

"How have I lived for so long without this in my life?"

"I blame myself," Summer said. "We didn't spend enough time together. I promise to make it up to you. Let's do this weekly."

"You're on," Megan murmured and moaned with delight when her technician began massaging her scalp. "Oh my God…"

"Our work here is done, Gabs," Summer said, and Gabriella readily agreed. Her phone beeped, and she let out a small whine. "That sounds like reality calling."

"Can't you tell it to go away for a little longer?" Gabriella asked.

"I wish," Summer replied as she looked at her phone. "Change of plans. The painting took a bit longer than the guys thought, so we're going to do dinner at our place so the fumes won't be as bad for you when you get home."

Gabriella hummed her approval.

"We're supposed to pick up some Chinese food and the guys will meet us at the house in about an hour," Summer added.

Both Megan and Gabriella straightened slightly in their seats. "So how do we need to do this?" Megan asked.

"Summer, why don't you head home and take care of Amber and do whatever you need to do before we all get there. Megan and I will pick up the food and then head over. Sound good?"

Nodding, Summer stood, carefully slid on her shoes, and picked up her purse. "Actually, it sounds perfect. Get me some crab rangoon, please," she said as she waved and made her way to the door.

Fifteen minutes later, Megan felt like a wet noodle as she slid into Gabriella's car. They'd already called in the massive dinner order, and really, all Megan needed to do was hold the box in her lap until they got to Summer's. There were worse ways to spend her time.

Once they arrived, Megan was surprised to see that the guys were there already. Zach came out to greet Gabriella, and Alex came out to take the food. When Megan didn't immediately move to get out of the car, Alex looked at her curiously.

"You okay?" he asked. "Shopping wear you out?"

She laughed softly. "You have no idea. Those two are lethal."

Zach and Gabriella had already walked into the house when Ethan came out. "Everything okay?"

Alex handed him the box of food with a laugh of his own. "It seems like shopping took a little more out of her than she expected."

For a minute Megan considered arguing that he didn't need to talk about her as if she weren't there, but she was too tired to.

"I can believe it," Ethan said. "Next time, pace yourself. Summer and Gabriella are like Olympic medalists where shopping and girls' days are concerned." With a smile and a quick wave, he was gone.

Alex crouched next to the open car door. "You gonna make it?" he teased.

With her eyes closed, Megan couldn't help but smile. "Go. Eat Chinese food. Save yourself. Just leave me here to sleep for a day or two."

"No can do," he said softly. "If you don't join everyone inside for dinner, I'll have to carry you in."

Turning her head to the side, she opened her eyes and looked at him.

Damn, why did he have to be so attractive? Here he was after moving furniture and painting all day, and he looked too good for words. She struggled to keep from leaning forward and tasting him. Her mind had to be playing tricks on her because Megan was fairly certain her memory of how Alex tasted and kissed was being overexaggerated.

He leaned in closer—or maybe she was the one who moved. Either way, they were a heck of a lot closer than they had been a minute ago.

Maybe it was the fact that she was feeling extremely mellow or maybe it was the fact that he was too damn tempting to resist. All Megan wanted was to know whether her mind had been playing tricks on her.

Alex whispered her name as he gently pressed his lips to hers.

Oh...

One of Alex's hands came up and cupped her cheek, and his touch was both arousing and familiar. Megan mimicked his move and marveled in the scratchiness of his jaw, the warmth of his skin. She sighed and moved a little closer, and the kiss went from chaste to inquisitive to a full onslaught in the blink of an eye. She wanted to pull him into the car or have him pull her out onto the driveway so she could feel more of him, but for now, this would have to do—the taste of him and being consumed by him.

No, her mind hadn't been playing games with her.

There had been no exaggeration.

Alex Rebat was sexy and sensual and completely lethal.

She pulled back because she couldn't breathe, but Alex's hand stayed where it was, gently caressing her skin. Megan leaned into it as she tried to catch her breath.

"It's still there," he whispered.

Her eyes drifted closed even as she nodded in agreement because she knew exactly what he was talking about.

"I know now isn't the time, but—"

"Did she fall asleep out there?" Gabriella called out from the doorway with a small laugh. "Come on, Megan! The food's getting cold!"

Alex stood and held out a hand to Megan. She accepted it and had to bite her tongue to keep from groaning at how good it felt to touch him. He gently tugged her to her feet, and for a brief moment, she was pressed up against him. Slowly she looked up at him and saw the same emotion on his face she knew was on hers.

Desire.

Plain and simple.

It would be so easy right now to reach up, wrap her arms around him, and pull him in for another kiss. As if reading her mind, Alex released her hand and said, "C'mon. Let's go have some dinner."

Mutely, she nodded, and they walked side by side into the house.

When they arrived in the kitchen, Zach and Ethan were arguing over some game that was going to be on later, and Alex immediately walked over to join them. Megan went to work helping set the table and putting the food out, and within minutes, they were all seated.

Dinner was loud and boisterous and filled Megan with joy—because not only was she surrounded by family, but the sound of laughter and being around other people were things she had seriously been missing out on for far too long. Back in Albany, whenever she did go out after work with coworkers, they tended to talk about work stuff. Here literally no one mentioned anything work-related. Part of Megan wondered if it was on purpose since most of them worked together or if it was because they were able to separate their jobs from their personal and social lives.

Actually, it was fascinating to observe.

"So did we redeem ourselves after the shopping disaster?" Summer asked after the guys went to the den to watch the game.

"I don't think you needed to redeem yourselves," Megan replied. "I wasn't prepared for that level of shopping. I feel like maybe I should have eased into it."

"That reminds me," Gabriella said as she put containers of food away, "all of your bags are still in the car. We'll need to bring those in."

Megan rose and stretched. "Ugh…any chance I can just will them to the guesthouse?"

"Do you need some help?" Summer asked.

But Megan waved her off. "It may take a trip or two…or five," she joked. "But I've got it. You relax."

"No arguments there. All the shopping and pampering was a treat compared to getting an infant to calm down when she's hungry," Summer said as she relaxed a bit in her seat.

Laughing softly, Megan made her way out to the car and opened the trunk. "Yikes," she murmured. How had she not noticed how much stuff she had purchased? Granted, some of the bags were Gabriella's, but the majority of them were hers.

Fifteen bags, she thought with disbelief. The last time she had purchased that many bags of anything, it had been groceries.

Grabbing the first batch, she walked around the house and made her way to the guesthouse. The space was fantastic and more than she needed, and she was beyond grateful for it. Placing the bags on the sofa, she stopped, looked around, and realized she had left her breakfast dishes in the sink and her coffee cup and a glass on the counter. The rest of the place looked pristine, and she needed to remember this wasn't her place and she should probably put a little more effort into keeping it clean.

"Note to self, be a better houseguest," she murmured on her way back to the car. She found Alex staring into the trunk. "Um…what are you doing?"

"Gabriella asked me to give you a hand. Is this everyone's stuff? Do we need to bring some of this inside to Summer?"

"Unfortunately, no," she said quietly.

Alex leaned in a bit. "What was that?"

She looked at him. "These are all mine. Well…those three are Gabriella's."

His eyes went a little wide with amusement. "Really? No wonder you were worn out."

Megan nodded. "Tell me about it. And I've already taken some into the house. I don't think I've ever shopped like this. I made one comment about wanting some new things, and—"

"How come?"

"How come what?" she asked.

"How come you wanted some new things? Did you leave a lot of stuff behind when you moved?"

Great. How was she supposed to explain how she was tired of being plain old Megan? How this move was about making changes that had nothing to do with her job?

"New job, new city…you know. I thought maybe some new clothes could go along with that."

He didn't comment. Instead he grabbed the rest of the shopping bags. Megan shut the trunk before following him to the guesthouse. Her heart was hammering in her chest at the thought of being alone with him with no prying eyes.

Would anyone notice if I shut the door and kissed him for a little while longer? she questioned herself.

The answer was most definitely a yes, so she quickly pushed the thought aside. Alex put the bags on the sofa next to the ones she had already placed there. "Thanks," she murmured. With nothing left to bring in, she suddenly felt awkward and unsure of what she was supposed to do or say. It wasn't an issue when they were sitting with everyone else, but when they were alone, it felt…strange.

Alex looked toward the door and then at her before he stepped in a little closer. "So…I was thinking. Maybe I could take you out to dinner one night this week. You know…we can talk and catch up."

Now it was Megan's turn to look over her shoulder and make sure no one was coming to see what was taking them so long. "Um…"

His expression—which had been mildly hopeful—fell. "What's going on, Megan?"

"I have so much going on right now, Alex," she said honestly. "I'm trying to settle in at work, and I need to take care of some other things before I start…you know…going out."

"You still have to eat, right?" he teased.

That made her relax a little, but she jumped when he took one of her hands in his. "I need to get a car and an apartment. I need to not be living here for too long because I don't like disrupting Summer and Ethan's lives." She paused and looked from their joined hands to his face. "I just need a little…time," she said carefully. "I don't think I could handle answering questions about us dating on top of everything else. This week at work is going to be crazy enough with new software coming, and I'm going to be training people, and…I need to be focused."

He nodded. "I understand. But you need to also take some time for you. I'm not saying it has to be with me," he added with a soft laugh, "although that would be my preference, but don't get into the same patterns you had in New York."

Part of her wanted to be annoyed at what he was implying. Unfortunately, he was spot-on. And she knew that he—more than anyone else here—had felt the effects of her work pattern.

Dammit.

"I'm trying not to," she admitted. "But it's only been a week, so—"

"I get it," he interrupted quickly. "And it's going to take time until you feel settled in, but don't be afraid to let people help you out."

Pulling her hand away, she gave him an irritated look. "I'm not afraid to ask people for help, Alex. I'm living here with my cousin because I didn't want to stay at a hotel and I wanted to take some time to get to know the area. I ride to and from work every day with Summer because I wasn't ready to commit to buying a car…I mean, how much more help am I supposed to ask for?"

He held up his hands in defeat. "All right, all right, my mistake," he said with a lopsided grin. "Sorry. I hate to think of you working crazy-long hours and still not getting settled because of that."

"Please, neither Zach nor Ethan will let me work the kind of hours I want to—and it has nothing to do with Summer being my ride. I'd be much further along in this whole transition and training at work if they'd let me do it at my own pace."

"Well, take it from someone who has worked with

your cousin—he learned to not live his life at the office. After his accident, he really…well, he really reevaluated what he was doing with his life. And I think seeing Zach go through that helped Ethan too. From what the two of them have shared with me, they were both workaholics."

"It runs in the family. Trust me."

Reaching for her hand again, he gave it a gentle squeeze. "Just…promise me something," he said softly.

His thumb was caressing her knuckles, and it felt so good—almost hypnotic—that she would have promised him anything. "Okay…"

"Promise me when you *do* get these things settled—the car, the apartment—you'll let me take you out."

Who was she kidding? It was easily going to be a couple of weeks before that happened, and by then, she'd have her emotions a little more under control. There was no way she *wasn't* going to go out with him. She knew that. She just needed to let all of these changes in her life settle in. She wasn't like the rest of her family. Change didn't come easily to her, and she took a lot longer to…process things.

But the possibility of picking up where they'd left off was certainly enticing. She wanted to sigh at the thought. When was the last time she had even felt like that?

Two years, to be exact.

Yup. She hadn't dated anyone since. Hadn't slept with anyone since. So agreeing to go out with Alex again? Um, yeah. That was a no-brainer.

She nodded. "I'd like that very much."

His smile grew. "Great," he said softly. "C'mon. We should get over there or everyone will be wondering what's taking so long to move a couple of shopping bags."

Megan laughed and then looked at the bags. "A couple? I think Summer and Gabriella knew exactly how long it was going to take to move them." Then she let out a small sigh. "Just the thought of going through all of them and hanging the clothes up has me exhausted."

"You could always wait until tomorrow. Or better yet, wait until you move."

The idea had merit, but she shook her head. "Somehow I don't think I'm going to be moving that fast, and that's a lot of bags to find a space for."

He nodded, and they walked across the yard and into the house to join everyone. Alex went to sit with Zach and Ethan while she went to the table where Gabriella and Summer were softly chatting. They both looked up at her with curious expressions.

"What?"

"That took…a while," Summer said.

Megan rolled her eyes. "There were a lot of bags." With a careless shrug, she sat. "So…what are we talking about?"

"Dessert," Summer replied.

"Didn't we just finish eating?"

They both nodded. "The baby's craving cake," Gabriella said. "Something gooey and chocolaty and…cakey."

"That's not a word, is it?" Megan asked with amusement. "I'm telling you, I wish I had a legit excuse to eat chocolate cake. As it is, I indulge way too often and then have to deal with the guilt."

"It doesn't show," Summer commented. "That black dress fit you like a second skin, and you have the curves to pull it off."

Megan didn't want to think about it. Not when

they were talking about cake. For something like what Gabriella was describing, the last thing she wanted to think about was fitting into a slinky little dress. Looking around the kitchen, she couldn't remember seeing any kind of cake. "Do we have anything cakey here? Did the guys bring something with them?"

"Oh, hell no," Gabriella said with a laugh. "We're going to have to send them to the store. All the bakeries are probably closed, but the local grocery store has a fantastic bakery department."

Megan knew she'd have to get used to the food and the culture. Back home she knew of every late-night bakery and where to get whatever she wanted to eat when she wanted to eat it. In time, she knew she'd feel the same way about Portland, but right now she wished she could be the one to get in a car and go get dessert.

Wait…why couldn't she?

"You know, if I can borrow a car, I can program the address into my phone and pick up dessert," Megan suggested. "That way the guys don't have to miss any of the game and we get to have a great dessert, and…honestly…I miss being able to drive. What do you think?"

Five minutes later, Megan had the keys in her hands and a smile on her face as she made her way out to the car.

Alex walked into the kitchen to grab something to drink and noticed Megan wasn't there.

"Where'd Megan go?" he asked casually, and Summer explained how Megan had offered to pick up dessert.

Well, damn.

With a nod, he turned to go to the den but then decided to ask a question or two.

"So how come she hasn't borrowed one of your cars to use regularly?" he asked Summer. "She mentioned earlier how she rides with you."

"Ethan and I don't keep a spare car," Summer said.

"And we got rid of our spare car," Gabriella added. "The Porsche wasn't practical with the baby coming, so we sold it. Now I've got the SUV, and Zach has the Lexus, so…"

He nodded again. "What about a place to live? Have you set up an appointment with a real estate agent yet for her?"

"I didn't want to overstep my bounds," Gabriella said with a grin. "It was more important for Megan to get here and start working. I don't think anyone's in any rush for her to move, but I know she's used to being on her own and doesn't want to impose. All we're doing is following her lead."

"Whose lead?" Zach asked as he walked into the room. Gabriella recapped the discussion, and now Alex felt silly for bringing it up. Zach looked at him as he pulled a bottle of beer from the refrigerator. "Believe me, I'm sure she's champing at the bit to find a car and a place, but Megan doesn't cut herself any slack. I suggested she take a day or two off so she can do the things she needs to do, but she doesn't want to do it. Personally, I have no idea how she's going to do any of it while working a full day all week long. I mean, she has the weekends, but I have a feeling she's going to make herself crazy on this."

"She's a typical Montgomery," Summer commented.

"Although she does favor the men in this family with her obsession with work."

"Surely she's got to have some hobbies," Gabriella commented and then looked from Summer to Zach and back again.

"Not that I know of," Summer replied. "She hasn't mentioned anything."

"What has she been doing with her free time?" Looking at Zach, she continued, "You're not letting her work late, so what does she do when she goes home?"

"Why are you looking at me?" he asked with a small laugh. "I'm here with you. I have no idea what she does after work."

"She eats dinner with us, but afterward she heads back to the guesthouse. I guess I just figured she'd be watching TV or something."

Alex zoned out of the conversation going on around him, a million thoughts racing through his brain as to how he might be able to help. The decision was not completely selfless; he knew by volunteering, he'd also be able to spend some time with her. Time he knew she'd put off until all the conditions were right.

And by right, he meant that not only would she need to be moved and settled into a new place, but it would have to be fully furnished and decorated and her new car would need to have several thousand miles on it.

Yeah. He hadn't pushed her earlier when they had talked, but he remembered some of their conversations from two years ago after she went back to Albany. She'd admitted to him back then that she worked too much, socialized too little, and wasn't big on dating. There wasn't a doubt in his mind that if something or someone didn't intervene, she'd put herself into that same pattern of behavior here in Portland.

And that's what he wanted to avoid. And not just for himself. For the three months after Zach and Gabriella's wedding when they had stayed in touch, Alex could hear the sadness in Megan's voice. The discontent. It was at such odds with the woman he first met and had spent an entire sexy weekend with. Even now when he thought about it, it made him hard.

Holding her close at the wedding while they danced…

Kissing her under the twinkly lights in the garden…

Barely making it through the hotel room door before clothes started flying…

"Alex?" Zach said, and Alex had a feeling it wasn't the first time he'd said his name.

"What? Um…sorry. My mind wandered for a minute."

"I was asking if you knew of any decent places to rent," Zach said. "The complex where Summer lived when she first moved here is good, and so is the place where Gabriella used to live. I think either place would be fine for Megan if they have any vacancies, but they were both a bit larger than she seems to want."

Summer made a tsking sound. "Why she only wants a studio apartment is beyond me. I like having space to move around. I don't think I'd be able to live in an all-in-one type of place."

"I thought she was more interested in getting a car first," Ethan commented as he walked into the room. "Don't you think it's a bit much for her to be doing it all at the same time? I mean, financially—"

"It's not like she's strapped for cash," Summer argued lightly. "I mean, let's be honest. She's probably the only Montgomery who doesn't use the name to her advantage."

"So what are we supposed to do?" Ethan asked. "Do we take her car shopping?"

"It's too bad we got rid of the Porsche," Zach said.

"No," Gabriella replied, shaking her head. "Megan would not have been comfortable driving it. She's more sensible than that."

"So what does that mean?" Alex asked. "A sedan?"

There was a round of "Oh yes" and "Definitely."

Everyone seemed to be talking at once, and Alex realized he had opened a hornet's nest and felt bad about it.

Alex thought about the car sitting in his garage. He normally drove a pickup truck, but he had a second car—a Nissan Maxima—that he used when he went on dates and didn't feel like being in the truck. It was three years old, and he hadn't driven it in a while, so maybe…

"You know," he began cautiously, "I have a spare car I'm not using. I'm not saying I'm looking to sell it or anything, but maybe Megan could use it for a while until she gets a little more settled. That way she has the freedom to come and go as she wants, and…I don't know… she can concentrate on finding a place of her own."

When no one commented on his offer, Alex figured it was a ridiculous idea. After all, it wasn't as if any of the Montgomerys were hurting for money. There was no reason Megan couldn't go out and buy a car. He was only throwing an option out there to be helpful.

Out of the corner of his eye, he saw Zach take a pull of his beer, his eyes never leaving Alex, but it was Alex who swallowed hard.

"That's not a bad idea," Summer said. "You could take her home with you tonight to pick it up."

And still Zach didn't say a word.

And neither did anyone else.

After a long, awkward moment, Alex spoke. "Look, the offer is out there, but I'll leave it up to you guys whether you want to say anything to Megan. My feelings aren't going to be hurt either way." He held up his hands and turned toward the den. "I think the game's about to start up."

He hadn't gone more than three steps when the front door opened and Megan walked in. She looked happy and carefree and relaxed with a big smile on her face as she breezed into the kitchen.

"That felt great!" she said. "I know it's crazy, but I've missed driving! I didn't realize how much until I pulled out of the driveway. And I got us several dessert options." Placing three bags on the kitchen table, she reached into the first one and handed a box to Gabriella. "Chocolate truffle cake. It was the chocolatiest thing I could find."

Gabriella let out a happy little squeal of delight.

Reaching into the second bag, she turned toward Zach. "Apple pie," she said. "I seem to remember it being one of your favorites, and—" She pulled out a half gallon of vanilla ice cream. "Just in case you wanted it à la mode."

Smiling, Zach stepped forward and placed a kiss on her forehead. "It's official. You are my favorite cousin."

"Like there was any doubt," she teased. Finally, she reached into the third bag and pulled out a package of Double Stuf Oreos, which she hugged to her chest. "Sorry, this one is primarily for me. These are my favorite. But I might consider sharing."

Alex remembered her Oreo obsession. They'd talked about it on more than one occasion, and the last time they'd been together, they had grabbed a package and ate them in bed. He caught her eye and knew the exact moment she remembered it too.

Turning away, Alex looked toward the den and caught a glimpse of the TV; sure enough, the game was on. He figured he'd saunter away and let everyone talk without him being there, but first Gabriella asked if he wanted coffee, then Summer asked which option he wanted for dessert, and Ethan questioned whether they could sample all the desserts.

And Zach continued to watch him.

Figuring dessert was the best diversion, Alex suggested they let the girls take their share of the sweets first and they'd come back and get theirs after checking the score. Ethan agreed, and they walked to the den.

Zach followed.

Here it comes…

"Were you serious about your offer?" Zach asked, his voice low.

"Of course I was. Why wouldn't I be?"

Zach shrugged. "It seems like you're being awfully accommodating where my cousin is concerned all of a sudden."

Alex swallowed hard. "Look, Zach, that's who I am. I see a problem, I try to fix it. The way I see it is as a friend helping a friend."

"You don't even know Megan."

"I know you, and I know your family," he countered. "And it's just a car."

"I know, and…sorry I got weird there for a minute."

"It's fine. Really," Alex assured him. "We're cool."

And with that covered, they turned to the television to check the score. When the game went to a commercial, Ethan grinned at them. "We can have dessert now, right? That was enough time for the girls to claim their dessert choices, right?"

Laughing, the three of them walked into the kitchen, where the girls were giggling over something. Alex helped himself to a slice of pie, a scoop of ice cream, and a stack of Oreos. He winked at Megan as he walked away.

"Wait!" Summer called after him. "You need to come here for a minute!"

Turning, Alex walked to the table as he put a whole Oreo in his mouth.

"You need to tell Megan about your offer!"

Megan's eyes went wide when she looked at him, but she didn't say a word.

He forced himself to swallow the cookie without choking. Looking over at Zach, he tried to convey his need for help. Luckily, Zach took the hint.

"Megan, we were talking while you were out, and Alex mentioned he has a car you can use."

"But…I'm planning on buying one."

Zach crouched beside her. "I know, but maybe you can use his for a little while so you don't have to deal with car shopping right now. It would be a temporary thing, and it would take some of the pressure off you."

She looked over at Alex and smiled. "Wow…thanks. If you're sure it's not going to inconvenience you—"

Alex quickly explained his situation with his vehicles.

"It's just sitting, so it would be a good thing for someone to be driving it."

Her smile grew. "If you're sure, then…yes! Thank you!" She breathed a sigh of relief. "One less thing on my plate! Now I'll be able to go out apartment hunting without bothering anyone!"

Both Gabriella and Summer cleared their throats.

"What? What was that about?"

"There's no rush," Zach quickly replied. "The car seemed like a quick and easy fix right now."

"Oh. Okay," she said hesitantly before looking over at Alex. "So do you want to drop the car off here one night this week, or maybe Summer and I can swing by on our way home after work sometime, or…"

"Um…Alex?" Summer said with a grin.

He knew what Summer was getting at, and as much as he wanted to ask Megan, he was afraid she would take it the wrong way.

So he hesitated.

And then the silence became awkward.

Finally, Zach took the decision out of his hands. "I think you should go home with Alex tonight."

Chapter 4

For the life of her, Megan had no idea how she got to this place.

Two weeks after Zach had suggested that she go home with Alex—to get the car—she was sitting in the guesthouse and listening to the loudest snoring she had ever heard in her life.

And it was coming from a fifteen-pound dog.

It was a Saturday morning, and Ethan and Summer—along with Zach and Gabriella—had gone out of town for the weekend for a friend's wedding and left Megan in charge of Maylene. It wasn't that Megan wasn't a dog person—she was—but the snoring was making her a wee bit cranky.

"How loud can one dog be?" she murmured as she poured herself another cup of coffee. It was fairly early—a little after ten—and she had nothing planned for the day other than dog-sitting. But if the damn dog didn't quiet down, she'd seriously consider putting her in the main house and checking on her occasionally.

Her laundry was done, all of her dishes were in the dishwasher, and the house was spotless. And now she had nothing left to do.

Well, that wasn't completely true. With the entire day to herself and no chance of anyone coming over, she could indulge in her secret hobby. In the past several years, she hadn't had the free time to indulge as much as she would have liked, but with her shorter working hours, she'd already crocheted four baby blankets with matching sweater, hat, and bootie sets. She was going to have to look into the local hospitals and women's shelters here in Portland. Her stash of yarn was almost depleted, so finding the closest craft store could be on today's agenda.

Besides, it wasn't as if she *had* to stay home—the dog did not require round-the-clock watching. Thinking about her options while she showered, Megan went about putting an effort into getting ready. Thirty minutes later, she was back to sitting and listening to the dog snore.

What to do? What to do?

She could always go to the office. With both Ethan and Zach out of town, no one would know that she put in extra hours. She couldn't think of any other ways to spend her time, and when she let that thought settle in, it depressed her.

She was in a new city, and there was so much she hadn't seen yet; she knew she could easily pass the time driving around and exploring. Then she could find the craft stores and maybe the local hospital, where she could bring the items she'd already made. Feeling slightly optimistic, she grabbed a pair of sneakers and then decided to let the dog out before she left.

"C'mon, sweet girl," Megan called to the dog, who immediately perked up. "Let's go outside!"

The dog was practically dancing at this point and began scratching at the door to be let out. Megan opened it, and together they stepped out into the yard. There was a fence, so there was no need to slip on her leash, and once the door was open, Maylene dashed out and ran around the yard. Megan watched her for a few minutes and then saw the mailman driving by. Feeling confident that the dog was going to do her business and would probably prefer to do so without an audience, Megan slipped out the gate and went to grab the mail.

On her way up the driveway, she sorted through the envelopes and picked out the few that were for her. From the yard, she walked over to Summer's back door, stepped inside to put their mail on the kitchen table, and then locked up and went back to the guesthouse while opening her Visa bill. She heard Maylene barking and knew she did that whether a person was in the yard or if she saw the shadow of a bird flying overhead. Without much thought, Megan walked into the guesthouse, put the mail on the coffee table, and grabbed her phone—figuring she'd do a Google search of some points of interest nearby so she could take off once the dog was inside.

She stepped out into the yard. "Maylene? Hey, sweet girl! It's time to come in!"

Nothing.

"Maylene?" she called out again and then began to frantically look around the yard. For a solid minute, she kept calling out to the dog in hopes that she was playing around, but when Megan turned around, her heart stopped.

The gate was open.

She had forgotten to close it when she came back with the mail.

Immediately she ran out of the yard and down the driveway, calling for the dog. With every minute that passed, her panic increased. Where would the dog go? Would she know to stay close to home? Megan had no idea. And what was worse, she had no clue where the dog might run to.

There was no way she was going to call Summer and upset her—at least not yet. It didn't look like any of the neighbors were out, and knocking on doors seemed like wasting precious time, and…

She had only one choice.

She needed help, and she knew of only one other person who would have a calm head in this type of situation.

She called Alex.

—⁓—

Alex was drinking coffee and looking out at his backyard. He loved his home, his property. Living in the suburbs was something he had always wanted to do, and when he found this house, it had everything he needed—lots of green space and room for him to put in the pool he now had and the kind of landscaping that ensured his privacy. He wasn't antisocial or trying to avoid his neighbors, but he had thought if he was able to work with clients out of the house, they'd appreciate the privacy.

With June almost here, the weather was starting to turn warm, and he'd opened up the pool the previous weekend. The water level was perfect, and so were the chemical levels. The pool was heated, and maybe in another week or two, he'd be able to start using it.

Off his back porch was a hot tub, and for now that worked fine.

He was considering changing and doing a little soaking when his phone rang. When he saw Megan's name on the screen, he was pleasantly surprised.

"Hey," he said when he answered and hoped his enthusiasm wasn't too obvious.

"Oh my God, Alex," she began breathlessly. "I've lost Maylene!"

"Um…what?" She immediately relayed what had gone on, and she was getting to the point of near hysteria. "It's going to be all right."

"You don't understand, Alex! I had one job to do—one stupid job!—and I screwed it up. I have to find her, and I have no idea where to look!"

He was already grabbing his keys and locking up the house. "I'm on my way. I'll be there in ten minutes, and I'll be on the lookout for her as I drive over."

"What do I do? Where do I even begin to look for her?" she cried.

"Go and grab her leash and start walking up one side of the block and then down the other. I'll be there as soon as I can. I promise."

He heard the shaky breath she let out. "I have to find her, Alex," she said quietly. "I can't believe I lost her."

"You haven't lost her, Megan. She's a handful—Ethan talks about that all the time. She's gotten out before, so we will find her. Trust me."

"I…I don't know…I'm not sure where to even start…"

At that moment, he hated how he wasn't there already with her. He could hear the devastation in her voice and knew she was going to have a serious meltdown any minute. "Megan," he said, his voice going firm and authoritative, "you need to do what I'm telling you. Get Maylene's leash, and then start walking down the block to the right of the house. I have a feeling that's the direction she'd go in first. Start there, and I'll be there as fast as I can."

That seemed to work because by the time she hung up, she sounded a little more in control of her emotions. Back when they had dated—and he used the term loosely—he had never seen Megan get emotional. She got frustrated, sure. But never emotional—never to the point of tears. And he wasn't sure how to react to it. His initial response was…well…it made him like her a little more. It softened her and showed how she wasn't as cold as she'd seemed when they had ended things.

That memory instantly got pushed aside because now was not the time to be focusing on it. The important thing right now was to get to her and help her find Maylene.

Luckily, traffic was on his side, and he didn't hit any red lights and turned onto Summer's block six minutes later. Alex immediately spotted Megan and pulled over, rolling down his window. "Megan! Hop in! We'll hit the other side of the street now."

Nodding, she quickly jogged over and climbed into the truck. It was pointless to ask if she'd had any luck—the simple fact that there wasn't a dog on the end of the leash told him she hadn't. He pulled over close to the right side of the road and drove slowly. They each called out to the dog as they went. After two blocks, Megan rested her head on the back of the seat and sighed loudly. He pulled over.

"It's no use," she said miserably. "She's gone. She's just…she's gone! I'm going to have to break it to Summer that I lost her dog!" She looked over at him, her brown eyes brimming with tears. "She loves that dog! Do you have any idea how much this is going to kill her?"

Unfortunately, Alex did know how much Summer

loved her dog, and no doubt this was going to be devastating for her. Reaching over, he took one of Megan's hands in his and gently squeezed it. "We're not giving up, okay? We'll keep driving around. We'll knock on doors. We'll put up posters and post on social media if we have to. I'll drive around all night if that's what it takes. All is not lost here, okay?"

The hesitant look on her face told him she didn't think it would do any good, but he refused to quit. Not after only two blocks! With her hand in his, he started driving and was relieved when she turned and called out to Maylene again.

They drove for several more blocks and then turned around and made their way up the other side. By the time they were back in front of Summer's, Alex decided to pull into the driveway and park. "We'll knock on doors now," he said.

"Maybe we need to go off the block," she suggested.

It was possible, he thought, but he had a feeling if they were on foot, they'd have more luck. "Why don't you go and grab a handful of her treats? This way if we spot her and she thinks we're playing, we can lure her over with a snack. What do you think?"

"Sounds good." Megan took off up the driveway, and Alex watched her disappear around the back of the house and into the yard. A minute later, she called his name, and he quickly jogged back to her. At the gate, he spotted her pointing to the far corner of the deck. When he stepped closer, he started to chuckle. "Don't you dare laugh."

He knew she was trying to sound intimidating, but there was a hint of laughter in her own voice.

There, sitting in the corner of the deck in Ethan's hammock, was Maylene—peacefully sunning herself. Alex glanced at the dog and then to Megan. "Um…"

"She was *not* there earlier. I swear."

"Okay."

"I'm serious, Alex! She didn't come when I called her, and she wasn't there when I brought the mail in and put it inside either of the houses. I heard her barking when I came out of the main house, but by the time I came out of mine, she was gone!"

"I believe you," he said carefully and took a step closer to her. "I'm sure she was just playing with you."

She shot him a bland look. "Seriously? That's what you're going with?"

He laughed a bit, unable to help himself. "I'm not sure what else I can say. The thing we should be focused on here is that she's not lost. She's home and in the yard, and even though I happen to know for a fact that Ethan doesn't like her sitting in the hammock, it's better than the alternative."

"I know it is," she said softly. "But now I feel like a complete idiot."

"Why?"

Her eyes widened as she looked at him. "Seriously? I almost had a complete mental breakdown over a missing dog who wasn't actually missing." She groaned and turned to walk over to the dog, gently chiding her.

Alex watched her and couldn't help the smile pulling at his lips. Personally, he was thankful Maylene had pulled this little stunt today if for no other reason than it giving him a reason to spend some time with Megan without her cousins and their spouses. Not that he had anything against them—they were his friends, after all—but he wanted some time alone with her to talk things out. About their relationship and how it ended and how he wanted to try again. Today might not be the best time to bring it up, considering her emotional state, but he had a feeling if he didn't do it today, there was no telling when he'd have another chance.

"Now we're going to go inside and think about what we did," Megan gently scolded the dog as she walked by Alex on her way to the guesthouse.

Chuckling, he followed behind her and silently closed the gate on the way. Without asking, he followed her into the house and shut the door behind him. Megan put the dog down, hung up her leash, and then collapsed on the couch with relief.

He chose to sit beside her—but not too close.

"You okay?" he asked.

Her eyes were closed, and her head was thrown back against the cushions. "That aged me about ten years."

He laughed softly. "But everything's okay now." For a moment he considered taking her hand in his so he could touch her, but he decided to resist the urge. He needed to figure out how to get her to relax and talk to him. "So how are you settling in? The job going okay?"

Megan turned her head toward him and gave him a small smile—as if she knew he was trying to change the subject and distract her. "Things are going well. Work is…well…there's always a certain level of confusion and frustration when a new system is going in, but I think I'm addressing the issues and keeping employee upset to a minimum."

"That's a good thing, right?"

She nodded. "It is. I guess I'm the one who's a little frustrated with the whole thing."

"I thought you said it was going well," he said, confused by her comment.

With a shrug, she explained. "Both Zach and Ethan are big on not letting me work long hours. I could be twice as far in this whole process if they'd let me work at my own pace. I'm feeling…restricted." Then she shook her head. "I'm being ridiculous, I know that. I know they're looking out for my best interests, but right now it's making mè a little crazy. Before Maylene took off, I was considering going in to the office today."

"On a Saturday? Really?"

"It would make the most sense. I'd get a lot of work done without any interruptions, and I'd feel a little more in control of the situation."

Alex knew what she was saying made sense, and he agreed with her to a certain extent. However, he wasn't about to admit that. Right now he wanted to be a little selfish and have this time with her. Looking at his watch, he had an idea.

"I don't know about you, but I haven't had lunch yet," he said casually. "Want to go and grab a burger or something?" When she didn't answer right away, he went on, "Or I can go pick something up and bring it back. You know, if you're worn out from all the excitement earlier."

She chuckled. "And now I do feel silly because it wasn't such a big deal, and yet…I'm telling you, I'm exhausted!"

He laughed with her and figured at least she wasn't turning him down. It gave him hope. Standing, he smiled at her. "Okay, tell me what you're in the mood for, and I'll go get it. What do you say?"

And when Megan smiled back at him, he felt a glimmer of hope.

—◦◦◦—

Okay, so maybe hanging out with Alex wasn't the smartest choice for the day, Megan thought as soon as Alex walked out the door.

She already felt emotional and overwhelmed from thinking she'd lost the dog, and it wouldn't take much more for her to do something ridiculous—like throw herself at him.

Yeah, she was already teetering on the edge.

With a sigh, she paced the small living room and tried to force herself to think about something else—like how she should have opted to go out with him rather than staying in. It wasn't that she didn't like the guesthouse. She did. The place was cute, and Summer had impeccable taste. All in all, she was happy here, but it was one thing to be hanging out here alone and another to do so with Alex.

Alex.

So many things were swirling in her mind where he was concerned. The obvious was how the attraction not only was still there but felt even stronger than it had before. Keeping her distance when he was near was a total act of self-control. But she wasn't stupid. There were issues that had to be dealt with, and confrontation was something she tended to avoid at all costs.

It was one of the most un-Montgomery things about her.

Her family was known for going after what they wanted and not being afraid to get in people's faces. Megan preferred to fly under the radar and blend in.

Normally that wasn't an issue. Honestly, she didn't ruffle feathers at home or at work. Her relationships with men tended to end amicably.

Except with Alex.

Yeah, she'd really screwed that one up, and she knew it was time to deal with it.

Or distract him with seduction. That could work, right?

"No, no, no," she sighed as she walked over to the kitchen table and began clearing away the decorative place mats and napkins to make room for their food. As appealing as seducing Alex was—really, truly was—this was something that had to be dealt with first.

Then she could seduce him.

Or hope he'd seduce her.

A small grin crossed her face at the thought of how thoroughly he'd seduced her the day of Zach and Gabriella's wedding.

Tugging at the hem of her dress for the hundredth time, Megan silently cursed the fact that she'd let her mother talk her into it. The navy-blue fabric clung to every ample curve and was shorter than the dresses she normally wore, and she was feeling very self-conscious about the whole thing.

She was surrounded by family and knew she shouldn't be feeling anything but happy to be here, but old insecurities still lingered. Okay, maybe they had resurfaced thanks to her ex constantly harping on her about losing weight. Megan wasn't fat—she knew that—but she was definitely not slim. She envied her cousin Summer. She had the kind of body Megan had always wished she had—slim—and she looked good in everything. Whereas Megan had to worry about how every article of clothing she had would fit or if it would be too clingy.

Another tug at the hem of her dress as she looked around to see where Summer was. They didn't get to see each other nearly enough and maybe—

"Excuse me?"

Megan turned and saw the most attractive man she had ever seen in her life. He was tall with sandy-brown hair and a smile that seemed almost too perfect. She swallowed hard, convinced he couldn't possibly want to talk to her.

"Would you like to dance?" he asked, and Megan's heart beat wildly in her chest.

She looked around and wondered whether someone had put him up to this. But he didn't look the least bit insincere. If anything, he seemed slightly amused by her confusion.

She cleared her throat and nodded. "Um…yes. Thank you."

His smile broadened, and it was almost lethal. He had dimples too. She had to stifle a sigh when she noticed them.

"I'm Alex Rebat," he said, extending his hand to her. "I'm a friend of Zach's. And you are…?

Blushing because his voice was as magnificent as the rest of him, she replied, "I'm Megan Montgomery. Zach's cousin."

She shook his hand, but he didn't release hers. Instead, he led her onto the dance floor where a slow song was playing. At first, Megan felt a little self-conscious about dancing with a stranger, but as soon as Alex gently wrapped his arm around her waist, all negative thoughts disappeared.

They swayed together to the music as if they'd danced together for years.

They talked as if they'd known each other forever.

And they were both more than ready to move off the dance floor and find someplace quiet to talk after their fourth dance.

Alex kept her hand in his as he led her from the banquet room to the lobby and finally out to the garden. The sun had gone down, and the entire area was lit with hundreds of soft-white twinkly lights. To Megan it looked like something out of a fairy tale while she felt like she was living in the middle of one.

Hand in hand they walked along the paths as Alex told her about his job as a physical therapist, and the more he spoke, the more she wanted to know about him. He had confidence and passion as he spoke about his work and his life, and she found herself hanging on his every word. And when he asked about her—her job, her life—she felt inferior in comparison.

So she'd given him a brief overview of her IT career and her life in Albany before turning the conversation over to him. The smile he gave her told her he knew what she was doing.

"Not big on talking about yourself, huh?" he asked with a knowing smile.

Megan blushed as she shook her head. "There isn't much to tell. My job is fairly boring compared to yours. What you do really makes a difference in people's lives—and after seeing all you did for Zach, I'm in total awe of you."

They stopped walking, and Alex moved so he was standing in front of her. "Don't be," he said, his voice a little gruff. "Zach did all the hard work. I was merely there to help. Not every case is as successful as his. He had the drive to do it, and he worked hard to make it happen."

Both his words and his voice were so intense that Megan was overwhelmed with the urge to reach out and touch him—not just hold his hand but… soothe him. Comfort him.

And she did.

Reaching up with her free hand, she gently caressed his face and heard his sharp intake of breath. This wasn't her—she didn't do things like this, wasn't this forward—and yet she couldn't help herself.

"Megan," he said softly as his head lowered toward hers.

She wasn't an overly romantic person and didn't believe in things like this actually happening, and yet the instant Alex's lips touched hers, Megan swore she saw fireworks. Normally she was a little more timid, inhibited, but something about Alex changed that. Wrapping her arms around him, she melted against him—reveling in the heat of his body, the feel of his lean frame against hers. The feeling must have been mutual because she heard a low growl come from him as he pulled her even closer.

Never before had she been kissed like this—it was the kind of kiss that started slowly, and they both sank into it until it kept going and neither wanted it to end. Megan's hands raked up into his hair, and when they *were finally forced to break apart for breath, in only a matter of seconds they dove in for another taste.*

For a few glorious moments, they had been cocooned in their own little world out in the garden, but it didn't take long for other wedding guests to start coming out and walking around, and the mood was broken. Alex never stopped touching her, though—everywhere they went her hand was in his, and she found she was thankful for the constant connection.

Over the course of the wedding reception, they danced again and talked and laughed, and Megan was nearly bristling with anticipation by the time Gabriella threw the bouquet. At that point, she knew she and Alex could leave. When she noticed other guests getting up to go, she looked over at Alex and said, "So…"

He was sitting beside her, and the expression on his face told her everything she needed to know.

He wanted to leave.

And he wanted to leave with her.

Casually they walked around and said their goodbyes separately. Out in the lobby, Alex took her by the hand—or maybe that time she took his—and they made their way down the massive hallway that connected the banquet hall to the hotel. Several times Megan had looked around to make sure no one saw them—and not because she was embarrassed but because she didn't want the interruption. If she didn't get Alex alone soon, she thought she'd spontaneously combust!

The ride in the elevator seemed to take forever, and she swore the walk to her room was a mile long. But once they were inside and the door was closed?

Perfect.

Something made Maylene bark, and Megan snapped out of her reverie. Even now, if she closed her eyes, she could still feel Alex's hands and mouth on her—the way his jaw was just scratchy enough against her skin. Her hands twitched as she remembered the way his suit jacket had felt in her hands as she pulled it off him and how the smell of his cologne had surrounded her.

In the middle of her kitchen, she found her heart beating fast and her skin feeling too warm. Alex would be back soon, and she needed to pull herself together. Making quick work of setting the table and putting drinks out for them, she found it hard to stop the movie in her head. And really, she didn't want to. It had been playing for almost two years. Why stop it now?

All the lights in the room were on, and Megan had a moment of complete panic as Alex peeled her dress off. She was left standing in her heels and blue-lace panties and bra, and all she could think was how there was no way to hide herself—he was going to see her every imperfection, and the thought of it almost paralyzed her. Then, as if sensing her fear, Alex took a step back but gently caressed her face.

"You're beautiful," he said gruffly. His eyes raked over her entire body—as bold as any caress—before he looked into her eyes. "All night I wondered how you'd look." Then he smiled. "And you're even sexier than I imagined."

Then he was pressed up against her, still fully dressed except for his suit jacket, and he was kissing her. And just like that, all of her insecurities were forgotten and the only thing Megan could focus on was getting more of him—more kisses, more touching, more...skin. She needed to be skin to skin with him.

And he didn't disappoint.

Together they worked on his tie and then his shirt until they were discarded. Megan managed to whip his belt off and let out a small giggle at her smooth move. Alex grinned at her as he walked her backward toward the bed. Her legs hit the mattress and she lost her balance and fell, bouncing on it. He followed her down, and after that, she was thankful for the lights because he was a sight to behold.

The beautiful expanse of lean muscle.

The way he looked at her.

The expression on his face as they began to move together..

Yeah. If she had missed all of that due to the lights being off, she would have regretted it.

This time Maylene's bark alerted her to Alex's return, and she was quick to fan herself as she scrambled to make sure everything they were going to need was out on the table. By the time he walked in the door, her breathing was a little more under control. Then he smiled at her.

And her heart rate was off the charts again.

Dammit.

Alex put the food down on the table and began unpacking it. "This is one of the best delis in the city," he said. "Trust me on this one. I end up getting food from there way more than I should, but it's completely worth it."

Forcing herself to relax and be normal, Megan looked at the food in front of her. "Um...there seems to be a lot here."

Chuckling, Alex sat. "Well, once I got there and saw some of the special salads they had in the case, I thought you might not mind trying some with me."

Megan picked up one of the wrapped items and looked at him. "This does not feel like a salad."

"Okay, this one is totally brownies," he said with a grin. "I made an executive decision on dessert."

And Megan couldn't help but laugh as she put the brownies down. "Good call."

He placed her sandwich on her plate and then served himself, and for a few minutes, they were both quiet as they started to eat. Finally, Alex paused and looked at her. "So? What do you think?"

"I think I may be ordering from this deli a lot!" she said with a grin. "We already know cooking isn't my thing, and I hate bumming meals off Summer, so I'm happy to know there is good food close by."

Over the course of the meal, Alex told her about some of his other favorite places to eat that were close by, and the conversation stayed in fairly generic territory. It wasn't until they were finished and cleaning up that Megan felt the need to broach the subject they were both clearly avoiding.

"So…um…I know I kind of interrupted your day," she began nervously, "but I was wondering if you have some time for us to sort of hang out and…talk."

She didn't need to explain because the look on Alex's face showed he knew exactly what she was referring to. With a nod, he picked up his glass and walked over to the sofa to sit. After refilling her own glass, she followed.

Unable to help herself, Megan let out a shaky breath as she looked at him. "I am so sorry for the way I handled things. I don't know if I ever got to say it...you know...back then." Then she waited for him to respond.

But he didn't.

Actually, he was studying his glass of iced tea.

Frowning, she went on. "At the time, I...I don't even know what happened. How could I have forgotten something as important as you coming to New York? Honestly, I don't have a good reason. I could make excuses, but what would be the point? I screwed up, and I hurt you, and I'm sorry."

Still no reply.

"I felt awful, Alex. I still do! But after...you know... I thought we were on the same page. It just wasn't going to work for us."

He arched a brow at her. "Seriously? That's what you thought? Because that wasn't where I was going with it at all."

Okay, now she was confused. "But...we talked. I got caught up at work, and I didn't get to the city to meet with you, and when I called you—"

Alex slowly came to his feet. "When you called me, I had already been waiting for you for two hours."

"I...I know that, and I explained to you why I wasn't there. The computer system at work crashed, and—"

"I don't care about the computers, Megan!" he said with frustration. "The fact is you used your job as an excuse."

"It wasn't—"

He held up a hand to stop her. "Yes, you did. The only one keeping you from leaving the office was you. It was why we only talked late at night."

"There was the time difference, and you said that worked for you," she argued.

With a loud sigh, he began to pace. "Fine. That was one thing going for us. But every time I tried to make plans with you, you always had an excuse. If you didn't want to be with me, then you should have said so."

"But I did!" she cried, and she hated the sting of tears that came with her words. "I told you from the beginning that I worked too much—that I didn't know how to change that. And you said you understood! Every time we talked about it, you said you understood." Swiping at the first few tears that fell, Megan went on. "So if you had a problem with it, then maybe *you* should have said so!"

Staring at her, Alex gave a curt nod. "Fair enough. You're right. I should have said something. But in my defense, after we finally agreed on getting away for a weekend together, I thought we would have time to talk about it. There's only so much I'm willing to talk about on the phone or in a text, Megan. We needed to have some conversations face-to-face."

"I know that. I do. But…if it was so important to you, you could have come to Albany. It was only a few hours' drive, and—"

"Do you even hear yourself?" he demanded. "I had already flown across the country to see you, and then you wanted me to drive another few hours to get to you after you messed up?" He huffed with frustration and began to pace. "How much more was I supposed to do, Megan? It couldn't all be on me!"

And then she didn't wipe away her tears; she couldn't. They were falling too fast and furiously as her heart squeezed painfully in her chest. She had known things had ended badly, and she knew how hurt she had been. She just hadn't realized Alex had felt the same way.

"I didn't know what to do," she sobbed. "I just thought that you'd...you'd—"

"What, Megan? Tell me!"

"I don't know, okay? Everything about you was always so kind and sweet and agreeable that I guess I just thought you'd forgive me!" She dropped down onto the sofa, covered her face with her hands, and cried.

"So basically because I'm a nice guy, I deserved to get stood up like that? After I flew three thousand miles to see you, it was okay to blow me off because I'm agreeable—is that what you're saying?"

She heard the anger, the frustration in his voice, and honestly, she didn't know what to do. "I'm so sorry, Alex. You have no idea how much."

He let out a slow breath and paced away to look out the front window.

"I would have come," she said weakly. "Later that night. While we were on the phone, I was in my car and going home to pack."

But he shook his head. "It wouldn't have mattered."

"You told me not to come, Alex," she reminded him. "You didn't give me a chance to make up for it."

Turning, he looked at her. "I was angry," he said and then instantly clarified. "I was hurt. It made me realize that you meant more to me than I did to you."

She jumped to her feet. "No! No, it wasn't like that. I swear—"

"Your actions said otherwise."

This time she did wipe the tears away and looked at him. "What is it you want me to say? What can I do? I can't change what happened! I can't undo it, and nothing I say is going to make it better!" Megan tried to relax. "When I saw you at Zach's that first time, you were the one asking me out. If you're still this angry at me, why would you even want to?"

Leaning against the cushions, Alex raked a hand through his hair and let out his own weary sigh before meeting her gaze. "Because we needed to do this, Megan," he said, his voice void of emotion. "We needed to talk this out—face-to-face."

"Then why did you kiss me?" she asked and cursed the catch in her voice.

His first response was a weak smile. "I think we should agree that we kissed each other."

She rolled her eyes and couldn't help her own smile. "Fine. Then I know why I kissed you. Why did you kiss me back?"

It was the most childish conversation she could remember having, and yet…it was helping to lighten the mood.

Slowly, Alex walked up to her. "Because I've wanted to kiss you since the first time I saw you. That hasn't changed, Megan."

"Oh." Her voice was a breathless whisper.

"And I'm going to want to do it again," he said, moving a little closer.

She swallowed hard, secretly hoping he meant right now because she would totally be on board for that.

"But I'm not going to," he said, and at least he sounded like he wasn't particularly happy about it. "I think we still have some things to talk about."

She nodded. "Okay." Then, because being close to him was too much temptation, she moved to sit in one of the chairs.

"You're right," he said as he sat back on the sofa.

"Nothing can change what happened. It sucked, and I was pissed off, but…it's over now. I forgive you."

Megan almost sagged with relief. "Thank you."

"Back then, logistics weren't on our side. But that was the least of our problems." He paused. "I can understand why you didn't want anyone seeing us leave Zach's wedding together. Hell, I felt the same way—partially because I didn't want the interruption but partially because I didn't want him or your brothers or any of the Montgomerys coming after me. I heard what Ethan went through, and honestly, I was happy to avoid that. But afterward—"

"I know, I know," she interrupted. "No one has ever been overprotective of me. Probably because I didn't date much. I spent more time in the library on Friday nights than I did out on dates. But because I did know how everyone was with Summer no matter whom she dated, I guess I wanted to avoid that." Looking at him, she gave him a weak smile. "I'm a very private person. I don't like having everyone know my business, so keeping my family out of it was important to me."

"And what about now?"

"What about now?"

He laughed softly. "Megan, I think we can both agree there's still something between us, and if we are going to move forward, I'd prefer not to have to hide it from your cousins."

Damn. She hadn't given it that much thought. Living in Summer's guesthouse wasn't going to afford her much privacy when she started dating.

"I'm not saying we have to ask anyone's permission," he explained, "but I'm also not going to lie to Zach."

"I don't see why we have to say anything to anyone.

At least not right away. For all we know, this might not go anywhere. I meant what I said that day, Alex. I have a lot on my plate right now, and I'm not ready to start dating yet."

His gaze was intense as he watched her, and she wasn't sure if he was angry or just thinking about what she'd said. It wasn't as if she was asking him to lie. Not really. Just maybe…keep things quiet until they figured things out. That wasn't so wrong, was it?

"Is it dating in general you're not ready for, or is it dating me?" he asked.

"Dating in general," she replied honestly. "This whole move has been a little hard on me. I lived in New York my entire life. I always imagined that if I moved, it would still be in the northeast region where I could drive to see my parents. And then when I was finally asked to join Montgomerys, I thought it would be in my father's branch or Christian's."

"But I thought Christian was in San Diego."

"He is, but in my mind I thought I would stay with my own family." She shrugged. "There was no reason for me to think that way. It was all in my own head."

"Then why didn't you ask to be placed with one of them?"

"There wasn't a need for an IT person in either place. What Zach is doing is new for the entire company, and he wanted to be the first to do it. If all goes well, I'll work with the IT teams at all the locations—if they need me—to help make the transition go more smoothly. Not that I think I'm going to have all the answers, but that's the plan."

"So you'd be traveling quite a bit," he observed, his voice neutral.

"Possibly. I don't think it will be much, but there is that small chance. It's still months away from happening. Honestly, I can't even think about that because there's so much going on now. I'm frustrated with Zach restricting my hours, and…" But she stopped herself. "I don't want to think about that right now. We were talking about us. Not work."

He seemed to relax a little. "Well, it was your job that caused issues for us in the past, so I think it's a topic worth discussing."

That wasn't the response she was hoping for. Truthfully, she didn't want to talk about work, and that was a first for her. "Can we…can we maybe talk about something else for now? It's not like the topic of my job is never going to come up again, but maybe we can talk about you for a bit and how your job is going, or maybe you can recommend something I can do this weekend to get to know the area a little bit better."

He considered her for a moment. "All right, let me ask you something—if you were in New York, what would you be doing right now?"

Megan looked at him like he was crazy, but after a minute, she replied, "We've talked about this already, Alex. Working."

He chuckled. "Oh yeah. That. Every Saturday?"

"Yup." She nodded. "The company I was with didn't have a new system like what Zach's doing, and because it was older, I was constantly doing updates and trying to find ways to make it run more efficiently, speed things up, that kind of thing. It was a challenge, and it pretty much consumed me."

"What about when you weren't doing that? Did you…I

don't know…go to the library? Museums? Or maybe go walking in the park or jogging…anything like that?"

She gave him a bland look. "Do I look like someone who goes jogging?" she asked with a mirthless laugh. "I know you only have experience with the outdoorsy Montgomerys, and trust me when I say I'm not one of them."

Sliding his palms over his jeans, he studied her. "Have you ever tried to be?"

"Be what?"

"Outdoorsy."

She laughed again. "Alex, I told you I spend my free time finding ways to make computers perform better. What do you think?"

"I think maybe you need to try something new," he suggested. "Maybe with this whole new change thing you've been talking about since you moved here, you might try doing something different other than working shorter hours."

"Like…being outside?" Her nose wrinkled with distaste.

Now it was his turn to laugh. "You don't have to look at it quite like that! But…yeah. How about instead of driving around…we go for a walk in the park?"

She eyed him suspiciously. "We?"

He nodded.

"Just walking, right? You're not going to try to get me to hike up a mountain or go camping or anything, are you?"

"Not on our first trip," he said seriously, but then his lips began to twitch, and she knew he was teasing.

Or at least she hoped he was.

"Alex—"

"Come on," he interrupted quickly. "Look, how about tomorrow I'll drive us to the park and show you all the points of interest between here and there, and then we'll walk around."

"What park?"

"Washington Park," he replied. "You'll love it. It's one of the oldest parks in Oregon, and there is a ton of history to it, and because I was born and raised here, I'll be able to tell you all about it." He paused and eyed her curiously. "And I have a feeling you're a history kind of girl, right?"

She looked like she was seriously considering his offer. "And by history, you're not talking about silly stuff, right? Like you're going to be telling me true historical facts."

"Silly stuff?"

Megan rolled her eyes. "You know, I'm not looking for facts about the guy who used to sell snow cones there or about the time some college fraternity built the largest human pyramid," she said and sounded a little amused at her examples.

Something flashed in his eyes, but before she could question it, it was gone. It was on the tip of her tongue to ask, but she decided to let it go for now. She was probably imagining it anyway.

"I'm going to want to know statistics on the park— when it was created, how many acres, what changes has it undergone since it opened…that sort of thing."

Rather than say anything, Alex started to laugh.

"What's so funny?" she demanded.

He sobered immediately and looked at her. "That's a lot of pressure on me and my knowledge of state history.

And I have a feeling no matter what I tell you, you're going to come home later and go online and make sure I wasn't lying." Then he chuckled again. "Honestly, I don't think I've ever met anyone who demanded I be able to entertain them with geographical statistics on a state park."

"Okay, maybe I'm being a little silly—"

"You think?" he asked and then gave her a big smile.

And the dimples were out, his eyes were twinkling, and she was pretty much about to melt into a puddle right there on the spot. Knowing she needed to do something to divert his attention or he'd be reading her mind in no time, she stood and walked toward the kitchen. "What can I say? I'm a history buff. I find it interesting." She found the container with the brownies and turned toward him. "How about some dessert?"

"That depends," he said, his voice going serious again.

Really? He was going to negotiate over brownies?

"On what?"

"There's still a lot of daylight left today. How about we have dessert and then go for a drive?" he suggested.

"A drive?"

He nodded.

"I've kind of already taken up the bulk of your day, and you're talking about spending the day with me again tomorrow," she reasoned. "I feel like I'm monopolizing your entire weekend."

"And I'm not complaining."

Really, she had nothing else to do, and he was offering her help with something she'd been meaning to do and kept putting off. So what was she waiting for?

"Okay," she finally said. "But brownies first."

———

Thirty minutes later, Alex was sitting in his truck waiting for Megan to come out. She'd said she had to let Maylene out and wanted to grab a sweater for herself. Out of the corner of his eye, he saw her coming out of the guesthouse. Her hair was in its ever-efficient ponytail, and she had on a pair of faded jeans and a sweater. It still amazed him when he tried to compare the woman from Zach and Gabriella's wedding to the woman he was looking at now. He knew people put a little more effort into how they looked for a wedding, but he couldn't understand why she seemed to go to such extremes to downplay her looks.

Megan was beautiful no matter what: honeyed hair, brown eyes, and a body that—even though she hid it under unflattering clothes—still made his fingers twitch with the need to touch it. Explore it. Feel it moving underneath him.

He let out a huff of frustration and forced himself to look away. "Think about what to show her—points of interest, places she'll find helpful," he said to fill the silence. Another glance out the window, and he spotted her running into the house.

"Must have forgotten something," he murmured. And sure enough, two minutes later, she was walking out.

His phone beeped with an incoming text, and he welcomed the interruption. After reading it, Alex replied to the text—his Tuesday client confirming their appointment—and looked up in time to see Megan turning around and heading toward the house again.

Seriously? he thought.

Shaking his head as he laughed, he decided to find out what was going on. Stepping out of the truck and onto the driveway, he saw Megan coming back out, and she seemed to be talking to herself.

"Everything okay?" he asked.

She startled at the sound of his voice. "What? Oh… um, yeah. Everything's fine except…" She stopped and shook her head. "No. Everything's fine."

Alex walked toward her. "Megan, come on. What's going on?"

Her shoulders sagged, and the look on her face was so sad it was almost comical. "People do this all the time, right? Why is it so damn difficult for me?"

"Um—"

"This shouldn't be so hard!" She threw up her hands in frustration and stalked over to the truck.

Alex followed her. "What exactly are we talking about?"

She spun around as if she had forgotten he was there. Then she sighed. "All I wanted to do was go out and…I don't know…drive around. Get to know the town and see where everything is. We talked about this thirty minutes ago, and I know it's not a big deal, and now I can't seem to get myself together, and it's freaking me out."

"O-kay," he said slowly. "Um…why, exactly?"

"First, I left my phone in the house."

He didn't see a problem with that, so he nodded.

"Then I went and got it, came out, and thought I was ready to go when I realized I left my purse inside when I grabbed my phone."

Ah. Now he was starting to see her frustration.

"So, here I am, thinking how I'm ready to go, but am I? No."

He looked her over from head to toe and couldn't see anything that was obviously missing, so he waited for her to explain.

"And now…" she began, but her voice cracked, "now I'm thinking 'Why are we even doing this?' and 'What exactly am I going to see?' and I feel like it shouldn't be so hard for me to get out of my own damn way—out of my own head—and go!" She was rambling and breathless, and her eyes were huge, and all Alex could think to do was hug her.

So he did.

She didn't fight him. She willingly went into his embrace, and he could feel her trembling.

All of this is over going for a drive? he thought.

For a few minutes, he simply held her. When he no longer felt her shaking, he pulled back and smiled down at her. "You okay?"

Nodding, she stepped out of his arms and gave him a weak smile. "Sorry. I didn't mean to come off as some sort of weirdo."

"I don't think you're a weirdo."

"Oh, please," she scoffed. "If I was in your shoes and someone had a meltdown because they couldn't figure out how to go for a drive around town, I'd think they were weird."

He shrugged. "Then it's a good thing you're not in my shoes."

Shaking her head, she laughed softly. "I guess I tend to overthink things, and I'm not used to having so much free time on my hands."

"I'm sure it's a little unnerving for you, but I think if you let yourself relax, you'll kind of enjoy it."

"Maybe..."

He had no idea how to handle someone quite like her. He could work with people with physical limitations, and he could encourage them and give them hope. *How much different could this be?* he wondered.

"Look, this is a little like a physical therapy session," he said, and she gave him a confused look. "Hear me out—you're doing something you've never done before, but it's going to help you and be good for you."

"Alex, don't patronize me," she said, but she didn't sound angry.

"I'm not," he countered. "You're looking to change some of your habits, right? Well, learning to relax is part of it. So, we're going to take it slow. No one's expecting you to make this big transformation overnight. But it's going to take some effort from you to make it happen and to develop patterns that are going to stick and be helpful in the long run."

She rolled her eyes. "Seriously?"

He nodded. "When I first start working with a client, our first few sessions are the hardest. Do you know why?"

She shook her head.

"Because we have to get to know one another and we have to test the limits of what we can and can't do."

"I don't see how this applies to us driving around, Alex."

Rather than acknowledge her comment, he contin-ued. "Today we'll drive around. No destination in mind. Just covering some basics that might help you this week.

Then tomorrow, we'll hit the park and get you outside and moving. And then, maybe next weekend, we'll see about hiking up a mountain. Baby steps."

And then the greatest thing happened.

She laughed.

A genuine laugh.

Her eyes lit up, and the sound of her laughter was enough to make Alex feel like his entire day was made.

"So what do you say?" he asked. "You ready to check out your new city?"

"Lead the way!"

Chapter 5

ON SUNDAY MORNING, ALEX WAS FINISHING HIS COFFEE AND contemplating the day. The weather was perfect—blue skies, temperature in the sixties…it was a great day to be outside doing something. Anything.

His usual routine had him working in the yard a bit—mowing the lawn, weeding, the basics—and then when he was done he'd make himself something to eat and soak in the hot tub to relax his tired muscles.

An image of Megan sitting in the hot tub with him flashed in his mind, and he was about to go with it when he heard a car door slam.

Speak of the devil…

They had driven around the city yesterday with Megan sort of dictating where they went based on what she specifically wanted to see. It wasn't the most exciting tour of Portland, but it was the most practical.

At first he wasn't sure what he was expecting. He simply figured he'd point out the banks, the grocery stores, and some of his favorite restaurants. And he did. But as they drove around, Alex noticed Megan commenting distractedly on places like the hospital and women's shelters. Then it was human services and day care centers. He had been about to comment on the things she probably wasn't even aware she was talking about when her attention turned to craft stores. At that point he figured she was thinking about decorating ideas, but he never got the chance to ask her about it because they drove by a Best Buy and she started talking about getting a new computer.

After they had gotten back to her place, he had decided to be bold and ask her to meet him at his home today for their trip to the park. He figured she would appreciate the chance to drive around and find the place on her own—even though she had been here once before—but the main reason was because he wanted her to see his house. To come inside and see it like he'd wanted her to on the night she came to pick up the car.

He heard her soft knock on the door and immediately went to answer it. She was about fifteen minutes early, and he was a little surprised.

"Hey," he said warmly as he opened the door.

"Hey," she replied with a shy smile. "I know I'm a little early, but I wanted to give myself some extra time in case I got lost."

Stepping aside, he motioned for her to come in. "I was finishing my coffee, and I'm not quite ready," he said. "I need to put on some sneakers, and we'll pack up a couple bottles of water and maybe a snack to bring with us. Sound good?"

Megan nodded and followed him inside.

"Help yourself to some coffee," he said, leading her into the kitchen and motioning toward the coffeemaker. "I'll be right back."

Funny how much he was looking forward to a day strolling in the park, he thought as he walked up the stairs to his room. It had been a long time since he'd done anything but jog or cycle around the park paths, and now he was anxiously grabbing sneakers and getting ready to spend the day simply strolling and playing park guide.

Well, knowing that Megan was going to be with him had a little something to do with it…or everything, whatever. Alex loved to be outside and to be active, but once in a while a quiet day at home was appealing. He always found it curious that people—like Megan— didn't go out more, and he was hoping to help her change that part of herself.

Granted, she might hate it. She might be the type of person who wasn't outdoorsy. And he could accept that. Sort of. But if she enjoyed their trip today, he'd suggest maybe going to the Japanese garden next weekend.

His mind was instantly swirling with places they could go together: not only the touristy sites the city was known for, but some spots the locals enjoyed— bars, restaurants, music festivals. He knew if she gave him a chance, he could have their weekends booked for the next six months easily.

"Don't get too ahead of yourself," he murmured. "She's clearly still testing the waters here where we're concerned. One thing at a time."

And that still didn't make much sense to him, but for now he was willing to accept it and do his best to prove to her he wasn't going to push or rush her to go on a date with him.

Even though technically that's what they could call what they were doing today.

And he was smart enough to know not to mention that to her.

Especially if he wanted to spend the day with her again.

With some sense of direction, Alex walked to the kitchen, and…Megan wasn't there. He called her name, and she answered from his living room. It was one of his favorite rooms in the house. There was a massive stone fireplace with built-in bookcases on either side, and the room boasted a twenty-foot ceiling with exposed beams. It was a little rustic, but it was the kind of space he absolutely loved.

He found her looking at his collection of books. Walking over to her, he waited to hear what she thought.

"This is the most eclectic library I've ever seen," she said, placing a book on drum making back on the shelf.

"Aren't all libraries eclectic?" he asked. "I mean, they have to have a book on pretty much everything."

Megan looked at him with amusement. "Okay, Mr. Technicality, let me rephrase that. This is the most eclectic personal library I've ever seen."

"Ah…much better," he teased. "And thank you."

"Seriously, how many of these have you read?"

"I'm not big on watching TV, but I love to read."

"Clearly." She laughed, motioning to the filled shelves. "You seem to have pretty much covered all the bases—you've got biographies, mysteries, how-to books…" She scanned the shelves again. "So many classics here. I remember reading most of these when I was in school—primarily as part of the curriculum—but there are some I reread later on for my own enjoyment."

"Like I said, I enjoy reading. But if I had to choose my favorite genre, I'd have to say science fiction. I have to read a lot for work—I like to stay up-to-date on new therapies being used and review case studies. I find that kind of thing fascinating."

"I get that," she agreed. "I read a lot of tech magazines and follow along with any new systems coming out. It's dry reading, but it keeps me thinking of ways I can enhance the systems I'm working with or help the company I'm working for."

"What about fun? What's your go-to genre when you want to relax?"

"Hmm…" While she looked like she was considering the question, Alex noticed the slight flush to her cheeks.

"And not what you think you should say, but what you really read," he clarified.

She glared at him before looking at the shelves. "Fine, but…no judging."

Alex made a motion across his chest. "Cross my heart. Now come on. What's your go-to?"

Megan huffed loudly. "Romance." She paused. "Go ahead. Make fun."

He frowned at her. "Why would I make fun?"

Now she fully turned to face him. "Why? Because everyone does," she reasoned. "Especially people who own the classics. I've heard everything from 'it's nonsense' to 'they're not real books' to—"

"Okay, okay, okay," he interrupted before she got herself too worked up. "And for the record, I don't think those things, but I've heard people say them, so…I get it. Personally, I don't see anything wrong with romance novels. I've read a few myself, and I'll admit I enjoy a lot of the fiction stuff I read when there's a romantic element."

"Really?"

He nodded. "Really."

She smiled at him and then moved over to another set of shelves displaying some framed photos. Part of him liked how she was taking an interest in him, but he was also feeling anxious about getting her to the park before she found an excuse to not go.

Picking up one of the pictures, she turned toward him. "You were so young here!"

The immediate pang of guilt he always felt when he looked at *that* particular picture hit, and then he pushed it aside. Walking over to her, Alex gently took the picture from her hands. "It was from the summer after I graduated high school. A bunch of us went camping for the first time without any parents or chaperones. We thought we were pretty cool." He forced himself to smile and think of the fun he was having when that picture was taken.

"And who's that with you?"

"That's Danny," he replied. "We grew up together, lived next door to one another pretty much our whole lives."

She was still smiling. "That's nice. Do you still keep in touch?"

"I see him once a week. Every Friday. Without fail."

"Every week? Wow! That's a committed friendship!"

"Actually, he is…he's one of my clients. We have a standing appointment every Friday," he said a little stiltedly.

Megan looked at him oddly, and he knew she would ask more questions—questions he wasn't willing to deal with right now. This was going to be a good day. He wanted to make it a good day for her, and talking about the darkest point in his life wasn't going to make that happen.

"I've never been camping," she said, surprising him. "It's totally not my thing."

"How do you know if you've never gone?" he teased.

"Let's just say I'm pretty sure I wouldn't enjoy it."

"But what about—?"

"How about we tackle walking in the park before we

continue this?" she said, laughing. "For all you know, you'll figure out by the end of the day that I'm not the outdoorsy type."

And before they lost this bonding they were clearly doing, he nodded toward the kitchen. "Come on. Let's grab some drinks and snacks and head to the park. There are more than fifteen miles of trails and—"

"Alex, I have no intention of walking fifteen miles today," she argued lightly.

He laughed as they worked together in the kitchen getting supplies. "I know, and I wouldn't ask it of you. There are more than four hundred acres to the park, so it is not a see-it-all-in-one-day type of place. Today I thought we'd walk around a little and see where the mood took us. There's a Japanese garden I'd like to take you to maybe next weekend. What do you think?"

"That sounds like it would be lovely," she said with a smile.

He bit his tongue before he blurted out, *It's a date*.

―⁓―

"You're in an awfully good mood today," Summer said on Monday while she and Megan were heading to lunch. "You never told me what you ended up doing this weekend. I hope Maylene didn't give you any trouble."

"Well…she did give me a scare on Saturday," Megan began hesitantly. At her cousin's wide-eyed look, she relayed the story of how the little pug had gotten out and where she eventually found her. Much to Megan's relief, Summer laughed. "Sure, it's funny now, but at the time, I was freaking out."

"I guess I should have warned you about that. She

does get out of the yard from time to time, but she never goes far, and she always comes back. For some reason she is obsessed with sitting in Ethan's hammock."

"Um, yeah. It would have been helpful information to have at the time," Megan deadpanned. "Thanks."

They walked into the café and were seated almost immediately. "So Alex came over and helped you look for her, huh?"

Megan nodded.

"That was nice of him," Summer said casually as she glanced at the menu. "And did you happen to…oh, I don't know…invite him to stay over?"

"What?" Megan cried. "Why would you even ask?"

Gently placing her menu down and taking a sip of her water, Summer gave her a look that could only be described as an evil smile.

"I have waited two years for you to come clean, Megs. I saw you and Alex at Zach's wedding. I saw you dancing and flirting, and then I saw you leave together. Twice," she added with an ever-growing grin. "And you were noticeably absent for the remainder of the weekend. And so was Alex. Now, is there something you'd like to tell me?"

With an exaggerated eye roll, Megan grabbed her glass of water and took a sip—figuring she could let Summer stew for a moment.

"You know, you could have asked before now," Megan began.

"And you would have told me?"

"You? Of course. Anyone else in the family? Probably not."

Summer laughed. "That I can totally understand.

They all mean well, but sometimes they manage to make everything worse."

"Well, I've never had to deal with that—not like you have. My brothers never seemed to take much notice of who I was dating."

Summer gave her a bland look. "That's because you didn't date much."

"I was studious. That's not a crime."

Reaching across the table, Summer grabbed Megan's hand. "You're right. There's nothing wrong with it, but I have to ask…why?"

"Why what?"

"Why was it so important to you? The grades, the studying? I mean, we all knew you were smart, Megan. I don't think you needed to spend so much time proving it."

"Easy for you to say. You were good at everything you did, and you weren't interested in being part of the Montgomery corporate machine."

"And yet here I am," Summer said with a small smile. "And you felt like you had to…what…prove you were capable of being a part of it?"

Megan nodded.

"Oh, sweetie. Why? I mean, I can't imagine anyone ever saying you couldn't work for the company. That's crazy!"

"My father wanted me to be groomed to be a corporate wife. That wasn't what I wanted. It was important for him to see me for who I was—am!—and respect that."

Summer studied her for a long moment.

And then kept studying her.

"What?" Megan finally asked. "What's so wrong with that?"

"Do you realize how many…let's say…problems working for this company has caused?"

"What are you talking about? You're here, and you obviously love it, so—"

Summer shook her head. "We are a family that is notorious for being workaholics to the point of not having lives! My brother James moved out when he was sixteen because he didn't want to be a part of the business. And you have a brother who fought long and hard to make a name for himself outside of Montgomerys, and you know how much stress that put on everyone."

"Okay, I get that," Megan countered, "which is why I'm trying to fit in. I want to be a part of it! James and Carter had fights because they wanted out. I want in!"

"But at what cost?"

Megan looked at her quizzically.

"If you truly love what you do, then I'll never bring this up again, and we'll go back to what I wanted to talk about—which is you and Alex. However, did you choose to go into IT because it's what you're passionate about, or was it to prove yourself?"

"I…I…"

Summer held up a hand to stop her. "Just…think about it, okay?"

Honestly, Megan couldn't have answered at that moment even if she had to. It wasn't the first time this topic had come up, and she had a feeling it wouldn't be the last. But it was something she was going to have to think about because now that she was starting to incorporate some changes in her life, would they still work now that she had finally gained the position she had fought so hard for?

Their waitress came to take their orders, and it wasn't until she walked away that Summer finally leaned back in her seat with another huge grin. "So…you and Alex at the wedding! I'm going to need some details!"

Rolling her eyes, Megan couldn't help but laugh. "Really?"

"Hell yes! I may be a happily married woman, but Alex is a very sexy man, and I have waited way too long to hear about this!"

Megan could feel herself blushing from head to toe, but she was excited to finally talk to someone about this.

"Ooh…I can tell it was hot by the way you're blushing!" Summer said excitedly. "Come on, you have to tell me! Did you sneak off and fool around in one of the supply closets?"

"What? Oh my gosh, no!" Megan's hands flew to her face to cover her embarrassment. When she lowered them, she told Summer about their walk in the garden, their first kiss, and how they made their quick exit from the reception and up to her room.

And that's where she stopped.

Sort of.

Well, her cousin didn't need to know everything, did she?

Summer fanned herself with her napkin. "I'm telling you, I was watching the two of you, but I didn't say a word to anyone because I didn't want to draw attention to you and have someone ruin whatever was happening."

"And I appreciate it."

"So? What happened next? Have you two been in touch all this time?"

Unfortunately, Megan had to tell her about the

romantic weekend that never was and watch the disappointment on her face.

"How could you just not show up? I don't get it!"

Megan shrugged. "I don't either. I flaked. I was so engrossed in a problem at work that I was working fifteen-hour days and lost track of everything. Next thing I know I'm on the phone with Alex and trying to apologize, and…it was awful, Summer. I felt so incredibly stupid, and Alex was so mad, and—"

"Can you blame him?"

She shook her head. "No."

"How was he when you saw him again? Did you guys reschedule the trip?"

Megan shook her head again. "The next time I saw him was the night at Zach and Gabriella's when the guys were getting ready to paint."

"No!"

Now she nodded. "Yup."

"Wow."

"Tell me about it."

"So…wow…um…was it really awkward?"

Megan let out a weary sigh. "More than you can even imagine. I mean, I knew I was going to see him. I think he was actually a large part of the reason I was so willing to take the job here and move."

"But?"

Megan shrugged again. "But I hadn't planned on it being so soon or so—"

"In front of everyone?" Summer supplied.

"Exactly! Then it felt even more awkward because we never told anyone about us, and now I don't know how to do it, and—"

"It isn't anyone's business," Summer said firmly. "I'm sure Zach will get all defensive because...well... he'll be offended that no one told him, like he was when it was me and Ethan."

"But you're his sister. It's different."

"I'm telling you, on principle, he's going to be offended. Just...prepare yourself. And Alex."

"Well, I don't think it's going to be an issue because we've talked about it, and we sort of hashed things out, and we're friends."

Summer smirked and delicately took another sip of her water. "Really?"

Megan smiled. "Really."

"So there are no lingering sparks? No chance of the two of you picking up where you left off?"

"Right now, I'm not interested in dating anyone. Not even Alex."

"Because you're dead inside?" Summer teased and then started to laugh. "Megan, come on! That man is like the perfect male specimen! How could you *not* want to get involved with him? And on top of that, he's one of the nicest people on the planet! Seriously, he helps everyone with everything! Look at what he does for a living—he *heals* people!"

"Okay, dramatic much?" Megan teased.

Crossing her arms over her chest, Summer grinned. "You can pretend all you want, but you're not fooling anyone. You can say all you want how the two of you are friends, but the only one you're lying to is yourself. And you know what? The only one missing out on something great is you."

"You really should have stayed with the theater

work," Megan said dryly. "Or maybe it was the psychology—"

"Make fun all you want, but I'm telling you, Alex would be perfect for you. What are you afraid of?"

That was a good question, and luckily Megan was saved from answering by the arrival of their food. Quickly taking a bite, she hoped to buy herself a little more time. But as usual, Summer wasn't fooled.

"I'm going to let this go for now," she said simply. "But you really should work on some of these issues of yours."

Rather than say anything, Megan simply nodded.

"Okay, new topic," Summer said cheerily. "Gabriella's baby shower! Any chance you can buy another baby blanket like you bought for Amber? Gabs has been admiring it and the sweater set."

For a moment Megan could only stare.

"I know it's short notice and all, and you probably need to special-order those things in advance, but I know she'd love it!"

"Um—"

"Anyway, I know I'm a little late on getting the shower planned, but I think between the two of us, we can come up with something great!"

On Wednesday, Alex was going over his schedule for the rest of the week. It wasn't like he needed to; he'd been working with this same list of clients for several months. But for some reason today he found himself looking at his Friday schedule and feeling…defeated.

Danny.

Raking a hand through his hair, Alex sighed.

Eight years. He'd been working with Danny on his own time for eight long years, and lately doing so had been getting harder and harder. Every week Alex walked in with a smile and a positive attitude, and by the time he left, he was mentally and physically exhausted and knew he was losing hope.

They both were.

Growing up, Danny Mathis had been his best friend. They lived next door to one another, and not a day had gone by when they were in school when they hadn't hung out together. They'd even picked the same college—University of Oregon. Alex always knew he would go into physical therapy, but Danny had been unsure of where he saw himself.

It hadn't taken long for Alex to realize that Danny was struggling at school—missing classes and partying too much—and he stepped in when he could to help him out by tutoring him and even doing some of his assignments. At the time, he thought he was helping him, but Alex realized too late that all he was doing was enabling Danny.

Spring break of their junior year, Danny and Alex—along with several guys from their fraternity—opted to go camping and hiking. It was something they'd all enjoyed doing, and looking back now, Alex still couldn't believe he hadn't realized how dangerous the situation had actually been. There had been drinking, and although Alex rarely drank more than a beer or two, most of the guys spent a large part of the trip wasted.

On their second-to-last day in the woods, they decided to try something epic—diving off one of the higher cliffs. They'd been doing it all week from the lower ones but wanted to end the week in a big way. Alex had agreed but wasn't so sure he'd actually jump. Once they were all at the top, Danny had come up with an even bigger challenge.

"Human pyramid!" he shouted excitedly. "And the guy at the top jumps first! It will be awesome! And then everyone dives in after him! What do you say?"

Not everyone was on board—including Alex—but no one stopped it from happening either. As everyone talked about their position in the pyramid, Danny called the top spot, and again, no one said anything. Alex could still remember seeing Danny stumbling a little as they were setting up, and that's when he approached him.

"Dude, it's ten in the morning. Please tell me you haven't been drinking already."

Danny looked at him with a cocky grin. "You need to lighten up, Alex. I was a bit hungover and thought the best way to ease the pain was with another beer. Or three." Then he laughed.

"Danny…maybe you shouldn't—"

He never got to finish because everyone was already getting into position and Danny made fun of Alex for trying to be the mother hen of the group. It was an ongoing joke, and rather than fight it, Alex held his tongue.

If there was one moment in his life he wished he could go back and change, that would be it.

Danny dove to the left rather than the right and ended up going headfirst into shallow water. He'd broken his neck instantly. There had been nothing but chaos as the next few guys dove down, oblivious to what had happened. Alex could still hear the screaming—the panic—when someone finally realized something was wrong.

It seemed to take forever for the paramedics to arrive and even longer to get Danny to the hospital. Critical time had been lost, and it took several days for the doctors to determine that Danny had shattered his first and second vertebrae—which meant his skull and spine were not connected. He was paralyzed from the neck down.

Guilt ate at Alex, and he had cried more in those first days after the accident than he had in his entire life. He would sit next to Danny—who was in a medically induced coma—and beg for forgiveness. He had even gone to Danny's parents and begged their forgiveness. They never blamed Alex; they told him how they were aware that Danny was prone to taking risks and how his behavior had gotten out of control. If anything, they blamed themselves for not stepping in and trying to help him sooner. Together they would all sit, consumed by their guilt.

Alex had finished college the following year and was then accepted into a PT program. With every new technique he learned, he would visit Danny and try to work with him. But there was never going to be a cure for his friend. No amount of therapy was ever going to make him walk again. Over the years he'd had to overcome so many health crises, and all Alex could do was keep him moving to help alleviate issues like atrophy.

But Danny had lost the will to live. He'd all but begged Alex to stop coming and let his body break down so he could be free from this prison, but Alex couldn't bring himself to do that.

Swallowing hard, Alex closed his calendar and

leaned back in his chair. A shaky sigh came out just as it did every time he allowed himself to think about that day. He had to come up with a way to inspire Danny—to give him some hope. Maybe he'd see about taking him out rather than doing exercises. Once in a while they did that. It wasn't an easy task, but the healthcare team that took care of Danny always helped him make it happen.

With a renewed sense of spirit, Alex told himself to look forward to Friday—to have a positive attitude. He'd been doing it for years, and he knew he could do it again.

And again and again.

He had to.

The following Sunday Megan knocked on Alex's door, practically bouncing on her toes. They were going to go to the Japanese garden today, and she had packed up a lunch for them to bring. She had casually mentioned to Summer how Alex was taking her sightseeing—as a friend—but the grin on Summer's face told Megan she wasn't fooling anyone. This wasn't a casual outing with a buddy; this was turning into something more.

Maybe Megan would talk to Summer more later on after she got home, but for now she was feeling too good to think about making excuses or explanations to anyone. For today, she was going to live in the moment and enjoy herself.

Their trip to the park the previous Sunday had been much more enjoyable than she could have imagined. Not only was the park itself beautiful, but Alex was an amazing tour guide. He seemed to know so much about the park and answered all of her questions—and there were many—and he did it all while walking at a pace she enjoyed. Megan had a feeling if it were up to Alex, they would have been doing the tour at a faster rate—mainly because he was so athletic—but he was considerate of her, and she found she liked that about him.

Actually, she was finding more and more just how much she liked about him.

If she took out their history, Megan realized she would have been drawn to Alex no matter what. He had a great personality, he was funny and caring, and there wasn't anything he wouldn't do for his friends. They had long conversations and found they had much more in common than she'd thought they would.

And the fact that he was incredibly good-looking didn't hurt either.

During the week their schedules hadn't meshed—he started work early in the morning, and he didn't keep regular hours. Gabriella had mentioned to her how Alex had customized the therapy schedule he'd done with Zach when he was recovering from his accident, and Megan figured that was something he did with all of his clients. While she hadn't seen him all week, they had texted almost every day and had talked on the phone last night to confirm their plans for today.

"We're still on for the Japanese garden tomorrow, right?" he had asked, his voice hopeful.

"Absolutely! And I'm handling the food, so don't worry about that," she'd responded. She couldn't wait to go to the deli and pick out the meal this time.

And once that was covered, they'd stayed on the phone for more than an hour talking about their weeks while Megan worked on a new baby blanket for Zach and Gabriella. It felt good to multitask, and the more she crocheted, the more relaxed she became. She was appreciating her free time more and more with each passing day, and she was loving listening to Alex talk. By the time they hung up, she found herself staring at the clock and willing the time to go faster so she could see him.

And here they were.

Two friends hanging out, doing some sightseeing. It was actually pretty nice. Not only was she having a good time, but Alex had been great about pointing out different points of interests while they drove. Now she knew where to get the best pizza, Chinese food, and sandwiches close to home, as well as a good dry cleaner and coffee shop. She had found out more about her new neighborhood thanks to one car ride with Alex than she would have on her own. And to make sure his advice was accurate, Megan had tried all of those places this week and had been thoroughly pleased.

If she were a more fanciful woman, she'd consider today a date. But Megan was many things, and fanciful wasn't one of them. She was practical. Levelheaded. There was a definite difference between going for a walk in the park with a friend and a romantic day at the park with a lover. And she and Alex were definitely not—

Wait a minute…

Her heart rate kicked up, and she felt her cheeks flush.

"No," she murmured. Sure, they had kissed that weekend at Zach and Gabriella's, but nothing even remotely inappropriate had happened since.

Inappropriate? she thought and rolled her eyes. She was a grown woman, and Alex was definitely a grown man. Nothing they'd done could be considered wrong or…inappropriate. It was a fling, right? People had flings all the time. A sexy weekend between two consenting adults—there was nothing wrong with that. And they had tried to extend it beyond that, and…

Okay, no more thinking about that, she chided herself. They had moved on, and even though there was still a definite attraction between the two of them, Alex was respecting her boundaries and allowing her to decide if and when she was ready to see if they could possibly explore their attraction again and…date.

She jumped when Alex opened the door and smiled at her.

Then her heart kicked hard for a completely different reason.

Oh yeah, she thought. *We are definitely going to explore this attraction. Soon.*

"Hey," he said. "We ready to go?"

Megan didn't trust herself to speak. Taking a step back, she waited as Alex locked up and then followed him to his truck.

"So what's on the menu?" he asked.

Okay, safe topic.

"I went to the deli where you got our lunch last weekend and had them make us a couple of sandwiches. I remember you saying how much you liked their turkey clubs, so I had them make one of those for you, and I got myself a chicken salad sandwich on whole wheat."

"Good choice," he said with a grin as he started the truck. "What else is in there?"

"I brought a couple bottles of water, chips, and two giant chocolate-chip cookies." She paused and laughed softly. "They had just come out of the oven and smelled too good to resist."

"No Oreos, huh?" he teased.

She blushed at the memory. "I didn't see any Double Stuf ones. Otherwise I would have grabbed those too."

Alex pulled out of the driveway and immediately began talking about the history of the Japanese garden. Megan sat back and listened to him talk. Occasionally he'd point out places they were passing that he thought she'd want to know about—the mechanic he used, a hair salon, and a day spa.

"I have to tell you, I never thought of myself as the kind of girl to go to one of those spas, but after going for mani-pedis with Gabriella and Summer, I have a feeling I'll be going again."

Alex looked over at her for a moment. "If you think that's good, you should do the all-day thing. Besides the mani-pedi, you can get a facial and a massage. It's supposedly very decadent, and I'm told every woman enjoys that."

Megan thought about it for a moment. "I'm sure it would be nice," she said thoughtfully. "I've never had a facial. Or a massage."

"Wait…what?" he asked with disbelief. "How is that possible?"

"I don't know. I never thought of going for one. Or… either. I never needed a massage, and a facial seemed like a waste of time. I've got good skin and…" Another shrug.

For a minute, she thought he was going to say something else, but he didn't. They drove in silence for a bit, and then Alex went back to talking about the garden. By the time they arrived, she was even more excited about what they would see.

After they parked and started walking, Alex took the cooler bag from Megan and reached for her hand. It seemed like the natural thing to do, so she didn't question him. For today, she promised herself to be content and go with the flow.

Baby steps.

"Okay," she said as the sign came into view, "what are we going to see first?"

"That depends," he said casually as they strolled along at a leisurely pace. "Was there anything you wanted to see first?"

"Hmm…there are…what…eight different types of gardens?"

Alex nodded.

"I guess we'll start with whichever one comes first," she said, and as they walked through the entrance, she chuckled. "Or we can choose to go left, right, or straight."

Beside her, Alex laughed too. "Why don't we go counterclockwise and make our way around?"

"Sounds like a plan."

The paths were lushly lined, and Megan realized that no matter what she had thought they were going to see, it didn't even compare to the reality. Never before had she seen anything so beautiful, so peaceful. This sort of place was never on her radar as something she'd want to see, and now she realized just how wrong she had been.

As they walked, Alex pointed out the different flowers and different statues they passed, and as they approached the first garden, she found herself thoroughly enchanted by it all.

"This is the tea garden," Alex said softly as they turned to the right.

Megan gasped with delight. "Oh my goodness! This is amazing! How is it possible a place like this exists in the middle of a city?"

"It is something, isn't it?"

"I swear, if I had a yard of my own, I would love to do something like this. It's like an oasis."

For hours they walked around, and with each new garden they encountered, she became more and more enamored with them. She had grown up in a big city and then gone to school and worked in one; things like gardens had never captured her attention. But after today's explorations, Megan knew she was going to be doing some serious thinking about where she wanted to put down roots and what she wanted that space to look like.

They walked the paths, enjoyed tea in the authentic tea house, and then picnicked with an amazing view of Mount Hood. Megan sighed as she took in the scenery.

"Was that a good sigh or a bad one?" Alex asked.

She turned her head and looked at him. "A good one. A really good one." Pausing, Megan took a minute to appreciate the sights and the smells and the sounds all around her. It was peaceful. Tranquil. Even though there were a ton of people all around them, it didn't feel crowded.

"This is so different from anything I've ever experienced," she explained. "And I can't believe I'm twenty-six and just now learning to appreciate nature."

Beside her, Alex was still for a moment. "I think we all get used to the way we live and sometimes don't realize how much else is out there to see. This is where

I grew up, which made it easy to want to be outside and explore. If I grew up in a big city, chances are I'd be drawn more to going to museums and restaurants and clubs and that sort of thing."

Now she studied him. "Do you enjoy those things? The museums and such?"

"Yes, there are some great museums to see around here too." Then he shrugged. "I figured I'd introduce you to some outdoor stuff first."

"And I'm glad you did." Moving a little closer, Megan rested her head on Alex's shoulder, and for a few minutes, they were both content to stay that way. "What are you thinking for next weekend?" When Alex didn't answer right away, she wanted to kick herself. Maybe he had other plans or didn't plan on being her permanent tour guide. She was about to correct herself when he spoke.

"How about the Portland Audubon Society? There are some great walking trails, and we can go bird-watching. How does that sound?"

"Bird-watching?" she asked with amusement as she lifted her head. "Seriously? That's a thing people do?"

Looking at her, he smiled, and everything in Megan simply melted. To her, there could never be a more per-fect moment than this one—their day had been amazing, their lunch was delicious. And the smile on this man and the sheer happiness she saw there…it was everything. Before she could second-guess herself, she leaned in and gently pressed her lips to his.

If Alex had been surprised, he didn't let on—but he also didn't immediately respond or take control. He let her kiss him—gently. Softly. Once. Twice. And then? Then they both sort of eased into it, sighing with pleasure as if this was what they'd been waiting for all day. It was slow and sweet, and Megan felt herself melt against him as his arms slowly banded around her. She remembered their first kiss had been in a garden, but at the time she hadn't paid any attention to that detail because her focus had solely been on Alex. And their first kiss had been all heat and need. It was the total opposite of this, and yet it felt the same. She already knew she was falling for him. Again. And with even the slightest encouragement, she'd be willing to get in the car right now and drive home and have another wild weekend of sex with him. Only...

It was Sunday.

She had work in the morning.

Dammit.

Alex lifted his head and placed a small kiss on the tip of her nose before resting his forehead against hers. "Where'd you go?" he whispered.

"What do you mean?"

"One minute you were right there with me—kissing me like...well...exactly like I remembered. And then the next I could tell you were distracted."

Megan didn't move. "Do you remember the first time we kissed?"

"The garden at Zach and Gabriella's wedding. We were in the corner, and there were those little white twinkly lights woven in the greenery. The music was barely a whisper, and it felt like we were cocooned somewhere in a world of our own."

So...yes. He remembered.

"It came to me that when we kissed there, I didn't

even pay attention to where we were. It was all about finding a place to be alone, and that kiss was wild and untamed, and—"

"It was so damn sexy, Megan," he said huskily. "God, you have no idea how turned on I was."

She smiled and felt herself blush. "I think I have a pretty good idea. We left the reception not too long after that."

"And didn't come out of the room for almost two days," he added, tucking a finger under her chin so she'd have to look at him. His expression was serious. "I'm not asking for another sex-fueled weekend," he began and then let out a small laugh. "I wouldn't say no to one, but that's not what this is about. I'm enjoying getting to know you. Nothing about our relationship has been… conventional, and I want you to know I'm willing to wait until you're comfortable taking this to the next level."

She swallowed hard. "You mean sleeping together again?"

Alex shook his head. "Eventually. Right now, Megan, I'd like to know that you see me as someone you want to be with—someone you'll go to dinner with or sit and watch a movie with on a Thursday night." He shrugged. "I'd like to think you'll give us a chance."

And that was what she wanted too. She knew that now. It was a bit terrifying because for so long, her work was what defined her and filled all her free time. To be in this new job and trying to meet all the commitments it required while starting a new personal relationship seemed almost too overwhelming to comprehend. Which was what she said to him.

"We'll take it slow," he said. "I know you have a

demanding job. I get it. And my schedule isn't exactly traditional either." He stood and took her hand in his, gently pulling her to her feet. "What do you say we walk around for a little bit more and then head home and talk about it? Later on, we'll maybe grill some burgers and watch some TV. Very casual. Nothing crazy."

She nibbled her bottom lip as she pretended to consider her options.

Alex leaned in and kissed the spot her teeth had just worried. "But you should know this," he said, his voice low and thick and full of promise, "I'm going to want to kiss you again, and I'll want to hold you close while we watch TV. And with even the slightest bit of encouragement from you, I'd even be willing to skip the dinner and television and feast on you."

She gasped softly at the image but didn't discourage him either.

He pulled her in close and placed a kiss on the top of her head. "But…the ball is in your court, Megan. We move at your pace. Okay?"

Right now, her pace was to find a secluded spot and have a throw-down in the garden.

She kept that idea to herself.

Clearing her throat, she said, "Let's finish walking around the gardens and head home and then…take it from there." Pulling back, she looked at him. "Is that okay?"

His smile was sweet and sexy and had her knees buckling. "I already told you we're gonna move at your pace. I've waited two years for you, Megan, and I don't mind waiting a bit longer."

Oh God. Two years.

She hadn't had sex in two years!

Seriously, what am I waiting for? she wondered.

"C'mon," he said. "Let's go and walk off this lunch."

Personally, she could think of a much better way to work it off, but for now, she opted to behave.

There'd be plenty of time to misbehave later.

—⁓—

They'd walked.

They'd talked.

They'd laughed.

There was not one damn thing they'd done in the past two hours that should have been considered sexy, and yet…everything about Megan was, and Alex had a feeling she was completely unaware of it. Now as they pulled into his driveway, he had to remind himself to not get too anxious because there was a very real chance they were going to go inside, order a pizza or eat burgers, and simply…watch TV.

And that would be great.

It would be fun.

It would…totally not be his first choice. Or his second. Okay, fine, it would maybe be his fourth or fifth choice, but he'd promised they'd take things at her pace, and he'd meant it.

At the time he had.

Now? Not so much.

The entire drive to his house they had talked about different options to tour next weekend—places that weren't in the same vicinity of the park. Hell, if it were up to Alex, they'd do some serious hiking, but he knew she wasn't ready for that yet. They'd tossed out the idea of doing some museums or more touristy locations, but those were things they could do anytime, and maybe they'd save them for a rainy day—literally.

"How do you feel about waterfalls?" he asked as they stepped into his house.

Megan put the cooler bag down next to the door and kicked off her shoes. "I don't think I've ever given them much thought. Why?"

"There's a great park about an hour south of here in the foothills of the Cascade Mountains called Silver Falls. It's a state park, but it's known for—"

"Its waterfalls?" she finished for him with an arched brow.

"Exactly. I haven't been there in years, but it's a spectacular sight. Lots of walking like we did today, but it's worth it. If we leave early enough, we can get in before the crowds show up and have some of the spots all to ourselves."

She smiled, and he saw she was seriously thinking about it.

"We'll pack a lunch like we did today, and on the way home we'll stop someplace for dinner and make it a full day. What do you think?"

He'd thought talking about parks and walking around would distract him. But as Megan began to walk toward him, he saw how the look in her eyes had nothing to do with waterfalls and everything to do with him. Them.

Yes.

When they were toe to toe, she looped her arms around his shoulders and pressed herself close. "I think I like the sound of that," she said softly.

"Yeah?"

She nodded. "Yes."

"And I like the sound of that," he said gruffly, gently banding his arms around her waist.

"The sound of what?" she whispered, her voice a little breathless and dazed.

"You saying yes." He dipped his head toward hers and captured her lips with his. For a split second, Alex cursed himself for acting so quickly—especially when he'd sworn they were going to take things at Megan's pace—but judging by how quickly she seemed to be on board, he felt confident that this pace *was* her pace.

His hands moved to her bottom and squeezed right before he lifted her. Megan's legs wrapped around his waist, and he had to make the decision to move them either to the sofa—which was close—or to his bed—which was all the way upstairs. She moaned his name as she moved her lips from his and nipped at his ear and his jaw, and the decision was made.

The sofa.

Walking them over, he laid her down and stretched out on top of her.

Yes.

This was what he'd been dreaming about—fantasizing about—for too damn long. The feel of her underneath him, her lush curves, the sound of her moaning as they fit their bodies together? Yeah, it was sexy as hell and had him harder than granite.

Don't rush, savor, he mentally told himself, but Megan's movements were making that hard to do. With her legs wrapped around him, her hands raking up his back and then into his hair, and then her lips claiming his again…um, yeah. Hard.

Her hands moved from his hair to the hem of his T-shirt, and he smiled against her lips when she began pulling it up. Rather than fight the movement, he pushed himself up and finished the job for her. Before he dove in for another taste, he watched the look on her face — the heat and desire as she looked at his chest and then reached out to touch it.

Skin on skin.

Megan's hands on his abs, his chest, were like hitting the launch button.

He was about to move, to close the distance between them, when Megan crossed her arms in front of her and pulled her own shirt off, tossing it to the floor beside his.

And then Alex simply forgot how to breathe. She was perfect. The pale-pink lace against her skin looked almost too delicate to touch, and yet that's exactly what he did—slowly, reverently. At the first touch of his hands, Megan's eyes drifted closed. His fingers skimmed, caressed, and trembled as they did so. Then he grew bold, he cupped, he kneaded, and her back arched as she pressed herself more firmly against his hands. She was so responsive to his touch—just like he remembered.

"Megan," he whispered and then groaned when she licked her lips, her slumberous eyes looking at him. And then he forgot what he was going to say—words escaped him. There wasn't anything he could say that would even begin to describe the way he was feeling or how much he wanted her.

She gave him a knowing smile as she skimmed her hand around his neck and slowly guided him down to her.

He inhaled her perfume, felt the heat of her skin, and

as his chest pressed gently to hers, they both sighed in unison. It felt so good. So right.

"Alex?"

"Hmm?"

"Kiss me."

And he did. And he kept kissing her, stroking her, caressing her, until he thought he'd go mad. He cursed his decision on the couch because there simply wasn't enough room. He wanted to see her sprawled out on his bed—her hair fanned out on his pillow as she panted his name. They were adults, and they could have the patience and restraint to wait until they made it up a flight of stairs, couldn't they?

He moved before he could question himself but not before Megan could. "Where are you going?" she asked, almost frantic as she tried to pull him back.

Alex took her hand in his and quickly pulled her to her feet.

"I want you in my bed," he said gruffly. "I've fantasized about it for two damn years, and now that you're here, that's where I want you."

"Oh…" she said breathlessly, her dark-brown eyes slowly raising to meet his gaze. "I want that too."

Satisfied, he began to lead her toward the stairs when her phone rang. They both stopped in their tracks, and his heart beat wildly in his chest because the moment had been so perfect that he was afraid of any distractions.

"Ignore it," she finally said, and Alex felt himself relax. They had gone all of two feet when his phone began to ring. Megan looked at him. "It's a coincidence, right?"

It could be, but a strange one. His head dropped forward, and both phones stopped. He waited a minute, and sure enough, they both started again. Looking over at her, he said, "I think we need to answer those."

Megan readily agreed, and as she reached for hers, Alex saw Ethan's number on his screen. He immediately answered. "Hey, Ethan, what's up?"

Beside him, Megan answered her phone, and he heard her gasp.

"Dude, did you hear me?" Ethan said.

Dammit, he hadn't. "Sorry…um, what?"

"They're taking Gabriella to the hospital now," Ethan was saying. "Zach's a mess, and Summer and I are two hours away. Can you get over there and stay with him until we get there? Summer's on the phone with Megan, so hopefully she'll go over too."

"Not a problem. I'm on my way," Alex said.

Chapter 6

THEY RACED INTO THE ER ENTRANCE AND IMMEDIATELY went to the desk to inquire about Gabriella. The woman at the desk asked them to take a seat and said she'd see what she could find out. Megan paced away from the desk but didn't want to sit. She was too revved up and nervous for her cousin and his wife.

Pulling out her phone, she texted Summer to let her know they were at the hospital and waiting to talk to Zach. Beside her, she noticed Alex texting. "Are you texting Ethan? I texted Summer."

"No, I texted Zach and let him know we're out here if he needs us," he replied, raking a hand through his hair. "You doing okay?"

Megan nodded. "Just scared for them. It's too soon for the baby to come, and I can't even believe it might be a possibility. Gabriella's the picture of good health and the perfect pregnancy."

"Sometimes that has nothing to do with it," he said. "Unless something traumatic happens, no one knows why some babies want to come out and meet the world sooner than they should."

She paced a bit more. "But…a baby born right now at this stage of the pregnancy could survive, right?" Alex might be a physical therapist and not an obstetrician, but she knew he had way more medical knowledge than she did.

He nodded. "Unless there's something wrong—"

Megan held up a hand to stop him. "I can't. I don't even want to think about it. I wish—"

"Here comes Zach," he said, and they both turned to wait for her cousin. He looked stressed and tired and so unlike himself. "How is she?"

Zach let out a weary breath and sat. They followed and did the same.

"She's resting right now. The contractions have slowed, so the doctors are going to observe her for a little while."

"What happened?" Megan asked. "Was it sudden? Did her water break?"

Zach shook his head. "Last night Gabriella was saying her back hurt. We didn't think anything of it because…you know…she's pregnant, and with the weight of the baby, we were told that sort of thing would be normal."

"O-kay…"

"Then she woke up around seven and said the pain wasn't getting any better. I knew she hadn't slept well because she'd tossed and turned and couldn't seem to get comfortable. So we looked up how to do some safe massages and things that can help with pregnancy muscle aches, and we tried them. It seemed to help a bit, and she slept for about three hours." He let out a mirthless laugh. "So did I. I wasn't exactly compassionate at that point because I was exhausted."

"Understandable," Alex said. "Why didn't you call me? I would have come over and brought one of the massage chairs and helped her out."

Zach rested his head back on the chair. "We didn't

think it was a big deal. When we woke up, we had something to eat, and she said the baby was being aggressive—kicking hard, moving a lot, but it wasn't like anything she'd felt before. So we called her OB and told her what was going on, and they suggested we start timing the pain and movement. Three hours later they told us to get to the hospital, and…here we are."

"If the contractions slowed down, that's a good thing, right?" Megan asked.

"It is, but it's only because they gave her something to slow them down. After doing a full exam, it isn't like she's in active labor—there's no dilation or anything like that, but the force of the contractions was a little too strong for them to be Braxton-Hicks."

"Are they going to keep her overnight?" Alex asked.

"We don't know. For right now they're going to monitor her for a couple of hours and take it from there." He sighed, and for a moment it looked like he was about to fall asleep. But he sat himself up and looked at the two of them. "I appreciate you coming and hanging out. I hate that I bothered anyone. I just…I didn't know…"

"Do you want me to call anyone?" Megan asked. "Your parents? Gabriella's parents?"

"No, but thank you. I'm hoping we're going to get the okay to go home, and then we'll chill. I'll pick up dinner on the way and see about changing my schedule at work tomorrow and—"

"Okay, okay," Megan gently interrupted. "How about this—if you get the okay to take her home, Alex and I will leave ahead of you, get dinner, and bring it to your house. You focus on getting Gabriella home. And tomorrow—because I know you're going to be freaked out about leaving her alone—I'll stay with her. The computer stuff can wait a day, and then we'll take it from there. One day at a time."

"I don't know if I want to leave her. I'd feel better if I was there—"

"And you'll hover and make her crazy. Trust me," she said. "Let's wait and hear what the doctor has to say, okay?"

Zach stayed out in the waiting room with them for about an hour before going to check on his wife. Not long after, Summer and Ethan arrived with a sleeping baby Amber. When Zach came out again and gave them an update, he told them that the doctors felt it was safe for Gabriella to go home. She needed to rest until her regular OB could see her.

"Okay, so that's good news," Summer said. "Whew! I am so relieved. If you're okay, Zach, we're going to head home and get Amber fed and to bed, and I'll call Gabs and check on her later."

"Sounds good," Zach said, kissing his sister on the cheek. "I appreciate you coming and waiting with us."

"Please, I hate how we weren't here earlier, but if you need anything, call," she added.

"We're going to go and pick up some dinner and bring it to the house," Megan said.

And within minutes, everyone was heading in different directions. In the car, Megan rested her head against the seat.

"Well, that was scary," she said.

Alex nodded. "Hopefully her doctor will be able to see her tomorrow and confirm that everything's all right. I know being on bed rest will make Gabriella crazy."

They made small talk as they drove, but Megan's mind kept wandering to what had almost happened before they got the calls from Summer and Ethan. By now they would have been naked in Alex's bed and probably on round two—if not three. Memories of their weekend together played in her mind as well. She knew what she was missing, and as much as she wanted to say how she couldn't wait to get back to his place, she knew she was far too distracted for that tonight.

Or maybe she was still too scared about taking that next step now that they were out of the heat of the moment. Why was it so hard for her to just let go like she had before? That weekend should have unleashed the side of her that tended to overthink and second-guess her every move in personal relationships. Why couldn't she just get out of her own way and be happy?

"Would you be disappointed if we…you know… don't—"

Before she could finish, Alex reached over and took one of her hands in his. "I'm not going to lie to you, Megan. I really wish we hadn't been interrupted, but I understand what you're saying, and…there's no rush."

She instantly relaxed.

"Just…promise me something," he said.

"What?"

"That you'll be honest with me. If we're moving too fast or if you're not comfortable, you'll tell me."

"I'm sorry." And when he looked at her, she saw the sadness and understanding there.

"Me too," he said softly.

They drove in silence for several minutes before she told him what else was on her mind.

"So…I'm thinking I'm going to offer to stay with Zach and Gabriella tonight," she said carefully.

He looked at her briefly before returning his attention to the road. "Oh…okay."

"Zach's exhausted, and he needs to sleep, and I think it would be helpful for someone to be there for Gabs to talk to and distract her for a bit. I imagine she's a little nervous about everything that happened."

He nodded again. "If that's what you think is best, then…sure. I can pick you up from there tomorrow after Zach gets home or—"

"We'll see how it goes," she said quickly.

When they were all back at Zach and Gabriella's, they ate and talked and laughed, and to the casual observer, nothing was wrong. But Megan knew everyone's head was not fully in the conversation they were currently having—about the health benefits of salmon.

How the hell had they started talking about that?

Alex helped Megan clean up the dishes while Zach helped his wife get comfortable on the sofa.

"Hey," she said softly even though her cousin was out of earshot, "why don't you take Zach outside and shoot some hoops or something—anything to distract him a bit."

"Good idea," he said.

When the front door closed, Megan walked over to Gabriella and sat on the sofa opposite her. "So…talk to me. How are you doing?"

"Honestly, I'm fine. They did an ultrasound, and I was able to see for myself that the baby is fine. I think I freaked out, which in turn freaked Zach out. I've got a call in to my OB, and I have no doubt she'll see me tomorrow." Then she smiled and rubbed her hand over her swollen belly. "I'm tired, and I know Zach is too."

"If it's okay with you, I'd like to stay tonight," Megan suggested. "This way we can force Zach to get some sleep so he can go to work tomorrow, and I'll be here in case you need anything."

Gabriella's smile grew and then turned a bit knowing. "Are we trying to avoid someone?"

"What do you mean?"

"Your cousin may be clueless and unobservant, but I'm not," Gabriella said. "I saw the little glances between you and Alex—and not for the first time, might I add—and I'm curious if your offer to stay here tonight isn't about maybe not going home with him."

Megan groaned. "Summer warned me that you are freaky good at reading people."

"It's a gift. So spill it. Distract me."

When it was worded like that, how could she refuse? So she shared how things were progressing between the two of them and even told her about their wedding history. "And we were kind of heading to the bedroom when Summer called."

Gabriella frowned. "Okay, so…you're clearly into him, right?"

"Oh yeah."

"And the feeling is mutual?"

"Definitely."

"Then I don't understand why you're not more excited about picking up where you left off. If this is something that's been building, then why put on the brakes now?"

"Because now that the lust fog has lifted, I have to think about stuff. It's what I do. It's annoying as hell, but…I get into my own head, and I have to reason everything out. How smart is it for me to get involved with Alex while I'm settling in to a new job? My job is what messed things up for us the last time."

"What did your job have to do with anything?"

Ugh. Where did she even begin? "You know how much I worked, right?"

Gabriella nodded.

"Well, let's just say that it was worse than you imagined."

"How is that even possible? The sheer number of hours you put in each week was crazy! How can it be worse?"

She gave a small shrug. "It wasn't just the hours. It was like…nothing else existed for me. It was like I couldn't think about anything else."

"And what about now? Do you feel like that with this job?"

"No," she said confidently. "And being that I'm spending more time at home and with you and Zach and Summer, I've had time to really think about why I was the way I was. To a certain degree, anyway."

Gabriella looked at her expectantly.

"There was nothing else for me back in Albany. Nothing that I was passionate about, no place else I wanted to go, and nothing else I wanted to do. After Colin dumped me, my self-esteem was shot, and my job—my office—became my safety net. I didn't want to put myself out there for anyone to hurt me again."

"But you let Alex in," she said softly. "Clearly you

felt comfortable enough with him to not only spend a weekend with him but to try to take it a step further."

"And yet in the end, I couldn't do it. I flaked. I reverted to type and ruined what could have been a great relationship."

Sitting up slowly, Gabriella reached out and took one of Megan's hands in hers. "You have a second chance here, Megan. I know it won't erase the past, but the fact that you're still single and Alex is still single has to tell you something."

She thought about it for a moment and couldn't believe it could possibly be this easy. "What if things go badly? How am I supposed to handle that with all of you being friends with him? And I'm driving his car! Right now there are far too many things to consider."

"There's a simple solution to that, you know," Gabriella said.

"Oh really? What? Because my mind has been racing through every scenario, and I can't seem to find anything that even resembles simple, and all of this is causing me more stress!"

"Well now, I think you need to pick things up where you left off, and it will help you alleviate a whole lot of that stress," she teased.

"Not helpful," Megan murmured.

"Okay, fine. Besides the whole job and car thing, what's holding you back?"

Shrugging, she said, "I don't know. Everything about Alex…intimidates me. He's so…passionate about everything he does, and he is the most put-together guy I've ever met. Meanwhile, I'm a hot mess who was content to work eighty hours a week and have no social life.

He's showing me around the city and getting me out, and it's great. But I know I'm going to eventually revert to type and screw it all up."

"You can't know that, Megan. You are capable of change."

"Am I? Because it doesn't seem like I am. I keep repeating the same patterns—"

"Because you never had a reason not to," Gabriella interrupted. "You weren't motivated to change. Now you are." She paused. "How are things going at work?"

"They're going great. I love it."

"And from what I can tell, everything's on track with the new system, right?"

Megan nodded.

"From where I'm sitting, it seems to me like things are all falling into place for you. It's okay to have a life outside the office."

"I'm just…it doesn't feel…natural. It's the way I've always been."

"Like I said, you're capable of changing—if you want to."

And that was the million-dollar question, wasn't it? Did she want to change?

The immediate answer was a "Hell yes!" especially if changing meant going to Alex's house and finishing what they had started earlier.

But the last time they had jumped into bed together, she had done it because she'd wanted to be more care-free and he had been too tempting to resist. Then she had spent the next two years feeling like she could never be that girl again.

"What if…what if I try," Megan began hesitantly,

"and...I can't do it? What if this truly is who I am, and it's not enough?"

Gabriella gave her a sympathetic smile. "You should be who you want to be and be true to yourself. If you want to change, then you have to do it for you and not because you want someone else to like you."

"I'm so confused," she moaned and slouched on the couch, wishing like hell that she had her crocheting basket with her right now.

"Then it's a good thing you're staying here tonight, right?"

"Finally!"

Alex was going to make a snarky comment, but he figured he'd let Zach have his moment. After all, it had been months since he'd won their two-out-of-three rule at racquetball. So he took it in stride and smiled as he shook Zach's hand. "Good game, man. Good game." It had been a week since Gabriella's hospital scare, and Alex found himself on the racquetball court and frustrated beyond belief.

Zach did a victory lap around the court with his arms in the air, and all Alex could do was laugh.

"I guess it's a good thing you came here and had a win before heading to the office, huh?" Alex asked.

Slowing down, Zach looked at him before touching his toes to stretch. "What are you talking about?"

"Work," Alex said. "Megan said you guys are putting in a lot of extra time on this computer system transfer. New system giving you problems, or is it not as user-friendly as the last program you were using?"

Zach straightened and looked at him like he was crazy. "I have no idea what you're talking about. The new system is like a dream. Megan got it all switched over and even worked out all the glitches in record time. The last IT guy we had took three times as long to get us up and running. I'm telling you, my cousin is a tech genius. Not once did she have to stay late or work a weekend." He stretched again. "You must have misunderstood her or something."

Yeah…or something, he silently seethed.

Right now he wanted to demand to know where Megan had been all week—hell, where she was today!—but he didn't want to get into an argument with Zach over it, so he tried a different approach.

Raking a hand through his hair, he said, "Yeah. Probably. I guess I figured something like that would take a lot of time. You know, based on her previous job."

Before he responded, Zach grabbed his water bottle and took a long drink. "She helped Ethan set up his home office one night, and then she did the same for me another night. Don't get me wrong, we both had a decent setup, but after seeing what she did for the office, we asked if she would be able to amp up our home offices."

Alex nodded. Okay, so that was two nights. Why had she lied to him and said she'd been working late all week? Where was she going and what was she doing to avoid him? She hadn't taken any of his calls, and most of her replies to his texts had been short and to the point.

And again, why?

Zach started to gather up his things, and Alex asked,

"So are the girls out doing one of those spa day things now that Gabriella got the all clear from her doctor that she can resume normal activities?"

That was clearly the one that gave him away. With his back to him, Zach hung his head. When he turned to Alex, he didn't look happy. He also didn't look too pissed, so Alex took that as a good sign.

"For crying out loud, Alex, if you're interested in Megan, can you please spit it out already? All of this beating around the bush is more exhausting than the damn games we just finished playing."

Well…shit.

Alex let out a long breath and figured if they were going to fight about it, he'd rather it happen now than later. Plus, it would be a huge relief to get it out in the open instead of trying to keep hiding it.

"Okay, look," he began diplomatically, "yes, I'm interested in Megan. We've been spending a lot of time together, and I thought things were going great, and this last week she's been telling me she has to work late. And then today she told me she had to go in to the office because of issues with the new system. It's a Saturday, and I figured maybe she wanted to work with no distractions. So now I'm wondering what I did wrong that she's blowing me off."

With a muttered curse, Zach walked over to the lone bench against the back wall and sat. "On principle I feel like I should kick your ass, but you're too damn nice of a guy. It would be like kicking a puppy."

Not the manliest of comparisons, but if it kept him and Zach from fighting, he'd let it slide.

"We've been going out every Sunday," Alex

explained. "I've been showing her around Portland and getting her to do stuff that was...you know...outside. From everything she's said about her life in New York, all she did was sit in her office all day and work. So I thought I'd show her around and help her see how the outdoors can be fun."

Zach chuckled. "Megan always had her nose stuck in a book from the time she was little. Don't expect miracles." He paused. "Maybe that's why she's hiding out on you—too much pressure to be outside. For all you know, she's hanging out at the library."

Alex frowned and sat on the bench too. "Well, that would suck," he muttered. "I don't want her feeling like she has to lie to me because I'm making her uncomfortable."

"It's probably not...wait a minute...is that why you offered her the car? To show her around? Because you were hoping to score some points with her?" Zach asked, and this time, he sounded more than a little irritated.

"It wasn't like that!" Alex shouted defensively. Damn, this wasn't what he was planning on, but...might as well get it all out there.

Standing, he paced a couple of feet away and then turned. "Megan and I...we *did* meet at your wedding, and we...we hit it off."

Zach glared at him for a minute. "Did you hook up with her?"

All Alex could do was nod.

"Shit." Another pause. "Wait...is Megan...is she the woman you were telling me about? The one from a while ago who told you—"

"Yeah," Alex murmured. "I had no idea she was moving here until you mentioned it that day on the court. I swear. And then…I took it as a sign—like this was a chance to see if what we had was more than weekend chemistry."

Zach began to pace, and he mumbled under his breath the entire time about friends hitting on his family members and how much he hated it, and Alex felt like crap. He remembered the stories about Ethan and Summer, and while he could see the similarities, the fact remained that Megan was his cousin and Zach had already admitted how he thought Alex was a good guy.

"I didn't plan this, Zach," he said. "I swear. I saw her at the wedding and was drawn to her. We danced, and we talked and laughed, and one thing led to another."

"Please…I don't want any of the details."

"Understood."

They were both silent for a long while, and Alex wasn't sure what he was supposed to do or say in this situation. He had promised Megan to not tell Zach about their weekend, but what choice did he have?

"So what are you going to do?" Zach finally asked.

"Do you know where she is today?"

Zach shook his head. "Gabriella's at home resting because the baby was kicking all night. Summer and Ethan were going to visit some friends up in Vancouver for the day. As far as I know, Megan hadn't made plans with either of them."

"Dammit."

"Are you going to call her or go and find her?"

Huffing with frustration, Alex replied, "I'm going to go and find her and ask her straight up what her deal is and why she's avoiding me. She probably wouldn't answer the phone if I called her, anyway."

"Like I said, I don't want any of the details, and I want you to know that I'm not...thrilled with this—"

"I know."

"But...I need your word that if you talk to her and she tells you she's not interested in dating you, you'll respect her wishes and leave her alone. If you can't handle hanging out with her when we all get together or her driving your car, then you need to be honest and tell me. I don't want to get in the middle of it, but she's my cousin, and you need to understand that she comes first." He stared at Alex for another long moment. "Deal?"

"I don't think it's going to—"

"Do we have a deal?" Zach repeated.

With a curt nod, Alex held out his hand, and Zach shook it.

One Montgomery down. Now all he had to do was find the other one and figure out what her deal was.

Six days.

He hadn't seen Megan in six damn days, and he had been willing to accept her story about working. Now that he knew she was lying? He was beyond pissed. Part of him knew she was scared—she was used to living her life a certain way, and he had been doing everything humanly possible to break her out of her rut and routine—but he also knew the other part of her was enjoying the sudden freedom she had discovered. Every time they talked, she was happy and laughing. Whenever they went out, she enjoyed herself. And when they kissed? He sighed because he knew neither of them had wanted to stop.

And yet they did.

When Zach had said Megan was ahead of schedule and he hadn't asked her to work on a Saturday? That had been Alex's breaking point. If she would have just talked to him, he would have respected her wishes and taken a step back. He had no problem with it. Hell, he'd stepped back as far as a guy could for two damn years! And now he was done being jerked around. He wanted her, and she wanted him, and it was time they stopped dancing around the topic and dealt with it.

And knowing now they essentially had Zach's blessing, Alex felt like a giant weight had been lifted from his shoulders. Honestly, it was nobody's damn business what he and Megan did. Alex understood that Zach was her cousin and was protective of her, but she was a grown woman, and she was capable of making her own decisions. And on top of that, after Zach and Megan had lived on opposite ends of the country for almost ten years, Alex didn't believe Zach should have a say in any of this.

It was between Alex and Megan and no one else.

No matter how the Montgomery family tended to think.

The entire drive over to the office Alex had built up a good head of steam. It wasn't the smartest way to go about approaching her, but she needed to know how upset he was that she'd lied to him. If nothing else, he expected honesty from her. He believed in being exactly who he was at all times, and he required the same from the people in his life. And if this was what she was going to do, then he needed to know that now so he could come to grips with the fact that they were never going to be.

The Montgomery offices were located in a large high-rise in downtown Portland. There were easily twenty other businesses in the building, so getting inside wasn't a problem. Finding her was possibly going to be—especially if she really wasn't at work and was off hiding someplace.

Like the library.

Or a day spa.

Or any one of a thousand places he'd mentioned to her and pointed out over the past couple of weeks.

Inside the lobby he looked around and found it nearly deserted. He took the elevator up to Montgomerys' floor, and when he stepped out, it looked empty as well. A wall of glass divided the elevator space from the office with a set of double doors in the middle.

"Now what?" he said with a huff. Out of the corner of his eye, he saw someone walking around in the office. He stepped closer and saw a familiar ponytail. Reaching for the door, he pulled, but it was locked. With no other choice, he knocked.

Megan stopped in her tracks and turned toward the sound, and the only thing Alex could think of was how she looked like a deer stuck in the headlights.

Busted.

There was no way she could pretend she didn't see or hear him, and her expression went from shocked to resigned in the blink of an eye.

Not a good sign.

At first she didn't move, and then her eyes went a little wide as she walked hurriedly to the door. Unlocking it, she flung it open. "Is everything okay? Is it Gabriella? I had my phone turned off and—"

Stepping into the office, Alex said, "She's fine. That's not why I'm here."

"Oh."

He looked around, and the silence and stillness were almost unnerving. Behind him, Megan locked the door again and came to stand beside him. She looked tired and a little defeated and…so damn beautiful it almost made him forget he was mad.

"Why'd you lie to me?" he asked.

"I…I don't know what you mean," she said quietly, but she wouldn't meet his gaze.

Tucking a finger under her chin, he gently forced her to look at him. "I played racquetball with Zach this morning. He told me you're ahead of schedule. You haven't been working late, and he had no idea why you said you were working today." He paused. "Care to explain?"

Megan took a step back and then another before turning and walking away.

What the…?

With no other choice, he followed her. She turned into an office in the far corner, and once he stepped inside, he knew it was hers. There was computer equipment everywhere and huge binders all over the floor. The space was a bit disorganized, and yet…it fit the exact way he had envisioned how her office would be.

Megan sat behind the desk, and Alex immediately stepped behind her to see what she was working on.

"Solitaire? You're here on a Saturday so you can play solitaire?" he demanded. "What the hell, Megan?" He spun her chair around, and her gasp of surprise only spurred him on. "What is your deal? You are so un-freaking-predictable, and I'm going crazy trying to keep up with you!"

"I've been busy," she said weakly.

"Bullshit," he spat. "I talked to Zach, and—"

"And Zach doesn't know everything, Alex," she countered with a little more heat this time. "I work my ass off here all day long. Yes, I got the system up and going faster than we thought, but my days are filled with training everyone on how to use it. Twice this week I went home with one of my cousins to help with his computer."

"I already know this," he said tightly.

She looked up at him, her brown eyes huge and looking a little bit helpless. "I needed some time, Alex."

"Time for what? Because I believe I told you—multiple times—that I would never push you or rush you. Last weekend we were on the same page. If Ethan and Summer hadn't called, we both know what would have happened, and you didn't seem too concerned about needing time then. If you remember correctly, you kissed me first."

She rolled her eyes. "Seriously, that's what you're going with?"

"What else should I say?" he cried. "Look, if you've changed your mind? If you don't want to see where this thing between us goes? Then at least have the decency to tell me. All I'm asking is for you to talk to me, Megan!"

"I don't—"

"Two years ago you had the excuse of living on the other side of the country, but now you're on the other side of town! Barely! It's not fair for you to blow me off without an explanation. I deserve to know where I stand with you."

He was breathless and angry and so frustrated he wanted to scream.

"You scare me!" she yelled, and it took him by surprise. "Excuse me?"

She nodded. "You do. I mean, not physically—I know you would never hurt me—but...you're just so damn much, Alex! You're like a force of nature! You're confident, and you know what you want, and I'm not like that! I am someone who takes things slowly, and I think everything through from every angle. The only time I was ever impulsive was that weekend with you!"

"Was it that bad?" he asked, his voice gruff and thick with emotion because...holy shit. He'd thought she was scared of getting involved with anyone or breaking out of her comfortable routine; he'd had no idea it was *him* she was afraid of!

Megan shook her head. "No, it wasn't. But...it's not me. The woman you slept with? That's not who I am! I dressed differently that weekend, I acted differently...I need you to know that this"—she motioned to herself dressed in yoga pants and a sweatshirt—"is the real me! I went shopping and let Summer and Gabriella pick out all new stuff for me, but at the end of the day, this is who I am!"

Taking a chance, he took a step closer to her. "I didn't think that you walked around in clingy dresses and stilettos. Although...I would be on board if you ever wanted to try it again."

She laughed softly. "I'm being serious, Alex. You were attracted to a woman who really doesn't exist."

Shaking his head, he took one of her hands in his. "That's where you're wrong. I was attracted to a woman with a great smile. I was attracted to a woman I enjoyed talking with. I was attracted to a woman who kissed like a dream." He tugged her gently so they were toe to toe. "And I'm still attracted to that woman. The dress and the heels? They looked great on you. But the yoga pants and sweatshirt look just as great. It's not the clothes, Megan, or the hair or the makeup. It's you."

His heart was hammering in his chest because that was pretty much everything he had. He was laying it all out there for her, and he had no idea what she was going to do with it. For all he knew, she wasn't as into him as he'd thought, and he was going to have to live with the fantasy of what could have been.

"I want to believe you—"

With his free hand, Alex cupped her cheek, caressed her soft skin. "You can. I'll never lie to you, Megan. Ever."

She swallowed hard, and Alex could see the uncertainty in her eyes. Why? What was it she was struggling with? He was at a loss for what else to do, what else to say, and as he was about to retreat, Megan grasped his wrist.

Uncertainty turned to panic and then pleading. "Alex," she began, "please."

He knew that *please*.

It had haunted his dreams for two years.

Alex quickly looked over his shoulder toward her open office door and considered his options.

"No one's here," she said, her voice a little soft, a little trembly.

It was almost too much to hope for, he thought. This wasn't the way he envisioned making love to Megan again for the first time, but right now, he certainly wasn't going to argue with it.

"Tell me you're sure," he said firmly.

"About no one being here?"

He smiled and hauled her in close. "No." Lowering his head until their lips were almost touching, he asked her again.

Her hand came up and gently raked through his hair. "I'm very sure."

"Thank God."

His lips claimed hers, and he felt himself relaxing for what seemed like the first time in two years.

Only for him.

Megan wrapped herself tightly around Alex as she realized that no other man had the ability to make her want to lose control like this. It was wild and scary and exciting all at the same time. He kissed her like he wanted to consume her, and she was more than willing to serve herself up for him.

All week she had been at war with herself over this— over them. She'd crocheted more in the past six days than she had in the past six months! And with every slip stitch, she questioned why she was sitting home alone when she could be spending time with Alex.

And now she had enough blankets, hats, and booties for a small nursery full of babies.

When he'd knocked on the office door earlier, she'd known a large part of her had been relieved that he was finally there—that he was making the decision for her and not letting her hide anymore. Not that she had been completely hiding. She loved her cousins and was thankful for the closeness they shared, but even she was beginning to feel like it was too much. With them working together and hanging out after work, Megan knew she'd be more than happy to put some distance between them for at least a little while.

Alex lifted her and put her on the corner of her desk. There was barely any room because she tended to not be all that organized. Turning her head away from him for a minute, she breathlessly said, "Wait," right before shoving a stack of binders to the floor. Alex chuckled—a low, rich sound—and Megan turned and reached for him again, eager for his kiss.

This reminded her of the night of the wedding—by the time they had neared her room, she hadn't cared who could see them. It was hot and frantic and a little naughty, and that's exactly how everything felt right now. She shifted enough to grab the hem of her sweatshirt and had it up and off with only a slight disruption to their kiss. Alex groaned and reached for her breasts, and she was thankful that today she had chosen to wear some of her new lingerie.

His hands felt amazing, just as she knew everything about him would. Alex broke their kiss so he could focus on kissing other parts of her—the parts that led down to the breasts he was gently kneading. Megan's head began to loll, but she refused to give in to it. Instead, she did her best to pull Alex's shirt off so she could see and feel and kiss him like he was doing to her. Growling with frustration, Alex whipped his shirt off before reaching for her again.

"Is this crazy?" she panted, rubbing against him in desperation to get closer and ease the ache she'd been feeling for far too long.

"No," he said before nipping at the swell of her breast. "If it were up to me, we would have been doing this all week."

She laughed huskily. "I meant here…the office."

"My bed's too far," he said around another kiss. "Right now, the desk is fine."

Kicking off her sneakers, she used her heels to pull him closer, and she could feel his arousal pressed snugly against her. She cursed her yoga pants. She cursed his jeans. His name came out like a soft whine, and he laughed softly against her neck.

She cursed him.

"Patience," he said, and she wanted to scream.

Then his hands moved between her legs, and she did. *Oh God*, she thought. *So good. It's so good…*

"I've been wanting to do this for so long," he murmured against her skin as his hands did wicked and delicious things to her.

She wanted that too. Her breath began to quicken, and her head did fall back. "I want…I need…more. Alex," she breathed, "more. Please."

After that it was fast and furious and oh so damn perfect.

The rest of their clothes fell away, and a few more items fell from Megan's desk.

But neither cared. There were more important things to worry about—or focus on. Or just…do.

And when she thought she couldn't wait any longer— thought she'd have to beg even more—Alex was there with her, and it was everything she remembered and so much more.

Had it really been this good?

Had it really been this wild?

The answer to both those questions was yes, and before she got sucked into the thoughts swirling around in her own head, Megan forced herself to let go and simply feel.

And it was the best damn thing ever.

"Can I ask you something?"

"Sure."

It was hours later, and they had made it to Alex's house.

And bed.

After a much more thorough and leisurely round of lovemaking, they were snuggled up—Megan was curled beside him with her hand on his chest and their legs tangled together.

"You work a lot of hours, right?" she asked.

Alex nodded.

"And…that's admirable, right? Like…people tell you it's a good thing, right?"

He nodded again.

She sighed. "Then why is it frowned upon when I do it? I mean, plenty of people work a lot—are dedicated to their jobs—but when I say that I am, I get grief for it."

For a minute, Alex didn't say anything. Seriously? This was what she wanted to talk about right now? Then he realized how much this must be weighing on her mind if she was choosing now to bring it up. He knew what she was getting at, and he needed to think through his answer properly.

"Let me ask you something," he said softly.

"Are you answering my question with a question?" she teased.

Smiling, he placed a light kiss on her forehead. "Sort of," he replied honestly. "Do you feel like you have to work long hours? Is it part of the job requirement?"

"Depends on the job," she said. "Sometimes I stay just because I'm curious and am looking for ways to optimize a system."

"Okay, but…why?"

Megan pulled away and looked at him. "I don't follow."

"I guess I'm curious as to why you feel the need to always be looking for more work. Do the other people in your department do that?"

"Well…no."

"Have any of your previous employers accused you of not doing enough work?"

"No."

He looked at her as if the answer was obvious. "Well…?"

She sighed again. "From the time I was little, I knew how important a good work ethic was. I watched how hard my father worked and how he talked about the people who worked for him. Then it was the way he started to train my brothers and was always telling them the importance of working hard and striving to do better no matter what job they had."

"And what did he say to you?"

She shrugged. "Nothing. I was a girl, and girls weren't supposed to worry about working. In his mind, I should have a good education so I could be a well-rounded individual, but he believed in things like making sure I had good manners and grace and my being groomed to be a good corporate wife someday."

"Um…wow. That's an outdated way of thinking. Even back then."

"I know. My mother put me in all kinds of dance classes, and I took piano lessons and…ugh. It was awful. I hated it. All of it. That's when I started studying so hard. I decided that I wanted to show him I was just as smart as my brothers." She paused. "Not that he noticed. Not until I was in college did it finally occur to him I had real dreams and ambition beyond being a wife, mother, and hostess."

Ah…suddenly it was all making a lot of sense.

Megan didn't actually *want* to spend her life holed up in an office working eighty hours a week; she felt like she *had* to in order to prove herself.

"That's a lot of pressure you're putting on yourself, you know."

She nodded. "The thing is, I don't know any other way now. I've been doing it for so long that I can't seem to help it."

"And how does your father feel about your career? Is he impressed?"

"Not really. Not the way he gushes over Christian and Carter. Although it took him a long time to gush over Carter mainly because he opted not to be a part of the Montgomery corporate world. But Christian? Oh my gosh… It's like he can do no wrong."

"That's got to suck for your brother," Alex commented, and Megan looked up at him like he was crazy. "Think of the pressure you put on yourself to try to get your father's approval."

"Right."

"Now think of how much pressure your brother must be under because of how your father follows him. I know you think that because he has your dad's approval that it should be easy, but I think it makes things so much harder. Your brother's always looking over his shoulder to make sure he's doing things the way your father wants him to or trying to keep up the image your father wants him to have." Alex shuddered. "I'm telling you, I wouldn't wish that kind of pressure on anyone."

Megan relaxed against his shoulder. "I never thought of it like that. I automatically assumed that out of the three of us, he had it the easiest."

"Nope. I'd say he has it the hardest. You're in the middle, and Carter's the lucky one."

"Why?"

"Because the only one he's concerned with pleasing is himself. He was brave enough to break the cycle and do something he was passionate about."

"Hey," she said, leaning up. "I'm passionate about what I do!"

"I don't doubt it. But you're making it harder on yourself than it has to be because you think you have to. Because of pressure you put on yourself, you're not getting the enjoyment out of it that you could."

She pouted. "I enjoy it."

Alex leveled her with a look. "Really?"

"Okay, not always, but…I enjoy reading up on new technologies and new systems and programs and—"

"And you could still do all that while putting in regular hours that allow you to have a life after you walk out the office doors."

"I'm working on it," she mumbled.

Reaching up, Alex guided her head to his shoulder. "I know you are, and I'm proud of you for it."

Snuggling closer, Megan placed a light kiss on his chest, and it made Alex smile. This was what he'd been thinking about and hoping for—to have this time with her where they could be intimate and talk and know the clock wasn't working against them. Everything about that weekend had been rushed because they knew Megan was leaving town at the end of it.

"I wish sometimes *he'd* tell me that," she said, and Alex realized they were still in the middle of talking about her life.

"I'm sure he is," Alex said because he didn't know what else he could say.

"It's not like he's mean about it or anything," she went on. "He's supportive in his own way, but…he doesn't gush like he does over Christian. Or Carter. I don't think he knows what to do with me."

"Have you ever tried to talk to him about it?"

"I wouldn't even know what to say. I'm always sharing what I'm doing and the cool stuff I've learned about, and he just sort of smiles and nods and asks if I need anything."

"Need anything? Like…what?"

Laughing softly, Megan pushed up so she could look at him. "You're obviously familiar with my family. You know we're fairly…um—"

"You're rich, Megan," Alex said with amusement. "It's okay to admit to that."

She laughed again as she shook her head. "Growing up, I never wanted for anything. We had the best of everything, we traveled, and there was never any pressure to get a job while we were in school." She paused. "Of course, it didn't mean we didn't all intern at Dad's office."

"Naturally."

"I don't think my father knew what to do with me."

"Well…now he does," he pointed out. "He saw what you were capable of and was smart enough to hire you."

"Maybe. But that just happened, it wasn't like it was planned."

"No, but…I would imagine this whole thing makes him happy."

"I guess."

Alex could tell she wasn't convinced, and he had so many questions he wanted to ask her—like why was she being so hard on herself or what difference did it make if her father said he was happy or not?—but something else sort of niggled at the back of his mind. He hesitated to ask because he didn't want to upset her, but…

"I have one more question, and then we are changing the subject," he said. "Deal?"

"Deal."

"You said yourself that your family is rich."

"Technically, you said it," she teased, resting her head on his shoulder.

He chuckled. "Fair enough. But…you moved here, and you're staying with Summer, and you were agonizing over things like rent and car payments, and…I don't know…it would seem to me that you wouldn't have to worry about that sort of thing—even saying how your parents ask if you need anything. Why not let them help you?"

"I've always made my own way since I finished school. I never wanted anyone to look at me and think I was relying on the family name or for it to look like I couldn't make it on my own." She paused. "I know a lot of people wouldn't do what I'm doing, especially when they could have it easy and live off their parents. That's not what I wanted or who I wanted to be."

He was finding more and more to respect about her, but at the same time, she seemed to make life harder on herself no matter what she did.

"You must think I'm crazy," she murmured.

Yes, he wanted to say.

But he didn't.

Instead he maneuvered them until she was beneath him—a position he was more than happy to keep them in—and smiled down at her. "I think you're beautiful," he said, kissing her cheek. "And smart." He kissed her other cheek. "And funny." He placed a light kiss on her forehead. "And incredibly sexy."

This time when he leaned down, he captured her lips with his. It wasn't light or sweet. It was the kind of kiss that put an end to their serious conversation and started something new.

And he took that very seriously.

Beneath him, Megan wrapped herself around him. She was all silky limbs and soft curves and...

"Alex?" she asked breathlessly, turning her head away from his slightly.

"Hmm?" He couldn't stop tasting her—her shoulder, her throat...anywhere his mouth could reach.

"Promise me something," she said, writhing beneath him.

"Anything." He had no idea where she was going with this, but right now, he'd promise her the sun, the moon, and the stars.

"Promise me…oh, that feels so good…promise me…"

His mouth found her breast, and he gently suckled as she tried to find her words.

"Yes, like that," she panted, raking her hands into his hair to hold him in place.

Would it be wrong if he didn't remind her that she was trying to ask him something? Because right now, with the way she was moving against him, the last thing he wanted to do was talk.

His name was a whispered plea before she said, "Promise to not let me leave tonight."

Lifting his head, Alex gave her a wicked smile. "Sweetheart, that was never going to be an option," he said before he silenced her with another kiss.

understood. "Okay. Got it. Not a problem. I'm sure it won't be a problem at all."

Summer's entire face lit up. "Really? You're sure? I know it's a lot to ask, and I feel like a horrible mom for even asking it but...oh my gosh," she said as she collapsed in one of the chairs facing Megan's desk. "I'm exhausted. The thought of a full-night's sleep is even more appealing than going out with my husband!"

"Maybe mentioning how I'm not going to get a full-night's sleep isn't the best way to convince me to babysit."

"Too late! You already agreed." The look of pure satisfaction on her cousin's face couldn't be missed. "And besides, it's not like you've been getting a lot of sleep lately anyway."

For two weeks, Megan had spent every night at Alex's. After that first weekend, she had come to work on Monday, dragged Gabriella and Summer to lunch, and pretty much told them everything—from Alex showing up at the office, all the way through the quickie in the shower that morning.

Who knew she would enjoy talking about her sex life so much?

She could feel her cheeks heat even as she smiled. "And I'm not even a little bit sorry about it."

"Good for you! Seriously. I think Alex is great, and I love seeing you smiling so much and looking so happy!" Summer's smile grew. "And I also have to say how much I am loving the way you are rocking your new wardrobe!"

Yes, on top of everything else, Megan had decided to finally start wearing all of the clothes her cousin and Gabriella had convinced her to buy. While she knew all looked good—the pencil skirts, the button-down

Chapter 7

MEGAN WAS READING OVER SOME REPORTS WHEN SUMMER knocked on her office door.

"Got a minute?"

Smiling, Megan put the paperwork aside. "Absolutely! What's up?"

Summer said brightly, "Ethan and I are dying for a night out. Like a date night. Alone."

"Ah. Gotcha."

"Right, so…obviously it would mean Amber would need to sleep over someplace or…someone would have to sleep at our place and we would have to sleep out."

"Say no more. I would love to babysit Amber. Seriously. It's not a problem. Just give me all the baby paraphernalia, and we'll have a sleepover at the guest-house. This way we'll be close enough to you if we need to be but far enough that you can have a bit of a break. Consider it a done deal. Friday night?"

"Oh…um…okay. I guess," Summer said hesitantl

"What? Was that not what you had in mind? I confused."

"I just figured with all the time you've been spen at Alex's that you wouldn't mind babysitting there. paused. "If Amber's close by, I know I'll feel the to check on her and then I'll end up bringing her and all of my efforts for a night off will be for no

Megan's eyes went wide for a moment and t

blouses, the stilettos—she seriously missed her yoga pants and sensible shoes.

Alex had commented on how much he was enjoying her new clothes, so she even tried to stay in them until he got home at night after working with a client. And that was really a feat because by the time she got home, all she wanted to do was strip off the shoes and the bra and the rest of it and get comfortable.

Luckily, Alex didn't mind helping her with that as soon as he walked in the door.

"You're happy, right?" Summer asked after Megan didn't immediately respond to her.

"I really am," Megan said. "Like…I can't even believe how happy I am."

"So, really, the two of you would be playing house this weekend."

Megan looked at her funny. "What do you mean?" Then she realized what Summer meant. "Whoa," Megan said, sitting up straight in her chair. "It's a little soon to be thinking about babies, so…just stop."

Summer gave her a knowing smirk. "You can't help it. No one can. It's the nature of the beast, so again…get yourself mentally prepared for it."

"I didn't think babysitting for a five-month-old required this much mental preparedness."

"Believe me, it does."

"Is it too late to back out?"

"Yup."

For a minute Megan debated messing with her cousin a bit more but decided against it. It didn't matter how much sleep she missed out on, the thought of having Amber for the night was something she was already looking forward to. Spending time with her honorary niece had become a favorite pastime since she'd arrived in Portland, and she adored her. There was something about a sweet baby snuggling in her arms that made Megan melt a little.

"You've already got the look," Summer said knowingly.

Megan immediately looked away and busied herself straightening papers. "What look?"

"The 'I love babies' look."

Shaking her head, she glanced at Summer. "No, it's more of an 'I love my niece' look. It's completely different."

"We'll see." Summer stopped and gasped.

"What? What's the matter?"

"Do you need to talk to Alex first? I mean, sure, it's fine for us to sit here and speculate on how cute this is all going to be, but maybe he doesn't want to babysit. Maybe he isn't into the whole baby thing."

Megan immediately waved her off. "Please, every time he's around you guys he can't take his eyes off Amber. He's always talking to her and trying to make her laugh. But if it makes you feel better, I'll text him right now and find out."

Summer instantly relaxed. "Yes. Please. Because as much as I want a night out, I don't want to put you in an awkward position."

"You're not. Trust me."

"Let's check with Alex first."

Megan nodded in agreement as she quickly typed a text to Alex. She hit Send and put her phone on her desk. "I'm not sure when he'll see the text, but I'm still confident that he's going to be fine with this."

"I forgot to tell you how much I love the dress you

bought for Amber last week," Summer said while they waited for Alex's response. "I put it on her yesterday, and…Megan, it's just amazing how much it reminds me of great-grandma's work! I know she isn't the only person who ever crocheted, but the details on it just make me think of her! You have to give me the name of the website you're ordering from because I'd love to pick out some stuff too."

"Oh, uh…I don't remember it offhand, but I'll get it to you," she stammered and glanced at her phone. "But about Friday…you have nothing to worry about because—"

Her words were interrupted by the sound of her phone alerting her that she had a new message. She picked up the phone, looked at the screen, and started to laugh.

"What? What's so funny?" Summer asked.

Megan turned the phone around and held it up for Summer to see.

"Wow…that's a lot of exclamation points and smiley faces."

Nodding, she put the phone down. "So as you can clearly see, babysitting is *not* going to be an issue. Just make sure you pack everything we could possibly need and then a little bit extra. It's been a long time since I've spent an entire night with a baby."

"When have you ever spent an entire night babysitting?" Summer asked.

"The summer after I graduated high school I worked as a nanny for a month for our neighbors. It was exhausting, and the pay was crappy."

"So is the pay for this babysitting gig," Summer deadpanned. "But if you're lucky, I'll bring some snacks for you and Alex to share."

"Double Stuf Oreos or the deal's off," Megan countered seriously.

Sighing dramatically, Summer said, "Fine. But you have to supply your own milk."

"Done."

Walking around the desk, Summer leaned down and hugged her. "I really appreciate this. No one tells you how this is the downside to not having grandparents living close by. I know if my mom was here, she'd have Amber sleeping over every weekend."

"That is the truth. But it's kind of nice how you have your brother and now me here to lend a hand, right?"

"Absolutely. And soon, you'll probably be getting approached by Zach to babysit for them too."

"And I'll love every minute of it."

"Oh! Did you order one of those blankets for Gabs? I know we talked about it—and I'm not trying to pressure you or tell you what you have to buy her for the shower—but I know how much she wanted one."

Sheesh…Megan thought. How had her crocheting become such a big thing?

"It's taken care of," she responded. "As a matter of fact, it already arrived."

Summer looked at her oddly. "Really? That's odd."

"Why?"

"Well, you haven't been home much, and I've been bringing in your mail, and I don't remember seeing any packages come to the house for you."

Dammit! Why hadn't she thought of that? Maybe she should just come clean and admit that there was no website, that she was the one making all of the baby stuff and—

"Summer?" Zach asked as he stepped into Megan's office. "We have that meeting in five. You ready?"

Saved by the proverbial bell…

"Absolutely," she said to Zach before turning back to Megan. "Okay, I need to get back to work, and I'm going to let Ethan know you're okay with babysitting."

Megan gave her a thumbs-up and then a wave as Summer and Zach left the office.

Her phone rang, and she saw Alex's name on the screen. Smiling, she picked it up. "Hey, you," she said softly.

"So? Is it definite? Are we getting Amber for the night?"

Unable to help herself, Megan laughed. "Are you being for real right now?"

"What? What's wrong with being excited?"

"It's not that you're excited, it's that you're…super excited," she said, still laughing.

"First of all, some would call it adorable, but whatever," he said seriously. "And second of all, I am *great* with kids. I love kids. And while I know Amber's just a baby and can't do much, I think it's going to be so much fun having her over!"

"You realize she's primarily going to eat and sleep, right?"

"Why are you trying to make this not fun?" he said, but she knew he was teasing.

"I just don't want you to be disappointed."

"Baby, the thought of spending the night babysitting with you could never be disappointing. It will be like one of those team-building exercises the big companies do. We'll have each other's backs and make sure sweet little Amber doesn't miss her mommy and daddy too much."

And just like that, her heart melted. "You really are adorable."

He chuckled. "I know, right?"

She relayed Summer's schedule of events to him to get his reaction.

"Sounds easy enough. Any idea what time they're going to pick her up on Saturday?"

"You know, that was the one thing she didn't mention."

"No big deal. We'll play it by ear, and if they want a little extra time alone, we'll take Amber to the park and go for a nice walk. The weather is supposed to be beautiful this weekend. What do you think?"

"Sounds good to me. But I have a feeling that for all their talk about needing a night alone, they're going to miss Amber, and we may end up all having an early-morning breakfast together."

Alex laughed. "Then I'll be sure to have all the makings for extra pancakes just in case."

"Mmm…you do make really good pancakes."

"Don't tell anyone. I kind of like when it's just the two of us sharing them in bed."

She smiled at the memory of him serving her breakfast in bed last weekend. "That probably won't happen while Amber's there. I have a feeling we'll be totally catering to her."

"There's always Sunday."

"I'm going to hold you to that."

"Sweetheart, anytime you want to hold me is fine by me."

―〰―

On Friday night, Alex kept Megan company while she babysat Amber.

"I don't think she's happy."

"How can you tell?"

"I don't think she's blinked in over a minute."

Megan looked closely at her niece's face and saw what Alex meant. "Or maybe she's just completely in awe of what a great job we're doing at babysitting."

Alex laughed softly, but he had a feeling that wasn't it. "All we've done is lean over and look at her."

"In all fairness, Ethan and Summer have only been gone for, like…ten minutes."

"Then it's been ten minutes since she's blinked."

"Oh stop," she said, swatting him playfully. "Let's get her out of her seat and see what she wants to do."

It was on the tip of his tongue to tell her Amber wasn't going to have a clue—nor could she tell them—but he sat back and watched as Megan lifted the baby from her seat and snuggled her close as she cooed and talked softly to her.

"Is this one of the dresses you got her?" he asked. "I heard Summer talking about all this handmade stuff you've been getting for her."

"Mm-hmm…" she hummed as she kissed Amber on the cheek.

His heart squeezed hard in his chest. They had talked about Summer's comments about them picturing this as being them sometime in the future. He just didn't expect it to happen quite so fast. The sight of Megan holding the baby made him feel like the last piece of the puzzle had fallen into place.

She was it for him.

It was crazy and maybe a little stupid to be thinking that so soon, but…there it was.

At first Alex feared he had spent so long building up his time with Megan from two years before that he wasn't seeing things clearly. But in the past few weeks he had come to the realization that he hadn't been wrong. He knew from their first meeting—those first few words they spoke to each other at the wedding—she was the one for him.

It wasn't something he'd ever thought would happen to him. Sure, he always knew he was going to meet someone, fall in love, get married, and have kids, but he didn't think that person would come in the form of a weekend hookup who he wouldn't see again for two years. But really, did it matter? The fact was that she was here now and things were going great.

Their biggest problem currently was their schedules. Alex accommodated his clients and didn't keep traditional hours, whereas Megan's were sometimes untraditional because she would work twice as long as everyone else. So he was up and leaving while she was still warm and sleepy in his bed. Never before had he dreaded getting up for work like he had in the past two weeks. And that was beside the fact that he wasn't getting much sleep because…well…she was right there beside him in the bed.

Just the thought of it made him grin.

So he'd leave for work and then two hours later, she would. He'd come home in the middle of the day or he'd meet her or some of his other friends for lunch and then head out for his evening clients. Megan always arrived home before him, and she'd read or just relax (she claimed). His hours never used to bother him before, but now they did.

When Megan had texted him about the two of them babysitting for Amber, he had taken out his calendar to reschedule his Friday evening clients. That had prompted him to take a hard look at his entire client list to see when his schedule might change. If his projections were correct, he had about another eight weeks before he had more of his evenings back. In the grand scheme of things, it wasn't a lot of time, but he was afraid if left to her own devices, Megan would start finding excuses to stay late at work, and then all of the progress she had made would be shot.

And he didn't want to see her moving backward this soon after she was finally moving forward with changing her work habits.

Not that it would change how he felt about her—he doubted anything would. But he knew Megan was trying so hard to make these changes in her life, and he wanted to be supportive of her. Unfortunately, he was the type of person who wanted to help everyone achieve their goals—it was a key element to his job as a physical therapist—but sometimes that meant letting people do it for themselves.

That was where he had the problem.

Hopefully he would know when to be supportive and when to be there to help. With his clients, his role was easy—he knew what was expected of him and how he had to conduct himself. In a personal relationship? Um, yeah. That one was going to be way harder.

"Who's a pretty girl?" she said from beside him as she played with Amber's toes, and he smiled again.

In the short time since she'd arrived in Portland, he had seen so many changes in her—she was more relaxed, she smiled more, and there was a softness to her now that wasn't there before.

But the woman sitting beside him? She was amazing and strong, and Alex wasn't so sure if he'd be able to do what she did—picking up and moving to the other side of the country—even if he did have relatives who lived there. She had taken a huge leap of faith, and he wasn't sure if she even realized it—if she knew how much she had already accomplished just by moving.

He had to get out of his own head because their focus tonight needed to be on Amber and he'd been looking forward to this all week. Moving closer to the two of them, he immediately tried to make the baby smile, and when she did, Megan looked over at him like he had done the greatest thing in the world.

"You look surprised," he said softly. "I told you, I'm good at this."

"I've been trying for five full minutes to get her to smile. You say two words and tweak her belly, and suddenly she's got this giant grin on her face."

Leaning in, he kissed Megan on the cheek. "What can I say? I've got a way with the ladies."

Amber seemed a little more at ease, and soon they had her laughing as they all played on the floor. Alex was making goofy faces and sounds to entertain her while Megan held Amber in her lap. After a few minutes, he kissed the baby's feet before looking up and suggesting, "How about I get dinner started? Summer said if you fed Amber first, she'd be content to hang out while we eat."

"Sounds good. All day I've been thinking about the

burgers you said you were going to make. Those are my weakness."

He stood and kissed her on the top of her head. "I thought I was your weakness," he teased as he walked to the kitchen.

Megan stood and followed him, with the baby in her arms. "Oh, you definitely are, which makes this one heck of a double treat—you *and* burgers? If we weren't babysitting, you would have gotten *very* lucky."

Right then and there he thought she was adorable— babysitting wasn't going to hinder a thing.

"In case you've forgotten, Ethan told us Amber will go to bed around eight, and then we shouldn't expect to hear from her again until around four a.m. If we keep her up until nine, that gives us until five a.m." Walking over to Megan, he leaned in until his tongue could trace the shell of her ear. Megan shivered at the light caress. "And last I checked, we've been functioning on far less than eight hours of sleep."

When he stepped away, he was feeling kind of smug—like he had her. She couldn't argue his logic.

"But," Megan said in a singsong voice, "Ethan also said she doesn't sleep as well when she's away from home. So we just don't know, do we?"

Damn. He had forgotten about that part.

"I guess we'll have to wait and see."

While he began making dinner, Megan set up Amber's baby seat in the kitchen and went about getting her food ready. They talked as they worked, and their conversation ranged from their day at work to where they wanted to explore on Sunday.

Alex stepped out onto the deck to put the burgers

on the grill and looked out at his yard. Everything was starting to bloom, and his landscapers were doing a great job. Maybe he'd ask Megan if she'd like to invite friends and family for a barbecue—not this weekend, but maybe next.

Looking toward the house and through the glass in the French doors, he could see Megan feeding Amber. It looked like she was singing and making airplane moves with the baby spoon, and the sight made his heart feel lighter. Happier.

With a sense of contentment, he flipped the burgers and stared up at the sky. The sun was setting, the temperature was mild, and everything was peaceful. Dare he say it was a near-perfect night? He took another glance into the house and knew he was wrong.

It *was* the perfect night.

Megan wanted to believe she knew what she was doing, but as her niece looked up at her with huge blue eyes, she wasn't so sure.

Bath time.

Was she really qualified to be giving a baby a bath? Amber was slippery and splashing, and she didn't seem to be enjoying herself at all. Summer had said bath time was their favorite time of day.

Clearly not *this* particular bath time.

"Everything okay in here?" Alex asked as he walked into the bathroom carrying a towel and a change of clothes for Amber.

"I think she can sense my fear."

Alex laughed softly, knelt beside Megan, instantly

began to talk in soothing tones to the baby, and—once again—had her smiling and laughing in no time.

"No fair," Megan mumbled and then wanted to splash him when he gave her a smug smile.

Again.

"Fine. You're the king of babysitting," she said as she stood. "So rather than me traumatizing her any further, you can finish giving her a bath."

"I'm not going to argue with that," he said and then spoke to Amber, "Am I, sweet girl? Who can argue with giving such a pretty girl a bath? We're going to get you all clean and in your jammies, and you're going to sleep like you're at home in your own bed."

Amber blew spit bubbles and laughed at him.

Megan imagined the baby was telling him to dream on.

It was still a little early—barely seven o'clock. She knew they had at least an hour before they could try to put Amber down for the night. Not that Megan was in a rush—for the most part, the baby had been no trouble at all. She was sweet and quiet and seemed to be fairly content.

It was good.

Almost too good.

Off in the distance, she heard a phone ring and could only guess it would be Summer calling to check in. She ran to answer it and smiled when she saw her cousin's name flashing on the screen.

"Your daughter is fine. She ate all her dinner, gave several healthy burps, pooped more than a child that small should, and is currently enjoying a bath. All is well, so stop worrying and enjoy your night," Megan said before Summer could even utter a word.

"Well, you certainly told me," Summer said with a laugh.

"When we hang up, I'll go take a picture of her in the tub and send it to you to put your mind at ease, okay?"

"Thank you."

Two minutes later, she was sending a picture of Amber with a crown of bubbles on her head as well as a bubble beard.

"I don't think Summer's going to find that as amusing as you do," Megan softly chided Alex.

"Then tell her to show it to Ethan. He will," he said with a laugh as he rinsed Amber off. When she was bubble-free, he turned off the water and pulled the plug before reaching for her towel, his gaze never leaving Amber. He spoke to her the entire time, and Megan watched in awe. It was one thing to hear him talk about how much he loved kids; it was quite another to witness it for herself.

Alex cradled Amber in his arms and talked softly to her as he walked to the vanity, grabbed her diaper and pajamas, and then walked to his bedroom where he gently put her down on the bed. The entire time Amber's blue eyes studied him. Almost as if she understood everything he was saying to her. It was beyond sweet, and as much as Megan wanted to go over and join them, she didn't want to do anything to ruin the moment the two of them were having.

Quietly, Megan pulled out her phone and snapped a couple of pictures. If Alex heard her or noticed, he didn't say anything. His attention stayed on Amber. When he had the baby fully dressed in her pink footy pajamas, he picked her up and placed a small kiss on her nose.

"What should we do now, Aunt Megan?" he asked in a playful tone. "Should we go downstairs and read or maybe play with Mister Bunny and Lamby?"

Unable to help herself, Megan laughed. "I think a little playtime first and then a story. How does that sound?"

"Perfect," he said with a smile.

For the next hour, they played and acted silly and pretty much put on an entire theatrical production starring all of Amber's toys. Amber yawned widely but didn't seem like she was quite ready for bed. Megan picked her up and rocked her as she talked to her about how much fun they'd had and how now it was time for sweet dreams.

"I'm going to take her up and try to put her down," she said quietly.

Alex stood and handed her another one of Amber's books. "Just in case," he said and leaned in to kiss the baby on the cheek.

"Thanks."

"I'm going to straighten up while you put her to bed," he said. "If she won't settle, call out to me, and I'll see if I can help."

Megan frowned at him. "Seriously?"

"What?"

"I couldn't get her to smile, but you did. We were having a total bath fail until you swooped in. And your rabbit voice was perfect," she grumbled. "So far I have totally sucked at this."

Pulling them in close, Alex hugged them both and kissed Megan soundly. "You have not sucked at this. It takes teamwork. I told you that. Hell, even Summer said she and Ethan do all of this nighttime stuff together. Personally, I think the night was a complete success. And if we can get her to go to sleep and stay asleep, even better."

There was no way she was going to voice her concerns where that last part was concerned. Instead she smiled and walked up the stairs to the guest room where they'd set up Amber's Pack 'n Play. There was only one small light on in the room, and Megan sat in the upholstered chair in the corner and got herself comfortable.

For fifteen minutes, she read some of Winnie the Pooh's many adventures and watched as Amber's eyes began to drift shut. Then she waited another few minutes to make sure she was asleep before slowly standing and moving across the room to place her in her bed. Never in Megan's life had she ever moved so slowly and cautiously, but she was genuinely afraid of waking the baby up.

After she straightened, she stood there in wonder and held her breath until she was certain Amber was going to stay asleep. Then, ever so slowly, she tiptoed backward toward the door, and all of those stealth moves were almost for nothing when she turned and found Alex standing in the doorway. She jumped and almost screamed, but luckily she caught herself before she did.

Alex placed a finger over her lips, motioned to the baby monitor he had in his hands, and gently led Megan out of the room and across the hall to his bedroom. He quietly closed the door and put the monitor down on the bedside table.

With her hand still in his, he pulled her close and then

kissed her slowly—as if he just wanted to savor the feel of her, the taste of her. When he lifted his head, he rested his forehead against hers and smiled. "Good job."

"With the kiss?" she teased.

He shook his head. "With Amber. The monitor was on, and I heard you reading to her and talking to her, and…it was amazing," he said softly.

It was possibly the greatest compliment she had ever received.

"Then I came up and saw you putting her down, and I could tell you were afraid to wake her, but I think not only did we exhaust her, but you totally relaxed her and made her feel secure."

High praise coming from the babysitting king, she thought, and she was flattered.

"That was scarier than the bath."

Alex's smile was still in place. "I think you deserve a reward for all of your stress and worrying tonight."

"I wouldn't say I was stressed—"

"There's a hot bath waiting for you, and when you're done, I'm going to give you a massage."

She gasped with delight. "Really?"

He nodded. "I normally do them for much different reasons—you know, as part of a patient's therapy—but I believe I know how to make it relaxing and sexy."

"You had me at relaxing," she teased. "But the sexy is a total perk."

Taking her gently by the shoulders, Alex turned her around and gave her a gentle push in the direction of the bathroom. "Go before the water gets too cool, and I'll be waiting out here."

Megan had only taken a few steps when she looked

over her shoulder at him. "And what are you going to be doing while I'm in the tub?"

"Reading." To prove his point, he reached over to his nightstand and held up his iPad. "Don't worry about me. Go and enjoy your bath."

It would have been easy to do that—after all, she knew a hot bath would be glorious. Hell, if he hadn't suggested it, she was going to see if he wanted to spend a little time outside in the hot tub. But now that she thought about it, it was better for them to stay close to Amber. Even with the baby monitor, she knew she'd relax more being close by.

"Well," she began hesitantly, "I guess reading is good, but…"

He arched one brow at her.

"But the bathtub is big enough for two," she said, walking toward him. "And I'm sure we can start this whole massage thing in there." Up on her tiptoes, she gently kissed his lips. "As a matter of fact, I think it would be a great way to help me relax."

A slow smile played at his lips. "I think we both know if I join you in the tub, the only massage you're going to get isn't going to be for relaxation purposes."

"And I can say with great certainty that I wouldn't mind. You can give me a massage tomorrow. But right now, what I want more than anything is for you to come into the bathroom with me, get naked, climb in that giant tub, and…massage anything you'd like."

Taking a step back, Alex whipped his shirt up and over his head and carelessly tossed it across the room, and Megan had to stop herself from laughing out loud. He was unbuttoning his jeans before she could even blink.

Clearly, he took getting naked seriously.

"We don't want the water to get cold," he said when she hadn't made a move to take anything off.

"I was enjoying the show," she said coyly, turning and walking toward the bathroom. It wasn't until she was next to the tub that she began to undress. Even without looking, she knew Alex was standing in the doorway watching her, so she decided to remove everything slowly.

First, she pulled her shirt up and over her head, dropping it to the floor beside her. Then she stretched. Next, she shimmied out of her yoga pants, taking her time peeling them down her legs before straightening and gently kicking them aside. Next came her bra. Bending over the tub, she tested the water and heard Alex groan behind her. Her panties were black and tiny and barely covered her bottom.

Doing her best to look a little seductive, she straightened and slipped her panties off before carefully dipping one foot into the tub—letting it slide into the water slowly. Then she stepped in and lifted her other leg in before slipping down into the water.

And man, did *that* feel good.

When she finally looked at Alex, he was standing in his boxers, and his erection was beyond impressive.

"If you hadn't climbed into the tub, I was going to take matters into my own hands and take you right there as you bent over."

She pouted. "Had I known that was an option, I would have waited."

It was like hitting the launch button. He whipped off the dark cotton and climbed in behind her. Megan leaned forward to make room for him, and when he gently pulled her back against his chest, he whispered in her ear, "Brace yourself."

And then his hands were everywhere.

His lips were everywhere.

It didn't take long for her to start panting his name, arching her back, and begging him for more. If this was what he was capable of in the confines of a tub, she could only imagine how amazing a massage from him would be when they were sprawled out on the bed. Either way, it was making her feel good.

So, so very good, she thought.

———

Monday night, Megan was back at her place and took advantage of a little alone time to do some crocheting. Alex had an evening client, and rather than going right to his place, she had stopped at the guesthouse to get a couple changes of clothes together to take to Alex's. She was deep into a little blue hat when her phone rang.

Her mother.

She contemplated not answering it. Not that she didn't enjoy talking to her, but she hadn't told her about her relationship with Alex yet and wasn't really ready to. Mainly because she wasn't ready to answer any questions about how serious it was or if they were talking about a future yet.

Yes, her mother was a firm believer in short engagements and long marriages.

Basically she believed in fairy tales.

The phone rang again, and Megan relented and answered it. "Hi, Mom!"

"Megan, I have a somewhat…delicate matter to discuss with you."

Oh, Lord, she thought. "Um…sure, Mom. What's up?"

"Well, it's about your Aunt Janice and Uncle Robert."

That was not what Megan had been expecting to hear at all, so she was instantly intrigued. "What's going on?"

"Well, with everything that happened with Gabriella and the false labor, your aunt is feeling anxious and wants to come back to Portland before the baby is born."

"O-kay—"

"And I'm sure you heard about the awkward incident she had while staying with Summer and Ethan."

"Uh-huh—"

"Well, I guess everyone sort of assumed you would have found a place of your own by now, and no one wants to stay at Zach's because they don't want to add to Gabriella's stress, so…" She let the silence hang for a minute until Megan caught on.

"Wait, are you saying Aunt Janice wants to stay at the guesthouse?"

"Yes!" her mother said with a loud sigh of relief. "Oh, I'm glad you said it and I didn't have to. You understand, don't you? It wouldn't be right for her and your uncle to have to stay at a hotel, after all."

"Um…no. Of course not. I guess I can stay in the guest room at Summer's while they're in town, and then—"

"No, no, no," her mother quickly interrupted. "I can't say with any great certainty, but I think the boys will be coming along soon too."

"So what am I supposed to do, Mom? I can't find an

apartment and move out in the next week. That's a little unreasonable!"

"Well…I'm sure you could find someplace to stay temporarily—"

"I suppose I could go to a hotel," Megan murmured, more than a little annoyed with the whole conversation. If this was going to be an issue, she wished it had been Summer to bring it up to her.

"That's ridiculous, Megan. It would cut you off from everyone, and I know how antisocial you can get."

"Seriously? Now I'm antisocial? When did that become my thing?" she demanded. Most of the time her mother was one of the most levelheaded people to talk to, but for some reason she seemed a little off tonight. "What is going on, Mom? You're not making any sense."

Eliza sighed. "Okay, fine. Here's the thing…why would you bother paying to stay at a hotel and being by yourself when you could maybe go and stay with…Alex?"

Megan immediately began to cough as she gasped at her mother's statement. How the heck did her mother even *know* about her relationship with Alex? They hadn't talked about it! Not that it was a big secret, but she knew it was something she hadn't brought up to her.

She was going to strangle her cousin when she saw her in the morning.

"Megan? Megan, are you all right? Put your hands in the air. That will make the coughing stop."

It took a minute, but eventually she was able to breathe normally again. With a steadying breath, she replied to her mother, "Why would you even suggest such a thing?"

"Oh, please. I may be your mother, but I'm not a prude. I know you're dating Alex, and I believe you lost your virginity some time ago, so don't sound so outraged by what I'm suggesting."

"Prude? Virgin? Mom! Seriously, what in the world?" Megan cried.

"Don't be so dramatic." Eliza sighed again. "Honestly, you'd think you'd be happy to have such a hip mother."

Oh, good grief.

"Mom, I love that you're so…hip," Megan forced herself to say. "But you're essentially asking me to ask Alex to let me move in! That's not hip, that's a little…brazen!"

"For crying out loud, like I don't know that this is the way most young couples are these days? I think it's wonderful that you're in a relationship with Alex!"

"And you know this how?"

"Unlike you, Summer talks to her mother, and imagine how I felt having to hear about this from Aunt Janice. You're dating this wonderful young man—who this entire family adores for all he did for Zach—and this is the relationship you choose to hide?"

Great. Here comes the guilt…

"I'm not saying you have to move in with him permanently," her mother went on, "although that would be extremely acceptable and make me happy, but maybe give it a test run for a few weeks and see how it goes."

For the life of her, Megan couldn't believe she was having this conversation. Actually, she wished she wasn't. "Mom…I don't think it's appropriate to—"

"Are you dating Alex?" her mother quickly interrupted. Like she could honestly deny it? "Yes."

"Have you…spent the night with him?"

"Mom…" she whined.

"I believe I have my answer to that." Then she paused. "I think it's the perfect solution to this situation. Right now it's very important for your aunt and uncle to be close by and for there to be room for your cousins too. This is a big milestone for their family. After almost losing Zach, no one thought they'd see this day."

And while Megan knew there was a part of that statement that was true—a very small part of it—she thought her mother was blowing this way out of proportion.

"And with Gabriella having complications and Summer having an infant of her own, I think it would be best if you cleared the way for their family to be together."

"I will talk to Summer about this in the morning, Mom. Okay?"

"Why? Why talk to Summer? Why don't you talk to Alex and make it easier on everyone?"

This was an argument she simply didn't want to have. She'd talk to Summer and then talk to Alex. There was no way she was going to just go to him first and put him in a potentially awkward position—especially if it was all for nothing. She didn't mind giving up the guest-house to her aunt and uncle, but if Summer didn't mind having her in the house, then she'd rather do that. And if the rest of her cousins came in? Well, they'd deal with that when the time came.

She looked at the yarn in her lap and sighed. If she moved in with Alex—even temporarily—it would mean outing her hobby. Not that she thought he'd judge, but it was still something that she kind of liked keeping to herself. It wasn't hard to envision sitting in Alex's living room with a fire going in the fireplace and sitting on one end of the sofa crocheting while he read and…

Ugh…how had her sexy dreams of the two of them turned to domestic ones so fast?

Across the room was the pile of clothes she planned to put into her weekender bag. It was getting to be a bit of a chore going back and forth. Still, it might be weird for her to just come out and ask him if she could stay—

"Megan? Are you still there?"

She laughed softly. "I'm here, Mom. Sorry. I just zoned out for a moment."

"Well, your aunt is planning to be there this weekend, so…you need to think about this and make it happen so it's not awkward when everyone shows up."

"Trust me. I don't believe I'll be able to think of anything else," she murmured as she put her crochet hook down and tried to think of how she was going to pack up all her stuff.

―◊◊◊―

Alex's legs were burning, he was sweating, and his heart was beating like mad.

And it felt great.

"What's the matter, Rebat? Can't handle a little bike ride?" Zach mocked as he sped past him.

Laughing, Alex let the razz roll right off him. It was a beautiful day, the sky was blue, and he was getting in a ride on one of his favorite trails while Megan was out shopping with the girls.

"Geez, Alex, if I can pass you, then you're really off your game," Ethan said as he pedaled by.

Okay, that one hurt.

With a renewed sense of purpose, he picked up the pace, and soon he was waving to Ethan and then Zach as he passed them. The burst of speed felt good, but he knew he was going to pay for it later. Images of spending some quality time in the hot tub came to mind, and then the image of Megan in there with him.

Alex had already racked his bike on his car by the time Zach and then Ethan arrived. After some teasing, they headed to one of their favorite pubs for lunch. Zach and Ethan rode together, and Alex followed.

Fifteen minutes later, they were seated in a booth and were grabbing at menus. "I don't know why we even bother," Ethan said. "We come here so much that we've memorized the damn thing. Why can't we just give the order as soon as we sit down?"

Zach laughed. "Because the one time we do that will be the time they've added something fantastic to the menu that we'd miss."

Alex looked at Ethan and grinned. "True story."

They each perused the menu, and when their server approached, they ordered. She looked at them and quirked a brow. "So…the same as usual?"

"I told you," Ethan murmured.

"How are you doing, Alex?" she asked. Her name was Frannie, and she was young and cute, and there had been a time when Alex had been mildly interested. Nothing had ever come of it, but she always flirted.

"Doing good, Frannie. How about you?"

She gave him a sweet smile. "Can't complain." Then she paused. "Well…maybe I can. We haven't seen much of you lately. Where've you been hiding out?"

Alex could actually *feel* Zach's glare.

He gave her a charming yet bashful smile. "I've been showing my girlfriend all around Portland—doing the parks and hiking and that kind of thing."

Frannie's smile fell a little. "She's a lucky girl. I'll have your drinks right out," she said as she walked away.

Before anyone else could speak, Alex looked directly at Zach. "Did I answer correctly?"

Ethan burst out laughing. "Seriously, Zach. You should have seen your face!"

"He's dating my cousin and flirting with another woman right in front of me! What exactly did you want me to do?" Zach asked.

"For starters, you can relax," Alex replied. "And I wasn't flirting with anyone. I was merely being polite to the woman who has the opportunity to spit on our food."

"Eww…" Ethan groaned. "Seriously, why would you even put that out there?"

Zach started to speak, but Alex cut him off. "We've come here often enough that you've seen Frannie talk to me like that. This isn't new information, and it's not a big deal. I'm not looking for anyone else. I'm perfectly happy with Megan."

"Yeah, well—"

"Here are your drinks, boys," Frannie said with a slightly less enthusiastic smile. "Your burgers will be out shortly."

"You totally ruined her day," Ethan said as he reached for his drink. "If she's going to spit, I hope it's only on yours."

"Nice," Alex said and picked up his own beverage. Beside him, his phone beeped, and he looked down to

see a new message from Megan. Smiling, he swiped the
screen and found a picture of her holding up a red-lace bra.

> **Alex:** I hope you're sharing this because
> you're buying it
>
> **Megan:** I'm thinking about it ☺
>
> **Alex:** You should probably buy more than one
>
> **Megan:** ???
>
> **Alex:** One in every color they have
>
> **Megan:** That can be arranged
>
> **Alex:** Buy them now and meet me at my place
> ASAP!
>
> **Megan:** LOL!
>
> **Alex:** Go and buy pretty things and I'll see you
> later
>
> **Megan:** Tell the guys I said hello

When he looked up from the phone, he saw the
smirks on their faces.

"What? What's so funny?"

"So…we get mocked for talking about our wives and
babies, but you can sit there with a goofy-ass grin on your
face while texting Megan? How is that fair?" Ethan teased.

"Maybe it wasn't Megan," he said and then instantly knew what was coming.

Before he could stop him, Zach pulled the phone from his hands, looked at the screen, and then cursed, thrusting it back at Alex. "Dammit."

"Serves you right," Alex said smugly, putting the phone screen-side down on the table beside him.

"Oh, God. Were they sexting?" Ethan asked, a pained expression on his face. "Please tell me there were no pictures!"

"Let's just say...nothing and move on from this," Zach said miserably. He took a steadying breath and let it out. "What are we going to do next weekend? Are you rescheduling your barbecue?"

Alex shook his head. The plan he'd had to have them all over to his place had fallen through due to weather, and then Amber had a cold and Gabriella wasn't feeling well, so they had yet to try again. "Megan's been a good sport about doing all the outdoor excursions I've been taking her on. Next weekend she wants to see some museums and walk around the city."

They talked about some of the more interesting spots to take her while they waited for their lunch. Alex knew Megan had already printed a list of places she wanted to see in the order she wanted to see them. She was incredibly organized—borderline OCD at times—but it was cute as hell. And when he saw that side of her come out, he realized how much she was trying to break out of it—especially because she'd been going with the flow on their trips.

Her organizational skills became increasingly apparent when she moved some of her stuff into his place this past week. She was emphatic about not taking up too much space and even insisted on putting the bulk of her belongings in the guest room. He had no idea what was in most of the boxes and cases she'd brought over, and it didn't look like she'd unpacked any of them. He'd questioned her about them, but she'd just kept saying they weren't anything important, so he'd let the subject drop.

Frannie brought out their meals and refilled their drinks, and for those first few bites, no one spoke. It was always the true sign of a good meal.

Or of people who were starving.

"What about camping next weekend?" Alex asked. "Nothing crazy or far away, but just to hike out someplace and maybe do some fishing? You guys in?"

"Too close to Gabriella's due date," Zach said. "I wouldn't be able to relax and enjoy it."

Ethan nodded. "I wouldn't mind a night or two away to fish, but maybe when Amber's a little older. Summer and I share the whole getting-up-at-night thing. It wouldn't be fair to leave her to handle it all. You should ask Megan."

Both Alex and Zach started to laugh.

"Trust me, Megan is not a camper," Zach said.

"That's what she's said a time or two to me, but I'm hoping she'll eventually change her mind," Alex replied.

"Don't hold your breath. You know it's not something all people enjoy. You've gotten her to go out and do the parks with you; just be happy with that."

But Alex shrugged. "I still think it could happen."

"Summer's not particularly outdoorsy either, and yet she spent that weekend camping out in a teepee at the springs," Ethan said and then looked at Zach. "Remember that?"

"Wasn't that the weekend you secretly hooked up with her? Do you really want me to remember that?"

Ethan grinned and gave Alex a sly wink. "I was simply referring to the camping aspect. You're the one who took it to the hookup."

"Oh, for the love of it!" Zach said.

"Okay, okay…everyone just drop the camping topic," Alex interrupted diplomatically. "We'll revisit that topic in a year when the babies are older and you two are allowed to go out and play again."

That seemed to break the tension.

"What about the three of us doing something early next Saturday morning?" Zach said. "We can bike again or maybe get a couple other guys and play some basketball. What do you think?"

Both Alex and Ethan nodded.

"I've got a few guys I can call," Alex said.

"Me too," Ethan agreed.

They discussed times and whom they'd ask and the conversation moved to pro sports and what games were going to be on the TV over the weekend. This was good. This was what they did, and even though he was having a good time, Alex's mind kept wandering to the picture of the red bra. He couldn't wait to see Megan wearing it for him.

And then he couldn't wait to see Megan not wearing it.

He fought the urge to smile because he knew the guys would jump all over him again for it. But mentally, he was grinning from ear to ear.

Tonight he was taking her out to dinner at one of his favorite Italian restaurants. It was the kind of place to dress up for, and he found that while they had thus far stuck to casual places, he was looking forward to taking her someplace nice. Weekends were the only times they could relax. Alex did his best not to schedule clients on Saturday, but sometimes it couldn't be helped. And even though they were both off doing their own things right now, he knew they'd make up for it later.

Especially with red lace.

Damn. He had to stop thinking about that until after he and the guys had parted ways.

Frannie cleared the table and asked if they wanted any dessert, but they declined and asked for the check.

"Whose turn is it?" she asked with a grin.

Ethan raised his hand. "I came in last today, so I'm guessing it's on me," he grumbled. "It's a stupid rule."

Zach and Alex looked at each other and grinned.

"Says the loser," Alex said.

"What have you got going on for the rest of the day?" Ethan asked.

"Once Gabs comes home from shopping with Summer and Megan, we were planning on grilling some salmon and relaxing. My parents won't want to give up Amber, so you guys can come if you like."

"How does Gabriella feel about everyone coming in already?" Alex was relieved no one had said anything about Megan moving in with him since Robert and Janice had arrived.

"I think she's fine with it, but she's been pushing herself to get everything ready. The last of the baby furniture came this week, and she spent way too much time yesterday doing that…what do they call it…nesting? I swear, she washed everything—all the baby clothes, blankets, and sheets—and then she had me moving furniture this way and that. It was crazy. I was kind of surprised she even wanted to go out today because there isn't one damn thing we need."

"It's not really about the shopping," Ethan said. "It's just an excuse to go out. I'm sure they're going to do lunch and the nail thing too."

"Maybe," Zach said, playing with a straw wrapper.

"And besides, women are always going to find something to buy," Ethan went on. "Just because she's shopping doesn't mean it's for the baby. I know Summer mentioned wanting to relax and then something about a pedicure. But I wasn't paying attention to whether that was today."

"Dude, how long have you known your wife?" Ethan asked with a small laugh. "Gabriella rarely sits still, and it's just shopping. It's not like she's out hiking or doing anything strenuous. You know Megan and Summer wouldn't allow her to overexert herself."

Zach visibly relaxed. "You're right," he said, leaning back in his seat and raking a hand through his hair. "I just worry about her." Alex's phone beeped, and when he went for it, Zach smacked his hand over it. "Do *not* look at it. I swear, it is asking too much for me to sit here while you exchange sexy texts with my baby cousin."

Alex rolled his eyes. "She's not a baby. And how do we even know it's her?"

"Who else texts you?" Zach deadpanned.

"Fine. I'll wait," he said, but his curiosity was killing him.

Ethan's phone beeped. "Um…am I allowed to see what that's about, or are you afraid your sister is going to be sending me a sexy text?" he teased and then started laughing as he picked up his phone. "Actually, I'm seriously hoping that's what this is."

"Could be a baby question?" Zach said. "Maybe Amber has a rash or she's crying because she misses you." He laughed at the crestfallen look on Ethan's face. "That will teach you to poke at me with anything sex-related about my sister."

"Way to kill a mood," Ethan said.

While they were arguing, Alex reached for his phone. "Um…guys?"

Ethan's phone beeped again. "It's been three years! You'd think you would have moved on by now and accepted it. I sleep with your sister. And she sleeps with me. Deal with it."

Zach's phone beeped, but he didn't hear it.

"Guys?" Alex said a little louder.

"What?" they both snapped.

"We need to go," Alex said as he slid from the booth and grabbed his stuff. "Like now."

"Why? What's up?" Zach asked.

Rather than say it, he picked up Zach's phone and held it up for him. "Because your wife's water just broke in the middle of the nail salon," he said with a grin. "I think you're about to have a baby."

"Holy shit!" he cried, sliding out of the booth. He looked panicked and unsure of where to go or what to do.

Looking at Ethan, who was reading his message, Alex said, "It looks like Summer and Megan are getting her to the hospital. Get Zach there, and I'll take care of the bill. I'll be two minutes behind you."

"Thanks, Alex," Ethan said as he stood. Clapping Zach on the back, he grinned. "C'mon! Let's go!"

Chapter 8

IT WAS ALMOST MIDNIGHT WHEN ZACH WALKED INTO THE waiting room, wearing a pair of scrubs and looking more than a little exhausted. Megan sat forward in her seat and held her breath.

"We have a girl," he said with a big grin on his face. "A beautiful, healthy baby girl with a head of black hair like her mother." Everyone jumped up to congratulate him—Megan, Alex, Summer, and Ethan, along with Robert and Janice Montgomery, who had left Amber with the nanny.

Megan leaned into Alex as he wrapped his arms around her while they listened to Zach talk about how Gabriella and the baby were doing. Reaching up, she swiped away a stray tear or two—which was so unlike her. She wasn't an overly emotional person, but some-how being here to experience something so amazing…it affected her more than she'd thought it would.

"You okay?" Alex murmured softly in her ear.

She nodded.

At first he didn't say anything, just kissed her on the temple. "It's pretty incredible, right?"

She nodded again.

"Look at your cousin's face," he said quietly, so only she could hear. "I've known Zach for a while now, and I've never seen him look so happy."

"I've known him my whole life, and I've never

seen him look like that," she replied and wiped away another few tears. "I'm so happy for him. For both of them. I swear I'm still in awe at how calm Gabriella was through the whole thing. Summer and I were freaking out, and Gabriella was the voice of reason." She paused and laughed softly. "We should probably apologize to her for that."

But Alex shook his head. "Nah. That's just the way she is. She's crazy efficient and always in control. I'm sure she was glad to have a distraction."

"I'm sure she was glad we were able to find our way out of the parking lot," Megan joked. "It was touch-and-go there for a minute or two."

"In about fifteen minutes, you'll be able to go down to the nursery to see her, but I think Gabriella would appreciate everyone waiting until the morning to visit with her. She's exhausted," Zach was saying.

"Have you decided on a name?" Janice asked, her voice thick with emotion, and Megan watched as her aunt wiped away happy tears of her own.

Zach smiled. "Willow. She is Willow Grace Montgomery."

And right then and there Megan's heart melted even more. If anyone would have asked her to speak, she knew she wouldn't be able to, and Alex must have sensed it because he held her a little tighter.

Zach excused himself and told them when to return, and for the next few minutes there was a flurry of excited conversation that Megan only listened to. Summer went for her phone to call her brother James while her mother called Ryder. Robert and Ethan were talking business, and Alex turned Megan in his arms.

"We missed our date tonight," he said, placing a kiss on the tip of her nose.

"This was just as good."

He smiled. "It wasn't quite the romantic setting I was going for."

Snuggling against his chest, she said, "I think the romantic element here was perfect." And she meant it. To get to be here—surrounded by family and friends—while a new life came into the world was…there were no words. They escaped her.

"I promise to make it up to you," he said. "We'll pick a night this week and dress up and go out and maybe even go dancing."

"Ooh…that does sound nice. But I'm really okay, Alex," she said, looking up at him. "I mean, I was looking forward to going out, but this? I wouldn't have wanted to miss it for the world. I never knew it could be so—"

He caressed her cheek. "I know. Me too."

Summer walked over and let out a happy sigh. "Now the whole family knows about little Miss Willow—even though it's three in the morning on the East Coast—and I called and checked on Amber. Once I can get a peek at our new addition and snap a picture or two, we're going to head home. This has been a seriously long day."

Megan and Alex nodded in agreement. "You're lucky Mrs. Knightley was able to stay all day with Amber and Maylene," Megan said. "And that she brought her up here for a little while."

"Oh, I know. Don't get me wrong, Ethan and I could have run home and grabbed her and brought her back here, but it would have been too much."

"I know this all happened at the last minute, but do you have everything you need for your parents to stay with you?" Alex asked.

"Yup. I feel like my mom was here not too long ago and now she's back," she said with a nervous laugh. "Ethan's already talking about boundaries and locking bedroom doors."

They all laughed.

"I'm kidding, and I appreciate you being willing to let them stay in the guesthouse, Megan. I feel awful about you having to move out—even temporarily."

But Megan waved her off. "It's fine. Really. And I understand the importance of all of you being together right now."

"I'm sure they'll head over to Zach and Gabriella's once they're settled with Willow, right?" Summer asked with a nervous laugh. "And then you can move back in. That is…if you want to."

"I don't think we have to decide tonight, do we?" Alex asked. "After all, it's late, and who knows how long they'll stay and who else is going to come and visit, so—"

Megan laughed softly. "What Alex is trying to say is we're good with the living situation right now and you shouldn't feel bad about it. Okay?"

"You guys are awesome. Thank you."

"We've got the apartment at my place, Summer," Alex suggested. "If your brothers show up and need a place to stay and they don't want to deal with a hotel or people in your guest rooms, they're more than welcome to stay there. Again, you don't have to make a decision tonight, but the offer's there."

She smiled at him. "You are too sweet, Alex. Once I know what's going on, I'll mention that to them as an option. Thank you."

A nurse came out and told them they could all come down to the nursery, and Alex took Megan's hand as they followed the group.

Willow was bundled tightly and had on a little pink knit hat, and when the nurse held her up for the group, Megan didn't even try to hold back the tears. The baby was so tiny and pink and perfect, and she couldn't even imagine how Gabriella must be feeling right now—if her emotions were this out of control, she would think Gabriella's were a hundred times worse.

After a round of pictures and a promise to come back in the morning, they said good night to Zach—who had come out to join them—and all headed out of the hospital.

It was late, and Megan was tired. Luckily, Alex must have been feeling the same because they drove home in companionable silence, holding hands, and it felt…nice. There was never a need to keep a conversation going or to think of something witty or interesting to say. Sometimes the silence was exactly what they needed.

Megan thought about his comments earlier about being disappointed that they hadn't gone out for their romantic dinner date. She smiled. She was amazed that Alex was the kind of man who thought like that. In her experience, dates were usually more of a big deal to the woman. And while she was a little disappointed, she also knew she didn't need to dress up and go to a fancy restaurant for their time together to be considered romantic.

Every day since she'd started staying over—and since he was up and out the door before her—he'd put a pot of coffee on for her, and he always left her a small note to wish her a good day.

Romantic.

Several times—when she had mentioned how she was going to be slammed at work—she'd found he'd packed a lunch for her with an encouraging message on the bag telling her to have a good day and to remember to get outside for a little bit.

Romantic.

The way he had been showing her around the city and letting her set the pace had been perfect. He always held her hand or would find her the most interesting things to see based on something she might have mentioned to him at one time or another.

Romantic.

He cooked dinner for her when she was tired, he rubbed her feet while they watched movies, and he made her breakfast in bed.

So, yeah. She was feeling like Alex had this whole romantic thing down pat.

They pulled up to the house and went inside, and Alex went right to the kitchen and opened the refrigerator.

"I don't know about you, but I'm starving," he said as he rummaged around for something to eat.

"The cafeteria food wasn't so bad—"

He straightened and looked at her with amusement and disbelief. "That was not the freshest sandwich I've ever eaten, and the only reason I finished it was because I was starving then too."

She couldn't argue with that. The food had been a bit on the pitiful side, but considering why they were there eating it, she had managed to tolerate it. But now that they were home, a late-night snack sounded pretty good. Walking over to the refrigerator, she peered inside too.

"What are you in the mood for?" he asked, bending to search. "We can have sandwiches, omelets…there's some leftover chicken from last night…I can whip up some pasta…"

"Oh, don't do that," she said. "Let's not make a big mess. Sandwiches are fine. Quick and easy and very little cleanup."

"Deal," he agreed.

Together, they made a light meal and cleaned up as they went along. Rather than sitting at the kitchen table, they walked into the living room and sat on the couch. Alex turned on the television, and they watched some classic reruns while they ate.

During a commercial, Alex looked at her and softly asked, "What are you thinking about right now?"

"Baby blankets. Something soft and pink and very feminine," she replied without really thinking. Not that it wasn't true; ever since she'd seen Willow, her mind had been going wild with ideas for something special for her.

"I suppose you'll be shopping online first thing in the morning," he said before taking another bite of his sandwich.

Being so secretive with him over her hobby was getting crazy. She knew that. Alex was nothing like her father, and she knew he wouldn't make fun of her or berate her for what she was doing. Maybe when they went upstairs…?

The idea had merit, but she decided to finish her snack and relax before saying anything to him.

When she was done, Megan let her head rest against

the couch. "Okay, that was exactly what I needed, but now I may have to sleep right here."

Alex's pose mimicked hers. "Because?"

"I'm tired, and now my belly is full. The thought of moving is not appealing at all." She yawned loudly. "Besides, we're grown-ups. We can sleep where we want, and this sofa is huge. I think it's bigger than the bed. Wake me when there's pancakes."

Beside her, she heard Alex's soft laugh. "Oh, no, you don't," he said, his voice a mere whisper. Even with her eyes closed, she knew he had turned off the television and was moving around, putting their paper plates and napkins in the trash. Before she could bring herself to open her eyes, Alex gently took one of her hands and maneuvered her until he could easily lift her into his arms.

"Alex—"

"Shh…you're way too tired to argue, and personally, I enjoy sleeping in a bed. Particularly if you're right there beside me, so…let me."

In all honesty, it was nice. She knew she should feel a little guilty he was carrying her around the house—and that's exactly what he was doing. With her in his arms, he was locking the doors, turning off the lights, setting the alarm. Megan rested her head on his shoulder and murmured sleepily. At this rate, she'd be asleep before they reached the bedroom.

"Oh, wait," he murmured, and she knew they were heading toward the kitchen. "My phone's almost dead. I need to put it on the charger."

As comfortable as she was, she knew it was ridiculous now to stay where she was. "Mine too," she said around another yawn. "Let me down, and I'll grab it."

"Where is it?"

"My purse."

Without releasing her, Alex walked over to where she'd put her purse down when they walked in. He found her phone, walked to the kitchen and plugged it in right next to his.

"Okay, now that's it," he said.

"You're sure?"

Nodding, he kissed her on the forehead. "Positive."

He walked across the room, turned off the last of the lights, and began to climb the stairs. Once they were up in the bedroom, he laid her gently on the bed and helped her get undressed. While she was barely able to stay sitting up, he walked over and grabbed one of his T-shirts for her to sleep in. She hadn't moved all of her things over, and on the nights when she did wear something to sleep in, it tended to be one of his shirts.

Gently, he slipped the garment over her head and helped her get her arms through the sleeves. Megan watched in amazement as Alex managed to pull the blankets down without disturbing her too much and then quickly undressed. They slid beneath the sheets together, and he immediately wrapped her in his arms.

Then she remembered she had something to tell him. Shifting slightly, she looked at him. "Alex, there's something I wanted to talk to you about."

Even though it was dark, she could hear him yawn. "Now?" he asked softly. "Is everything okay?"

Another yawn.

"Everything's fine. I just...I wanted to tell you about—" And dammit, now she had to yawn.

"Tell you what," he said, his tone going sleepy.

"Hold that thought, and we'll talk about it in the morning, okay?"

"Okay." Kissing him on the chest, Megan realized waiting a few more hours wasn't going to hurt. And besides, she was way too comfortable and sleepy to talk anyway.

"Good night, beautiful girl."

And just as she was about to fall asleep, she smiled at his comment.

Romantic.

The next morning, Alex stood in the middle of his guest room and watched as Megan took several boxes, cases, and baskets from the closet. When she had everything on the bed, she stood back and motioned to it all.

"What exactly am I looking at?" he asked.

That's when she started pulling things out—yarn, ribbons, scissors, crochet hooks, measuring tapes...

"Are you thinking of learning how to knit or something?"

With a small huff of exasperation, she faced him. "First of all, this is all for crocheting, not knitting. And—" With a short pause, she began to pull out some of the items she'd made. "This is what I do in my spare time," she said with just a hint of defensiveness. "I make baby blankets and hats, dresses, sweaters, booties—"

"So all the stuff you gave to Summer—"

"I made myself."

Then she really looked defensive as she seemed to wait for his response.

"O-kay," he began hesitantly, slowly stepping forward and looking at the tiny garments. Then he looked at her and smiled. "Megan, this is amazing! I mean, seriously amazing!" He held up a tiny sweater and marveled at the craftsmanship. It was delicate and soft and... "Why have you been keeping this a secret?"

She shrugged, but he knew her better than she realized.

"Who do you make these for? Or do you just keep an inventory of them for whenever you might need a gift for a baby?"

With a sigh, Megan sat on the corner of the bed, picked up one of the blankets, and studied it for a moment before she answered him. "My great-grandmother taught me how to crochet when I was a little girl. I was always in awe of the things she would create, and when I expressed an interest, she started to show me how to do it."

Silently, Alex sat down beside her and waited for her to go on.

"I got really good at it, and I started spending my allowance on yarn, and I would make afghans and scarves and whatever else came to mind." She placed the blanket back in one of the boxes and then faced him with a sad expression. "My father told me I was wasting my time and that it was a ridiculous hobby to have. He told me to find something useful to do with my time."

"Oh, Megan. Sweetheart," he said softly, taking one of her hands in his.

With a small smile, she said, "I didn't stop. I just made sure I did it when no one was home or in the privacy of my room with the door locked."

Alex looked at the sheer amount of yarn she had and the finished blankets and garments.

Remembering his earlier question, she finally replied,

"I donate them to hospitals and women's shelters." Her voice was quiet and a little uncertain—as if she was waiting for him to react the way her father had.

"Is that why when I first took you around town you made note of those places?"

She nodded. "I had planned on just doing a Google search, but being out and seeing them in person was the motivation I needed."

He squeezed her hand and pulled her close. With a kiss to her temple, he said, "You're an amazing woman. You know that, right?"

But she pulled back and looked at him. "Remember the day you came and found me at the office? The week after Gabriella went to the hospital?"

He nodded.

Looking down at their joined hands, she said, "Those nights when I said I was working, this is what I was doing." Then she looked up at him. "I don't expect you to understand, but…doing this? Crocheting? Making things for precious little babies? It relaxes me."

"Megan—"

"So I'm not completely hopeless, right? I mean, I do know how to step away from my work and relax and just…be normal."

And right there his heart broke a little bit for her. All this time she had felt the need to put on some sort of armor—something to prove she was a hard worker like the rest of her family, when really, there had always been this softer side of her she was too afraid to let people see.

He knew what he needed to do—what would help her feel comfortable about letting her secret come out.

"How about we have some breakfast, bring some of

these goodies to the hospital with us, and deliver them to the nursery before we go see Gabriella and Willow?"

Her eyes shone with unshed tears, and a slow smile spread across her face. "Really? You...you wouldn't mind?"

"Sweetheart, I think that what you do is incredible, and I can't wait to see the looks of delight on the nurses' faces when you bring these in."

One tear fell and then another. "Thank you."

Shaking his head, Alex leaned in and kissed her before wiping away her tears. "Nothing to thank me for. I'm the one who should be thanking you."

"For what?"

"For trusting me enough to share this with me." Then he paused and grinned.

"What? What are you smiling about?"

"You know now I'm going to want to go to the craft store with you and offer advice on what you should make for Willow, right?"

Her smile was dazzling. "Well? What are we waiting for? It sounds like we have a full day ahead of us!"

Monday morning, Alex walked into the rehab center carrying a tray of coffee for some of the staff. It was something he did from time to time, and today he was in a good mood and wanted to share it. He smiled and waved at the people he passed, and when he got to the therapy room, he saw people setting up and getting ready to work with patients.

"Good morning," he called out. Spotting Tony, Alex held up the tray. "I have coffee!"

"Thanks, man," Tony said as he grabbed a cup. "How was your weekend?"

Alex told him about the bike ride and then about Zach and Gabriella's new baby.

"That had to be cool for you."

"How come?"

"Zach was a patient," he said simply. "When you took him on, he had the worst reputation in our field. No one wanted to work with him, and really, no one was sure he'd ever walk again. Then you came along, and not only is he walking, he's out biking and playing sports again, and now he's married and has a baby. I know it makes me happy, and I don't even know them."

Smiling, Alex took a sip of his coffee. "I am happy. And yeah, it was way more emotional than I thought it would be. Like you, all of those things ran through my mind when he walked out of the delivery room in a pair of scrubs. I thought, 'Look at him. Look how far he's come.'" Alex willed himself to not get choked up again. "It was definitely cool."

Tony took a long drink from his cup before saying anything else. "I was at a conference this weekend, and one of the presenters used your buddy Danny's case in his lecture."

That wasn't anything new. Danny's accident had made the local news, and during the first few years after it, he had gone through most of the rehab centers in hopes of someone finding a therapy that would help him regain some movement.

But they'd all failed.

Then Alex thought of the difference between Danny

and Zach—both had traumatic accidents with very different injuries and outcomes. What Alex wouldn't give for Danny to have had the kind of recovery Zach had and to be living a life where he was celebrating with a wife and baby.

"Can I ask you something?" Tony said after a moment, interrupting Alex's depressing thoughts.

Alex nodded. "Sure."

"What are you doing here?"

Alex looked at him funny. Tony was a good guy—he easily had ten years on Alex—and he was the kind of guy who looked out for everyone. He was one of the lead therapists at the center, and as far as Alex could tell, he'd been doing physical therapy forever.

"What do you mean?"

Putting his coffee down, Tony crossed his arms over his chest. "Look, don't get me wrong, I love having you on staff."

"Okay—"

"But awhile back—maybe a year or two ago—you talked about branching out on your own and starting your own practice. Are you still thinking about it?"

He shrugged. "Sometimes," he admitted, "but it's not a priority. I enjoy being here, and I have some clients I work with on my own plus my work with Danny, but…I don't know. You know the old saying—if it ain't broke, don't fix it."

Tony chuckled. "I know that saying, but…dude, you have so much more to offer. You're young, and you're a gifted therapist. You're bouncing around from place to place. Why?"

"I'm not bouncing around," Alex argued lightly,

wondering where all this was coming from. "I'm here with the center, I have clients on my own—"

"You also work with patients over at Portland General and at Cornerstone Rehab," Tony pointed out.

"Is that what this is about? I'm working for the competition?" Alex asked incredulously.

"That's not what this is about." Tony leaned against the massage table. "I look at you, and I see so much of myself when I was younger—I was ambitious and loved my job and had dreams of starting my own practice. But I never did it. I had the stability of working here, and it was easier to stay than to go. I don't want to see that happen to you."

Well, damn.

"Look, I appreciate what you're saying, but…I'm happy with the way things are. I don't want to leave anyone high and dry, and maybe if the perfect place came along, I'd consider it. But for now…things are good."

Tony gave him a smile that said he understood all too well.

"Just think about it," Tony said after a minute. He straightened and shook Alex's hand before walking away.

Reaching for his coffee, Alex took another long drink and frowned. It had begun to go cold.

It wasn't as if he hadn't thought about starting his own practice. He had. A lot. It wouldn't be hard for him to find a location, nor would it be hard for him to find clients. He turned down requests all the time—most of them were athletes with sports-related injuries. Similar to Zach's but not as extreme. And maybe that was it—he didn't want to be the guy who was giving massages to athletes who pulled a muscle. He enjoyed working with people who required intensive therapy—exactly like Zach.

And Danny.

More than anything, however, he wasn't sure if the time was right, and why rock the boat when things were going so well?

He thought about Megan and how she took a chance—leaving everything and everyone she knew on the east coast to take a job in Portland. Granted, she had her cousins here, but it still meant taking a leap of faith.

Something maybe he should think about a little more.

He worked with the two patients he had at New Hope and left at lunchtime. The thought of surprising Megan at work was appealing, but his mind was still on his conversation with Tony, and he wanted some time to sort things out in his head before he talked to her. Driving around with no particular destination in mind, he began a list of pros and cons for branching out on his own.

Pros: Be his own boss, take on the patients he felt needed him the most, have a more regular schedule.

Cons: Let down his colleagues at New Hope, Cornerstone, and Portland General, say goodbye to his current patients there.

While the list of cons was smaller, it affected him more. One of the things Alex loved most in this world was helping people—helping them heal, helping them achieve their goals. How could he know if leaving was going to hinder someone's recovery? What if their next therapist did things differently and their progress suffered? He wasn't sure he could take that chance. It would be selfish, wouldn't it?

And Alex knew he had many flaws, but being selfish wasn't one of them.

With a sigh, he raked a hand through his hair and continued to drive—this time heading back to the house so he could grab something to eat and maybe work out for a little while to clear his head. It wasn't as if he was giving up on the idea completely, but for now he was going to stay where he was and wait until he knew the time was right.

He thought about Megan and compared their relationship to his current situation. From the moment he met her, Alex knew she was special, but the timing wasn't right. And now look where they were! Things were great and only getting better. Why? Because he hadn't pushed like he had wanted to, and eventually everything had worked out. Chances were—if he were patient again—it would be the same where his career was concerned.

Nodding, he reached out and turned on the radio.

He felt good, like he'd accomplished what he needed to. Waiting. It was the smart decision. The right decision.

But damn if it didn't leave him feeling the slightest bit disappointed.

—⁓—

Whenever the Montgomery family got together to celebrate, it was always loud. It was fun, but more than anything, it was loud. As Megan sat in Zach's backyard and looked around at all the people there, she felt happy.

Willow was only two weeks old, and yet the entire family felt the need to descend upon Portland to meet her. Uncle William and Aunt Monica had arrived with Megan's parents two days ago, and then her cousins

James and Ryder had flown in yesterday with their wives and kids. Summer and Ethan had offered to host the get-together, but Zach had insisted it was easier for him to do it so Willow could sleep in her own space and Gabriella wouldn't have to stress about packing her up.

If there was one thing Megan was coming to realize about her cousin, it was that Zach liked being in control, and if that meant hosting a big family barbecue only two weeks after the birth of his first child, then so be it.

"Megan!"

Looking up, she smiled. "Hi, Uncle William! How are you?"

He was a little grayer than the last time she'd seen him, but his eyes always twinkled with mischief, and when he smiled, it was impossible not to smile with him.

"Splendid. Just splendid," he said as he sat in the seat beside her on the massive deck. "This is one of my favorite ways to pass the time—celebrating another addition to the family."

"It's a wonderful thing."

"That it is," he agreed. "So, tell me how you're liking working in Portland. I'm hearing great things about you."

"Really?" she asked excitedly.

"Would I lie to you?"

Blushing at the praise, she began to tell him about all the things she'd done for Zach's office since her arrival. One of the things she loved most about her uncle was how he had a working knowledge of every aspect of the business; there wasn't a department he wasn't familiar with, and he was also on top of computer trends and technology. He was one of the few members of her family she could talk to without worrying about whether she was boring him.

All around them people were talking about babies and families, and Megan was happily chatting about her job. It hit her about ten minutes into their conversation. Was this normal? Shouldn't she be talking about Zach and Gabriella and Willow too? Deciding that she should, she instantly switched gears.

"It's so nice how everyone was able to come in for this," she said conversationally. "I know it means the world to Zach that the whole family wanted to celebrate with him."

Her uncle studied her for a moment, and she could tell he was a little surprised by her immediate change of subject. But he went along with it anyway.

"I was a bit disappointed that my boys and their families couldn't make it, but they promised they'd come for Willow's christening," he said with a smile. "It will be wonderful to have the entire family in one place. I believe the last time that happened was Zach and Gabriella's wedding." He seemed to beam with pride at the thought of it. "I have to say, they were my most challenging match to make, but I had faith that it would all work out."

Megan laughed softly. Uncle William's matchmaking skills and antics were well known in the family, and she had to wonder if he had any plans to start looking for potential spouses for her and her brothers. Christian and Carter weren't here today, but maybe she should feel her uncle out so she could give them both a heads-up.

"You do have a gift," she said with a sweet smile. "How many matches does that make for you? Five? Six?"

William nodded and seemed to relax a bit. "Well,

there were my boys—Lucas, Jason, and Mac. Then there were your cousins—Ryder, James, Summer, and Zach. Although, if you ask Ryder and James, they'll swear I had nothing to do with it. Summer and Zach were a little more appreciative."

She couldn't help but laugh at the imagery. "So what's next? Planning any matches for the grandchildren yet?"

Her uncle gave her a curious look that transformed into a bit of a secretive smile. "Well now, they're all a little young for that, but you never know. My oldest granddaughter, Lily, claims there's a boy in her class she has a crush on. I may have to check him out for myself and see if there's any potential there."

While she knew he was kidding, she could still imagine him doing it and thought it was incredibly sweet.

Her uncle sighed. "I don't know. I feel like everyone's on to me now. You seem very happy with your young man, and your brothers are…well…let's just say I know when to wave the white flag."

"Wait…you mean you're not going to try to find anyone for Carter or Christian?"

William shook his head. "I'm pretty certain Carter's avoiding me. I've been to all of his restaurants, and he's never around. And Christian?" This time his sigh was infinitely wearier. "That boy must have had something serious happen because he's very withdrawn and almost hostile when it comes to social situations. Even if I wanted to try to find the perfect woman for him, I have no idea where to begin."

"Never stopped you before," she murmured, reaching for her glass of wine.

"So how are things with you and Alex?" he asked. "You know, the first time I met him I felt like he was part of the family."

Smiling, Megan turned to try to find Alex in the crowd and spotted him talking to her mother and Aunt Monica. She chuckled at the wide-eyed expression on his face and had to wonder what they were talking to him about to put that look there. William followed her gaze and started to laugh.

"I don't know what has been going on between your aunt and your mother lately, but they've been as thick as thieves with one another. And it seems like they've cornered poor Alex. Do we need to go and save him?" he asked with a wink.

She considered it for a moment but figured Alex could handle himself for a little while longer. For now, she was enjoying her conversation with her uncle. "I'm sure he's fine. He's been around our family enough to know how we can be."

William nodded. "True." But he turned and looked at the three of them again. "Still…he looks awfully serious, and I don't think my wife has stopped talking for a full three minutes," he said with a small laugh. "I can't imagine what they're talking about."

Megan was kind of wondering the same thing.

"Whatever it is, I'm sure if he needs rescuing, he'll let someone know," William said.

Maybe, she thought. "So…you were mentioning Christian being hostile with social situations. I haven't noticed. What have you heard?"

"Oh, it's not what I've heard, it's what I know! I've been out to San Diego many, many times, and your

brother simply refuses to engage in anything social—
he'll go if it's a small family event—but anything
for the company, he refuses." He gave her a serious
look. "Ryder started up that office and had a tradition
of company events—holiday parties, softball games,
retreats—and Christian wants no part of them. Luckily
other executives have stepped up, but it doesn't exactly
present a good image for the head of the company not to
want to be around his employees."

"That does seem odd," she commented. "I wonder
why—"

"Megan?"

From across the deck, she heard Alex call her name.
Turning around, she saw him waving her over and could
barely suppress a grin. She looked at her uncle. "I guess
he needs saving."

He laughed as he stood and then held out a hand to
her to help her to her feet. "That's probably not a bad
thing. I'm curious as heck to hear what's been going on
over there, so if it's all right, I'll walk over with you."

"I'd love that."

Together they walked over to join Alex, and she saw
the immediate relief on his face when she was there.
He kissed her on the cheek and tucked her in close at
his side.

"So what are we talking about, ladies?" William asked
as he sat beside his wife and kissed her on the cheek too.

"Oh, we were asking Alex about his job and his
family," Monica said with a big smile. "I always worry
this group will overwhelm people, but Alex seems at
ease with all of us, and I was curious if he was from a
large family as well."

William looked up at Alex. "And are you?"

Alex shook his head. "I have one sibling, and my parents each only have one sibling, so really…comparably…we're a much smaller group."

"And he's close with them," Megan's mother said, sounding pleased.

Megan almost groaned. Her mother's interest in Alex she could understand. After all, it had been a long time since Megan had been involved with anyone and even longer since she'd brought anyone around her family. Unfortunately, that made Alex someone to be observed like an animal at the zoo or something.

"Is your family close by?" Aunt Monica asked. "Are they here in Portland? Is this where you're originally from?"

"I was born and raised here in Portland," Alex responded, "and my family—my parents—currently live about twenty minutes away in Burlington."

"How nice to have them so close by."

"Mom…" Megan said, and even though she was smiling, she put a hint of warning in her voice.

"What?" her mother asked innocently. "I think it's nice to have family close by. Not that I would know what it's like, but I can imagine it would be wonderful—especially for Alex's parents."

She groaned and began to wonder how she could have felt so happy and carefree just moments ago.

Alex's arm around her waist tightened slightly as if he was silently telling her he understood how she was feeling. "My folks travel a lot now," he said to the group of them. "And honestly, we only see each other about once a month and sometimes not even that."

Aunt Monica spoke before Megan's mother could. "All of our boys still live close to home. They're married now and have children, but it's so nice to have them nearby. Plus, they all work with William, so we see them all the time."

Megan's mother sighed. "Whereas my children scattered all over the country, and I have no grandchildren of my own." Then she looked directly at Alex and Megan and added, "Yet."

"Mom!"

Aunt Monica patted her mother's knee. "Now, now, Eliza...don't start pressuring the two of them. When the time is right, it will happen." Then she smiled up at Megan and Alex. "And the two of you look so happy together. It's been a pleasure watching you all this time."

"Um...thank you," Megan murmured, unsure what her response should be.

"I remember seeing the two of you dancing at Zach and Gabriella's wedding," she went on, "and I saw the sparks back then." She paused and smiled at Eliza. "And I know that, personally, I was thrilled when I heard you had finally moved here and started dating Alex. The two of you make such an attractive couple—just like I knew you would."

Out of the corner of her eye, Megan saw Summer watching her with amusement. "Um...if you'll excuse us, it looks like Summer needs us. We'll talk to you later!" And with that, Megan took Alex's hand and led him away. When they approached her cousin, Megan sagged with relief.

"Were you two getting the third degree?" Summer asked.

"Not so much me as Alex."

He nodded. "I don't know what kind of fascination your family has with me, but it's been going on almost since the wedding."

Both Megan and Summer stared at him in stunned silence.

"Um…I mean…they're just overly curious about me, and they ask a lot of questions and—"

"Wait, what do you mean they've been fascinated with you since the wedding? When have you seen them?" Megan asked.

Before he could answer, Summer did. "I knew Aunt Monica and your mom talked to Alex when they were here after Amber was born, but I just thought they had some physical therapy stuff they wanted to talk to you about."

He nodded again. "That's how it seemed at first, but their interest quickly turned toward more interest in me—personally."

"And what about before that? Amber's only a few months old, and Zach and Gabriella have been married for two years," Megan commented. "When else have you had conversations with them?"

"Yeah, Alex," Summer said, crossing her arms and studying him. "When?"

"I, um…I don't…" He looked nervously toward Megan's aunts and uncle, and Megan saw them looking back in return.

"Oh, for the love of all," she murmured. "Is this my uncle doing his matchmaking thing again?"

"I haven't talked to your uncle," Alex said. "This was primarily your mother and your Aunt Monica."

"Well, that's odd," Summer said. "Maybe they're just curious about you."

"Maybe. But—"

"But what?" Megan asked.

"Everyone!" Zach called out. "Lunch is served!"

And Megan knew she was going to have to wait for her answer.

—◦◦◦—

"Not so fast," William said when his wife went to join the group to get some food. He held her hand before leading her to the far end of the deck where he knew no one would overhear them.

Monica looked nervously over her shoulder as Eliza walked away. She turned to her husband. "Honestly, William, I'm starving. And those steaks and burgers have had my mouth watering for the past thirty minutes."

"And you'll get to eat as soon as you tell me what's going on," he said with amusement.

She looked at him with all wide-eyed innocence. "I don't know what you mean."

But he knew his wife well. He knew when she thought she was being clever. "You were grilling poor Alex a few minutes ago and then talking babies in front of poor Megan. She looked like a deer caught in the headlights."

She waved him off. "Oh, don't be dramatic, William. You know how much Eliza wants to see her kids settled like ours. And it's only natural to start making comments like that when you see a couple who is so perfect for each other."

He quirked a brow at her. "Really? And you know

they're perfect for each other after only being around them this one time?"

She looked away briefly. "Well…like I said, I saw them at the wedding together and thought how good they looked together and—"

"Looks can be deceiving," he commented. "For all you know, the two of them have absolutely nothing in common."

Monica looked up at him, and he swore he saw a hint of triumph in her eyes. "That's where you're wrong—both of them have strong work ethics and are close to their families. They're both fans of the same music and have similar tastes in food. And Megan—even though she's never been one for the outdoors—has said how much she wished she got out more. Alex has been taking her on little adventures every weekend since she arrived here."

He nodded approvingly. "And you learned all of this in the past few minutes?" *It was almost too easy to get her to confess all*, he thought.

"Of course not," she said distractedly, watching everyone getting food. "Eliza and I have been watching them ever since the wedding." Then she realized what she had said, and her hands flew to her mouth.

William leaned in and bent over until they were almost nose to nose. "Are you trying to take my place as the matchmaker in the family, Monica? You couldn't possibly know this would be a good connection for Megan," he said with amusement.

She gave him a smug smile. "That's where you're wrong. Eliza and I were very careful collecting our data. Seeing as how Megan is her daughter, it didn't take much for her to know her interests and what she was looking for. A couple of carefully worded inquiries in some conversations, and she had a good idea of the kind of man Megan was looking for."

"And what about Alex? How could you have possibly found information on him? The only time I remember you coming to Portland after the wedding was when Summer had the baby."

Another smug smile. "That was easy. Zach is our godchild, William, and I took a lot of interest in his recovery. Alex was on my radar long before I saw him dance with Megan. So I already had some insight into who he was. Every once in a while I would get an update from Janice on how Zach was doing, and let's just say that maybe—occasionally—I'd call Alex and talk to him about it. Nothing behind Zach's back."

He had to hand it to his wife—she was crafty. Clearly she'd been paying attention to how he did things these past several years.

"Admit it, William. You're impressed."

Why deny it? Leaning in, he kissed her softly on the cheek. "That I am, my dear. That I am."

"Who knows? Now that I've got this feather in my cap, I may see who I can fix up next!"

Wait…was she seriously thinking she could start matchmaking to the rest of the family? Not that there were many left, but…still.

He patted her on the shoulder. "You did a good thing, but…I'm still curious how you were going to handle this if Megan's job hadn't ended in New York. Opposite coasts is enough of a deterrent to keep people from being together."

"That was a little trickier."

"Monica," he said in hushed tones, "you didn't get that girl fired, did you?"

"Of course not!" she cried. "Honestly, William, that would be wrong on every level. I refuse to play God like that."

"Then how—"

"Megan knew her contract was almost up and had been worrying about where she was going to work next. Eliza dropped a couple of hints with Joseph, who talked to Robert, who—"

"Talked to me," William finished for her. *Son of a gun.* "So, really, I helped in this match."

She gave him a stern look. "You can't let me have this, can you?"

He shook his head, pleased. "I worked very hard to convince Zach to hire Megan."

"You did not," Monica argued. "Zach needed an IT person, and he has no issues working with family, considering his own sister works with him in his office along with his wife and all of his cousins throughout the corporation. So don't even go there."

With a hearty laugh, he hugged her close and kissed her soundly. "Fine. This one's all on you."

Now it was Monica's turn to look pleased. "Thank you." She paused. "Now can we go and eat?"

"Absolutely." And when they started to walk arm in arm toward the food, he said, "Of course, if I had handled this match, it wouldn't have taken two years."

Monica threw her head back and laughed even as she elbowed him in the ribs.

—⁂—

"Just think, in another six to eight weeks, we get to do it again," Megan said later that night as they walked into Alex's house.

"And there will be more of them, won't there?" he asked.

Nodding, Megan tossed her purse on the table and went to the kitchen to grab something to drink. "From what Gabriella was saying today, it seems like Willow's christening is going to be almost as big as the wedding."

"That can't be right."

"Okay, maybe that was a slight exaggeration, but this time the entire family is coming—all the cousins, all their kids—which makes for a large crowd."

He was aware.

Having known Zach for almost three years, Alex had met most of the Montgomery family, and for the most part, they were a great bunch of people—very personable. But this thing with Megan's mom and her aunts was getting…strange. Although, if anything, now was the time he should be expecting it. After all, he and Megan were dating, and things were serious between them, so he guessed it was only fitting that her mother would start grilling him on his intentions.

Alex laughed to himself at the image of how Eliza and Monica Montgomery would react if he told them his intentions and how he was more than ready to make a commitment to Megan and move the relationship forward. He imagined their eyes going wide and how pleased they'd be.

"Do you want something to drink?" Megan called out.

Megan, on the other hand, would probably freak out

if he announced to her family that he already envisioned them married with children.

And hell, he should probably talk to her about that before talking to her family.

"Alex?"

Oh, right. A drink.

"No, thanks," he said as he walked into the kitchen. It hit him—and not for the first time—how she was at home here. In his house. Since the first night they made love, she hadn't spent another night in Summer's guesthouse. Part of him felt guilty about it because she had seemed excited to have a place of her own and to be spending time with her cousin, but the other part of him was so damn happy to have her there with him.

Now when he looked around his house, there was a little bit of her in every room. She had put her stamp on so much of his space, and he loved it. Her crocheting basket sat next to the end of the sofa in the living room, and the afghan she'd made for them was currently folded on the ottoman in the corner. For a woman who didn't think of herself as soft or girly, she certainly had put a lot of feminine touches all around him. Just the thought of her not being here bothered him.

Would she want to move back to Summer's once the whole family went back to North Carolina? Was he making assumptions about her wanting to be here with him all the time because she was afraid of hurting his feelings? They hadn't talked about it since the night Willow was born.

One of the things he realized about the two of them was how they could talk for hours about a hundred different topics—like books or movies, his job, her job, her crocheting projects and techniques—but they never talked about them—as a couple.

"You're looking pretty intense over there," she said, closing the refrigerator door. "Everything okay?"

He nodded, reaching for her hand. "Did you have a good time today?"

She smiled. "I did. But then again, I usually have a good time with my family. I wish more of my cousins could have been there, but that will happen soon enough."

"Six to eight weeks," he said with a wink and led her into the living room. They sat on the sofa, and Megan reached for the TV remote.

"Anything good on tonight?"

Before she could turn it on, he gently took the remote from her hand and put it down. "Actually, I was kind of hoping we could talk."

Something in his tone must have alarmed her because her eyes went a little wide. "Oh, God…my mom and my aunt totally freaked you out, didn't they?" She muttered a curse. "Why didn't you come and get me sooner? Or why didn't you tell me how they've done this sort of thing before? If I had known, I would have put a stop to it!"

They were getting off track. He didn't want to talk about her aunt or her mother or the rest of her family. Not really. What he wanted more than anything was to see if they were on the same page.

"How did you feel about living in the guesthouse?" he asked, hoping she'd accept his sudden change of subject.

"Um…what?"

"I mean, I know you liked it because it meant you had

a space of your own and it kept you close to Summer, but…you didn't bring all of your stuff with you when everyone arrived, and I guess I'm wondering if you're going to want to go back there. You know…in between now and the next family invasion."

"Why? Do you…do you want me to go back there?" He saw her swallow hard, and she went to pull her hand away, but he wouldn't let her. "It's all my stuff, right? I sort of moved in here and took over and…" She looked around the room a bit frantically. "I realize we sort of fell into this routine, but if I'm overstepping some bounds here, that's totally fine. I get it. Really."

"Megan," he began, "that's not what I'm saying." He stopped and tried to find the right words to say. "What I meant is…I *like* how things are going. A lot. But I know we sort of just…'fell into this routine.'" He smiled as he used her words to make a point. "It wouldn't have happened like this if you lived in an apartment across town of your own, but I wanted to make sure I wasn't putting any pressure on you to stay here. With me. In the house."

Shifting his position so he could face her, he went on. "I know it was presumptuous of me to think you would want to pick up where we left off, and maybe lending you a car and offering to show you around the city and stuff made you feel…obligated—"

"Oh my God…do you think I'm sleeping with you because you lent me your car?" she cried, and this time she pulled her hand free before putting more space between them. "Seriously, Alex, is that what you're thinking? What kind of person do you think I am?"

Okay, he was screwing this up…

"That is not what I'm thinking, Megan. I swear! I'm

honestly thinking I'm the one behaving questionably! I don't want you to think I did all these things to… manipulate or orchestrate us getting together."

Sighing, Megan stood and paced a few feet away from the sofa before turning around and facing him. "Alex, I'm not going to lie to you, it did feel a little… I'll use your word, 'orchestrated.' And at first, I wanted to be annoyed with you about it. But the more time we spent together, the happier I was that you did it. If left to my own devices, I would have played hard to get because I thought it was what I was supposed to do."

Alex stood and walked over to her, happy that she didn't move away when he took her hands in his again. "And I'm not going to lie to you—I had a feeling you were going to do your best to blow me off. It didn't matter how many time we got thrown together because of your cousins, you were a little…aloof with me."

She blushed and looked at the floor.

"But," he went on, gently tugging her hand to get her attention, "I think we would have ended up where we are right now no matter what. Why? Because this is good, Megan. Really good."

She nodded but didn't respond.

"I think we landed in this place together without talking about it, and that's kind of what I was getting at. I'll admit my presentation wasn't the best, but that's what I was trying to do. I want us to talk about this. Us. Where we're going."

"Oh."

He couldn't tell if that was a good 'oh' or a bad 'oh.' It was kind of neutral.

Honestly, he was kind of hoping she'd say something

first. He felt like he was the one putting it all out there—
his feelings—while she was merely listening and commenting. Right now, he still wasn't confident about
where they stood.

Which was what he said to her.

"Alex, this is the healthiest relationship I've ever
been in," she began. "I spent a lot of years feeling inferior and not having a good self-image because of things
the men I'd dated had said to me or made me feel."

This is brand-new information, he thought. "You
never mentioned that to me," he said softly, leading her
back to the sofa to sit down.

She tucked a stray strand of hair behind her ear.
"I guess I always had a bit of an inferiority complex
because of my family. That part I told you. But…" She
sighed. "It got worse for me after college. I dated this
guy after I graduated, and we were together for a year.
He used to tell me all the time how I needed to lose
weight and that I looked frumpy and chubby, and…I
don't know. He got into my head. He was my first long-
term relationship, and for some reason I accepted the
things he said to me because I was afraid that if I broke
up with him no one else would want me."

With her hand still in his, he gently caressed her
knuckles and wondered what he could possibly say that
wouldn't come off sounding trite.

"When I met you at the wedding, I was so out of my
comfort zone. My mother talked me into buying that
dress and those shoes, and…as much as I resented her
for it at first, I also felt a little empowered by that outfit.
And then to have someone like you find me attractive?
That really boosted my confidence."

He couldn't help but smile at her words.

"That's why I was so insecure when I moved here and we reconnected. I knew what you were remembering, and I knew I wasn't that woman. Not really."

"Megan, we've been over all of that. The woman you are right now is who I want. She's the woman I'm drawn to." He paused. "She's the woman I'm falling for."

Her big brown eyes went wide as she gasped at his words. "You're…you're…"

He nodded. "I think about us all the time. I wish things had been a little more conventional where we're concerned, but…I kind of like that this is us too. We're a little unconventional, but it works. And I want it to keep working. I don't want you to be a temporary houseguest here. I want us to talk about life beyond Willow's christening."

"Oh, Alex—"

"I know it's scary—you're still finding your way with the job and Montgomerys, and I know how you like to have time to think things through, but…how am I supposed to know if you're thinking about these things if we don't talk about them?"

She laughed softly. "I think about it a lot too."

Now it was his turn for his eyes to go wide. "Really?"

"Uh-huh. Actually, I think about it—us—all the time. I was afraid to jinx things by mentioning it. Everything has been going so well that I didn't want to mess it up."

"Baby, you never have to worry about that with me. I want us to talk—I want you to feel comfortable coming to me and talking about your fears and your hopes and… everything!" Relief washed over him as he pulled her into his arms and kissed her.

When she lifted her head a moment later, she smiled at him. "I really like when you do that."

"Oh yeah?"

She nodded. "Yeah. Definitely."

"Well, how do you like it when I offer to take you upstairs to our bedroom and make love to you in our bed?"

He hoped she caught on to the emphasis on the word *our*.

Her smile was slow and sweet. "I like it when you do that too. But you know what I like the most?"

He shook his head as he rubbed his thumb on her cheek.

"I really like it when we wake up in our bed all wrapped up in one another and make plans for how we're going to spend the day together." Then she gave him a shy smile. "And then we put those plans on hold to make love again."

Alex carefully stood and pulled her to her feet. "Then brace yourself, because you are going to be one very happy woman starting right now."

Chapter 9

IF THERE WAS ONE THING MEGAN LOVED ABOUT ALEX, IT was how he was a man of his word. So when he said to brace herself, she did.

And she was *very* happy about it.

The sun was starting to come up, and they were tangled together, and even though they couldn't have had more than a few hours of sleep, she felt perfectly content. Snuggling closer to Alex, she placed a kiss on his chest and felt his arms tighten around her.

"You can't be awake already," he said sleepily. "If you're awake, that means I've overslept."

Megan laughed softly and kissed him again. It was true that he was the early riser of the two of them. She was content to stay in bed and hit the snooze button on her alarm several times when she needed to get up, whereas Alex didn't even need an alarm.

"It's a Sunday," she softly reminded him. "You can't oversleep on a Sunday. It's impossible."

Placing a kiss on the top of her head, he said, "I disagree. What if we had plans to leave the house early and go…say…camping."

That had her laughing a bit harder. "There are so many things wrong with that sentence that I don't even know where to begin."

Alex pulled back and looked at her with mild amusement. "What could possibly be wrong with that?"

"For starters, no one leaves on a Sunday morning to go camping. That's just crazy. And secondly, I would never go camping. Like, ever. So…you never have to worry about saying I've overslept for that."

"You should try it."

She shook her head. "Nope. I enjoy sleeping in a bed, indoor plumbing, and having heat in the winter and air-conditioning in the summer. Oh, and electricity," she added while fighting the urge to laugh again. "I'm a big fan of electricity."

He shook his head. "Everyone should camp out at least once. I'm not saying it has to be a weeklong thing—"

She placed a finger over his lips and shook her head again. "The closest you will ever get me to camping is sitting on the back porch making s'mores over the fire pit. That's it."

"You don't know what you're missing," he said casually.

"Bug bites, a bad night's sleep, getting eaten by a bear…the list is endless, I'm sure."

This time he laughed. "What if I promised to take you to a bear-free campsite? Would you try it?"

Megan held firm. "Sorry. No can do. I'll go walking in the park and even do a little hiking, but beyond that, it's a hard no."

"And here I was thinking I had found the perfect woman," he said as he rolled over.

"And someone who camps is your perfect woman?" she asked, maneuvering so she was now lying on top of him.

Nodding, he said, "Definitely." Then he sighed.

"Well, we gave it a try, and it didn't work." Another sigh. "I guess we'll look back on this someday and laugh and...ow!" he cried out with a laugh when she smacked him on the arm.

"How would you like it if I told you my perfect man wasn't outdoorsy? How would that make you feel?" she questioned.

Alex anchored a hand in her long hair and gripped it. "I wouldn't like it because I'd know you were lying. Or teasing," he added, guiding her closer. His voice went husky when her lips were almost to his. "Just like I'm teasing right now. I don't care if you don't want to camp, Megan. Don't get me wrong, I would love to do that with you—to have that experience with you—but it's not so important to me that I'd give this up."

Her smile was slow and sexy as she wiggled against him and felt how he was already aroused. "Good. Because I don't want you to give this up." Then she kissed him and hummed her approval as his free hand smoothed down her spine. He squeezed her bottom as he moved against her.

The kiss went from slow and languid to wet and untamed. When Megan moved to catch her breath, Alex gently nipped at her neck. "Is this what you were talking about last night?" he murmured against her skin. "This kind of tangled-up morning where we forget about everything else?"

With a moan of pleasure, she continued to move with him. "Yes..."

"Then you know this was all part of my plan when I told you to brace yourself last night," he said, rolling them so she was beneath him. He took her hands in his and pinned them above her head on the pillows. "And there's nothing I want more in this world than to make you happy."

Alex was good with words.

But his actions were even better.

A week later, Megan was sitting in her office when her phone rang. Looking down, she saw her father's name on the screen. Panic instantly filled her because her father never called her. Something had to be wrong.

"Dad?" she answered anxiously.

Joseph Montgomery chuckled. "Did I catch you at a bad time, Megan? You sound a little out of sorts."

She instantly relaxed and let out a breath. "I… no…I'm fine. I guess I was a little surprised to see your name on my phone. I thought something was wrong."

He laughed again. "I can see why you'd think that. Your mother is usually the one to call, and then I simply get on the phone and say a quick hello."

At least he's aware of it, she thought.

"So what's up, Dad? Everything okay?"

"I've been hearing a lot of good things about you," he began. "It sounds like the transition to the new programs and new system went more smoothly than anyone expected. As a matter of fact, you now hold the record of the fastest and most efficient installation in company history."

"Really?" she squeaked, unable to hide her glee at the praise.

"Really," Joseph said. "I'm not going to lie to you, I wasn't so sure you were up to the task when we first talked about offering you the position. The company you were working for in Albany is tiny in comparison to Montgomerys."

"It was, but computers are something I'm good with, Dad. And once I had everything set up, it was just a matter of training the staff properly. We had a great system in place to work with everyone in smaller and more diverse groups, and Zach was pretty emphatic about our time management, so all in all, it was the perfect combination."

"I'm proud of you, Megan," he said. "I know I don't say that to you nearly as often as I should, but it's true. I'm seriously impressed with all you've accomplished."

She wanted to put the phone down and do a little victory dance right there next to her desk, but she knew she'd have to wait at least a little while to do that.

"Thanks, Dad. That means a lot to me."

"I was in a meeting with your Uncle William and Uncle Robert, and we want to extend a position to you."

Her eyes went a little wide. "Oh?"

"I know we talked about it when you were first hired, but after seeing the kind of results you've achieved, we want you to keep going with it throughout the company."

Megan's heart began to race. This was it! This was what she'd been waiting for! "O-kay—"

"We're going to need you to hit our San Diego office and work with Christian and his staff, then come to North Carolina to work in Charlotte with Uncle William's people, and then Chapel Hill for Robert's people. Then you'll come to New York and work with my staff. How does that sound?"

"It sounds like I'll be living out of a suitcase for a

while," she said with a nervous laugh. Thinking about having the position was one thing; planning it and seeing how time-consuming it was going to be was quite another.

"Don't be ridiculous. It's not all going to happen at once—although we are all looking forward to making the transition sooner rather than later. And you won't be working alone, so it's not like you'll have to stay in any one place for an extended period of time. You'll have a team of people working under you who can handle most of the grunt work. You're going to be the executive IT director, Megan. That means you can delegate responsibilities. What we most want from you is to make sure things happen in the same timely manner as they have in Zach's office."

She breathed a little easier. "Oh. Okay. I can do that."

"I know you can," her father said confidently. "William is on the phone with Zach now discussing when he feels will be a good time for you to step away and meet with Christian first. No one wants Zach to be left shorthanded, so the two of you will have to work out who will cover your responsibilities while you're gone or if Zach will have to hire someone to take over the position."

"But…I enjoy working here," Megan said defensively. "I'd like Portland to be my base office, Dad."

"And it can be, but Zach is still going to need someone there to handle any problems while you're gone. That's common sense."

"I get that, but—" Then she stopped herself. "I'll talk to Zach about it."

"Very good. Once you get a timeline in place with

him, we'll have a conference call to get things going and put your travel plans in place."

"How come I'm starting with Christian? I would have thought I'd start with either you or Uncle William."

"Christian's got a smaller staff, and the process should go faster. Plus I'd like for you to check on him."

"Check on him? Why?"

"I'm hoping that having you work there will force him to interact with his staff a little more. We've had several complaints about his disinterest in working with just about anyone. Which is a complete change from how he was with our London office. So naturally, we're concerned."

"Dad, this isn't new information. Everyone's been going on about this for years. Obviously this is who he is now. If people are so upset by it, why not send him back to London?"

"Because he doesn't want that either," Joseph said sadly. "I don't know what to do with him."

Thinking about the conversation she and Alex had had a while back, she said, "It's a lot of pressure for him, don't you think?"

"What do you mean?"

"Well…Christian was—for a while—the only one of the three of us to work for Montgomerys. I'm sure he felt a lot of pressure to make you proud and do things in a way that would meet with your approval."

Her father didn't make a sound, and she questioned whether to go on but ultimately did.

"We all want our parents' approval, Dad. That's natural. But…what if this corporate life isn't what he wants anymore and he doesn't know how to get out of it?"

"I guess I didn't want to consider that," he said in a low voice. "It wasn't an issue with any of your cousins—they all willingly went into the business. Part of me was a little embarrassed at how my own kids didn't want to follow suit."

"I did," Megan said, her voice equally low.

"I didn't want that life for you. I wanted to see you with someone who would take care of you. This world—this corporate world—there are times when it leaves little time for a life. It's not what I wanted for you, Megan."

"It wasn't your choice to make," she said, her heart hammering in her chest at how brutally honest she was being. "I'm not saying this is the perfect life, but I enjoy what I do. I worked so hard for so long for you to notice me and not pass me over as some sort of…I don't know…trophy child or something."

"Megan, you see how much I worked when you kids were growing up, you're seeing how miserable Christian is now—can you honestly say you want that for yourself?"

Suddenly she wasn't so sure.

"But that's not the case for everyone. Summer's found a balance between work and motherhood, Zach has cut back on his hours—"

"Zach fell off of a mountain. He didn't have a choice but to reevaluate his life."

"Okay, maybe Zach's not the best example. But Mac and Jason and Ryder and Lucas…they're all making it work," she argued, but she wasn't sure why.

"But it was a rocky road for them. Remember that." He paused. "No matter what you do, Megan—whether it's working for Montgomerys or not—I'm proud of you and want you to be happy."

"Thanks, Dad."

"And I'm sure you have work to do and want to talk to Zach about scheduling, so—" He stopped and sighed. "Just know you can talk to me. It doesn't have to be about work. I enjoy hearing about your life. I should say that a little more, huh?"

Unable to help herself, she smiled even as she felt the sting of tears at his heartfelt words. "I could say it too."

"We'll both have to remember to try a little harder, right?"

"Absolutely."

They talked about how she was enjoying Portland and about some of the places Alex had shown her and how much she was doing in her spare time.

And then he specifically asked about Alex.

"And he treats you well?" he asked, sounding very much like a disapproving parent.

"He treats me better than I ever imagined a man could treat a woman," she replied. "He's kind and considerate, and he makes me laugh, and he challenges me to try new things," she explained, and then paused and thought. "But more than anything, Dad, he accepts me for who I am. I've never dated someone who did that."

"Everyone tells me how wonderful he is," Joseph said begrudgingly, "but in my mind no man is ever going to be good enough for you."

And her smile grew. "Alex is. Trust me. He's just… he's everything."

Joseph said, "Then I guess I'll have to approve. I don't want to. You're my baby girl, after all."

"Aww, Dad…"

Then he cleared his throat, and she knew this senti-mental time was over. Her father didn't do sentimental for more than a few minutes at a time, if at all. And she was glad she'd had those few precious moments to experience it.

"So I guess we'll talk soon," he said, his voice getting businesslike again.

"As soon as I talk to Zach, we'll set up a conference call."

"Okay, then. I'll be looking forward to it."

"Me too."

"Good."

"Okay," she said and was about to say goodbye when she felt a little choked up with emotion. "Thank you, Dad. For believing in me."

"I always have, baby girl."

And when she hung up the phone, Megan spun in her chair, and rather than jump up and do her victory dance, she wiped away those few tears she couldn't hold back and let herself relish those last few words.

They never talked about it, and she realized how she had missed the signs—mainly because they weren't the same ones he was showing to her brothers.

There were ones that were especially for her.

If she hadn't been so busy looking at how Christian and Carter were being treated, maybe she wouldn't have felt forced to work so hard to be successful. To be seen.

Another pothole to working hard that she walked right into.

Another missed opportunity because she had been

so focused on her own goals or what she thought was expected of her.

This was who she'd been—who she was—for so long that she wasn't sure what she was supposed to be from this point on. More than anything, she wanted to talk to Alex and share her good news. He was always a good sounding board for her, and right then and there she knew that as soon as she got home, they'd talk, and he'd help her make sense of everything.

He'd make everything all right.

—⁓—

"Stop. Please."

Alex looked up and gave a weak smile. "This is very important. You know this. We've gone over it so many times. We need to keep your muscles moving so—"

"Alex," Danny said, his voice weak and breathless, "please. I need you…to stop and listen…to me."

The fact that his friend's voice sounded labored bothered him. It was happening more and more lately. And it wasn't surprising to him; in fact, he knew it was only a matter of time until things like this started to happen.

He just wasn't ready for it.

Stepping away from Danny's bed, he sat down. "Okay. I'm listening."

Danny stared at him for a long moment, and for the first time in a long time, Alex saw how different he looked. For the most part, he always saw the face of the boy he had grown up with, but this time he was seeing him as the man he currently was.

He was tired.

He was broken.

"You're the only one, you know?" Danny said, and when Alex looked at him oddly, he explained, "You're the only one…who still comes to see me." He paused and caught his breath. "After the first year…they all stopped."

Alex knew exactly who he was referring to and it ticked him off. They were all there that day—everyone had played a hand in what had happened, and it simply infuriated him how they could all go on with their lives without taking any time to help with the life they all destroyed.

"I'm always going to be here," Alex said, swallowing the lump of emotion in his throat. "You and me? We've been friends forever."

Danny smiled, but it was small. "Tell me how things are going…with Megan."

Every week since Megan had moved to Portland, Alex had talked about her during his sessions with Danny. It was their thing—Danny would agree to the therapy as long as Alex talked and told him about all the things he was doing. At first he felt guilty about doing it—about talking about all of the great things going on for him when Danny would never again get to experience any of them—but it seemed to make his friend feel better. So he would talk and Danny would listen, and they'd get through the exercises.

"I found out she has a secret hobby."

Danny's eyes went wide with curiosity.

"She crochets."

And then Danny's expression turned to confusion. "Really?"

Nodding, Alex explained. "She makes things for babies—blankets and sweaters and stuff—and then donates them to the hospital and shelters." He smiled as he remembered how excited the nursing staff had been the day he had gone with her. "She's incredibly talented, and it's such a contrast to how she normally presents herself, and it's just…I'm seriously impressed."

"She sounds more amazing…every time you talk about her." With a pause to catch his breath, Danny added, "So things are good?"

"Things are going really great," he said, relaxing in the chair. "We had a long talk Saturday night about her not being just a temporary houseguest."

"And?" Danny asked, his voice a little wheezy.

"And we both agreed it's what we want." Alex raked a hand through his hair and grinned. "I feel like…man, it's so weird, but…I feel like I've been waiting for her for, like…ever. The day she moved in—even though I thought it was temporary—the minute she started to unpack, it was like, 'Okay, this is what I've been missing.' It's strange, and I can't even describe it, but…she's the one. I know she's the one."

"You deserve to be happy, Alex." Danny paused and took a few moments to focus on his breathing. So much so that Alex almost called for a nurse. "You…more than…any person…I know…deserve happiness."

"Danny…"

"It's…true…"

Alex stood when Danny began to cough violently. He looked around, and fortunately, a nurse came in. It took a few minutes to get Danny to calm down and for his breathing to return to normal, and for the first time in years, Alex began to fear his friend wasn't going to get better.

"Remember to talk slowly," the nurse reminded Danny and then looked at Alex. "He's getting tired, so maybe you should do more of the talking."

Alex nodded and waited until she was out of the room. "She's right. I don't want to cause you any more pain. So…why don't we wait and talk more next week?"

He stood closer to the bed, and something in Danny's eyes held him there. "Just…one…more…thing—"

"Danny, you need to rest. It's important."

"You've…blamed…yourself…" He started to cough again but not as badly as he had moments earlier.

"Stop," Alex begged. "Just…this time you need to stop."

"It…wasn't…your…fault," Danny rasped. "Never."

And then it was Alex who couldn't breathe. In all the years since the accident, they'd never talked about it. The last thing he wanted to do was cry in front of his friend, and yet he knew he couldn't stop the tears from starting.

"I should have stopped you," he said, his voice cracking. "If I had tried harder, you wouldn't have jumped. You wouldn't be here like this right now!"

"You…couldn't…stop…me. Never could," he added and gave him a weak smile. "My fault. Not…yours."

But Alex shook his head. "I knew you had been drinking, and I knew that stunt wasn't safe. I should have spoken up and taken the razzing from everyone about being the buzzkill of the group!"

"It would…have made…me…want to…jump…more."

Alex hated to admit that Danny was right. Their whole lives he could never talk his friend out of anything he had set his mind to.

But it didn't change how Alex felt. The guilt. The anger.

"It's okay…to be…mad," Danny said, and that's when Alex realized how his face must look at the moment. "You…can…yell. It's okay."

But he couldn't.

He wouldn't.

What good would it do either of them?

Instead, he squeezed Danny's shoulder. "Rest. I'll see you next week, okay?"

And there was that look in his eyes again, and it nearly gutted Alex.

He was about to say goodbye—that had been his plan—but something else entirely came out. "I'm sorry," Alex said, his voice breaking. "I'm so damn sorry."

"I'm…the one…who's sorry," Danny rasped. "My fault. Stop…blaming…yourself."

Alex shook his head, and tears began to fall.

"Forgive…me."

Shaking his head again, Alex said, "There's nothing to forgive. I need you to forgive me!"

The slight shake of Danny's head was the only response.

"Dammit, Danny!"

"Forgive…me," he repeated, and when Alex was about to respond, the nurse returned and told him he needed to leave.

With one last look at his friend, Alex said, "We'll talk next week." Walking around the room, he collected his things, and as he was about to leave, he heard Danny repeat the phrase one more time.

When he got out to his truck, he sat for a long time

behind the wheel and cried. He cried for the loss of his friend's ability to move and for his role in it.

But mostly, he cried because he felt like a failure and a fraud.

Champagne was chilling.

Candles were lit.

Her little black dress was showing off her curves.

And Megan played with her hair to give it a bit of a sexy look as she waited for Alex to walk in the door.

She couldn't wait to share her good news with him—praise from her father and the position she'd been hoping for? It was probably one of the best days ever for her. Of course…it meant she'd have to spend time away from Alex, and then there was the chance that things might not go as smoothly as they had in Zach's office and…

Stopping the negative thoughts, she forced herself to think positively. For all the years she had felt inferior to the rest of her family—after all, most of her cousins were overachievers and way more successful than she would ever be—this was finally her time! She was going to be able to prove she was just as dynamic as all of the Montgomerys, and she was going to rock this position and show them all that she was…

What?

Their equal? That didn't seem right. No one had ever made her feel inferior or that she wasn't keeping up with them. That was her own issue. So really, the only one she was proving anything to was…herself.

And that took a little wind out of her sails.

Still, if this was going to make her feel better about

herself, wasn't that a good thing? A great thing? Maybe this newfound confidence would help her in other aspects of her life? Like…like…

She was stumped.

Right now, life was pretty damn good. She had a job she loved working for Zach, she was making friends, she was going out and socializing and had an amazing relationship with Alex. So…what exactly was she still looking for?

The sound of the door opening broke her out of her reverie. Turning, she smiled, and when she saw Alex, she knew immediately something was wrong. She cursed the fact that she'd set the scene for seduction and immediately blew out the candles and turned on the lights.

"Hey," she said softly. "What's going on?"

Alex kissed her distractedly and looked around. "Did you just blow out candles?"

"Um…yeah. I had lit some and…but you looked like…"

He turned and faced her as he placed his keys on the kitchen counter. He spotted the champagne. "What are we celebrating?"

And just like that she watched him transform. Gone was the solemn look of a minute ago, and in its place was the relaxed and happy man she was used to seeing. She easily could have been distracted by the change in his demeanor, but she wasn't fooled.

"It doesn't matter. I want to know what's wrong. You walked in here looking like you'd lost your best friend."

The devastation was back, and she knew she'd hit a nerve.

"Alex?"

He raked a hand through his hair, walked into the

living room, and collapsed on the couch. Megan was instantly beside him and then sat in stunned silence as he told her all about his relationship with his friend Danny and the accident that had left him paralyzed. She looked over at the framed picture he had of the two of them, and her heart broke.

Taking one of his hands in hers, she lifted it and kissed it. "So...every Friday..."

He nodded. "I go there every week. He has a therapist who works with him, but I go because I always felt like I could make him do it—I could be the one who got him to feel or move again. Our whole lives we've encouraged one another, pushed one another. And I wanted so damn much to be the one who did that for him—showed him that he shouldn't give up." He paused as his voice cracked. "But he is. I can tell. He's...his body is working against him, and he's not willing to fight it anymore."

"Maybe he was having a bad day," she said softly. "I'm sure—just like everyone else—he gets overwhelmed."

But he shook his head. "I've witnessed him have a lot of days like that. This was different, and...and it just about killed me. It brought all of it back—not that it's ever far away. But the guilt about how I could have prevented this..."

Megan squeezed his hand to get his attention. "Alex, you don't honestly believe that, do you?"

He didn't answer.

"I know I wasn't there, and I didn't know you back then, but it sounds to me like Danny is a pretty strong-willed person. Chances are you might have tried a little harder to get him not to jump, but he was going to do

it no matter what—and just to prove to you he could!"
She paused and watched as a myriad of emotions played
across his face. "It was an accident. A horrible, horrible
accident. Has he ever blamed you?"

He shook his head again. "Never. Even today he tried
telling me it wasn't my fault."

"That's because it wasn't."

Alex jumped to his feet and began to pace as he
furiously explained all the ways she was wrong—how
Danny and everyone else were wrong. "I knew he
couldn't do it—or shouldn't do it. I could have stopped
him, and then he'd be walking around, having a life!
And because of me, he's lost everything! Every week I
go and I try and different therapy options, and…I should
have healed him!"

"You're not God, Alex!" she cried as she came to her
feet. He instantly stilled at her words, and she saw the
anger written all over his face. "Do you hear yourself?
You could have stopped him? Everyone has free will!
There are no guarantees you could have stopped him.
And as for healing him? He broke his neck, Alex! I may
not know a lot about the workings of the body like you
do, but even I know there's no cure for that."

"I could have—"

"No!" she said fiercely, going to him and taking
both his hands in hers. "You couldn't have. You can't
save everyone! You can't heal everyone!" Pausing, she
took a moment to collect her thoughts. "Alex, you are a
gifted therapist. My family and I saw that firsthand by
what you did for Zach, but can you honestly stand here
and tell me every patient is a success story? That every
person you've ever worked with was healed?"

He stared down at her, but his expression never changed. He was angry, she could feel it radiating off him, but she knew this was something they had to talk about. They might not have known each other long, but she had a feeling this was a side of himself he didn't show very often.

If ever.

Pulling away from her, Alex stalked across the room and went to look out the window that gave him the view of the backyard. But Megan wasn't deterred. She walked right over and started talking again.

"I get that you're angry, Alex. I even understand your guilt. That's something you have to come to grips with, and it doesn't matter what anyone says. But you have to know that sometimes things happen that we can't change. Accidents happen every day. Good people get hurt and lose their lives every day. You've done more than most people would have done, and Danny knows that. You're hurting, but so is he. Every day is a struggle for him to survive." Swallowing hard, she said the hardest thing she had ever had to say. "Who are you fighting so hard for—him? Or you?"

When he looked at her, his expression went from rage to sadness to…nothing. "I'm going to the gym," he said, his voice void of emotion.

And before she could even blink, he was gone.

—⁓—

All the lights in the house were off when Alex got home, and even though the car was in the driveway, that didn't necessarily mean she was here.

Hell, he wouldn't be surprised if she'd left after the way he'd carried on earlier.

He'd gone to the gym and punched the bag until his hands went numb and then ran on the treadmill until his legs were about to give out. And the entire time he was there torturing himself, all he could think was how she had been right. When she'd asked who he was fighting for, he knew the answer, and it shamed him.

He was fighting for himself.

To clear his conscience.

To make everything right.

Even now as he walked through the darkened house, he was disgusted with himself. He didn't turn on any lights; he simply walked up the stairs to the bedroom and hoped Megan was there. The bedroom door was closed, and he took that as a good sign. Slowly, quietly, he opened the door and could see her huddled under the blankets on their bed. The clock on the nightstand read eleven o'clock, and he hated how he'd stayed away so long.

Closing the bedroom door, he walked over to the bed, stripped down to his boxers, slid beneath the blankets, and fought the urge to move close to Megan and pull her into his arms. He needed to feel her and apologize to her and…hell, he just wanted to talk to her. She was the only thing keeping him sane right now, and he wasn't sure if—

"Alex?" she said sleepily.

He took his first easy breath in hours as he rolled toward her and gathered her into his embrace. "Hey," he said softly.

Megan willingly moved closer to him and even hugged him tightly. "I was worried about you."

Alex inhaled deeply, loving the smell of her shampoo, and let the breath out slowly. Placing a kiss on the top of her head, he said, "I'm sorry. I…I don't even know what else to say."

Megan kissed his shoulder and snuggled closer. "You were hurting, and I pushed, and I'm sorry too. That wasn't very fair of me to do. I…I had no idea you've been struggling with this, and it wasn't my place to make those observations or assumptions."

His heart hurt even more as he listened to her. Tucking a finger under her chin, he gently nudged her to look at him. "You don't owe me an apology. I was angry because…you were right. I…I never had anyone state things as plainly as you did, and I lashed out because you forced me to look at myself and…I didn't like what I saw."

They both fell silent for a long moment.

The last thing he wanted to do was talk more about this—he was emotionally raw and needed to let everything settle in.

"I ruined your night," he said finally but quietly. "You had champagne and candles, and…I ruined that. What were we celebrating?"

Beside him, Alex felt her shrug. "It was nothing. It's not important."

Reaching over, he sat up and turned on the bedside light so he could see her. They both blinked for a few seconds as their eyes adjusted to the brightness. "Megan, don't. Don't make light of it. Obviously, you had something planned, and you had a good reason for it. Please. Tell me what's going on."

Megan sat up too and sighed. "My father called me today," she began. "And…I got the promotion. I mean, I guess it's a promotion." Her eyes met his, and she gave him a small smile. "I'm going to be handling the transition to the new systems for the entire company."

Alex's eyes went wide, and he smiled proudly at her. "That is amazing news!" Pulling her into his arms, he kissed her but then immediately pulled away and sprang from the bed. "Wait! Wait right there!"

Dashing from the room, he went down the stairs and into the kitchen. It didn't take long to find the champagne and the glasses she had set out earlier. Scooping them up, he took the stairs two at a time to get back to her. The sound of her laughter when he all but jumped on the bed beside her was like music to his ears.

"Alex…this is crazy! We don't have to do this now! It's not a big deal. Really." But she was still laughing as she said it.

With little effort, he popped the bottle open and poured them each a glass. Raising his, he said, "I am so proud of you. You worked hard, and I know you're happy to have your father and everyone acknowledge all you've done and how amazing you are."

Her shoulders sagged, but her smile grew.

"I've always thought you were amazing. I'm glad everyone can see it now." He touched his glass to hers. "Here's to your dream job."

Tears welled in her eyes as she whispered, "Thank you."

They each took a sip, and Alex turned and adjusted their pillows so they could sit back and relax. "So tell me about this new position. I know you mentioned all it might entail a while ago, but now that it's official, what's going to happen?"

She told him about their schedule for each location

and in what order she was going to be doing them. "I talked with Zach today, and we think that for now we're going to see how things go with me being in San Diego. If they find that there is too much for my department to handle while I'm gone, he may need to either promote someone or hire someone as my full-time assistant."

"Do you really think that's going to be necessary?"

"At this point? No. The new system is a dream and shouldn't require having a team of people on constant alert. And I'm not going to be gone that long—at least not with this first install."

He took another sip of his champagne. "So when do you start? When do you have to leave?"

With a small grimace, she said, "Sunday night."

"As in…the day after tomorrow?"

"Yup."

Well…shit. The last thing he wanted to do was be the one to hold her back—especially since she seemed to finally be comfortable in her own skin and getting the praise and acknowledgment from her father she'd been craving—but he hated how it was all on such short notice.

"How long will you be gone for on this first trip? Do you have to stay from start to finish?" he asked and prayed he didn't sound too clingy or needy.

"This is just preliminary. I want to meet with Christian's IT people and see how things are functioning with their current system."

"Don't all the offices have the same system?"

She shook her head. "Some are a little older, and it's not just the system but also how well the team works with it. I've seen some weird patches put in place and shortcuts that slow down the system and have people working way harder than they should. I want to get a feel for the employees so I can get a read on how easy or hard they'll be to train."

After another nod and another sip, Alex realized she'd never answered his question. "Will you be back for the weekend, do you think?"

"That's the plan as of now. I'll fly down on Sunday and be home Friday night, maybe Saturday morning. I'd like to spend time with Christian too. I'm going to stay with him so we'll have a chance to hang out together. It's been a while since we've seen each other.

"Just tell me when to drop you off and when to pick you up, and I'll be there," he said with a smile. Reaching over, he took the champagne from her hand and put her glass along with his on the bedside table. Then he maneuvered them both until they were lying down again. "I'm excited for you, but I'm going to miss you too."

Megan gave him a small smile. "My schedule for all of this isn't quite nailed down, but I'm going to request to not be away for extended periods of time."

And as much as he loved her for trying, he knew it wasn't practical. "That means a lot of traveling for you. Back and forth from San Diego isn't going to be much, but once you're going from coast to coast, I think you're going to find it will be easier for you to stay longer."

She snuggled closer to him. "I don't want to think about that right now. I want to get through this first stage with Christian, and then I can see how things go from there."

"Okay," he said softly, enjoying the feel of her in his arms.

What he wanted more than anything was to kiss her and make love to her, but after the way they had argued earlier, he wasn't sure that was the best thing to do. So he convinced himself to be content. Beside him, Megan yawned, and he realized he had sort of woken her up.

"C'mon, let's get some sleep," he said and turned to shut the light back off. "We'll talk about your itinerary tomorrow."

She yawned again and nodded, and they settled under the blankets—limbs tangled, Megan's head on his shoulder, her hand over his heart.

Closing his eyes was easy; getting his mind to stop racing was not.

They hadn't settled anything, and there wasn't going to be time before she left. He didn't want to spend what little time they had together this weekend rehashing their argument.

Hell, he didn't want to argue at all.

His issues with Danny were his own, and there wasn't anything anyone—not even Megan—could say to change them. This was why he never talked about the situation with anyone. No one would understand. And for the most part, he was fine with that. More than fine with it because it worked for him. The one time he did bring it up, look at how it had turned out! He had wasted a perfectly good evening with Megan and ruined her big celebration.

He'd have to rectify that tomorrow by doing something nice for her—dinner, flowers, another bottle of champagne…the works. It would be a romantic evening on steroids.

That brought a smile to his face.

But they'd do all of that at home. Knowing she was leaving Sunday had him feeling a little selfish and wanting to have her all to himself. This was the perfect distraction after the night they'd had. He was thinking about what he could make for dinner when he felt Megan shift a little closer.

Hmm...

Her nails lightly raked over his chest, and she kissed his shoulder.

Even better.

Megan carefully glided over him until she was stretched out on top of him. His hands immediately moved to her legs and skimmed up and...

No panties.

How did I ever get so lucky? he wondered.

"Something I can do for you?" he asked, his voice low and gruff.

In the moonlight coming through the curtains, he watched as she lifted her nightie over her head and then shook out her hair.

"Actually, there's something I want to do for you," she said softly.

Alex swallowed hard. "Really?"

She nodded.

"And what's that?"

Leaning forward, she placed a gentle kiss on his lips right before she said, "I want to love you."

With a groan, he wrapped her in his arms and gave himself over to her.

~~~

She was dazzled.

There was no other way to describe it.

When Megan had come down the stairs the following evening, it had been like stepping into the most romantic setting in the world. There were dozens of candles lit as well as a fire in the fireplace. Soft music was playing, and there were bouquets of flowers scattered all over the living room and dining room. A fresh bottle of champagne was chilling, and Alex was dressed in a pair of dark trousers and a crisp white dress shirt.

He was so handsome that he took her breath away.

Placing her hand over her heart, she looked around the house in awe. "Alex," she whispered as she smiled at him. "When did you have time to do all of this?"

With a careless shrug, he walked over and kissed her thoroughly. When he lifted his head, he said, "I moved some things around and rescheduled some clients so I could shop. I wanted to celebrate properly since we didn't get to last night."

"It really wasn't—"

But he placed a finger over her lips to stop her words.

"I don't want to talk about yesterday. I want to have tonight to hear all about your new role and how much everyone loves you."

She laughed. "That isn't going to take all night."

His smile turned a little wicked, a little sexy. "That's good. Because I have other plans for us tonight that don't involve talking about work."

All kinds of sexy images came to mind, and she hoped they matched what Alex had planned. Alex took her by the hand, led her over to the dining room table, and held a chair out for her. She looked at all the delicious food he had prepared—stuffed mushrooms, shrimp cocktail, a salad, and dinner rolls.

"Oh my goodness, how many of us are eating?" she teased.

Taking the seat beside her, Alex grinned. "Just the two of us. I knew these were some of your favorites, so I thought it was a good place to start. Then I've got salmon, rice pilaf, and a vegetable medley for dinner."

Her eyes went wide. "That's a lot of food!"

"We'll take a break in between," he said mildly and then motioned to the food in front of them. "No rush tonight. We'll eat at our leisure."

She didn't need to be told twice. There had been so much to do at the office today that she had skipped lunch, so right now, she was starving. Every bite she took was like a little taste of heaven. The man had some serious skills in the kitchen.

And everywhere else.

And he was all hers.

"What are you smiling about?" he asked.

Busted.

With a flirty grin, she confessed. "I was sitting here and smiling because you made all this wonderful food and you're just so…good with everything that you do. And I'm lucky to have you."

"Wow…that's some serious thinking over a stuffed mushroom," he teased.

But she shook her head. "I'm being serious, Alex. You are so amazing and…and…" She sighed happily. "Some days I still can't believe someone like you would want someone like me."

He frowned. "What's wrong with you? Any man who didn't want you is a fool," he said fiercely, and then he seemed to relax. "Although their loss is my gain, so why am I complaining?"

They ate in silence for a few more minutes before he asked about her itinerary for the next day.

"Christian is picking me up when I arrive in San Diego. We'll go right to the office, and I'll work the rest of the day with him." Then she gave him a rundown of what she had planned for the week. "I'm going to come home Saturday morning. I wanted the opportunity to stay late on Friday in case we make some decent progress. And if we can leave the office at a reasonable time, then I'll enjoy having dinner with my brother."

"Sounds like a good plan." He reached for her hand again, and his thumb stroked the inside of her wrist. "Promise me you'll call when you land."

Her heart simply skipped a beat at the look in his eyes and sincerity in his voice. "Of course. And I'm going to call you every night before I go to sleep because that's one of my favorite times of the day for us. I love talking to you until I can't keep my eyes open anymore."

"I love that too."

When they finished the appetizers, Alex rose, held out a hand to Megan, and gently pulled her to her feet. Music was still playing softly, and he moved them into the living room where he pulled her in close and began to sway to the music.

Seriously, she almost swooned right then and there.

It was beyond romantic—the candles, the flowers, the music—and they didn't need to talk. Sharing the moment was enough.

One song turned to two. Two songs to four, and Megan was simply enjoying the intimacy of being close to him. It occurred to her how she was finally learning to enjoy life after five o'clock. For the first time in her life, she had…a life. Something to look forward to, someone to come home to. And suddenly, the thought of leaving and taking on extra responsibilities at work didn't seem quite so appealing.

Alex kissed her on the cheek and pulled back a little. "I'm going to get our dinner started. Why don't you go up and take a nice hot bath and relax, and I'll call you when everything's ready?"

That sounded glorious, but her mind was still racing with whether she wanted to leave in the morning. Before he could walk away, she said his name.

"You okay?" he asked.

"I…I was thinking…maybe…" She paused and sighed. "Maybe I shouldn't do this."

"Do what? Take the bath? It was just a suggestion," he said lightly, kissing her one more time before heading toward the kitchen. "I'd be just as happy to have you sitting here and talking with me while I cooked. Then after dinner we can sit in the hot tub for a while. How does that sound?"

Well, that sounded even more glorious, but it still didn't put her mind at ease.

Alex was in the kitchen, and she could hear him moving pots and pans around. "What if I'm making a mistake?" she called out, and all activity in the kitchen stopped.

The look on Alex's face as he walked back toward her showed how confused he was. "So this isn't about the bath, is it?"

She shook her head.

"What's going on?"

"Remember all those times we talked about me

wanting to change my life? And how working so much wasn't good for me?"

He nodded but didn't say anything.

"Well…I'm having a life," she said, her voice cracking on the last word, and then she took a moment to get her thoughts together. What she wanted most was for Alex to wrap her in his arms and tell her it would all be okay, but he was keeping a little distance—probably because he didn't want to influence her.

Because he was good like that.

"I'm finally at a place where I'm happy and comfortable in my own skin. And that's all because of you," she said softly. "And even though this job is something I thought I always wanted, now that I have it…I'm not so sure."

He let out a long, slow breath and then closed the distance between them. With his hands on her shoulders, he gently squeezed. "It's okay to be nervous about this, Megan. Like you said, you've wanted this for so long, and I'm sure there's a lot of anxiety about it. I think anyone starting a new job feels that way."

"I don't know—"

But he silenced her words with one finger over her lips. "Then it's a good thing your first project is with your brother. Talk to him about how you feel. He's worked for the company for a long time, and even though you've been here with Zach and Summer, I have a feeling you'll be more comfortable taking advice from Christian."

He has a point, she thought. But it still seemed like she wasn't completely comfortable with this whole thing.

Now he did pull her into his embrace and kissed her

on the lips—slowly. Thoroughly. When he lifted his head, he smiled at her. "Go and spend the next week with your brother and see how you feel. If you're really not into it, when you get home on Saturday, we'll talk about it some more. Okay?"

Silently, she nodded.

It wasn't quite what she was hoping for from him. She wanted some guidance, direction.

She wanted someone to tell her what to do.

Alex took her by the hand, led her over to the kitchen island, and motioned for her to sit down. He poured her a glass of wine and then began to talk to her about a food truck rodeo that was going to be in the city next Sunday. It was a great distraction, and for now, she'd take it.

Chapter 10

FRIDAY AFTERNOON ALEX WAS IN THE CAR AND HAD MEGAN on speakerphone. "So? How do you feel about the way things are going? Are you working late tonight or going to dinner with Christian?"

"Dinner with Christian. Definitely," she said, and he could hear the weariness in her voice. "I can't wait to come home though. Now I wish I had planned to fly home tonight. I miss you."

He smiled because she was so much more at ease with sharing her feelings now. Hell, she was so much more at ease with almost every aspect of her life these days, and it was wonderful to see. And he wasn't arrogant enough to believe this was all his doing, but he felt good knowing he had played a small part.

"I miss you too," he replied. "But this time tomorrow, you'll be home. Do you already have plans for when you need to leave again?"

"Unfortunately, Tuesday morning. I was going to try for Monday, but I wanted another day at home before I head out. Am I being too selfish, do you think? If I go Monday, maybe I'll get done faster."

He knew she would continue to second-guess herself, so the only thing he could do was stop her with a distraction. "How about we talk about it when you get home tomorrow? You land at noon, and I have everything we need here for lunch and dinner, so we can come home and chill all day. Actually, I was planning on going to the deli in the morning and getting our lunch stuff, but I did shop for dinner. I'm planning on making those shish kabobs you like, and I stocked up on some of that triple chocolate ice cream for dessert. Does that sound good?"

She laughed softly. "I know what you're doing."

And he couldn't help but laugh with her. "Is it working?"

"Talking about chocolate is always a good distraction. Unfortunately, it doesn't solve anything."

"I think you should enjoy dinner with your brother and relax tonight. Tomorrow you'll be home before you know it."

She hummed softly. "I seriously can't wait. Don't get me wrong, I have loved having some time with Christian, but…" She sighed. "He hasn't been as fun to be around as I'd hoped."

Alex laughed again. "Fun? With all the work you had planned, I didn't think you were looking for fun."

"Everyone's made comments and observations about him over the past couple of years—he's too serious, he's not engaging—but I didn't see that side of him because whenever I did see him, it was at a family function. But now that I've seen him in work mode? Um…yeah. He's a different person. And not in a good way."

"Yikes. Have you tried talking to him about it?"

"That's my plan tonight."

Alex pulled into the parking lot of the long-term care facility Danny had called home for the past six years. It was the third one he'd lived in, and in Alex's opinion, it was the best place for him. He parked and looked at the clock.

"Okay, he may be a little hostile toward you questioning him because he's heard it all before," he said evenly, "and if he seems resistant, just…find something else to talk about. Something neutral so you don't spend the night arguing."

"Now I wish you were here," she said with a nervous laugh. "I almost feel like I might need some sort of mediator to help me out."

"It won't be so bad. He may surprise you."

"Let's hope so."

They were quiet for a long moment. "I'm sorry, but…I have to go," he finally said. "I have an appointment."

Megan gasped softly. "Oh, I'm sorry! I wasn't even paying attention to the time."

"It's all right. Go and have a good night, and let's plan on talking when I pick you up tomorrow, okay? Text me when you get on the plane so I know you're on time."

"I will," she said softly. "And Alex?"

"Hmm?"

"Thank you."

He smiled. "For what?"

"For always knowing exactly what to say to put my mind at ease."

His smile grew. "It's my pleasure."

After they said goodbye, Alex sat in the car for a moment longer and let everything Megan had shared with him sink in. Between the job and worry for her brother, he had a feeling she was going to come home far more tense than when she'd left. The image of giving her a sexy massage to help her relax came to mind, but before he let the thought verge on the X-rated version, he forced himself to remember where he was and what he was here to do.

Gathering his duffel bag and his bottle of water, Alex climbed from the car and made his way into the facility. Everyone on staff knew him, and he waved and said hello to everyone he saw. At the door to Danny's room, he ran into one of the staff therapists.

"Hey, Dennis," Alex said, smiling. It was a little awkward to run into a fellow therapist here—mainly because he never wanted anyone to think he was stepping on their toes. He didn't come here in a professional capacity. His only concern was to spend time with his friend and maybe enhance the therapy he was getting.

"Hey, Alex," Dennis said with an easy grin. He looked over his shoulder into the room and then motioned for Alex to follow him down the hall a bit. At a small seating area, he stopped, and his smile faded slightly.

"Something wrong?" Alex asked.

"I'm glad I ran into you." He paused and let out a small sigh. "Danny isn't doing well—it's been a bad week."

"Why? What's going on?"

"He's got fluid building up in his lungs," Dennis said quietly. "And he's not responding to the antibiotics the doctor prescribed. So his breathing is labored, and he's sleeping a lot." He looked Alex in the eye with a hopeless expression. "I don't think there's going to be anything anyone can do at this point." Reaching out, he placed a hand on Alex's shoulder. "I know how far back the two of you go, and…I thought you should be prepared."

Everything in Alex went cold. He'd known it was coming…had seen it last week, and yet…he'd never be okay with it. He'd never be ready for it.

With a curt nod, he murmured, "Thanks," and turned to go to Danny's room. His heart hammered in his chest, but he didn't stop to think; he just walked in like he always did—with a big smile on his face and ready to tackle any and all of Danny's objections to their therapy.

"Hey, buddy," he said happily. "What's the word today?"

Normally Danny would at least crack a smile, but today he was barely awake. Placing his bag and his water down, Alex stepped close to the bed and studied his friend.

He was pale, and his breathing was labored. Alex swallowed hard and had to fight to keep his own breathing in check. He felt sick; his heart ached. Bowing his head, he fought the tears.

"How's…Megan?" Danny whispered.

Inhaling deeply and letting the breath out slowly, Alex met Danny's gaze and smiled. "She's doing great. She's in San Diego right now working with her brother, but she'll be back tomorrow."

"Good."

"That's how I feel too." He realized he was going to need to keep the conversation going. They weren't going to do their exercises today. Today was about simply hanging out and…visiting. "She's only been gone a few days. But she'll have to return next week."

"How…long?"

Alex shrugged. "I think this is going to go on for at least a few weeks. Then she's going to be doing this on the east coast for the rest of the company branches." He raked a hand through his hair and tried to not sound quite so negative. "She won't be able to fly home every week, but…we'll deal with it."

"Marry…her," Danny rasped.

Alex laughed softly. "Maybe someday." Although he already knew he wanted someday to come soon. He had told Danny a week ago that Megan was the one for him, and he'd meant it. Marriage was something he and Megan still had to talk about.

"You…love…her." It wasn't a question.

"I do. I really do." He paused. "But I haven't told her that yet. I mean, we've talked about our feelings, but neither of us has used the l-word."

Danny grinned. "Afraid?"

Alex matched his grin. "Terrified, actually. I've never said that to anyone before. But I want to. I…well…there hasn't been the right time to say it. And now with her new work schedule and all the pressure she's feeling, the last thing I want to do is add to that by maybe saying I love her when she might not be ready to hear it."

"Don't…wait."

"Danny—"

"Trust…me," Danny said weakly. "No…tomorrows."

And damn if that didn't gut him right there. He knew exactly what Danny meant. He squeezed his friend's shoulder, even though he knew he couldn't feel it. "I do trust you. Always," he said. His throat felt tight, and he had to remember to breathe through his nose to keep himself together.

"You're…going…to…be…all…right."

But Alex shook his head. This wasn't the way the conversation was supposed to go. This wasn't what he came here for. Unfortunately, he didn't have a clue how to turn the conversation around—couldn't think of something funny to say to distract them. There wasn't anything he could do, and that's what hurt the most.

There wasn't anything he could do.

"Marry…Megan…and…be…happy." He paused. "For…me."

Well…shit.

Fighting back tears, he looked Danny in the eye, and right then and there, he gave him the words he knew he needed to hear. And they were the truth.

"I am going to marry her," Alex said, his voice low and gruff and raw. "And we're going to be happy, and every day I'm going to live life to the fullest and do all the things we always talked about doing."

Danny seemed to relax a little. His eyes closed, and his breathing seemed to settle a bit.

Reaching behind him, Alex pulled his chair a little closer. He kept the other hand on Danny the entire time. He needed the connection—needed to maybe give him some of his strength even now.

"It's…going…to…be…okay," Danny whispered. "I'm…finally…going…to…be…okay."

Alex forced himself to nod and to keep his tears at bay.

And for the next hour, he talked about all of the crazy things they'd done when they were kids, and when he finally got up to leave, Danny had fallen asleep with a smile on his face.

She had a strategy.

Start with casual and have a glass of wine.

Talk a little about the transition to the new computer system over appetizers.

And have a glass of wine.

By the time they were having their entrée—and on their third glass of wine—her brother should have unclenched enough to talk about what was going on with him.

Megan was grabbing her purse when Christian walked into her office space.

"Would you be opposed to grabbing some Chinese food on the way home?" he asked. "I know we talked about going out, but I think I would prefer to just hang at home. What do you think?"

She thought it was going to make her plan go even more smoothly.

With a big smile, she said, "Sounds perfect to me. Let's go!"

Christian drove, and they walked into the restaurant and scanned the menu together, laughing about the things they used to refuse to eat as children but now loved. As they waited for their order, Megan kept the conversation light and casual—hoping to get her brother to relax. She already knew he had an extensive wine collection at his house, so there was no need to make any other stops.

At the house, Christian set up the food while Megan quickly excused herself to change into her comfy clothes. Five minutes later, she was strolling into the kitchen in confusion.

Where was her brother?

Where was the food?

"I thought dinner out on the deck might be nice," he

said as he walked into the kitchen to grab a bottle of wine.

He definitely looked more relaxed, and even though he was still basically wearing what he'd worn to work—minus the tie and jacket—his hair was a little mussed, and he didn't seem quite so uptight.

Outside, they had a fantastic view of the ocean, and even Megan had to admit it would be hard to be stressed out with a view like this outside your window every day. Within minutes they each had started to eat.

"So, what are your thoughts on how it's all going?" Christian asked.

Considering they had been talking for the past forty minutes about everything but work, she figured she was okay with talking about it now.

"I think it's going well," she replied. "You have a great team, the system you have in place is running fine, and your employees are all knowledgeable on how to use it. Personally, I don't think any of them are going to struggle with the new system at all. Like anything else, there's always a learning curve, but this will go much more quickly than Zach's transition."

He smiled. "Good," he said with a hint of cockiness. "It will be fun to be able to tease him with that knowledge at a later date."

She laughed, and when Christian joined her, the last of any worry left her. Growing up, Christian was usually the more serious sibling, but he had a great laugh and an even greater smile. And right now with the ocean breeze blowing his dark hair and his blue eyes full of mischief, she saw the first signs of the boy he'd been before the corporate machine of Montgomerys had taken over.

Megan was about to comment on that when her phone rang. Excusing herself, she walked into the house to grab it and saw it was her father calling.

Tenth time since she'd arrived.

Opting to let it go to voicemail—and not feel guilty about it—she carried the phone out to the table and sat back down.

"Everything okay?" Christian asked.

"Just Dad calling. Again," she said with a small laugh. "I'm sure he's leaving a message. I wanted to be able to enjoy my dinner without talking business with him again."

Christian nodded and gave a mirthless laugh. "You better get used to it. This is going to become your new normal."

She looked at him oddly. "What does that mean?"

Christian put his fork down, reached for his wine-glass, and took a sip before answering her. "It means Dad likes to micromanage. And not just at the office. He has a tendency to want to know what you're doing at all times and then tell you what you *should* be doing." He paused and looked out at the water. "Sometimes I wish he'd back off. I look at how Uncle William is with Mac and Lucas and Jace and wonder why Dad can't be more like that. They all work together but Uncle William doesn't hover."

Unable to help herself, she laughed. "Are you kidding me? Are you forgetting how he meddled in their lives and played matchmaker to them?"

Christian looked at her, and what she saw in his eyes almost broke her heart. "He did it to make their lives better. Not control them."

Okay, clearly they were getting somewhere…

Reaching across the table, Megan took her brother's hand in hers. She did not want to jump in and ask him what had happened, so she decided on a more round-about approach. "Have I told you about Aunt Monica's attempt at matchmaking?"

A slow smile spread across Christian's face as he shook his head.

She relayed the story about how Aunt Monica and their mother were essentially grilling poor Alex before and after they had started dating. "I'm telling you, that day at Zach's, the look of sheer panic on his face was almost comical."

"I'm sure Uncle William was ready to jump right in after that," he said with a small laugh.

But Megan shook her head. "I think he's ready to move on to his grandchildren now."

"Seriously? They're all under the age of ten. How much matchmaking can he do?"

She laughed. "For now I think he's just observing, but you never know."

They ate in companionable silence for a few minutes before Christian spoke again.

"Don't you wish…I don't know…maybe our parents were more like that? More concerned about our happiness than about business?"

"I think Dad struggles to try to keep up with Uncle William where business is concerned, and he's a little more uptight about appearances. He and Uncle Robert share that trait."

"That's for sure."

"But…I had a good conversation with Dad last

Friday," she said, relaxing back in her chair. "A really good one, and I thought we had turned a corner. But since I got here he has been all over my every move."

"Like I said, get used to it." He paused and took another sip of his wine. "What made you think you had turned a corner with him?"

She told him about their conversation about Alex. "For the first time in my entire life, he told me he wanted me to be happy."

Christian snorted with disbelief. "Right. He lulled you into a false sense of security to convince you to take the job. Then he'll do everything he can to monopolize your time so you can't possibly be happy. Trust me on this one, Megan."

She was about to question him, but the Pandora's box was open, and he was more than willing to explain it all.

"He'll praise the hell out of your work ethic and tell everyone how great you are at your job. But the minute you don't do what he wants, he won't have a problem guilting you into seeing things his way, and he won't care about who you're with or what his demands are costing you."

"Christian, what in the world happened?"

Finishing off his wine, he quickly poured another glass and pushed his dinner plate away. "Do you have any idea how much I loved living in London?" he asked defensively, but he didn't wait for an answer. "It was a dream come true because it got me away from everyone. Then…Dad starts taking trips over to see how things are going. I was involved with someone—she was my assistant, actually—and he got all over me about how unprofessional I was and how I was jeopardizing the company reputation."

"That's ridiculous! Look at Lucas and Emma! And Jason and Maggie! Hell, even Zach and Gabriella!" she cried in outrage for him.

But he shrugged. "At the time, there was no Zach and Gabriella, so…" Then he shook his head. "Anyway, he started staying for longer periods of time, and things became strained with Poppy."

"Poppy? Seriously?" she asked and had to hide a smirk.

"Yeah, yeah, yeah…ridiculous name, I know," he murmured. "Anyway, things were getting tense between us and Dad was always there, and then he went and hired a new assistant for me and transferred Poppy to work with my VP, David."

"Oh…wow. How…? I mean…how could he possibly think he had the right to do something like that?"

"At the time we were involved in working some major deals—one of the biggest financial deals of my career. If I could stay focused on contract negotiations and making the client happy, it would be the ultimate victory for me. The kind of deal I had worked for my entire life. And I thought if I could prove to him I could handle an account of that magnitude, he'd back off."

Megan was on the edge of her seat. "So what happened?"

"I closed the deal. Made a shit-ton of money for the company," he said, his voice void of emotion.

She gave him a bland look to let him know that wasn't what she was referring to.

"Closed the deal on a Friday. Dad called and asked me to meet him at the office on Saturday morning. I thought it was odd because we had planned on meeting for lunch, but he insisted I come to the office first." He took another long drink of wine. "When I arrived, he wasn't there. But Poppy and David were."

At first she didn't understand what he was saying.

And then she did.

"Turns out the two of them had been carrying on for quite some time," he said. "And somehow, Dad had found out about it. As I was standing there screaming at the two of them and demanding to know how they could do this to me, in strolls dear old Dad to say I told you so."

Her eyes went wide. "Are you kidding me?"

"Do I look like I'm kidding?" he deadpanned.

"But…how did he know?"

Christian shrugged. "He claimed he noticed some lingering looks and caught them whispering with one another a few times and then he hired a private investigator. When he knew he had the proof…well…there we all were."

"So…then what?" she asked hesitantly.

"Then I fired them both, told Dad to leave, and then spent the better part of a month getting the company in order because I wanted out. Luckily that was around the time Ryder was looking for someone to come here and take over temporarily so he could take a break. And then it just worked out that he didn't want to come back and I had no place else to go."

"I…I don't even know what to say. Does…does anyone else know about this?"

He shook his head. "You're the only one I've told, and I doubt Dad has shared the story."

They sat there in silence, and Megan's mind reeled. "Is that why—"

"I don't interact with any of my employees any more than I have to," he said, knowing where she was going. "I'm not looking to be anybody's friend, and I don't want anyone to misconstrue anything I do or say. It's better this way."

"Is it?" she asked sadly.

His expression was equally sad when he looked at her. "I'm getting used to it."

"I don't think you are," she countered. "You're obviously miserable here. You're miserable at work, in your personal life…I think it's time you started to live for yourself, Christian."

"Like you?" he asked snidely. "You seem like you're finally happy, you're in a relationship with a guy you say is amazing, and yet you're diving into this project that will ruin all of that. Is that what you want?"

She sighed. "Why isn't it this way for any of our cousins? How is it possible that it's just us?"

"It's not. James walked away from it all, and Zach moved across the country to avoid working with Uncle Robert. Maybe we're just bad about setting boundaries."

And that sounded exactly right. "How do we fix that?"

"Hell if I know, kiddo." Looking at her, he gave her a sad smile. "But promise me something."

"Anything."

"You're not too deeply entrenched in all of this yet. You know if you wanted to, you could work for Zach and be perfectly fine there. You don't need to take on the whole company. Learn from my mistake. Don't give up something that could bring you a lifetime of happiness for the few bits of praise and approval Dad's going to throw your way."

"Do you really feel like you gave up a chance at happiness with Poppy?"

He shook his head. "No. I didn't see that as a forever type of relationship. But now I'm so paranoid about any type of relationship that I'll never have the chance to find out if I could have one."

And damn if that wasn't the most depressing thing she'd ever heard.

This was the exact kind of thing she was planning on talking about with Alex when she got home. She didn't want to make the wrong decision, and she didn't want to sacrifice what they had for the sake of a job. The only thing holding her back was the fact that for as comfortable and as confident as she felt in their relationship, they had yet to talk about the future.

Well, they had talked about her moving in with him, so that was a good sign, but…it certainly wasn't a promise of forever.

And she wanted forever with Alex. She knew that now.

Honestly, she had known that since the first time he'd kissed her.

She needed to be brave and believe in herself—in them—and show him she no longer was the woman who lived for her career or for her father's approval. The only one she wanted to please was herself.

And him.

As if sensing her inner thoughts, Christian refreshed her wine and refilled their dinner plates. When she looked at him questioningly, he smiled. "So tell me about Alex."

—∾—

Saturday morning Alex was up early and anxious for Megan to arrive. He went for a run, and on his way home he stopped at the deli to pick up some salads and some of Megan's favorites for lunch. She'd only been gone for six days, but it felt like so much longer. It was important for everything to be perfect when she got home and for them to have everything they would need for the weekend so they wouldn't have to leave unless they wanted to.

And he seriously hoped she wouldn't want to.

With his arms loaded with groceries, he stepped into the house and immediately began to put things away. Once that was done, he looked at the clock and saw he still had two hours before he had to leave for the airport. Muttering a curse, he went upstairs, showered, and got dressed.

And then he only had an hour and forty-five minutes to wait.

"It's like the clock isn't even *trying* to move," he muttered.

So he went downstairs and double-checked on what he had planned for dinner, ran the vacuum, and then sat down to look over his schedule for the week. He had cleared everything from his schedule for Monday so they could spend the day together and he hoped she was able to do the same. Maybe Zach would need her to come in to the office, but hopefully not for the entire day.

His phone beeped with an incoming text.

On the plane! Some storms here earlier, but we're supposed to take off soon. May be fifteen minutes late.

Putting the phone down, he wished he had asked her to call him so he could have at least talked to her for a little while. A fifteen-minute delay wasn't the worst thing in the world. Still, he hated the thought of her taking off under those conditions. She'd be home soon enough, but right now he missed the sound of her voice. Actually, he just missed *her*.

And after he got her home and they spent several hours exhausting one another, he planned on taking Danny's advice and finally telling Megan how he felt. What was he waiting for? If he had been smarter, he would have planned this better—instead of simply welcoming her home, he would have set everything up for a romantic proposal.

"Way to think of this great idea ninety minutes before she comes home, idiot," he chided himself.

And while his mind raced with possibilities, there wasn't time for him to get it all done.

"For the love of it…there has got to be something I can do!" Beyond frustrated, Alex stood and tried to think of something productive to do to pass the time. He was so damn organized and practical in his everyday life that there was literally nothing that needed to be done.

And for once, that gave him no pleasure.

He needed something to do. A distraction.

He wished he had opted to run those two extra miles this morning.

It was too late to go ring shopping, and there wasn't time for him to plan the kind of romantic gesture he wanted when he proposed, so he was back to square one. Deciding to give Zach a call and maybe feel him out about Megan's schedule on Monday, he almost jumped when the phone rang as soon as he went to reach for it. The phone number on the screen wasn't familiar, but that wasn't anything new. A lot of times he received calls from doctors or other therapists who were looking for a referral from him or even to refer him to a client in need of his services.

Swiping the screen, he answered, "Hello?"

He listened for a solid minute as his heart began to beat so hard in his chest that it verged on painful. And then everything in him froze as the phone crashed to the floor.

Danny was gone.

—⁓—

Megan stood outside baggage claim and huffed with impatience. She'd landed almost thirty minutes ago and had missed a text from Alex. It said Zach was coming to pick her up and he was sorry.

Nothing else.

She'd tried calling him, but the calls went directly to voicemail. What could have possibly come up?

And to make matters worse, Zach wasn't here yet and he wasn't answering his phone either. Now she had no choice but to stand and wait. Well, that wasn't completely true. She could at least try to find some answers. Pulling her own phone from her purse—again—she dialed Summer's number.

"Hey! Are you home already?" Summer said as she answered.

"Hey, um…I'm back, but…I'm kind of stranded at the airport."

"What do you mean?"

Megan explained about Alex's text and Zach being late.

"That doesn't sound like Alex," Summer said. "Or Zach. My brother is annoyingly prompt. Hang on, let me see if Ethan knows what's going on."

"Why would…?" But she could hear Summer talking to her husband. Now she was even more frustrated. If either Alex or Zach answered for Ethan and not her, she was going to seriously be ticked off.

A few seconds later, Summer was back on the line. "Okay, Alex's line went right to voicemail, and he's trying to find Zach. Do you want me to come get you?"

"No, but thank you. I'm sure Zach is on his way, but I just wish I knew when he was going to get here. Do you happen to know if there's some sort of accident or anything nearby and he's maybe caught up in it? Or what if…" She gasped. "What if Zach has been in an accident? What if I'm standing here getting annoyed when he's hurt on the side of the road somewhere?"

"Okay, okay…you're kind of starting to freak out now…hang on." Again Megan could hear Summer and Ethan talking, but she couldn't make out what they were saying. They kept on talking until Megan thought she'd go mad.

"Summer?"

"I'm here," Summer said, her voice sounding a little grim. "Um…Zach left his phone at home. Gabs said he should be to you any minute. He only got the text from Alex about an hour ago, and he left as soon as he could, so—"

"Okay, now you're starting to freak me out. What's going on?" Her heart began to hammer hard in her chest. "Does Gabriella know why Alex couldn't come?"

"She said Zach was driving the SUV, so look for that."

"What's going on? What happened? Is Alex all right?" she asked frantically.

"He's fine. I mean, he's…he's not hurt—"

"Summer!" she cried. "Just tell me!"

"His friend Danny passed away this morning. Alex is with the family right now, and…seriously, Zach should be there any minute!"

Her heart broke for Alex. She hated how she wasn't there for him and knew how devastated this was going to make him. Just a week ago they had talked—argued— about it, and now she wasn't there for him when he needed her most.

"Can you meet me at Alex's? I think I see Zach in this line of traffic pulling up."

Summer agreed, and when they hung up, Megan quickly flagged Zach down. As soon as they were on their way, she felt herself trembling.

She should have been there.

If she hadn't been traveling, she would have been there with him when he got the news.

"You okay?" Zach asked after they pulled out of the airport.

"I should have been here," she said quietly. "He was all alone when he got the news."

He nodded. "We'll all be there when he gets home," Zach said, his own voice quiet and reflective. "It'll be all right."

Megan only wished she could believe him.

At this point, she was going to have a houseful and she wasn't sure if that was the right thing to do, but she wanted to think that Alex would appreciate coming home to people who wanted to be there for him. And she knew if she asked them all to, they'd stay as long as he needed them. This was her chance to do something for him—the man who did everything for everybody else.

She practically sagged with relief when they turned onto Alex's block. Within minutes she was walking through the door and calling out his name. She ran up the stairs to their bedroom and looked for any signs of him.

As she walked back down the stairs, Summer and Ethan were walking in.

"He's not here," Megan said sadly. "Have either of you heard from him?"

"No," Ethan replied wearily. "I tried calling him again, and I texted him, but he never responded. I'm sorry, Megan."

She fluttered around the kitchen—offering drinks and snacks—and when she saw all of the food Alex had bought for them for today, it made her even sadder.

They were supposed to be celebrating today.

They were supposed to be happy.

"What should I do? Do I try calling him again? Text him and let him know I'm home? I honestly don't know," she admitted with a hint of embarrassment. Maybe other people felt comfortable in situations like this, but she didn't.

"I think you should text him and tell him you're home and you're here for him," Summer said softly. Then she looked at her husband and brother. "Why don't the two of you go and grab some sandwiches from the deli for us?"

As soon as they were gone, Summer took her by the hand and led her into the living room and onto the couch. "Text him, and then let's talk. I can tell you're totally not okay right now."

Nodding, Megan sat and typed out a message to Alex—Thinking of you. Missing you. Here for you. XOXO

Placing the phone down beside her, she looked at her cousin. "I should have been here. If I had come home last night instead of staying in San Diego, I would've been here with him."

Summer reached over and squeezed her hand. "You had no idea this was going to happen. No one did. You're here now, and you'll be here for him. I'm sure the next few days are going to be rough all around."

"I've never—" She paused. "I've never been in a situation like this. Other than our grandparents, I've never dealt with the death of anyone else—let alone someone young like Danny. What if I make things worse? What if I'm not...you know...the kind of person who is comforting?"

A small and understanding smile played at Summer's lips. "I get accused of being overly emotional all the time." She laughed softly. "I've heard that my whole life. And when Zach had his accident, I thought I'd be completely useless because I'd be so overwhelmed, and yet I found a strength I didn't know I had. You never know how you'll react until you're right in the middle of a situation. You need to just be here for Alex and see what he needs. Listen to him when he needs to talk, and be there to hold him when he needs to cry."

"That sounds almost too simple. I'm sure there's more to it than that."

Summer shrugged. "Maybe. Everyone handles grief differently. He may be the type of person who takes control of the situation and just powers through. He may need time by himself to reflect on the loss of his friend. He might get angry…we don't know. What you need to remember is that he's grieving and it may not look like you think it should look."

Nodding, Megan turned her hand and squeezed Summer's. "Thank you."

"For what?"

"For not talking to me like I'm some sort of weirdo because I don't know how to handle this aspect of a relationship."

"Can I let you in on a little secret?"

Megan nodded.

"We're all just winging it," Summer said with a wink and a grin. "Every day is like a new adventure, and sometimes it doesn't matter how long you're with someone, there are going to be certain scenarios that have never come up before and you have to figure them out. Then you learn from them for the next time."

And as strange as that all sounded, it gave Megan comfort. Maybe she was better at this whole relationship thing than she was giving herself credit for.

Before she could comment, Gabriella walked in carrying Willow. Hugging them both, she gave them what little information she had, and they all sat to wait.

—◦◦◦—

Alex pulled into the driveway sometime after seven, recognized all of the cars, and groaned. It had been a hellacious day, and he was talked out. He had been looking forward to coming home and holding Megan and relishing the quiet. She wouldn't push him to talk if he didn't want to. With a sense of resignation, he knew his friends all meant well, and he'd go inside and talk with them and accept their condolences, and hopefully they would see what he needed most was to just be alone.

With Megan.

He walked into the house, and Zach was the first one to greet him. Alex thanked him for his kind words and hugged him and then found himself being hugged by Gabriella. And then Summer. And then Ethan. Megan waited to the side, but she was the only one he could see. When he finally got to her, he clung to her like a lifeline.

All around him, Alex could tell everyone was moving—offering to get dinner, get him something to drink…anything he wanted.

But he had everything he wanted.

Right here in his arms.

It would have been rude to ask them all to leave. Chances were they had been there all day—at least since Megan had arrived home.

Resting his forehead against hers, he sighed. "I'm sorry I didn't pick you up at the airport."

With a small smile, she shook her head. "I was worried about you." She touched his face and kissed his lips, and for the first time since he'd answered the phone that morning, he felt like he was going to be all right. "Come on," she said softly. "Come sit down. Are you hungry? We ordered some pizza, but we grabbed sandwiches earlier, and Ethan picked up one for you too if you'd prefer that."

He wasn't hungry. He had no appetite. Right now the thought of food wasn't the least bit appealing. Sitting on the sofa, his head fell back against the cushions as he explained to everyone what had happened.

"Dennis said they were finishing up their morning therapy and Danny just looked at him and said to tell me I shouldn't be afraid. Things were finally going to be all right." His throat felt tight as he relayed the story. "When I saw him yesterday, we talked. Not a lot because he wasn't doing well. But it was like—" He stopped as the words caught. "It was like he was making sure I was going to be okay. All these years I've been trying to take care of him, and there he was wanting to make sure that I was all right."

Megan held his hand, and he saw both Summer and Gabriella wiping away tears.

Swallowing hard, he went on. "I know he's in a better place. All these years, I knew how much he hated living like that. I'd like to think that right now he's running the bases up with St. Peter or shooting hoops like we used to when we were kids." He stopped and wiped at his own tears. "I need to believe that because otherwise, it hurts too damn much."

No one spoke for a long time, and Alex was grateful for that. He needed a few minutes to let himself openly grieve. All day he had held it together for Danny's parents—he wanted to be there for them and be strong for them. He didn't cry until he was alone in his car. But the drive was short, and really what he wanted to do was howl and yell and cry.

And he would.

Eventually.

The doorbell ringing broke the silence, and Ethan was the first to jump up to answer it. Alex knew it was their pizza delivery, and he was thankful for the interruption.

For another hour, they ate and talked about things

that were meant to distract him—and they did. Megan talked about her trip and what it was like working with her brother. He sensed she was holding something back, but he'd talk to her about it later.

Maybe.

Zach and Gabriella talked about how much—or how little—sleep they were getting because Willow was a night owl, and Summer and Ethan chimed in with their own stories of how their lives were changing now that Amber was starting to become mobile. It was the perfect distraction, and Alex appreciated hearing stories that made him laugh and remember that life does go on.

"How about we meet at the park next weekend for a bike ride," Zach suggested as he was packing up to leave. "We'll do like we did the last time—meet up around eight, do the rounds, and then go for lunch. What do you say?"

For now he agreed because it was easier. Alex had no idea how he'd feel a week from now, but if he had to cancel, he knew Zach and Ethan would understand. "That sounds great. Thanks."

Once everyone was gone and it was just him and Megan, he immediately reached for her. She went into his arms willingly and wrapped herself around him. No words were spoken. They weren't needed. She locked the door, took him by the hand, and led him up the stairs to their bedroom.

Still quiet, she undressed him and then herself before joining him on the bed. They made love slowly, sweetly. And after, when he tucked her in close beside him and their legs tangled together, he stayed awake long after she fell asleep and simply listened to her breathe.

It was comforting.

It was soothing.

And it was reaffirming.

He must have fallen asleep because the next thing he knew, Megan was easing out of the bed. She never got up before him, so when his eyes opened, Alex was surprised at how bright the room was. Sunlight was streaming in, which meant…

"Good morning," she said softly, turning to look at him.

"What time is it?" His voice was husky, and he felt like he could still use another couple of hours of sleep.

"It's after nine. I was surprised to wake up and have you still in the bed." Her words were light, but he could sense she was being cautious as well.

Reaching for her hand before she could leave the bed, he tugged her back to him. The smile on her face was a little sweet, a little sleepy. "I was going to make some coffee."

"Not yet," he murmured. "Let's stay here a little longer. I hate that we didn't get to have any time together yesterday for me to hear about your dinner Friday night with your brother." When she made to correct him, he stopped her. "I know what you told everyone yesterday, but…I think there's more to it than that."

She relayed Christian's story of why he left London. "I'm telling you, Alex, I wanted to pick up the phone right then and there and yell at my father."

"What stopped you?" he said lightly.

Megan looked at him and laughed softly. "Too much of a chicken, I guess."

He shook his head. "Not true. You're one of the bravest people I know."

The look she gave him said how much she didn't believe him. "I'm glad I'm getting to have this time with Christian because it felt really good to sit and talk. I can't even remember the last time we did that."

"Then it's a good thing you took this job."

She made a face.

"What? What was that look?" he asked, frowning.

"Honestly? I don't know if I'm…keeping the job."

Alex straightened and looked at her. "What are you talking about? This is what you've been working toward for years. How can you walk away?"

"Because you helped me see there's more to life than that—my job shouldn't define me. I know I'm a good person, and I'm good at what I do. Zach has already told me he wanted me to use Portland as my home base if I took the promotion but how he'd be happiest with me doing what I'm doing now."

"Megan…all of your hard work—"

Now she looked at him funny. "You've been telling me for a long time—almost since we met—how I needed not to live for my job. And this promotion? It's going to have me living for the job. In the five days I was in San Diego, my father called me almost a dozen times to check up on my progress! He's already micromanaging me, and according to my brother, it's something I'm going to need to get used to."

"Maybe he's not the best one to be taking advice from, considering his history where your father and work are concerned," he commented.

"What's gotten into you?" she asked. "I thought you'd be happy about this. I thought this was good news. I wouldn't have to travel. We could—" She paused, and he saw the uncertainty in her eyes. "We talked about planning our lives beyond Willow's christening."

And at the time, it seemed like a good thing. But now? Nothing made sense. Who was he to be telling anyone how they should live or what was right or wrong? And on top of that, where did he get off trying to plan anything when the hard truth was that no one was guaranteed a tomorrow?

Losing Danny was something he knew was coming, and yet it was gutting him just the same. And right now, he wasn't sure if he could possibly put himself into the position of feeling like this ever again.

Even for Megan.

All night—or at least for part of it—he'd lain awake with his stomach in knots and his heart aching. Alex kept waiting for the moment when he'd feel okay. That moment when he'd be able to take a breath and not feel like he was suffocating. And even though he knew he'd slept, the light of a new day did nothing to ease the pain and anxiety.

He'd never see his friend again.

Ever.

For most of his life, Alex was a happy-go-lucky type of guy. He always looked on the bright side, he followed the rules, and he lived to help people. And where had it gotten him?

For the first time ever, he felt paralyzed by fear—by all the uncertainties of life. He was questioning why he was doing the things he was doing—his career, his hobbies, his friendships, and his relationship with Megan.

She'd once admitted to him that she thought he would be disappointed by the woman she really was because she wasn't packaged in a slinky dress and heels the way she'd been at her cousin's wedding. But that was all cosmetic and superficial. What he was was so much worse.

He was a fraud.

He couldn't help anyone. He couldn't save anyone. And at the end of the day, he wasn't the man he thought he was—the man anyone thought he was.

He was a failure.

"Alex?"

Looking at her, he felt…sad. For her. For him. For them. He shook his head. "I…I can't think about any of that right now, Megan. You should do what you've always planned on doing. Who am I to be telling anyone how they should live?" Moving away from her, he climbed from the bed, walked over, and pulled on yesterday's clothes.

Megan came up behind him, and as he straightened, she wrapped her arms around him. "You're an amazing and incredibly smart man. You helped me see things about my life I never saw before." She kissed his shoulder, but Alex quickly stepped away.

"Let's make some breakfast," he murmured and all but sprinted from the room. The last thing he wanted to hear was praise for himself. Didn't she realize what he'd done? Wasn't it obvious that he clearly didn't have his shit together?

He was down in the kitchen and pulling food from the refrigerator to make them breakfast before Megan was even halfway down the stairs. What he wanted more than anything was to just…not talk. Not think.

And just not…be.

Wordlessly, she came into the kitchen and put the

coffee on. They moved around the kitchen—around each other—and managed to make a small batch of pancakes without saying anything. They sat down together, and Alex struggled for something to say—something that wasn't about…anything.

"I was thinking about taking you to Crystal Springs today," he said casually. "We haven't been out exploring in a while. The weather's supposed to be great. We'll pack up the lunch stuff I bought yesterday to take with us, and then I can make what I had planned for last night tonight. What do you think?"

If she thought he was trying to avoid what they were talking about earlier, she didn't let on, nor did she bring it up. The rest of their breakfast conversation was neutral—as in she talked to him more about her conversation with her brother and how it made her feel.

But she didn't ask for his advice, and he didn't offer any.

If anything, they were carefully circling one another and talking like casual acquaintances.

And while it should have bothered him—and there was a time in their relationship that it had—right now he wasn't feeling anything.

He was numb, and he knew he was going to stay that way for a long time.

Chapter 11

FOR THE BETTER PART OF A WEEK, MEGAN HAD BEEN walking on eggshells. Alex was not handling Danny's death well—not that most people would notice. On the surface, he was behaving like his usual self, but she knew better. He was putting on an act for his family, for his coworkers. And to some degree, for her.

The funeral was both uplifting and heartbreaking. So many people had shown up to celebrate Danny's life, but the entire time Megan stood beside Alex, she could feel how tense he was. She wished he would cry or yell or vent in some way, but he didn't. He was the pillar of strength for everyone, and the eulogy he gave had everyone in tears.

Standing at the front of the large Presbyterian church, Alex had faced all the people who had loved Danny. After sharing stories of their childhood antics and poetically talking about his friend's lust for life, Alex turned somber.

"I feel like the first half of our lives was spent with me trying to guide Danny. I was the levelheaded one, the practical one. He always tried to get me to cut loose a little and have some fun—and I did—but at the end of the day, I did my best to get him back on track when he'd wander."

Pausing for a moment, he went on, "In the past few months, I feel like our roles reversed a bit. Danny had something to teach me, and at times, I didn't want to hear it. I didn't want to stay on track and listen. I knew if I did, then I'd have to accept what he was saying—and what he was saying was that it was time for him to let go." Another pause as emotion seemed to clog his throat and halt his words.

"You see, he was tired. He'd fought the good fight for so long that his body was too weary to go on. I kept thinking if I just helped him move his legs or improve his circulation, it would make a difference. But in the end, he was the one helping me make improvements in my own life." He swallowed hard. "People ask why— why did he have to suffer for so long? And I'll admit to thinking the same thing. But what I have come to believe is that Danny was here to help us all. We need to remember that life is precious. Every day is a gift. We need to cherish it. And each other."

Megan had sobbed openly. She didn't normally do that, and at a time when she should have been comforting Alex, he had stepped down from the podium and comforted her.

Which was so typical of him.

She had delayed going back to San Diego because she didn't want to leave him, though he had been fairly vocal about her needing to get back to work. Megan had argued that she was working—she was going in to the office with Zach every day—but she knew what he was referring to. He seemed to be deliberately pushing her away, and for the life of her, she couldn't understand why.

Okay, that wasn't completely true—she knew he was struggling with guilt. Or some form of delayed survivor's guilt. But he wouldn't talk about it. Every time she tried to bring it up, he shut down and would go for a run or claim he had to work on client files. She wasn't stupid; she caught on to his diversion tactic fairly quickly.

She just didn't know what to do about it.

Okay, and *that* wasn't completely true either. With her father calling her almost nonstop, she had finally conceded and made arrangements to head back to San Diego for a few days to work more with Christian's IT team to get the work and training done for the new system. Alex had seemed greatly relieved when she'd told him her plans, but she had been the one freaking out when he told her she should stay in California until the job was done.

Not a good sign at all.

But at the time, it seemed like the right thing to do because it would get her father off her back and maybe give Alex the time alone he needed to finally grieve.

It should have been the perfect plan—the right thing to do—and now that she was settled in with Christian, she realized that maybe it was a good thing for her as well.

Until Zach called.

She'd been away for five days when her cousin called in a state of near panic.

"When was the last time you talked to Alex?" he asked sharply when she answered the phone.

Her first instinct had been to be annoyed at his tone and his lack of a greeting, but his question put her on high alert. "Um…yesterday morning. Why?"

Cursing under his breath, Zach let out a loud sigh before answering. "I just got a call from Tony—he's one of the therapists Alex works with—and he said Alex quit."

"What?" she cried. "When?"

"Tuesday."

The day she had left for San Diego.

Megan collapsed in her chair and wondered why Alex would do something like that—why he would lie to her or simply not tell her what he'd done—which was what she asked Zach.

"I have no idea. I thought he was doing all right. I've been talking to him almost every day since Danny died, and he seemed like he was okay. Obviously, I was wrong."

"Did you call him after you spoke to Tony?" she demanded, now knowing exactly how he must have felt when he called her.

"I've been trying, but he hasn't answered. I went by the house, and he's not there."

Now she cursed. "He has to be somewhere, Zach! Have you called his parents? Has Tony tried calling him? I mean…someone has to have talked to him!"

Now she was getting frantic and hating the fact that— once again—she wasn't there.

"Okay, I think we both need to calm down a bit," Zach said evenly. "I'm going to keep calling and texting him. Why don't you do the same, and we'll talk again later?"

A sound by the doorway caught her attention, and she saw her brother standing there, concern written all over his face.

"Zach, you have to find him," she said fiercely as emotion threatened to choke her. "Please."

"I'm doing my best, Megan," he said solemnly. "I swear."

When she hung up, she looked at her brother.

"What's going on?" he asked, and she relayed her call with Zach to him.

"What am I supposed to do?" Megan cried. "I have no idea what I'm supposed to do at this point!"

Christian looked at her and frowned. "Megan, why are you even asking me this? You know I'm the last person to—"

"You're right," she said with irritation as she stood. She was done looking to other people to tell her what was right and what was wrong for her or simply what to do. Right now, she was doing what she wanted—what she knew in her heart was the best thing for her. "I need you to get the IT team in here right now for a meeting." Walking around the office, she began collecting her things, and when she looked at her brother, he was grinning.

And Christian hardly ever grinned.

"Anything else I can do?"

Stopping in her tracks, she studied him. "Yeah. You can smile more."

He laughed softly. "Anything else?"

Nodding, she said, "You can get me on the first flight back to Portland."

—∞—

Walking out of the airport, Megan looked around for her ride. Christian said someone would be here to pick her up, but she had no idea who it would be. Placing her suitcase on the pavement, she looked at the cars lined up outside baggage claim and figured she needed to look for Summer or Gabriella. The sound of a horn beeping made her jump, and she looked and saw Zach parked right in front of her.

He didn't get out of the car, and she simply threw her

luggage in the backseat. When she was seated and they were pulling away, she looked at him. "Well? Have you talked to him?"

Zach shook his head and focused on maneuvering through the traffic. "All I got was a brief text saying he's camping and wasn't sure when he'd be home. I have a pretty good idea where he is, but…I can't be sure."

"Can we go there now? Can you take me to him from here?"

Glancing at her, he said, "Megan, you need to think this through. It's great that you want to help him—"

"But—"

"But I've never seen Alex like this. I'm thinking maybe I should go or maybe one of his therapist friends. Having you here and waiting for him at the house would probably be a lot smarter than you going to him right now."

"Bullshit!" she cried. "I don't want to sit and wait, and it's not your call to make. I'm the one who's going to go to him! I'm the one who loves him, dammit!"

A slow smile played across Zach's face, and he quickly hit the Bluetooth and called Ethan. She was mildly confused when all he said to Ethan was "We're going with plan B" and hung up.

"I don't understand," she said. "What's happening?"

"Just…give me a few minutes, and it will all make sense," he said and was about to say more when her phone rang.

One look at the screen, and she wanted to scream.

It was her father.

Again.

Megan was frustrated enough to not ignore it. "Hey,

Dad," she said when she answered, but there was no hiding her annoyance.

"Megan, where are you? I called the office and was told you left for Portland. What's going on? You can't leave in the middle of a job!"

"Actually, I can, and I did," she said tartly. "Christian's team is doing fine, and they don't need me there to babysit. And on top of that, I'm turning down the position."

"What!?"

Her whole body seemed to sag with relief at saying those words aloud. "I don't want to live like this, Dad. I want to have a life. A life with Alex. And right now, he needs me. You can be angry or disappointed in me or whatever, but this is the way it's going to be. I'm staying in Portland, and I'm working with Zach, and… that's it."

"Megan, wait! This is ridiculous. You're not thinking clearly—"

"You know what? For the first time in my life, I think I am," she snapped. "I'm doing what I want to do, and you know what that entails? Being with Alex, being happy at my job, and crocheting all kinds of frivolous baby things in my spare time! And I don't care what you think about that!"

She was on a roll, but she noticed they were pulling up to Summer and Ethan's house. She looked at Zach questioningly, but he said nothing. "I have to go now, Dad. I'll talk to you when I can." And then she hung up.

Once they were in the driveway, Zach motioned for her to go into the house. Ethan was standing at the front door and moved aside with Amber in his arms. When they were all in the living room, Megan looked around. "Where's Summer?"

Zach held up a hand to stop her from asking any other questions and then began to explain.

"If all that was required here was a new outfit or a day at the spa, believe me, Summer and Gabriella would be here," he began. "But what you're looking to do requires a different approach."

She looked at Zach and then Ethan and then back to Zach. "I'm not following you. I'm going after Alex. What more is there?"

Ethan laughed softly. "Megan, you're not just going to go after him like you're walking into his house. He's camping—like in a tent near the lake. It's not a spot you can drive to, and there are no modern conveniences there."

"Or anywhere close by," Zach added.

"So…wait…so you guys are like…so this is…?"

"Remember the day the girls took you shopping?" Ethan asked. "Well, this is our equivalent to a girls' day. Just…a bit more sped up and a lot less glamorous."

And then she was so overwhelmed with emotion that she was laughing and crying at the same time. Both men looked nervously at one another and then at her.

"Um…Megan?" Zach asked.

She waved him off. "This is…this is seriously the greatest thing ever. I mean, I loved going shopping with the girls; that's what we're programmed to do. But this? What the two of you are doing? I don't think I've ever felt so loved. Thank you!" Reaching out, she hugged Zach and then Ethan. Then she took a moment to get herself together. With a steadying breath, she finally said, "Okay, what's first?"

For an hour, the guys explained to her how to pack her backpack, the proper clothes to wear, and the importance of being aware of your surroundings. Her head was spinning with all the information. They explained how to use the compass and made her practice walking around with all of her gear on.

"You won't need a tent. Alex will have one," Ethan explained. "But we've put a sleeping bag in with your stuff. You'll need to remember that you're sleeping on the ground, so there's not a lot of padding. Chances are you're going to be a little uncomfortable…"

"But," Zach quickly interrupted, "it should only be for a night or two, and I think you'll be fine." He glared at Ethan. "Don't make it sound horrible, dude. We're supposed to be encouraging her."

"I am encouraging her," Ethan argued lightly. "But it's also important that she be prepared for things like this so that she doesn't say something later on or complain and make Alex feel bad. He's already struggling, and you know he's the type who'll pack up and leave to make Megan happy even if he's not ready to go."

"Okay, let's all stop talking like I'm not here," she interjected calmly. "Look, I'm aware that this is going to be far out of my comfort zone and I am going to have to have a good poker face to get through it. But I'm willing to go and be miserable and sleep on rocks and pee in the woods if it means being there for Alex! So can we please get back to business so we can go?"

Ethan and Zach exchanged glances. "Geez, relax," Zach said with a small huff. "I'm just looking out for you."

She rolled her eyes. "And I'm very thankful for you.

For the both of you," she quickly amended. "But we are seriously losing daylight here. I have no idea how far away Alex's campsite is, and I'm nervous and anxious and, honestly, a little bit nauseous. I hate that he's out there all alone and hurting, and I just want to get to him. So can we please…wrap this up and get going?"

An hour later, Megan was wearing leggings, a T-shirt, a sweatshirt, and boots, and pulling her hair up into a ponytail. Zach was loading all of her gear into the car. When she stepped out of Summer and Ethan's guest room and into the living room, she stopped and smiled. Ethan was sitting on the floor singing to Amber, and she was laughing. It was a precious scene. Ethan caught sight of her and stopped mid-song. He scooped his daughter up and stood.

"So? You sure you're ready?" he asked.

Nodding, she said, "I am. Tell Summer thank you for letting me raid her closet."

He walked into the kitchen and then came back with a small cooler bag and handed it to her. "There are a couple bottles of water in there, some granola bars, two sandwiches, and two chocolate bars." He smiled and then seemed to blush. "You know…in case you really need something to calm your nerves."

Standing on her tiptoes, Megan kissed him on the cheek. "Thank you."

Outside, Zach beeped the horn, and her heart kicked hard in her chest. She looked at Ethan again, and her expression must have showed how nervous she was.

"Zach's going to walk you as far as he can," he assured her. "There's a battery pack in your gear, and we normally have some decent cell service when we camp out at that site, so if you need someone to come and get you, you can call any of us at any time. Okay?"

She nodded. The horn sounded again, and she thanked Ethan one last time before running out to the car.

Once she was seated and they were on the road, she turned to Zach. "Am I crazy? I mean, am I completely crazy to be doing this?"

He shook his head, but his eyes stayed on the road. "To be honest? I wasn't sure what you should do. I've never seen this side of Alex, and as much as I wanted to be the one to help him like he helped me, I knew I wasn't the one to do it." He shrugged. And then he looked at her and grinned. "And when you said you wanted to—and you were willing to trek out into the woods to do it?" He chuckled. "Then I knew beyond a shadow of a doubt that I wasn't the one to do it."

"I still have no idea what I'm going to say when I see him," she admitted quietly. "I've never had to handle a situation like this, Zach. I'm…I'm scared."

Sighing, Zach drove for a few minutes without saying anything. Finally, he spoke. "The mere fact that you're showing up is going to speak volumes to him. And I think you are going to have to take your cues from him. There isn't a speech you can prepare. I wish there was. He needs to know you're there for him—that we all are. But you need to be prepared for some things too."

"Like what?"

"Like he might not want to come home yet. He may need more time to come to grips with this situation."

"Oh."

They drove for a little while longer in silence. "When I met Alex, I had hit rock bottom. I'd pushed everyone away—doctors, therapists, friends, family...everyone. I didn't think I'd get another therapist because I had fought with so many of them and figured no one would want to help me. Then Alex showed up." He paused. "And he talked to me—he talked to me like there wasn't anything wrong with me. He didn't treat me like a patient or someone who'd suffered a trauma. We just talked—man to man." He shrugged. "That spoke to me more than anything else anyone had done since the accident. That initial conversation, he just...he asked my opinion—he didn't give his. Out of all the people I had been dealing with—and there had been more than I can even count, it seems—he was the first to try to get to know me, and he asked me what I wanted to do."

Her eyes stung with tears. "I never knew that," she said quietly.

She saw Zach swallow hard. "He gave me hope when I thought I had nothing left. But that's just him—that's the way Alex is. He has a gift, and when I think about him throwing that away—" He stopped and shook his head. "We can't let that happen. He has too much to give."

Tears streamed down her face. "I know. He's always there for everyone, and it's hard to imagine him off and hurting like this all alone."

Zach squeezed her hand. "Now he won't be alone. He has you."

"I feel very unqualified for this, but I'm not going to give up. If I have to camp out for a week, I'm going to do it."

Smiling, Zach pulled off the highway, and Megan saw the sign for the campground. It wasn't until the car was parked that he looked at her and said, "Let's hope it doesn't come to that."

She tried to laugh at his attempt at humor, but she just couldn't at the moment.

"The selfish part of me wants to be the one to hike into those woods and help him. To save him. The way he saved me," Zach said, his voice thick with emotion. "But then I realized that helping you get to him is going to be the best thing for him. That's my contribution to this whole thing." He hugged Megan close. "You've got this."

Megan hugged him back. Knowing that her cousin— her big, strong cousin who had overcome so much more than she could even imagine—had faith in her to save the man she loved gave her the confidence to do it.

––––––

The weather was perfect, the fish were biting, and everything was peaceful.

And he was miserable.

First he thought walking away from his job and the clients he couldn't possibly cure was the right thing to do. Then he figured having the house to himself would help. But all that accomplished was him sitting alone missing Megan and thinking about all the things he was supposed to be doing to fill his time.

That's when he knew he had to leave.

At least out here in the woods, the sights and sounds of nature distracted him.

Reeling in another fish, Alex wondered if he should quit for the day. He'd already caught four. More than enough to feed him for the next couple of days.

If he had refrigeration.

"Idiot," he murmured, removing the fish from the line. Maybe if he caught sight of any nearby campers, he'd offer them some. In the meantime, cleaning them and filleting them would help pass the time.

Except he was super efficient at that too.

Dammit.

Wrapping the fillets and placing them in his cooler, he contemplated what to do next. He stretched, looked at the lake, and sighed. It was so quiet and tranquil, and on some levels, it was soothing. There was something to be said for getting back to nature without any disruptions or people who made you—

"Son of a *bitch*!"

Alex turned—not so much at the words but at the voice.

Megan.

He looked on in shock as she made her way through the brush looking like someone who had stepped off the pages of a Land's End catalog. She huffed, pushed a tree branch aside, and jumped down from the small opening and onto the clearing where he had set up camp. When she spotted him, she looked incredibly relieved.

"Thank God," she murmured.

Alex wasn't sure which was the stronger emotion for him—shock or relief.

"What are you doing here?" he asked. He was glued to the spot, thinking maybe this was a mirage and he was starting to lose his mind.

And considering he'd slept maybe a total of twelve hours in the past week, that was totally possible.

Closing some of the distance between them, Megan

hefted her backpack off and let it fall to the ground. "I decided to give camping a try," she deadpanned.

As much as he didn't want to, he couldn't help but laugh at her statement. "How are you liking it so far?"

"If I wasn't carrying a small house on my back, I would probably like it more." Then she crouched down, opened up the small cooler bag that was hooked to her pack, and pulled out a bottle of water. She drank half of it before looking at him again. "I could also do with a lot less branches to the face."

"There was a path—"

Nodding, she stood. "And I followed it for as long as I could, and then some sort of wild animal was blocking the way, so…I had to get creative. No one told me I might need a machete."

Alex quirked a brow at her. "A wild animal?"

"Yup. Wild. Possibly rabid."

"Rabid? Or do you mean rabbit?" he teased.

She gave him a bland look and took another sip of her water. "It was bigger than a rabbit, and it had…attitude. I thought it was safer to fight my way through the trees."

It was hard to believe they were standing here in the woods talking like this. For months Megan had been adamant about never going camping, and yet…here she was. Last time he'd spoken to her, she was fully entrenched in her job and talking about how crazy things were and how busy she was and how much her father wouldn't leave her alone, and yet…here she was.

"Why aren't you at work?"

Her shoulders squared, and she whipped off her sunglasses and gave him a defiant look. "I quit my job."

Alex's eyes went wide. "Um…what? When? Why?"

With a careless shrug, she walked past him and toward the water. She peered at his fishing gear before looking at him over her shoulder. "Have you caught anything? I have a couple of sandwiches in my bag, but I've never had freshly caught fish."

This had to be a hallucination. The woman he knew would never willingly quit her job and hike into the woods. Uh-uh. No way. Shaking his head, he walked toward her and had to touch her to confirm whether she was real. Reaching out, he gently grasped her shoulders and pulled her close.

"I don't suppose you can catch lobster in a lake, can you?" she asked, her expression going a little soft as she looked up at him.

He laughed softly. "Is this your way of telling me you're hungry?"

"I had a granola bar," she commented, "but I was eating it when I was almost attacked, so I threw it at the beast and took off."

The urge to haul her in closer and kiss her was strong, but there was still an inner war waging within him. Maybe cooking some of the fish would be a good distraction.

"Then allow me to be a good host and make you something to eat."

She must have recognized what he was doing because she took a step back. "I have a sandwich if you're not ready to eat yet. It's okay." Without looking at him, she walked over to her pack and pulled out the food. She offered one to him. "There's two. You know…just in case."

And that's when he saw it—or…heard it. The vulnerability. She was here, and on the outside she looked completely confident and at ease, but inside? She wasn't so sure.

Taking the sandwich, he motioned to the log he'd been using as a seating area. He was expecting a comment or two on the lack of places to sit, but she didn't say a word—she simply sat down and opened her lunch.

He was halfway through his when he couldn't take the silence anymore. "What are you doing here, Megan?" he asked quietly.

Once she was finished chewing, she turned to him. "Do you remember when you flew to New York to be with me?" she began nervously.

He nodded.

"We had talked about all the ways it was impractical for us to be together—or at least that's what I kept saying. And every time I would say it, you would challenge me and come up with reasons why it made sense. I kept putting up these barriers, and you kept knocking them down. And you know what? That's what I needed. I just didn't realize it at the time." She paused and looked at him. "Now I'm here to knock down yours."

"Um…what?"

"You weren't willing to let me walk away from what we'd started," she said. "You took a risk, you flew across the country and planned this amazing weekend for us—"

"And you didn't show," he reminded her, but there was no anger to his words—he was simply stating a fact.

"I know. And I regret that more than anything." Her expression went from neutral to fierce in the blink of an eye. "I should have come to you. We talked, and we fought, and then we both gave up, and because of that, we lost two years. Well…I'm not giving up, and this is me coming to you. Maybe the gesture is two years too late, but it's here. And right now, you're the one having doubts, and I'm here to listen to you and talk them out with you and just…dammit, Alex, you have far too much to give to just walk away from it all."

"Megan—"

"No," she quickly interrupted. "You have too much to give to your clients, to your friends, and to us." With that, she reached out and took his hands in hers. "I love you. I love everything about you! Your struggles are my struggles, and when you're hurting, I'm hurting too. I know I can't possibly understand the depth of what you're feeling right now, but I'm here for you. I'm always going to be here for you."

Maybe she was still speaking, maybe she wasn't. All he could focus on was the fact that she loved him. She had said the words when he'd been too afraid all along to say them. His brave girl was finally realizing her own strength. He knew how out of her comfort zone all of this was—quitting her job, hiking out into the woods, and expressing her feelings first. So if she could do it, maybe…just maybe…he could do the same.

"I hate who I am right now," he said gruffly. "I hate that I'm letting my friend down because I can't seem to move on or move forward."

She squeezed his hand. "Alex, you have to allow yourself time to grieve! No one expected you to just get up the next day and carry on as if nothing had happened. Taking some time for yourself is a pretty normal thing to do."

But he shook his head. "It's more than that. All those

years I worked with Danny, and what did it do? You were right…that day when you asked who was I doing it for. It was me. I was doing it to try to ease my guilt about what had happened to him. So, really, I possibly extended his life—a life he didn't want—for my own selfish purposes. What kind of person does that make me?"

For a long moment, she looked at him, and he was certain she was thinking about taking her words back from earlier. Maybe now she was seeing the real him and was looking for a way out. And he wouldn't blame her.

"What was my cousin Zach like when you first met him?" she asked.

"Excuse me?"

"What kind of condition was he in when you first met him?"

The image of his friend on that first day came to mind—he looked like some sort of mountain man and growled louder than a grizzly bear—which was exactly what he said to Megan. "Essentially, Zach was a complete mess."

"I wasn't around much, but everyone in the family knew he wasn't doing well. He shut everyone out and was refusing therapy. What would have happened to him if you hadn't come along?"

"He would have hired another therapist," Alex said, but Megan shook her head at him, and he realized what she was getting at. No other therapist would have taken him on. At least not for long. "He probably wouldn't be walking right now."

"Earlier today, Zach told me about your first meeting," she said as she gently caressed his hand. "He said he had hit rock bottom. That wasn't the life he wanted to live. And then you came along and changed all of that for him because you cared. You took the time to get to know him and gave him hope. Is he the only client you've ever had who was a success?"

Alex shook his head.

"Have you ever had a client whose injuries were so significant that they couldn't regain use of their limbs?"

He nodded.

"And did you continue to work with them, or did you walk away?"

It was hard to swallow past the knot in his throat. "I stayed," he said, his voice low. "I always stayed."

Her expression softened, even turned a little sad. "And you stayed with Danny because he was your friend. It wasn't about an ego thing for you. Anyone in your position would have stayed because of the emotional connection. You don't walk away from the people you love when they can no longer walk or because they're no longer physically capable of being the person we want them to be."

And deep down, he knew she was right. He knew that even if he wasn't doing therapy with Danny, he would have kept going and seeing him every week because… that's what friends do.

"I never thought it would hurt this much," he admitted, his voice catching. "All these years, I always knew this day would come, and yet…I wasn't prepared for the pain. I keep thinking…hoping…"

She pulled him in close and held him as he cried. It was as if the dam had finally broken because ever since the morning of his friend's death, he hadn't let himself cry to the point of it hurting—to the point of almost not being able to breathe. And the entire time, she held him, stroked his back, soothed him.

Alex had no idea how long they stayed like that, but when he finally raised his head, he felt mentally and physically exhausted. He wiped away the moisture and was almost embarrassed to look at Megan. He never cried in front of anyone, and he hated that he had done it now. But when she cupped his face in her hands and gently forced him to look at her, all he saw in her eyes was love, understanding, and acceptance.

"I love you," he finally said. "I've loved you from the first time I saw you. And the thought of ever losing you like—" But he stopped and shook his head. "It all just overwhelmed me."

"And it's okay, Alex. You had so much to deal with. I want you to know you can talk to me about this kind of stuff. You've always listened to me go on and on about the things that scare me, and it's kind of nice to know you get scared and overwhelmed sometimes too." Then she gave him a small smile. "It's nice to know you're not perfect."

He laughed and rested his forehead against hers. "But I want to be. For you. Only for you, Megan."

"No," she said softly. "I like this much better because I know I'm not perfect by any stretch of the imagination. This levels the playing field. Besides, I think being perfectly imperfect is a good thing."

They stayed like that for a long time until Alex knew he needed more—and even if she wouldn't say it, he knew the damn log was crazy uncomfortable.

Clearing his throat, he said, "Um…you know…I have a tent right over there that's got more than enough room for two people to lie down and get comfortable."

Her smile was knowing. "I have an extra sleeping bag for a little more padding if you're interested."

Without a word, he stood and held out a hand for her. Together they picked up her pack, walked over to the tent, and set out her sleeping bag. Then he carefully tugged her inside, zipped the tent closed, and focused all his energy on showing her how much he missed her.

—⁓—

"I'm not going to lie to you—I really enjoyed that."

Alex looked at her and grinned. "I'm glad. Although I do wish it was a little fancier."

They were eating the bass he'd caught, and she genuinely was surprised at how much she was enjoying herself. "A salad would have been nice to go with it, but I'm kind of impressed at how you put together such a good meal with so little to work with."

"Well, had I known I was going to have company, I would have been better prepared."

"I still have my chocolate bars for dessert, and I'm willing to share," she teased.

"The only dessert I plan on having is you," he said silkily, and Megan knew she was blushing.

"And I am more than willing to let that happen and have the chocolate all to myself."

"Deal."

Together they cleaned up and packed away the left-over food and then huddled close around the fire. "This would have been a great time to make s'mores."

"Next time. I promise."

And the funny thing was she was already looking forward to it. She had a feeling that with a little preparation, this could be a really cool experience—with clothing that was actually hers, some food options, and possibly a bigger tent, she could be completely on board with coming out to the woods again.

"You're on." Alex was sitting behind her with his arms around her, and she could feel him chuckling. Playfully, she elbowed him. "What's so funny?"

"I was expecting a little more of a fight."

She shrugged. "Well, the food was good, the tent is almost comfortable, and other than the wild animal who I had to fight for my granola bar, this hasn't been all that bad. And…no bears." Another shrug. "I'm considering that a win."

"You realize that every time you talk about your trip into the woods, your encounter with what I'm guessing was a squirrel gets wilder and wilder, right?"

"If a squirrel roars, then I guess it was a squirrel."

He laughed harder. "Now it roared at you?"

She nodded furiously. "And its fangs were very scary."

Hugging her close, Alex kissed her on the head. "Then I guess you're lucky I'm here to protect you. Your last granola bar is safe."

"Whew!" Megan replied with a dramatic sigh. "My hero."

He kissed her again. "Always. That's always what I want to be."

"Then you have nothing to worry about because you've always been that to me." Looking over her shoulder at him, she smiled. "You came into my life, and you saved me."

His laugh was a little softer this time. "I don't see how. There wasn't anything wrong with you. You were fine."

But she shook her head. "No. I wasn't. You took me by the hand and showed me all I had been missing. And I'm so thankful for that."

They sat in silence for a few minutes, gazing into the fire.

"You realize we're both unemployed right now," he said lightly. "You may not have a choice but to enjoy this lifestyle. It could be our new home."

Megan laughed out loud. "I don't think so. When we get home, you know Tony and everyone else will welcome you back with open arms."

"Maybe..."

"Or—"

He pulled back and looked at her. "Or...what?"

"Or...this could be your chance to start something of your own. You know it's something you've always thought about, and maybe now is the time to do it." Megan knew she was taking a big risk to bring up something like this when they were seemingly getting back on track and he was more relaxed than he'd been in weeks. But for some reason, she couldn't help herself.

"I don't know...it would be a lot to take on. I'd have to find a place and order equipment and find clients and—"

"And you know none of that would take you very long. You already have some clients of your own, so that wouldn't change."

"I quit on all of them."

"And I'm sure they'd all take you back in a heartbeat," she countered. "And you know you have a big enough network within the medical field that you wouldn't have a problem finding more clients."

"That would still leave finding a place."

"Since we both have nothing but time on our hands, I imagine we could spend some of it looking at prospective locations," she said lightly. "And who knows, you might find something right away."

"Equipment isn't cheap, Megan. I have a decent amount of money in savings, but…I don't have a business plan in place."

She turned in his arms and looked at him. "Give yourself fifteen minutes with Gabriella, and she'll have one for you. She's scary smart and organized with stuff like that. Trust me."

"What about—?"

"Oh my gosh!" she cried out with a laugh. "We don't have to decide this right now, do we?"

He shook his head.

"Good." She kissed him soundly on the lips. "Just promise me you'll think about it."

With a nod, he said, "I will. But that still leaves you."

"Nah, I've still got a job with Zach. I'm just taking a short leave of absence. I told him I'd call him when we're home and let him know when I'll be back in the office but that he shouldn't expect to see me for at least a week."

Alex chuckled. "You think you could survive out here for a week?"

"Hmm…it wouldn't be my ideal way of spending my vacation time, but right now, I can't complain. I'm pretty happy right where I am."

His smile grew. "Yeah?"

"Yeah."

"And if you had your choice of where to spend your vacation time, where would you go?"

"It doesn't matter. As long as I'm with you, I'm a happy girl."

"But if you had the choice—"

She groaned dramatically. "If I *had* to choose…I'd have to go with something tropical. I've never gone to Hawaii or anyplace like that, and I've always wanted to. So…yeah. Someplace beachy would be nice."

Alex stood and stretched. "You know it's required that when you go on a beach vacation, you have to wear a bikini, right?"

She came to her feet and considered him for a moment. "I did not know that. But I'm not sure that's the right look on you."

Pulling her into his arms, he hugged her tightly. "Smart-ass."

"That's right, and you love that about me."

He looked down at her as he stroked the soft skin of her cheek. "I love everything about you, Megan Montgomery. And as much as I enjoy camping, we are going to pack up tomorrow morning and go home and book a flight to Hawaii right away."

Her eyes went wide. "Seriously?" she squeaked.

"Seriously," he said. "I think we both deserve a little private time away to think about this next phase of life. And you're right—the time is right for me to branch out on my own. But by doing that, it means it may be a while before I can go on vacation again. So let's do it now and do it right."

She looked over her shoulder at the tent. "And there's no way we can pack up right now, right?"

He laughed and hugged her again. "Too dark. But trust me, we'll be up plenty early and on our way."

When she frowned at him, he was confused. "I thought you'd be happy about that."

"You love camping, and now—because of me—you're leaving. I'm sorry. I'm being selfish. We don't have to leave in the morning. We should stay as long as you want to. Hawaii can wait."

"But I can't," he argued lightly. "Megan, I do love camping, but I can come and do this anytime. Going to Hawaii with the woman I love? I've never done that before, and you know how much I love trying new things and being adventurous."

She grinned. "And you think going on vacation with me is going to be an adventure?"

He leaned in and kissed her softly, thoroughly, on the lips before saying, "Sweetheart, the last vacation we planned, you didn't show up. I have a feeling getting you to the airport and keeping you out of work mode is going to be an adventure in and of itself."

She hated how he was kind of right.

"And once we land? I plan on keeping you busy exploring the islands during the day and then keeping myself busy exploring you all night."

She smiled sexily. "Sounds exhausting."

"Yeah, but you are more than worth it."

―⁓―

They didn't get to leave the next day for Hawaii, but they had a flight out for the day after. And as much as Megan was disappointed they'd have to wait, it meant she had a little more time to prepare properly.

"I can't believe how desperately I needed this."

"You camped out for one night. It was hardly as if

you were wandering the desert for a month," Summer teased.

"I would do it all again," Megan commented, "but I wasn't prepared for the lack of—"

"Being clean?" Gabriella offered. "Personally, I've never camped, but I know what Zach looks like when he comes home from a trip, and I'm always amazed how he can stand himself."

"I camped out once," Summer said from her massage chair. "Giant tepee, king-size pallet on the floor—"

"Hot spring right in your room," Gabriella finished for her. "Sweetie, that's hardly roughing it."

"For me it was."

Megan purred as her feet were massaged. "I think that sounds like my kind of camping."

"I thought you said you enjoyed camping with Alex," Summer said.

"I did. It was fine. But a hot spring right in my own personal tepee? That sounds way better!"

They all laughed and then sat quietly as their chairs massaged them and their feet were pampered.

This was definitely the best way to prepare for a trip.

"Do you have everything you need for Hawaii?" Gabriella asked.

"I think so. I'm not thrilled with my bathing suit, but Alex and I agreed we'd shop when we got there. As it is, he was bummed I was coming out with you guys today for mani-pedis."

"I'm sure he was fine once Zach and Ethan showed up," Summer commented.

"Oh, sure. Pizza and babies. Every single guy's dream Saturday," Gabriella said with a small laugh.

"Alex loves kids," Megan said with a serene smile. "He's going to make a great dad someday."

"Someday soon?" Gabriella asked with a grin.

With a shrug, Megan squirmed in her seat to get more comfortable. "Who knows? We're starting a whole new phase of life. It's anyone's guess what surprises await us."

"Ooh…I like the sound of that," Summer said.

And for the first time in her life, Megan realized that being hyper-focused on having a plan was overrated. She couldn't wait to find out what the future held for her and Alex.

And she wanted to be surprised by all of it.

Epilogue

Two months later…

"CAN YOU ZIP ME UP?"

Alex walked over to where Megan stood with her back to him and her slinky black dress open all the way down her spine. He moved in close, placed his hands on her hips, and kissed her nape. "It seems a shame to cover all of this."

They were standing in front of the full-length mirror in their bedroom, and he could see her blushing.

He loved to make her blush.

"How about I promise to let you uncover it all later," she said in a breathless whisper as Alex went back to raining tiny kisses along her spine.

"How about we just cancel and stay in?"

Megan laughed softly. "We can't cancel, Alex. It's our engagement party."

Straightening, he slowly worked her zipper up, and once it was in place, he gently grasped her shoulders and turned her to look at him. "Maybe it's just me, but it seems crazy to have an engagement party when we eloped two months ago."

In an act that still amazed him, Alex had suggested that they get married in Hawaii, and Megan had agreed. He had to admit that he'd first said it as a way of teasing her about her trouble with taking risks or doing things spur of the moment, but his girl had surprised him and said yes!

It was quite possibly the first time he didn't mind being proven wrong.

"Not everyone knows that," she gently reminded him.

"Our parents know, our siblings know, your cousins know—"

She gave him a patient smile and kissed him quickly on the lips before stepping away. "I know what you're saying, but you also said you still wanted to have a traditional wedding."

"I thought we both said that."

She continued to smile as she slid on a pair of mile-high shoes. "We did. So this is part of what goes with the whole traditional wedding scene. It's a small cocktail party—"

"For a hundred people," he murmured.

"Get used to it. The Montgomerys don't do anything small. You should know that by now. You've been to enough of our celebrations."

He laughed. "That's true, but it's a whole other story when I'm directly involved like this."

Next she put on her earrings. "Too late to back out now. You already married me."

And with a smile of his own, he walked over to her and wrapped his arms around her waist. "And I love you so much that I'm willing to marry you again."

That made her giggle, and he loved the sound. Actually, he loved everything about her. Looking at Megan right now, he was reminded of the woman he had first met back at Zach and Gabriella's wedding, and he was so happy to see her feeling comfortable in her own skin. Finally! She enjoyed her job with Zach, she enjoyed dressing up like they were tonight, but she also enjoyed lazing around the house with him wearing one of his sweatshirts with her hair up in a messy bun. He loved both those sides of her.

"Tomorrow everyone's planning on going over to Zach's," she reminded him. "I know you mentioned stopping in at the new clinic to see how much work the contractors accomplished today, but I'm hoping you can do that early in the morning. I want to be able to spend some time with my brothers while they're here, and I want you there with me."

Tonight was going to be his first time meeting Carter—which he was looking forward to—and Alex had to admit he was curious to catch up with Christian. Last time they'd seen him, he seemed to be in much better spirits, and Megan had mentioned—several times—that she thought he was dating someone new. Tomorrow would be a time for them to be able to be a little less formal and really get a chance to talk.

"Is Christian bringing a date tonight?" he asked.

"Not that I know of, but I'm hopeful!"

"Your aunt and uncle haven't been to San Diego lately, have they?"

Megan laughed and picked up her beaded purse. "Christian hasn't mentioned it, but you never know with those two. They can be pretty stealthy when they want to be."

Then she stopped and struck a sexy pose.

"You look beautiful," he murmured, moving in close again. "Are you sure we can't stay home? We'll text them all our wedding picture from Maui."

Megan swatted at him playfully. "Stop! It's going to be a wonderful night, and we're going to have fun. Remember that. Aren't you the one who's always reminding me to make the most of every day?"

Dammit, that did sound like him.

Actually, it sounded like Danny.

And with a silent prayer of thanks to his friend, he took his wife's hand and led her from the bedroom. "Come on. Let's go celebrate us."

One *More* Moment

Shaughnessy drummer Julian Grayson's personal life is in disarray and all he wants is to fly under the radar for a while. Enter social activist Charlotte Clark, who cheerfully undertakes the salvation of a guy she *thinks* is homeless and down on his luck.

Chapter 1

DIRTY, DUSTY. AND MORE THAN A LITTLE SWEATY, JULIAN Grayson tossed his keys on the table and stood in the entryway of the home he hadn't seen in three months. He'd say it was good to be home, but he wasn't a liar.

With a mixture of dread and curiosity, he forced himself to move. He'd been told what to expect, but if he'd learned anything over the last five years, it was that there were some things you just couldn't prepare yourself for.

Stepping into his massive living room, he froze. The place looked completely different—void of anything personal. It could have been a picture out of a decorating magazine, and as much as he hated it, he couldn't help but let out a sigh of relief.

Every trace of Dena and their life together was gone. *Good riddance.*

The entire room was white—the couches, the rug, the curtains. The back wall was made of windows, and with the sun shining through right now, it was almost blinding. Looking down at himself, he knew there was no way he could even walk further into the room—let alone touch anything.

He kept waiting to feel something. Anything. But after three months of riding his motorcycle around the country, he supposed he had dealt with most of his feelings on just about everything.

Maybe.

After walking out on the wedding, Julian had found a car waiting in front of the hotel and a valet holding the door open as if he'd known exactly when Julian was going to need it. Then he had gone to Mick's place and picked up the motorcycle he'd dropped there the previous day and the duffel bag that would contain the only things he'd need for however long he wanted.

Amazing how when the band traveled on tour, he required half a dozen pieces of luggage, but for this particular trip he had managed to condense it down to one duffel bag. And he'd made it work. He'd looked like hammered shit most of the time, but it worked. It fit his mood, and really, the only one he'd been hanging out with was himself, so what difference did it make?

There wasn't a doubt in his mind that most people thought he was crazy for what he'd done. Not just taking off on his bike for three months, but the whole wedding thing. Looking back, he knew it was the only way for him to do it. For years, Dena had been playing him and he'd been so blinded by love and loyalty that he'd kept taking whatever she threw at him. So many people had warned him and tried to talk him out of staying in the relationship, but Julian wouldn't listen. Couldn't. He'd been too determined to make things work.

It wasn't until a week before the wedding that he'd been confronted with the truth, and it hit him hard. Dena didn't love him. Probably never had. She wanted fame and money and he had been her ticket.

Given his tendency to cave where Dena was concerned, Julian knew the only way he was going to stay strong was to put some major distance between the two of them and not let anyone know where he was. He'd periodically checked in with his family, along with Mick and the guys, but other than that, Julian had spent the better part of the last ninety days on the back of his motorcycle and sleeping in some of the crappiest motels he had ever seen. It made staying under the radar and not being recognized a whole lot easier.

As if on cue, Julian's phone rang. Pulling it from his pocket, he grinned and answered. "You adding ESP to your list of skills, Mick?"

A low chuckle was the first response. "Nah, just know that you're punctual if nothing else. You said you'd be at the house at two. I figured I'd give you ten minutes to get in the door and get your first look around." He paused. "Everything okay?"

"I made it as far as the living room."

"My decorator, Joanie, did a fantastic job, don't you think?"

Julian shrugged even though Mick couldn't see him. "It's very…white."

"White's in. It's classic. Trust me, in time you'll love it."

———

As Julian stood on the deck staring out at the ocean two hours later, he had to admit, his manager had outdone himself.

The rental house was right on the beach in Malibu. It was prime real estate and the house itself was magnificent. The moment he walked inside he had felt at home, something he hadn't felt in a long time.

Along with giving him the address, Mick had

informed him that a housekeeper would be coming in tomorrow to do his shopping and cooking. Not a bad deal at all. Living here for the next several months certainly wasn't going to be a hardship, but he also knew he would have to start giving some serious thought to his future.

Part of the problem was how much he had isolated himself since walking out on his wedding. It was a completely selfish thing to do—after all, he did have a commitment to the band and they had all been talking about getting back into the studio. But even after all his soul-searching, he wasn't feeling much like making music. If he were honest, he would just admit that he was burned out. Besides all of his years with Shaughnessy, he had pulled double time trying to help Dena launch her own music career—which had failed. And on top of all of that, Julian realized that if it hadn't been for this career of his—his fame and notoriety—he wouldn't be in this position right now. Not the standing in a five-million-dollar home on the beach, but realizing that people weren't real or genuine. People would use you and betray you all because of who you were.

There was no way he was going to open himself up to that again. Ever.

⌇⌇⌇

The sun was coming up and Julian didn't remember seeing it go down. He'd been watching all kinds of boring documentaries since he'd first turned on the TV. Slowly he rose from the couch and stretched. With a quick glance around he spotted a clock and saw it was barely six a.m.

It didn't take long for him to realize he hadn't eaten anything the night before, but his body ached and after three months of either camping out or sleeping in crappy motel rooms on lumpy beds, he needed a decent night's sleep in a real bed.

With a shrug, he slowly made his way to the master bedroom, stripped down, and slid beneath the sheets. Everything in him began to relax. He had forgotten what Egyptian cotton sheets felt like or how incredibly satisfying a soft pillow was.

But after three hours of tossing and turning and willing his brain to shut off, Julian gave up the fight to get some sleep. It was annoying as hell to realize that after staying up for over twenty-four hours straight, he just couldn't relax enough to sleep. Off in the distance he heard his phone ring and kicked the sheets off. Naked, he stalked to the living room and grabbed the phone from the coffee table just as it stopped ringing.

"Son of a bitch," he hissed. A minute later a text came through.

> **Mick:** Housekeeper not coming today. She'll be there Wednesday.

So much for hanging around and not having to be responsible for anything. Just what he needed on top of his mental and physical exhaustion. Now he had to leave the house and actually go out into the real world.

To buy groceries.

If this was the start of his new life, it seriously sucked.

The line in the coffee shop was longer than usual and Charlotte Clark was thrilled that she had no place pressing to be until later in the afternoon. It would have been even more thrilling if she didn't have to work on a Sunday, but that was the way it went. Being a vocational rehabilitation advisor had her working more hours than she would have imagined, and sometimes those hours weren't conventional.

Some of the people she placed were fresh out of rehab or even prison, but most of the time they were simply people who were down on their luck.

Sort of like the guy standing in line in front of her. His clothes were rumpled, his hair was unkempt, and he looked like he hadn't shaved in a week. Silently she cursed herself for being judgmental. Maybe he was just a guy who didn't care about his appearance. That certainly wasn't a crime and she'd known many people like that, but everything about this guy had all of her senses on alert.

With a background in social work, Charlotte had learned to read people and notice things about them that maybe they were trying to hide or simply didn't want to share. If she had to venture a guess, she'd say this guy was tired and a little agitated. His posture and the way he kept shifting from one foot to another…and then the way he sighed—loudly—multiple times. Maybe it was the long line or the fact that the line wasn't moving that was bugging him, or maybe it was something else.

She shook her head and reminded herself that she needed to quit analyzing people. The guy was simply here to grab a cup of coffee just like she was. End of story. And even if it wasn't, it wasn't any of her business.

There was no way she could help everyone and there certainly was no way she would approach a total stranger. How could she walk up to him and ask him if he realized that he needed to fix himself up a little bit?

Bad Charlotte! Ugh…she hated when she couldn't get out of this mode. It was a beautiful day outside and she should be thinking about finding something fun and relaxing to do. Later she'd need to go over to the homeless shelter in Santa Monica and meet with her weekly group to see about setting up interviews for the coming week.

The line moved forward and she was relieved to see that she was almost to the front. Unkempt guy stepped up to order and she couldn't help but listen.

"Large black coffee," he snapped. "None of that overpriced fancy crap. Just your basic, regular coffee. Three sugars." He paused. "And let me get a blueberry muffin and…actually, make that two."

"Anything else?" the cashier asked.

He shook his head and waited.

At that point, Charlotte put her own focus on the menu board and thought a blueberry muffin sounded good too. Originally, she had only planned on getting herself a coffee—one of the overpriced fancy ones—and a fruit cup, but now that the idea of the muffin was there, she knew she'd be changing her order.

In front of her, the guy reached into his back pocket and cursed.

Loudly.

"Um…cancel my order," he told the cashier, his voice so low and deep it was almost a growl. "I forgot my wallet."

Without hesitation, Charlotte stepped forward and smiled at the young cashier. "Hi, Carly," she began, reading the girl's nametag. "If it's okay with you, you can add his order to mine." She was feeling pretty good about herself and her gesture, but when she turned and looked up at the man she was helping, she couldn't help but gasp.

Jet-black hair and silver eyes—which were currently glaring at her. There wasn't even a hint of a smile and if anything, he was borderline snarling.

"What do you think you're doing?" he asked.

Charlotte had met enough people who were down on their luck to know that sometimes pride was a huge deterrent to them accepting help in any form. "I heard you say you had forgotten your wallet and just figured I'd help."

"Why?"

Her shoulders relaxed even as her smile grew and she laughed softly. "What do you mean *why*?"

"Ma'am?" the cashier asked. "What can I get you? The line's getting backed up."

"Oh, right. Sorry." Although she was a little miffed at being called *ma'am*. At twenty-seven, she didn't consider herself old enough for *that* title, but she'd deal with that later. "I'll have a tall mocha Frappuccino and a blueberry muffin, please." Then she handed her credit card over before looking back at the angry man.

"I don't need anyone to buy me coffee," he growled.

Undeterred, she smiled and accepted her card back from the cashier. "Oh, please. I know I get cranky when I can't have my coffee, and you look like you could use it. It's not a big deal. Really." She stepped around him to go wait at the other end of the counter for their order. For a minute, she didn't think he would follow, and she had to hide her smile when he finally did.

"I could have just gone and grabbed my wallet and come back," he argued. His voice was low, but there was still heat in it.

She shrugged and offered him a smile. "Now you don't have to."

They stood in silence until their order was placed on the counter and Charlotte thanked the barista and then smiled at the man. He still hadn't picked up his coffee or muffins, and she wondered just how stubborn he was going to be.

"Look, if it bothers you that much, just...pay it forward," she said.

"Pay it what?"

"Forward. You know, next time you're in line and notice someone in need of a hand, help them out." Her smile broadened even as he looked at her as if she were crazy. "Anyway, enjoy and have a great day!"

Without waiting for an answer, she walked out of the coffee shop and across the street toward the park benches where she could sit and see the beach and enjoy the fresh air. It really was a beautiful day out and there was no way she wanted to waste it sitting inside.

Sitting down, she pulled the muffin out of the bag and was about to break off a piece when someone sat down beside her.

Her unkempt man.

With her sunglasses on, she was certain he couldn't read her surprise, and she did her best to sound casual as she asked, "Would you like to join me?"

About the Author

Samantha Chase is a *New York Times* and *USA Today* bestseller of contemporary romance. She released her debut novel in 2011 and currently has more than forty titles under her belt. When she's not working on a new story, she spends her time reading romances, playing way too many games of Scrabble or Solitaire on Facebook, wearing a tiara while playing with her sassy pug, Maylene…oh, and spending time with her husband of twenty-five years and their two sons in North Carolina.

Also by Samantha Chase

The Montgomery Brothers
Wait for Me / Trust in Me
Stay with Me / More of Me
Return to You
Meant for You
I'll Be There
Until There Was Us

The Shaughnessy Brothers
Made for Us
Love Walks In
Always My Girl
This Is Our Song
A Sky Full of Stars
Holiday Spice

Shaughnessy Brothers: Band on the Run
One More Kiss
One More Promise
One More Moment

Holiday Romance
The Christmas Cottage / Ever After
Mistletoe Between Friends / The Snowflake Inn
Holiday Spice

Life, Love and Babies
The Baby Arrangement
Baby, I'm Yours
Baby, Be Mine